THE FACE WAS STILL SMILING IN THE MANGLED PHOTOGRAPH

She cut the photo first into vertical strips, then into horizontal ones, until she created a mound of glossy confetti. She took Alex's photographic remains and tossed them into the toilet and watched them drown in the swirling waters.

Soon Alex would be gone, and everything would be right, the way it was supposed to be.

She put on the locket. "Thank you for my gift," she said softly.

She would wear the locket every night. During the day it would stay hidden, like her pain.

The metal was cold against her skin. She shivered and hugged herself.

She hated the waiting.

Other Avon Books by
Rochelle Majer Krich

Till Death Do Us Part

NOWHERE TO RUN

ROCHELLE MAJER KRICH

AVON BOOKS  NEW YORK

NOWHERE TO RUN is an original publication of Avon Books. This work has never before appeared in book form. This work is a novel. Any similarity to actual persons or events is purely coincidental.

AVON BOOKS
A division of
The Hearst Corporation
1350 Avenue of the Americas
New York, New York 10019

Copyright © 1994 by Rochelle Majer Krich
Cover photograph by Ron Rinaldi
Published by arrangement with the author
Library of Congress Catalog Card Number: 93–90654
ISBN: 0–380–76534–9

First Avon Books Printing: April 1994

AVON TRADEMARK REG. U.S. PAT. OFF. AND IN OTHER COUNTRIES, MARCA REGISTRADA, HECHO EN U.S.A.

Printed in the U.S.A.

RA   10 9 8 7 6 5 4 3 2 1

Many thanks to Manuel Katz, my colleague and friend, for an insider's view of Venice, California; and to my editor, Lisa Wager, for her expert advice and painstaking guidance—and some laughs along the way.

Chapter 1

The flash caught her as she was stepping inside the house and exploded into tiny fragments of blinding light.

Alexandra Prescott flinched. Instinctively, she lowered her head and started to raise her arm to shield her face, but there was no barrage of flashes, just a glee-filled, high-pitched chorus of "Happy Birthday, Alex!"

Circles of light still floated across her gray-green eyes. Alex pulled her lips into a smile and met the faces standing behind the crayoned banner taped to the ecru wall above the archway to the living room.

"This is . . . wonderful," she said, wondering whether her voice betrayed her emotion. "Just wonderful."

"I knew, but I didn't tell!" yelled Nicholas, her five-year-old stepson. "I knew the whole time, Mommy! Right I knew, Lisa?" he asked his sister, who was holding a Polaroid.

Alex's husband Warren came up to her. Pulling her close, he bent his head down and kissed her on her mouth. "You really *are* surprised, aren't you? I can feel your heart thumping." His grin deepened the faint lines around his eyes and mouth and softened the serious, almost square lines of his face.

She was instantly warmed by the pleasure and love she read in his deep amber eyes. They were kind eyes, caring eyes; it was the first thing she had noticed about him. Lifting her hand to his forehead, she smoothed into place several strands of dark brown hair that needed no smoothing. Touching him anchored her.

"I didn't suspect a thing," she whispered. "I must look a mess." She was dressed in stone-washed jeans, a red cotton knit sweater warm enough for the mild January day, and Adidas running shoes; wearing anything nonwashable to the Venice, California, preschool she ran was impractical and

1

expensive. In the morning, she'd pulled her thick, wavy black hair into a ponytail. She lifted her hand now to brush back the tendrils she knew had escaped.

Warren took her hand. "You look great. Except for the purple finger paint on your nose." Smiling, he rubbed the paint off her face.

Her vision was clear now, and she scanned the room, noting the friends and relatives who had come to wish her well. A human dowry, Alex thought—they had all been part of Warren's life long before they had become part of hers: the Lipmans and Greens. The Bennets and the Blairs. The McAllisters. The Judds.

Denise, Warren's former sister-in-law, stood with her boyfriend, Ron; she was smiling warmly at Alex. Lisa, Warren's fourteen-year-old daughter, was next to Denise, and Alex was struck again by the startling resemblance between aunt and niece. Same straight, shoulder-length, honey-blond hair; same high cheekbones; straight, short noses; porcelain skin; expressive, almond-shaped brown eyes. Lisa, tall for her age, was already five feet five inches, only two inches shorter than her aunt, and would clearly have the same slender, willowy build.

Paula Lewis was here, of course. She was part of the dowry, too—she had been the Prescott housekeeper from the time Lisa was an infant. Next to Paula were Mona and Stuart Hutchins—Denise's parents, Lisa and Nick's maternal grandparents. Mona flashed Alex a manufactured smile. Alex wondered fleetingly why she and Stuart had come.

Alex spotted Patty, an aide at the preschool, and Evelyn, her assistant and a close friend (not part of the dowry; Alex had cultivated this relationship on her own). Patty and Evelyn both knew Denise, and Warren and the kids, of course—they had known them, in fact, before Alex had—but they were standing apart, to the side. Alex was reminded of how she'd felt at her first high school dance—awkward, nervous, silently willing one of the pimply, gangly boys to transform her from a wallflower into someone who belonged. She walked over to them.

"Happy birthday, Alex," Patty said shyly.

"Thank you, Patty." Alex hugged her lightly. "I'm glad you came." She turned to Evelyn and, taking her hands, shook her head in mock accusation. "So that's why you asked me to take the afternoon shift!"

Alex usually left the school at three so that she could pick Nicholas up from kindergarten; Evelyn and Patty stayed and supervised the children whose parents needed day care until six.

Evelyn's smile lit up her angular face. "Guilty as charged. I guess you'll never trust me anymore."

"I guess not." Alex grinned, then turned to the others. "Thank you," she said to the roomful of people. "All of you. I don't know what to say."

"Say 'cheese,' Mommy!" squealed Nicholas. "Lisa, take another picture of Mommy."

"Say 'money,' " someone called.

"Say 'sex!' " Ron called, and Denise said, "Shhh!" but she was smiling and everyone laughed.

Prepared this time, Alex smiled into the camera. "Cheese."

Evelyn said, "How about taking a picture of your folks, Lisa?"

Something flickered in the girl's dark brown eyes.

"Go ahead, honey," Denise said and touched Lisa's arm.

"Fine," Lisa said. "Alex, move closer to Dad, okay?"

It was still "Alex," even though she and Warren had been married for almost two years. Maybe it would always be "Alex." Never "Mom." But that was understandable, she told herself, not for the first time. Lisa had been nine when her mother had died of complications less than two months after giving birth to Nicholas, twelve when her father had re-married; and unlike Nicholas, who had welcomed Alex happily and unconditionally, Lisa had been guarded, unapproachable, often bristling with an unnamed anger that Warren liked to label "the teenage thing" but Alex knew was something else.

Within the past few months, though, Alex had sensed a thawing of that reserve, an ebbing of the anger, and if Lisa wasn't yet affectionate toward her stepmother (God, how Alex hated the word!), at least she seemed to have accepted Alex as Warren's wife and a member of the family.

Alex posed. Another flash from the camera. Nicholas ran _____ lifted him high, and he planted a wet kiss on her cheek. She hugged him tightly, ruffled his tawny hair, then lowered him to the tiled floor.

"Do you like the sign, Mommy? Lisa drawed it, but I colored it in." Pride gleamed in his deep amber eyes. Warren's eyes.

"I love the sign, Nick." I love *you*, Nick. "Thank you, Lisa." She smiled at her stepdaughter.

Lisa shrugged, and whisked her blond hair behind her ear, but Alex could see from the sudden color in her cheeks that she was pleased.

Nick wedged himself between Alex and Warren. "Take one with me in it, Lisa," he ordered.

Denise stepped forward. "Why don't I take one of all of you? Go ahead, Lisa."

Lisa hesitated, then handed the camera to her aunt. Warren moved away from Nick to make room for his daughter, but she walked around Warren and positioned herself on his right.

Which was only understandable, Alex told herself. And it didn't mean anything. But she couldn't help noticing the look of mincing approval in Mona Hutchins's eyes.

It was almost midnight when Warren and Alex finished clearing things away and went upstairs to their bedroom.

"We should have left the rest for tomorrow," he said as he unbuttoned his shirt. "In fact, you shouldn't have had to clean anything. It was your party. And Paula told you to leave it for her till tomorrow."

"I know, but dried guacamole is not a pretty picture." She grimaced. And though Paula had offered, Alex suspected that in the morning, the housekeeper would have greeted a less-than-spotless kitchen with disapproval.

In many ways, Alex still felt as if she were on probation with the woman, constantly being tested by criteria she was supposed to intuit, more often than not failing. Tonight she'd thanked Paula for helping with the party preparations—Paula was easily slighted, Alex knew—but throughout the evening she had noticed a grim line around the housekeeper's mouth. Maybe Alex hadn't thanked her enough.

"Anyway," she continued, "you and Lisa did most of it. And if people had left at a decent hour . . ." She ____ced her Adidas, slipped them off, and unzipped her j____

"By 'people' you mean Mona and Stuart, right?" Warren shook his head and smiled. "They never know when to leave." He walked into the adjoining bathroom and tossed his shirt and T-shirt into the built-in hamper.

Or when not to come at all, Alex thought. In a casual voice, she said, "Actually, I was surprised to see them." Which wasn't exactly true. They came to the house constantly, often without warning. Of course, they were attached to their grandchildren, and to Warren, but still . . .

"Well, they *are* Denise's parents," Warren said, returning to the bedroom. "And Denise helped Lisa plan the party. Mona and Stuart would've been hurt if they hadn't been invited. And they like you, Alex."

No, they don't, Alex thought as she walked to the closet to hang up her jeans. They regard me as the woman who took over their dead daughter's husband and family. And house. And just about everything in it, including the English Provincial furniture, the blue-and-white willow-patterned dishes, the Waterford stemware.

Aloud, she said, "Did you see Mona on her hands and knees ___ng to get the stain out of the carpet with the club s_____ to her. She _____'s carpet. "She looked ridiculous."

up to her. She

_____ flamboyant version of Denise, Mona

_____, bright orange dress that, together with ____ hennaed, short-cropped hair and an orange-_psticked mouth, had made her look like a jack-o'-lantern. Alex smiled at the image.

Warren laughed. "She wasn't on her hands and knees. Anyway, Mona means well. It was a fun party, wasn't it?"

"It was a *great* party," Alex said warmly, meaning it. "And it was so sweet of your parents to phone."

Sweet, but not surprising. Bea and Phil Prescott were warm and affectionate and clearly approved of their new daughter-in-law. They lived in Chicago. So did Warren's sister Nora and her husband, Robert. They had all flown in for Alex and Warren's private wedding ceremony in the minister's study at the church Warren attended. Bea and Phil had returned to California several times since then, and Alex had enjoyed each visit.

On the phone tonight they had voiced their familiar complaint, that Alex and Warren and the children lived too far away. "We should never have let Warren go to Stanford for law school," Bea had said, only half joking. As always, it had been hard for Alex to hear the love and pride in her mother-in-law's voice and not think about her own parents. Two years ago, she'd broken a year-long silence to call and tell them she was getting married. "I see," her father had said; Alex had pictured his stern, tight-lipped mouth. Her mother had said, "I hope you'll be happy" in clipped, grudging syllables of unforgiving disapproval that twenty-two months and two thousand miles hadn't softened. Alex hadn't spoken to them since.

Don't think about them, Alex told herself now. Don't let them ruin your day. With forced cheer she said, "Warren, it was wonderful of Lisa to plan the party. I'm really touched. I'll get her a few CDs of her latest favorites." Alex was rewarded with his smile. "And I'll call Denise." She took off her sweater, folded it, and put it on the dresser.

"Good idea. Denise will appreciate it." He sat on his side of their king-size bed and picked up a law journal from his nightstand. "I'm glad you two get along so well, Alex."

Alex was relieved more than glad. From everything she'd heard, Denise and Andrea, Warren's late wife, had been extremely close, even though Andrea had been nine years older than her "baby" sister. And it had been clear to Alex that Denise had a special relationship with her sister's children, especially Lisa. Alex hadn't known what to expect—would Denise be hostile, or would she ignore Alex and pretend she didn't exist? But aside from an initial awkwardness, natural under the circumstances, Denise had been wonderful—warm, friendly, eager to introduce Alex to her own circle of friends. She'd offered to help Paula watch Lisa and Nick while Alex and Warren honeymooned in Hawaii. And she had tactfully and gracefully relinquished her role as surrogate mother. For that, Alex had been especially grateful.

"Denise looks happy, doesn't she, Warren? I think she really likes Ron."

He looked up from his journal and smiled. "I hope so. She loves decorating people's houses, but she's twenty-seven, and it's about time she settled down. She's very pretty. She's bright. She's got a great personality. I don't know why she hasn't married yet." He shrugged.

"Should I be jealous?" Alex said lightly. *I'm so lucky*, she thought as she looked at her husband.

A moment later he was behind her, his arms wrapped around her. "Never."

She leaned back against him, the top of her head tucked under his chin. "Not too bad for a woman of thirty-two?"

"Not bad at all." He slipped off her bra straps and kissed her shoulders. "Happy birthday, Alex," he whispered. His breath was warm on her neck.

It never failed to surprise her, the way his touch made her instantly tingle with desire. "You already wished me a happy birthday downstairs," she said softly. She fingered the hammered gold, heart-shaped locket that lay between her breasts. Then she turned and put her arms around his neck.

"That was for public," he said. "This is for private."

Alex stifled a cry as she awoke. She lay still, bathed in sweat, waiting for her heart to stop lurching in her chest. Warren was asleep, lightly snoring next to her, his bare chest rising almost imperceptibly with each trouble-free breath. She was tempted to wake him, to have him wrap his strong arms around her, to make love again and lose herself in the passion and tenderness of his embrace. But he would want to know why she was crying, and she couldn't tell him about the dream. She couldn't tell anyone.

The dream was always the same. Waking brought with it no relief, since the dream was not about monsters or demons that daylight or moonlight could banish. And it was not about any of a myriad of very real, horrifying events that could take place tomorrow, or the next day, or the next year, but probably wouldn't. The dream was about what had been, and there was no escaping it. Not even today. Not even lying here in this bed, with a husband she loved.

She clutched the locket Warren had given her as if it were an amulet with protective powers, despaired because she knew that it wasn't. She would have the dream again and again, and it would be merciless in its accurateness, terrifying in its inexorable sameness; and despite the sameness, the pain would always be sharply new.

"Happy birthday, Alex," she whispered to herself.

Chapter 2

The locket lay nestled against the ink-black velvet lining of the box.

She lifted the locket and opened it. At the birthday party she'd forced herself to smile with the others as Alex said, "Oh, Warren, it's so beautiful!" and watch as she kissed him on the mouth. The pain had sliced through her, but no one had seen. The next day she searched and searched until she finally found an almost identical, hammered gold, heart-shaped locket. She had intended just to try it on, to see how it looked on her, but as soon as she slipped it on and saw herself in the oblong mirror on the jewelry display cabinet, she knew that she had to buy the locket. He would want her to have it. "Shall I gift-wrap it?" the salesman asked, and she said yes, because it was a gift; of course it was a gift.

In her bedroom, she cut small hearts out of a piece of white paper until she had the exact size and shape she wanted. She placed her model heart on the Polaroid photo and outlined the shape with a fine-point, red felt-tip marker. Then, using cuticle scissors, she carefully excised the face from the photo and pressed it into the left half of the locket. The fit was perfect. She repeated the process with a snapshot of herself. She'd spent a long time choosing a photo, had selected this one because he'd taken it of her and she liked the way her eyes looked, soft and glowing. You have great eyes, he'd told her; don't blink.

Alex's face was still smiling at her from the partially mangled photo. She took the scissors and cut the beautiful face and long black hair and perfect body she sometimes hated so much. (Other times, in spite of herself, she felt herself drawn to Alex, but she had to fight those moments. They confused her, angered her.) She cut the photo first into vertical strips,

8

then into horizontal ones, until she had created a mound of glossy confetti. She took Alex's photographic remains and tossed them into the toilet and watched them drown in the swirling water.

She put on the locket. His locket.

"Thank you for my gift," she said softly.

It bothered her to see Warren with Alex, to know that they were sharing a bed. Making love. But soon he would see that Alex was wrong for him. Then Alex would be gone, and everything would be right, the way it was supposed to be. The way it had been before Alex came. Before she ruined everything.

She shut the locket. Standing in front of her dresser mirror, she undid the tiny clasp on the delicate gold chain and imagined that his hands were fastening the locket behind her neck. She would wear the locket every night. During the day it would stay hidden, like her pain.

The metal was cold against her skin. She shivered and hugged herself.

She hated the waiting.

Chapter 3

"**W**ell," Dr. Pearson said.

Lying on a disposable, thin white paper sheet on the cold beige vinyl examination table, Alex heard the note of guarded surprise in the gynecologist's voice and tensed. Something was wrong; she knew it. She tried to see his face between the V of her legs, but his graying, balding head was bent and his eyes were closed, as if in prayer.

"Relax your muscles," Dr. Pearson said gently but firmly. "We're almost done."

She obeyed quickly, letting her back sink into the vinyl, consciously expelling her breath, wondering whether the "we" referred to the doctor and her, the doctor and the myopic nurse in the room who was looking anywhere but at Alex, or the doctor and his veteran hands that had briskly, efficiently, and nonsexually tapped and kneaded her breasts and abdomen and were now exploring the most intimate parts of her body.

"Is that tender?" Pearson asked.

"No." It wasn't her breasts, Alex decided, because Pearson's "Well" had come after he'd examined them. Was it a cyst? Her mother had suffered from ovarian cysts.

"You can sit up now," Dr. Pearson was saying as he removed the latex gloves and tossed them into a tall waste basket. "When you're ready, come see me in my office." He adjusted his tortoiseshell glasses, smiled at Alex, and left the room, the brown-haired nurse trotting behind him like a setter.

Something was definitely wrong, Alex decided as she dressed. The last time, Dr. Pearson had smiled and told her that everything was fine and that he'd see her at her next annual checkup. Pearson had smiled now, too, but the smile had been noncommittal, an automatic manipulation of facial muscles that meant nothing and could be masking everything.

Smiles, she had learned, like their wearers, could often do that. She tried not to think of the grim possibilities, but the eyes that stared back at her from the mirror hanging on the wall in the tiny curtained cubicle were somber, more gray than green, like the ocean at dusk.

Dr. Pearson wasn't in his office. Alex had been in the room only once, when she'd first become his patient. The framed diplomas on the paneled walls testified to his competence, but that was small comfort to her now. She took a seat in front of his large cherry wood desk and checked her watch. It was one-fifty. During the day, with traffic, the drive from Los Angeles to Venice could take half an hour. She'd told Evelyn and Patty that she'd be back by two-thirty, but unless she left right now, she'd never make it on time.

I'd better call Evelyn, Alex decided, and I should probably find a gynecologist closer to home. But just then Dr. Pearson entered, and she sat upright in the navy-tweed-upholstered armchair.

"Well," he said again as he sat down. He opened a manila file in front of him and examined the top sheet. "You're thirty-two, is that right?"

Why was he asking her that? "Yes." Too young for anything serious, she wanted to say nonchalantly; still under warranty. But of course, there were no warranties on bodies as there were on toasters and dishwashers and VCRs, and even then the warranty always expired two days before the product did.

"You told the nurse your last menstrual period was three weeks ago?" He looked up at her.

Alex nodded. "It was right around my birthday." If it was cysts, she decided, she could live with that. The idea of surgery didn't thrill her, but surgery was manageable, survivable.

"Was it light?"

"Yes. It lasted only two days. I think I mentioned that." But Alex had been irregular for years; Pearson had known that since she'd become his patient when she moved to Los Angeles over three years ago. "Is there a problem?" Please let it be cysts, she thought, and now her hands were clutching the arms of the chair, her manicured nails digging into the reddish wood.

"Not at all, not at all. I didn't mean to alarm you. But

that's what threw me off, you see. Then, when I examined you and did an internal, and when I checked the results of the lab tests . . . " He smiled at her. "I would estimate that you are about ten weeks pregnant, Alexandra."

She stared at him. Her mouth was suddenly dry. "Pregnant?" The word was almost a croak. "But my period—"

"Please don't worry. It's not uncommon to experience bleeding in the first month or two. Of course, I want you to let me know if you have a recurrence of any bleeding at all."

"Are you sure?" she managed. "That I'm pregnant, I mean." Her hands were clammy. "There's no possibility that the tests are wrong?" There was a rushing sound in her ears, as if she were in a tunnel, and she leaned forward to hear his answer.

Dr. Pearson frowned. "You seem upset, Alexandra. I'm sorry. I assumed—that is . . . " He paused. "If you're unhappy about the pregnancy and want to terminate—"

She fell back against the chair. "No! Of course not!" She was quiet for a moment. "When—when am I due?"

"By my calculations, I'd say around August. But given the circumstances, I could be off by several weeks in either direction. We'll do some blood work and an ultrasound and get a more definite date." Pearson waited.

"I'm just so surprised," Alex finally said. "Because of my period." It had been another disappointing month, but she had become inured to disappointment, and she found it hard to comprehend that what Pearson was saying—what she had yearned for so long to hear—was true.

"You're definitely sure?" she asked again, but this time she was smiling, and Pearson was smiling, too, clearly relieved. And then she was only half listening as he talked about getting enough exercise and rest and having a diet rich in iron and all the essential nutrients, and all she could think about was telling Warren and how happy he would be about the blossoming life they had created together and how incredibly lucky she was—no, not lucky. How truly *blessed* she was.

Twenty minutes later, she left Dr. Pearson's office with a fee schedule, prescriptions for prenatal vitamins, an assortment of pamphlets on pregnancy, and a sample magazine showing a serene mother holding a chubby, beaming, dimpled infant.

And hope.

Driving home on Venice Boulevard, she thought about nothing but the baby. (She had been barely conscious of descending in the elevator or leaving the Cedars-Sinai medical towers, had been mildly surprised when she'd found herself in front of her red Jeep Cherokee.) Of course, in retrospect, everything made sense: The queasiness (she'd attributed it to the flu that had been going around), the sudden snugness of her jeans and two favorite dresses (too much junk food), the tiredness that pursued her throughout the day (again, the flu).

It was almost three when Alex parked the Jeep in front of the yellow-and-white-trimmed stucco, one-story building on Brooks Avenue. Her preschool. She still felt a thrill of pleasure every time she saw it, still marveled at how fate or luck had brought her here one Sunday, two and a half years ago, to a Venice Beach art festival, and had made her path cross with that of Cybil Manning. The two women had gotten into a conversation after admiring one of the artist's canvases—an oversized, sensuous, Georgia O'Keefe-like iris, Alex remembered. I wish I could paint, Cybil had said with a sigh, don't you? And Alex had mentioned that she used to paint, but was now a preschool teacher in Los Angeles and was thinking of starting her own preschool; she'd owned one before she'd moved to L.A. What a small world, Cybil had said; she had a preschool and was planning to retire, and was Alex interested in buying it? I don't think so, Alex had immediately replied, because how could she move to Venice, of all places? It was the last place on earth where she would consider living.

But Cybil had pressed her card on Alex. Think about it, she'd said. A week later, Alex had driven back to Venice and visited Cybil's school and immediately fallen in love with the cheerful, well-kept building and the gayly painted, multicolored gym facilities in the enclosed yard. And the children. Cybil and Alex had agreed that Alex would manage the school for six months; if she liked it, she would then buy it. If not, well, no harm done.

Of course, Alex had loved it. Evelyn Goodwin's warmth and cooperation and friendship had made the transition almost effortless. And despite having hesitations, Alex had immediately taken to Venice. It was a beach community with local color and quaint charm, with art galleries and outdoor cafés, with "walk" streets (no cars allowed) and paths where roller skaters and bicyclists whizzed by, and stretches of sand where bodybuilders flexed their oiled, highly defined muscles.

It wasn't the "Venice of America" that its founder, Abbot Kinney, had envisioned in the early 1900s. Alex had read about Kinney's dream of bringing a cultural Renaissance to America. He'd dug canals in the marshy land he owned; he'd built hotels, an auditorium, arcades, all with pseudo-Italian-style facades. The cultural Renaissance had never taken root; people who flocked to Venice, Kinney had quickly learned, were more interested in amusement than culture, and he'd filled their needs.

In 1920, six weeks after Kinney died, the pier he'd built burned down; in 1929 many of the canals were filled. For almost forty years Venice, suffering from benign neglect, slipped into seediness. Then the beat writers discovered it. The artists followed. Gradually, the once-famous resort underwent restoration and regained its popularity. Million-dollar homes now stood on property adjacent to the remaining canals in South Venice, but Kinney, Alex thought, would probably be disappointed by what had become of his dream.

For Alex, though, Venice had turned out to be perfect. And that was before Warren Prescott had made it clear that his interest in Alex went far beyond her role as his two-and-a-half-year-old son's teacher. She had retreated from him at first, like a turtle withdrawing into its shell—not because she wasn't attracted to him, but because she was. The possibility of starting over, of finding happiness, was exciting, tantalizing, and ultimately frightening. But his quiet, steady persistence had overcome her resistance.

And now she was pregnant.

The yard was empty. Evelyn and Patty were inside, doing story time with the fourteen full-day children. Of these, six stayed till six each day. There were an additional ten half-day preschoolers who stayed only till noon.

Alex stood in the doorway, unobserved by the boys and girls who were sitting cross-legged in a circle on the yellow-and-white-checkered vinyl tile floor. They were hunched forward, listening raptly as Evelyn read "Corduroy," taking their eyes off her only to glance at the illustrated pages Patty held up from time to time. It was a poignant story, one of Alex's favorites, about a little girl who fell in love with an imperfect teddy bear and took him home. Evelyn reads it with such feeling, Alex thought, and then, *I'll be reading it to my son or daughter soon.*

"The end," Evelyn said several minutes later, and of course there were cries of "More!" Then Alex joined Evelyn and Patty in supervising the children as they cleared away puzzles, crayons, Lego pieces, trucks, dolls.

"How'd everything go?" Alex asked as she reshelved books in one of the two-tiered bookcases that lined the walls.

"Fine. One tantrum. One bathroom accident." Evelyn smiled and ran her fingers through her straight, shoulder-length, medium-brown hair. "Patty and I managed. Why are you always so worried?"

"I don't know," Alex admitted. "Habit, I guess." *Children are a serious responsibility, Alexandra.* Her parents had instilled that concept in her early, had reminded her of it constantly. *You're not to watch television while you're baby-sitting, Alexandra. That's not what the Thompsons pay you for.*

"What about Bobby?" Alex asked Evelyn. "I noticed he wasn't in the circle with the others. Did he fight with someone?"

"With Richie, now that you mention it. Lately he's always fighting with someone, or crying. I don't think it's anything serious, though."

"Maybe," Alex said, unconvinced. Bobby Lundquist's moodiness troubled her. "I think I'll talk to his mother."

Evelyn frowned. "You'll just get her upset, Alex. It's probably just a stage. What about you? Everything okay?" she asked in an undertone.

"Everything's great." Alex smiled. "The fact is—" She stopped. She should really tell Warren first, shouldn't she? She'd called him from Dr. Pearson's; his secretary had told her that he was in a meeting with an important client. Alex hadn't wanted to give him the news via the Jeep's cellular phone. Too much static. Not enough privacy. "I'll tell you later," she said to Evelyn.

"Tell me what? What's the mystery?"

"No mystery. It's just—" She cast a look behind her. Patty was only a few feet away, but she was engrossed in helping one of the children with an art project. Alex turned back to

Evelyn. "Oh, hell, Ev, promise not to tell Warren you knew first. I'm pregnant!" she whispered. She could feel herself grinning as she said the words.

Evelyn's brown eyes were wide with surprise. "You're kidding! But I thought—"

"Dr. Pearson said that wasn't a period. Believe me, I'm just as shocked as you are."

"It's wonderful," Evelyn said. She hugged Alex tightly. "I know how much this means to you, and to Warren. I've been praying this would happen." Her eyes glistened with tears.

"Well, your prayers worked," Alex said softly. "You're a good friend, Ev."

"The best." Evelyn smiled. "But then, you make it easy."

Evelyn's smile, Alex always felt, added an extra measure of prettiness to her face and made her look far younger than her thirty-three years. She had a clear, almost translucent complexion and wore little makeup, just a hint of rosy blush on her cheeks and pale pink gloss on her soft, shapely lips.

"Well, now it's my turn to put in a good word for you," Alex said lightly.

"Not for a baby, I hope!" Evelyn laughed and blushed. "I think I should get married first, don't you?"

"Probably." Alex grinned. "What does Jerry say about that?"

Jerry was the computer-systems salesman Evelyn was dating. Six months ago, he'd come to the preschool to sell Alex a system. She hadn't needed one, but he'd met Evelyn and asked her out. "Love at first 'byte,'" Alex had teased.

"Nothing specific," Evelyn said. "But he's been hinting lately and doing all sorts of romantic things. Lots of flowers. You know. . . ." Smiling, she handed Alex a stack of books.

Alex shelved them in the bookcase. "I love getting flowers." She sighed. "Warren doesn't often bring me flowers, but when he does, it makes me feel like we're dating all over again. Sounds like things are getting heavy with you two," she added and grinned knowingly.

"I don't want to rush things," Evelyn said, suddenly serious. "I like Jerry. He likes me. But, well . . . it's easy to make mistakes."

Alex touched Evelyn's arm. "Of course. You're right." There had been a too-quick, too-short marriage after high school, Alex knew, and several subsequent relationships. Evelyn had alluded to them but hadn't elaborated. Alex hadn't pressed for details.

"Enough about me," Evelyn said. "Why haven't you told Warren yet? He'll be thrilled."

"I couldn't reach him from the doctor's, and now, well, I'm just as glad. I'd like to tell him in person."

Evelyn nodded. "I think you're right. What about the kids? Are you going to tell them right away?"

"Not Nicholas. August will seem like a million years away. That's when the baby's due," she explained. "About Lisa . . . I'm not sure what to do. What do you think?"

"If you tell her later, she might feel you kept something from her, shut her out." Evelyn's brows were concentrated in thought. "On the other hand, the two of you are just starting to get along better. She might feel uncomfortable about the idea that you and Warren are having a baby, that you're . . . " Her voice trailed off.

"Having sex," Alex finished for her. "Doing it." She grinned. "I know. I remember being a teenager and thinking about my parents having sex. It seemed unbelievable, embarrassing. Gross, almost. And I'm not even Lisa's mother." Alex sighed. Aside from feeling awkward, would Lisa resent the idea of Alex and Warren's baby? Or would the baby bring them all closer together?

"Ask Warren," Evelyn said.

"You're right. I will."

She told him late that night. They had just made love, and she was nestled in the crook of his arm, her leg draped over his. She ran her hand across his chest, then traced the outline of his square jaw, his wide mouth, the straight line of his nose. He was so handsome, she thought. If the baby was a boy, she hoped he would look like Warren.

"I went to Dr. Pearson today," she said.

"Everything okay?"

She heard his concern and pressed closer against him. "Everything's fine. Wonderful, in fact." She paused. "I'm pregnant, Warren." She smiled into the darkness.

The hand that had been stroking her arm stopped. "Are you

sure?'' There was an edge of wariness beneath the surprise in his voice. ''I thought—''

She repeated what Pearson had told her. ''Isn't it great?''

''It's great,'' he agreed softly. He was quiet for a moment, and she wondered what he was thinking. Then he said, ''When is the baby due?''

''Sometime in August. No school, no worries. Talk about perfect timing.'' She smiled. ''Dr. Pearson said he'll have a better idea after I have the ultrasound,'' she added.

''Speaking of Pearson, Alex, I think you ought to find an obstetrician closer to home. L.A.'s not far, but you'll have to go in every month, more often toward the end.''

Dr. Pearson had expressed the same concerns, had offered to refer Alex to a colleague in Venice or Santa Monica. She'd declined. ''I like Dr. Pearson, Warren. I don't want a different doctor. And he has privileges at St. John's in Santa Monica. That's less than twenty minutes from the house.''

It was an excellent hospital, Pearson had told her. It was smaller than Cedars and consequently offered more personal care; many Hollywood celebrities chose St. John's for elective surgery for that reason.

''That's fine,'' Warren said. ''But what about when you go into labor? It'll take Pearson quite some time to get to St. John's, won't it?''

''He said to call as soon as I start having contractions.''

''Okay, I guess. With a first child, your labor probably won't be fast.'' Warren paused. ''What about September, Alex? What will you do about the preschool?''

She felt a stab of disappointment laced with irritation. They were having a baby. She had expected euphoria, not talk about mundane details like her work and where she would deliver. ''Evelyn can handle things until I come back, and we'll hire a temporary assistant. And a nanny, too, of course.''

''Paula can take care of the baby, Alex.''

She tensed. ''Warren, I—''

''I know. Paula works for Denise three days a week now. But I'm sure Denise won't mind finding someone else. And Paula will be thrilled to be working here again full-time. She's always saying how much she misses the kids.''

How do I tell him? Alex wondered. Choosing her words carefully, she said, ''I was thinking about hiring someone younger." Someone new, not part of the dowry; someone who won't be measuring me as a wife and mother. Comparing me to Andrea.

"Paula's the best, Alex," Warren insisted with a surge of enthusiasm. "She was terrific with Lisa, and with Nick later on, when Andrea. . . . " His voice trailed off. "I don't know how I would have managed without her," he finished in a quieter, almost somber tone. He glanced at Alex. "Unless there's something about her that bothers you?"

Alex hesitated, then said, "No, not really." Coward! she told herself. "Let me think about it, okay?"

"Sure. I want it to be our decision, Alex, not mine." He smiled. "By the way, is Pearson concerned that you're having your first child? Because you're over thirty, I mean."

She pulled away and moved her leg off his. "Many women wait to have children until they're in their thirties. Thirty-two isn't exactly decrepit, Warren. You didn't think so three weeks ago at my party." She tried to keep her voice light, to hide the annoyance she felt.

"Of course thirty-two isn't decrepit," he said, clearly surprised by her pique. In a soothing voice, he added, "I'm sure everything will be fine, Alex. Maybe I should talk to Pearson, though, find out if there are any precautions you—"

"If Pearson has any concerns, I'm sure he'll tell me," she snapped. With an effort, she softened her tone. "Pearson said I'm in great shape, honey. And he's going to schedule me for an amnio to make sure the baby's all right. It's just routine, he told me."

"Okay." He stroked her arm. "Take it easy, Alex."

"I'm sorry. I didn't mean to bite your head off." Alex hesitated, then said, "This isn't the reaction I expected. We've been trying for months, and now that I'm finally pregnant . . . Aren't you happy about the baby?" Tears stung her eyes.

"Of course I'm happy." He leaned over and kissed her. "You took me by surprise, that's all. Weren't *you* surprised when Pearson told you?"

"Yes." Warren was right, of course. She wasn't being fair. His reaction to the news had mirrored hers. She was inventing problems, as always.

"My folks will be thrilled," Warren said. He hesitated, then said, "Alex, are you going to call your parents?"

She felt her stomach muscles contract. "I don't know."

"Alex, don't you think—"

"Not now, okay?" Again she regretted her tone. "I'm sorry. I don't want to deal with that tonight. Tonight is special." She moved closer to Warren and rested her head on his chest. He stroked her hair. "Warren, should we tell Lisa? I'm not sure how she'll react—maybe she'll be embarrassed. I don't know. But I don't want her to feel left out. In fact, this may be a way for us to become closer."

He thought for a moment, then said, "Let's not tell her yet. August is a long time away. I remember how impatient Lisa was when—" He broke off.

When Andrea was pregnant with Nicholas, Alex finished silently. Why can't you say it? "Okay. Father knows best." She lay down on her back.

"I love you, Alex." There was a quiet urgency in his voice.

"I know."

"I'm really happy about the baby. *Our* baby." He placed his hand below her abdomen.

"I know that, too," she said, covering his hand with hers, wondering why she felt the faintest twinge of a feeling she couldn't quite define.

Later, after he was asleep, Alex stole out of their bed. She tiptoed across the floor to the dresser and carefully opened the middle drawer. At the back, underneath a neat stack of panties, slips, and pantyhose, was a pale gray envelope. She took the envelope, sat on the floor, and opened it. As always, her hands were trembling as she spilled the contents onto her lap.

When she was done, she replaced the envelope, shut the drawer, and walked over to the French doors that opened onto the balcony overlooking the oval swimming pool. She pulled the drape aside and looked down at the reflection of the quarter moon, a silver-gold boat gliding on the black, still waters.

She heard the rustle of sheets. A moment later, his hands were caressing her bare shoulders.

"Alex?" Warren said softly. "You're shivering. Are you okay?"

"I'm fine." She let the drape fall back into place. "I couldn't sleep."

He turned her so that she was facing him. He touched her cheek. "You were crying."

She could tell him now, she thought. She could tell him now, and although the nightmares probably wouldn't stop, would never stop, at least she could rid herself of the guilt she added, layer by layer, day by day. *And the truth will set you free,* her father had always told her. But was that really so?

"It's Larry, isn't it?" Warren whispered, stroking her arm.

"Warren—"

"Alex, it's only natural that you're thinking about him, that you're sad because he died before you had children together. Is that why you're crying?"

The truth died somewhere in her throat. "I'm crying from happiness," she said. She saw the questioning look in his amber eyes. "And hormones, I guess." Her smile was tremulous. Her eyes threatened to betray her with fresh tears. She buried her head against his chest.

"Come back to bed," he said.

Chapter 4

"Can I come, too?" Nicholas asked Alex.

She was sitting on a hunter-green vinyl stool in front of her bathroom vanity, and he was standing near her, watching as she applied makeup.

"Lipstick," she said. She pointed to the Estée Lauder tube she wanted. He handed it to her. It was their ritual, and she loved it. She applied the coral lipstick, then handed the fluted gold tube back to him. "All done. Thank you."

" 'Welcome. So *can* I?" Nicholas moved away from the vanity.

"Nope." She scrutinized her face in the mirror and softened the blush on her cheeks.

Warren entered the bathroom. "What can't Nick—hey!" he said sharply to his son. "Get off there. You could crack your head if you fell in."

Alex turned her head quickly and saw Nicholas slide off the edge of the white tub.

Nick said, "But I'm careful, Daddy."

"Nick, Daddy's right. Bathtubs are made of very hard material." To Warren, she said, "Sorry. I didn't know he was sitting there."

"Nick's not going to do that again, right, champ?" Warren feinted a jab to Nick's cheek. "Come help me pick a tie."

They left the bathroom. A moment later Alex followed. Nick was sitting on their bed; Warren was in front of the dresser, adjusting his tie. Alex crossed the room, stepped into the large walk-in closet, and started flipping though her dresses.

"Why can't I come with you and Mommy?" Nick said.

"Because tonight is for grown-ups. Just your mom and me and Aunt Denise and her boyfriend Ron."

"I don't like Ron so much. He wears too much perfume."

"After-shave," Warren said. "Men don't wear perfume. And you don't have to like him. Denise has to like him."

"Lisa said Aunt Denise likes him a whole lot. Lisa said she thinks he's a fancy. What's *fancy*, Mommy?"

"Fancy?" Alex smiled. "*Fancy* means liking nice things."

Ron *was* fancy. Custom-tailored suits, expensive silk ties, custom shirts with monogrammed cuffs. Carefully groomed, slicked-back, thick black hair. Manicured nails.

Ron and Warren had been friends at Northwestern. A half year ago, Ron had relocated to the West Coast to manage the new Century City office of the New York investment firm he worked for. He'd contacted Warren; Warren had invited him to the house a few times and introduced him to Denise. The two had been dating for several months.

Alex reached for her jade-green, jacquard-silk dress, but it wasn't where she'd put it after she'd worn it last week. She found it next to another green dress and wished for the hundredth time that Paula would stop rearranging her dresses (these she did by color) and her purses and belts and shoes and makeup. And everything in the linen closet and pantry. ("So sorry, Alex," Paula said every time. "That's how Andrea liked everything. Old habits are hard to break, aren't they?")

Alex wasn't sure Paula was trying very hard to break them.

She shut the closet door so that she was out of view, took off her robe, and slipped on the dress. "I need help," she called to Warren as she stepped out of the closet, and waited until he came over and zipped the back of the dress.

"Very, very nice," he whispered in her ear. He ran his hands over her hips.

"But snug." Three weeks had passed, and she was just starting her fourth month. Her body was changing. Her breasts were fuller but no longer achy. Every morning after she showered, she followed the La Leche booklet instructions and toweled her nipples vigorously, preparing them for the tiny, demanding mouth. At night, lying in bed in the velvety darkness, she liked to touch the firm swelling, still low in her pelvic area, that was her growing uterus. Her baby.

"Lisa wouldn't tell me what *fancy* is," Nick said, swinging his legs back and forth. "She said it's a secret and Aunt Denise told her she couldn't tell anyone. Do *you* know, Daddy?''

"Okay, champ," Warren said. "No more questions. Mommy and I have to get ready, and you have homework to do, right?''

"Daddy!" Nicholas giggled. "Five-year-old kids don't have homework!" He hopped off the bed. "Lisa said it's French.''

"The secret is French?" Alex smiled and clipped on pearl earrings.

He giggled again. "That's silly! No, the word. *Fancy*.''

Recognition dawned. Not *fancy*. *Fiancé*. She looked at Warren. He was busy examining his cuff links. He knows, Alex thought. He knows. Lisa knows. But I didn't know. She turned away, trying to hide the flush that had suffused her face.

After Nick left the room, Warren said, "You're upset, Alex. Don't be. You know how close Denise and Lisa are.''

"I'm not upset." *Liar.* "I'm just surprised, that's all.''

"Look, it's no big deal. Ron's been hinting that they're getting serious. I told you that. Denise told me he proposed, but she hasn't said yes. She isn't sure.''

"When did you talk to her?''

"A couple of days ago. I don't remember exactly.''

Now Warren was lying. He remembered everything—names, dates, phone numbers, times.

"Why?" he was saying. "What's the difference?''

"No difference. Just curious." Alex picked up her brush, drew it through her thick hair a few times, then turned to face him. "Ready.''

"You look great." He smiled.

"Thanks." She knew he meant it, but she wished it didn't feel so much like a peace offering.

When Alex and Warren came downstairs, Lisa was lying on the light taupe carpet in the family room, her legs propped up on the navy tweed couch, her ankles crossed. She was surrounded by open schoolbooks, a loose-leaf notebook, and a bag of potato chips. She was munching on chips and talking on the phone, and she interrupted both to listen to Warren's instructions. If she noticed Alex's silence, she didn't say anything.

"Have a great time, you guys," she said and returned to the phone and the chips.

Alex and Warren left the family room and walked in silence through the hall and out the door that led directly to the two-car garage.

"Alex, don't tell Denise you know," Warren said as he opened the passenger door to the forest-green Lexus. "She'll be upset with Lisa, and—"

"Of course not. Don't worry. Your secret's safe." She smiled brightly and got into the car.

The beachfront restaurant had an outdoor dining area on a wide terrace facing the water, but the March night air was too chilly, and they sat indoors. Alex and Warren came here often for the food and the soft Southwestern decor, and for the shared memory of what had been a wonderful first date.

The center of the room was filled with small square tables covered with white linen cloths; the bleached wooden chairs were upholstered in teal leather, as were the booths that lined the perimeter of the room. Several potted yucca palms in over-size terra-cotta planters sat on the adobe tile floor. The walls, roughly textured, were painted a light sand, a perfect neutral backdrop for the varied canvases that adorned them—all on loan, all from local artists. As always, Alex lingered for a few moments to study the latest offerings. As always, she felt stirring within her the urge to paint again. Maybe now . . .

Alex and Ron sat next to each other on the inside of a semicircular booth; Warren and Denise sat at the ends. Alex looked out the floor-to-ceiling windows and watched the surf silently pound the shore. Even indoors, she could smell the salty air. She relaxed against the leather of the booth.

She was in a better mood. Warren had been right, of course. There was no big deal about Denise's telling Lisa. Alex was being oversensitive.

They studied the menu for a few minutes, then ordered. The waiter arrived with a bottle of white wine and filled their goblets. As soon as the waiter left, Ron took Denise's right hand and, over her laughing protest, extended it toward Warren and Alex. A large mabe pearl, encircled with diamonds, gleamed on her fourth finger.

"It's beautiful," Alex said.

Ron said, "A beautiful ring for a beautiful girl." He took a sip of wine.

"Woman," Alex said.

Warren smiled. "Alex is always on me about that."

Ron said, "I plan to replace this with a diamond very soon." He put down his wine goblet, lifted Denise's hand to his lips, and kissed it. "To the woman I love, and plan to marry."

"Ron!" Denise exclaimed in an undertone.

Alex said, "What a wonderful surprise!" and felt Warren's thigh nudging hers.

"We're not engaged." Denise removed her hand from Ron's. "I wish you hadn't done that," she said quietly. She was blushing.

"All you have to do is say yes, honey. Hey, Warren, can you help me out here? Tell her I'm the best thing for her. She doesn't seem to believe me. Either that, or I've got some competition I don't know about."

"He's the best thing for you, Denise," Warren said lightly.

"See?" Ron said. "He's a lawyer. Lawyers don't lie. Much." He laughed.

"Not as much as investment counselors," Warren said.

Denise smiled. "You guys." She shook her head.

"Time for a toast," Ron said, lifting his glass again. "To Denise and me, to the continued friendship of all of us at this table, to never-ending happiness, and most especially, to the two *women*"—he emphasized the word and winked at Alex—"who are gracing this evening with their charm and beauty."

"Real smooth, Ron," Warren said. "And I don't mean just the wine." He laughed.

Ron kissed Denise, then leaned toward Alex. "Do I get a kiss for that eloquent speech?"

"Absolutely." She smiled and turned her cheek, but his kiss caught her on the lips, and she wasn't sure if she was imagining that his mouth was open and that she sensed the tip of what felt like, but couldn't possibly be, his tongue. Flustered, she drew back quickly and looked at Denise and Warren, but they were studying their menus. Now Ron's arm was around Denise, and he was kissing her again, on the mouth.

"I want to make another toast," Ron said. "Here's to Warren and Alex and their baby."

"Their baby?" Denise stared at Warren, then at Alex. "You're pregnant?"

You make it sound like the aftermath of an unnatural act, Alex thought, feeling the color flooding her face. She looked at Warren. *How could you?* her eyes said.

"I slipped when I was talking to Ron the other day," Warren said quietly to Alex. "And, well . . . " He turned to Ron. "I asked you not to say anything." Warren's tone was pleasant, but there was a steely undercurrent of anger.

"Hey, what the hell? You weren't going to keep it a secret forever. Anyway, we're all like family, right?" Ron grinned, then said to Denise, "They *are* married, Denise. You ought to see your face."

"I'm just so surprised. It's wonderful news," she added quickly. There was a tremor in her voice.

Alex felt instant remorse. Of course, Denise sounded strained—she was thinking about her sister, Andrea. That was only natural.

"I had no idea you two were planning on having a baby," Denise said. "When is it due, Alex?"

"August."

"You must be thrilled."

Warren smiled and took Alex's hand. "We are."

Ron said, "Denise, just say the word, and you and I can make babies of our own. How about it?"

She shook her head and smiled. "Have you told Lisa, Warren?"

"Not yet."

"I think you should tell her soon, Warren."

"I will, Denise. When the time is right."

"She might be upset. Have you thought about that?"

They're talking as if I'm not here, Alex thought with a flash of irritation, as if none of this concerns me.

Ron said, "Hey, Denise, lighten up. We're celebrating."

Denise flushed. "You're right. I'm sorry. This isn't the right time, but Lisa is sensitive, and there are things . . . "

Warren placed his hand on hers. "Lisa will be fine, Denise. We'll all be fine."

"I just want to help." She looked at Warren, then at Alex. "Congratulations, both of you. I know you're going to make a terrific mother, Alex."

"She's already a terrific mother." Warren smiled at Alex. "She's a natural." He kissed her.

"Thank you," Alex said softly.

"Of course she is," Denise said. "I just meant with her own child." She sounded flustered.

Ron said, "Well, it's no wonder Alex is a great mom. She's got all those preschool kids to practice on, right?"

Sally Lundquist, Bobby's mother, was sitting on the padded folding chair in front of Alex's desk in the small office off the main classroom when Alex entered.

Alex had met her formally a year and a half ago, when she'd registered Bobby in the preschool, and saw her frequently when she picked up Bobby in her maroon Mercedes. She was a large-framed, overweight woman in her late twenties with straight, chin-length, light brown hair that added unnecessary roundness to her already bowllike face. She had a small, pink-lipsticked mouth, a short nose, and light blue eyes fringed by pale lashes.

"Thanks for coming, Mrs. Lundquist," Alex said as she opened another folding chair and placed it next to her. "Bobby's playing with a puzzle, and Evelyn's keeping an eye on him, so don't worry."

Sally Lundquist's hands, long and surprisingly slender, rested on the quilted black leather Chanel purse that lay on the lap of her dress. "On the phone yesterday, you said Bobby's been getting into fights, so of course Donald and I are concerned. But isn't that typical of four-year-olds?" She said the last with a pointed why-did-you-drag-me-down-here tone.

"All kids fight once in a while." Alex flashed what she hoped was a reassuring yet confident smile. "I've noticed for a while that Bobby's been moody. But lately he's been fighting more and more, almost every day, and . . . well . . . he seems generally unhappy. And angry." Sullen, combative. A bully. Not words you say easily to a mother.

Mrs. Lundquist recrossed her legs. They, too, were slender and shapely, an unlikely support for her body. "Are you a psychologist, Mrs. Prescott?" The voice was carefully cool, the annoyance stronger now, no longer camouflaged.

"No. And I wouldn't presume to make a psychological evaluation." It would be unprofessional. And illegal. Maybe Evelyn's right, Alex thought; maybe calling Bobby's mother was a mistake. Maybe I should end this conference now—just thought you should know, Mrs. Lundquist. See you at car pool.. Have a nice life.

"Bobby's bright," Sally Lundquist said. "*Very* bright. We had him tested." The eyes that looked at Alex for confirmation held a hint of defiance.

And something else. Anxiety? Guilt? Both were familiar to Alex. "Bobby *is* bright. He's above average in his phonics and prereading skills. His motor development is superior, too." She paused. "But I *am* concerned about him, Mrs. Lundquist. He doesn't want to participate in group activities— shared play, story hour, circle time. Even in the yard he won't join in the exercises. He sits by himself, either on a swing or in the sandbox." Alex hesitated. "He doesn't seem to have friends, Mrs. Lundquist."

Bobby's mother fingered the gold and black ribboned chain of her purse. "Does everybody have to have friends? Is there a crime in being shy, Mrs. Prescott?" Her smile was brittle. "I was shy when I was young. Bobby's an only child, as you know, so he doesn't . . . so he can't . . . "

Alex didn't answer. She felt the woman's unspoken pain.

"Is someone upsetting him?" Sally Lundquist demanded. "Is that it? If someone's upsetting him, I want to know!" Her voice was shrill, almost hysterical.

"No one's upsetting him," Alex said softly. "At least, not as far as I know." She paused. This was the most difficult part. "I was wondering if you'd noticed any unusual behavior at home, anything that would explain Bobby's . . . unhappiness."

Sally Lundquist drew in a sharp breath. "What are you suggesting? That . . . that *we're* to blame? That's ridiculous!"

"Of course not." Careful, Alex thought. "I just wondered—"

"Donald and I are loving, caring parents! I had a caesarian when Bobby was born, but I breast-fed him, even though the doctors told me to give him formula! And I've never left him for hours on end with a housekeeper the way some people do! Never!"

"I understand," Alex said, not really understanding, not knowing what else to say.

"Maybe it *is* someone in the school who's upsetting Bobby. How do you know the other children aren't picking on him, calling him names? Starting the fights? Maybe he'd be happier somewhere else! Maybe I should take him right now and find a different school!''

I want to take my toys and go home. Alex wasn't offended or angry; she felt sympathy for the woman sitting across from her whose eyes belied the words coming out of her mouth. Alex said, "We'd hate to lose Bobby, but if that's what you want . . .''

"No, that isn't what I want! I want—oh, God, I don't know what I want!'' Suddenly she was crying, the tears spilling down her plump cheeks onto the olive-green wool of her dress. Her nose and eyes were reddening; her lips were twisted in an effort to stop them from quivering. Her eye makeup had started to streak, giving her a raccoonlike appearance.

Grief should look more dignified, Alex thought sadly. "I'd like to help, Mrs. Lundquist,'' she said. Should she reach over and touch her? If one of the children were crying, Alex would comfort, caress, croon. *Tell me where it hurts. Let me make it all better.* Aloud, she said, "Can you talk to me? Can you tell me what's wrong?''

Bobby's mother shook her head, bit her lips. She opened her purse and rummaged furiously until she found a tissue, then blotted her eyes roughly.

Alex moved forward in her chair until her knees were almost touching those of the other woman. "Sometimes I see him playing with dolls. He's very angry when he's playing, Mrs. Lundquist. He slams the dolls against the walls, on the floor.''

"He's so good!'' Sally Lundquist whispered. Her fingers were twisting the wide, polished gold band on her left hand. "You have no idea! I love him so much, and I hate what's happening to him, and I can't . . . I can't . . . '' Sobbing, she buried her head in her hands.

Was she trying to tell Alex that Bobby was being abused? Alex hadn't seen any bruises, but that didn't mean they weren't there. And there were ways, she had read, to strike a child without leaving evidence. "Is someone hitting him?'' she asked, trying to soften the words, feeling them bounce against the walls like Ping-Pong balls and reverberate in the air. Hittinghimhittinghimhittinghim.

Sally Lundquist's head jerked up. "No one's hitting Bobby! It's—" She stopped. When she spoke again, it was in a calm voice. "I have to go. I'll talk to Bobby about playing more with the other children and not fighting. I'm sure everything will be fine."

"Mrs. Lundquist, have you thought about talking to a therapist? You might find that helpful. I could give you—"

"I don't want to talk to a therapist! And I don't need your help or anyone's!"

She jumped up. Her purse fell to the floor, and a second later, its contents were strewn across the linoleum. She squatted and began to retrieve the scattered items, stuffing them back into her purse. Alex bent down and located a lipstick that had rolled under the desk. She handed it to the woman.

"Thank you." Sally Lundquist stood up and smoothed the skirt of her dress. "Please don't call the house again, Mrs. Prescott. I'll make sure everything's okay with Bobby." The voice and the pink-lipsticked mouth were fighting for control.

"Mrs. Lundquist—"

"Please!" It was a desperate wail. "No one's hitting Bobby! Stay out of my business, damn you!" She turned and rushed out of the office.

Now what? Alex wondered. Do I leave it alone? And what are the odds that Bobby Lundquist will suddenly turn into a model child? Forget "model"—what about moderately happy? She was about to leave the office when she spotted a slip of white paper, almost unnoticeable on the white linoleum. It must have fallen from Sally Lundquist's purse. Alex picked it up and hurried out to the street, but the Mercedes and its occupants were gone.

Alex walked back inside and examined the paper. The top edge was jagged; the paper had probably been torn from a small memo notebook. There was no name, just a handwritten phone number and the letters EMER. She turned the paper over. There was nothing on the back.

She would call Sally Lundquist later and tell her she'd dropped the piece of paper—assuming, of course, that Alex got the chance to talk. The woman might just hang up at the sound of her voice; she'd told Alex not to call the house about Bobby.

Alex looked again at the slip of paper. Wasn't she using it as a pretext to call Sally Lundquist and . . .

And what?

Alex sighed and put the paper in her purse.

Chapter 5

"**H**ey!" Nicholas yelled. "You're squishing me to death!"

"Sorry." Alex released him. She'd been leaning against her Jeep Cherokee, waiting for his school day to end, and when she'd seen him bouncing across the lawn, swinging his Teenage Mutant Ninja Turtle lunch box with such joy and lack of worry, she'd felt like running to him and scooping him up in her arms. Instead, she'd hugged him. Too tightly, obviously.

"You okay?" she asked. "No broken bones?"

"Nope. I'm strongest! See?" He pushed up the right sleeve of his red knit top and made a muscle.

"Awesome," she said, touching the tiny bulge on his arm. "Arnold Schwarzenegger, watch out." She saw his grin. "Let's go."

"Front seat?" he asked, hope in his voice.

"Not yet." Even though he'd be secured, she worried about his hitting the dashboard and the glove compartment. She opened the back door and he scampered in. She adjusted his harness and belt, making sure that the strap diagonally crossing his small chest was far enough away from his neck and that the lap belt was resting on his hips, not his stomach.

Driving home, she stole an occasional glance at Nicholas in the rearview mirror; each time she thought again about Bobby Lundquist, and others like him, and shuddered. She couldn't understand how anyone could abuse a child. And in spite of Sally Lundquist's denial, Alex was certain Bobby was a victim of abuse. That would explain the alternating bullying and self-imposed isolation; the rage expressed in the boy's crayoned drawings, in the pummeling he vested on the other children and, more frequently, on the mute toys in the classroom.

Whom was he hitting—the father or the mother? she won-

33

dered as she pulled into her driveway on Cabrillo. Sally Lundquist had been tearful, anxious. A concerned mother. But what if that was a pose? Sally Lundquist had been angry, too. "Stay out of my business, damn you!" she'd warned.

And the father—Donald, was that his name? Alex had met him once or twice at car pool, but she couldn't recall much about him except that, like Bobby, he had dark, curly hair. Should she talk to him? But what if he was the one who was abusing Bobby? Maybe that explained why Sally Lundquist had been so nervous.

Evelyn had been upset when Alex had described her talk with Bobby's mother, but she'd advised Alex to drop the matter—It's not as if we have any proof that anything's going on, she'd said; maybe it *is* none of our business. Maybe, Alex had said, but Evelyn was on the timid side, not wanting to take risks, to get involved. Alex would talk to Warren about the Lundquists and her worries. Warren was objective, sensible, not one to rush into action. He was also the parent of a young boy.

Paula was in the service porch, ironing, when Alex and Nicholas entered through the side door. The housekeeper was of medium height, with a square build and almost no waist. In contrast to her body, Paula's face was narrow and her nose and chin were sharp. Her light brown eyes were ringed with black eyeliner. Her hair was straight and too long; several months ago, she'd started tinting it an unnatural black that made her features seem even more severe, especially when she wore it in a ponytail, like today. (Alex frequently wore her hair in a ponytail. She wondered fleetingly from time to time whether the housekeeper was imitating her. She supposed she should be flattered.)

Alex had to continually remind herself that Paula was thirty-eight, only six years older than she was. Paula seemed older somehow. Maybe it was her matronly manner and dress, and her speech, which tended to be stiff and formal. She seemed to carry the weight of the world on her shoulders.

Alex often wondered whether Paula had been different with Andrea. Maybe not. She was a widow and childless, Warren had said; she'd had a hard life. When Paula had been living in the house, Alex had seen a framed photo on the housekeeper's dresser of her and her late husband. Next to it had been a photo of a young child. Paula's nephew, Warren had told Alex.

"How was your day, Paula?" Alex said now.

"Fine, thank you. Hello, Nicholas, dear." Paula smiled at him. "There's a snack waiting for you on the counter."

"Thanks!" He put his knapsack and lunch box on the ceramic tile floor and headed for the kitchen.

"You forgot something, young man."

Paula bent her head for a kiss and pointed to her cheek. Nicholas ran to her and kissed her. She tucked his shirt inside his jeans and smoothed his hair with her fingers.

Alex was inexplicably irritated. "Any messages?" she asked as Nicholas skipped toward the kitchen.

"No. You're low on starch." Paula shook a can of spray starch and aimed it at the nightgown on the ironing board.

It was Alex's nightgown. Alex hesitated, then said, "Please don't starch that nightgown, Paula." How many times had she made the same request? Five? Ten? A hundred?

"I've always used a little starch on nightgowns. You won't feel it, and the look is so much nicer." She sprayed the front of the nightgown and deftly ran the iron over the material.

Say something, Alex told herself. Be assertive. Instead, she gritted her teeth, annoyed with Paula and herself, and went to the entry hall table for the mail. Paula had arranged it, as usual, according to the size of the envelopes. Alex was certain that the woman scanned the envelopes to see who had sent them. She'd mentioned that to Warren again the other day. So what? he'd said. It's not as if she's reading our mail. Why don't you like her?

Because she doesn't like me, Alex had wanted to say; because she resents me and blames me for the fact that she no longer lives here, that she's here only twice a week, that she has to iron in the service porch instead of in the room that was hers. Because she's watching me, waiting for me to make a mistake. Let's get rid of her, Warren; let's get someone who didn't love Andrea and raise her children.

But Alex hadn't said anything. Her feelings were so nebulous, so impossible to prove. Voiced aloud, they would sound so childish. And Warren would be annoyed.

Fifteen minutes later Paula came into the kitchen and an-

nounced she was leaving. Alex was drinking a glass of milk—
her third of the day. Calcium for the baby.

"Thanks for everything," Alex told her, eager to shut the
door behind Paula and reclaim her house.

"You're welcome. I see you're drinking a lot of milk lately,
Alex. If you're not careful, you'll gain weight." Her lips
curved into a knowing smile. "Your nightgown came out
lovely, by the way. See you on Tuesday, dear."

"Have a nice weekend, Paula." Bitch, Alex thought as she
closed the door behind her. That wasn't the first oblique reference she'd made to Alex's pregnancy. She'd obviously seen
the prenatal vitamins in Alex's medicine cabinet. Alex had
found the vitamins and other medications rearranged.

So what's new? she thought, and wondered again why she
didn't have the courage to fire the woman.

Warren came home after six-thirty, later than usual. Normally
he came home around six, then returned to the office for one
or two hours if he had work to finish. He'd had a rough day,
he announced when he took his seat at the dining room table.
Haven't we all? Alex thought, noting that Lisa was still in the
strange, leave-me-alone mood she'd been in all afternoon.
Probably a fight with a girlfriend, Alex decided. Or a boyfriend? When did teenage girls start getting into that? She
concentrated on her salad and on the news bulletins Nicholas
volunteered between mouthfuls of food. After a while, though,
she noticed that Lisa was staring at her.

"What?" Alex finally said to her stepdaughter. She put
down her salad fork.

"Are you talking to me?" Lisa asked.

"You've been looking at me." Alex quickly smiled to take
the edge off her words. "Do I have something on my nose?
Finger paint again?" It had been a family joke, after they'd
all looked at the Polaroids taken at the birthday party.

"No paint." Warren grinned.

"I wasn't staring." Lisa took a bite of hamburger.

Yes, you were, Alex thought. "Sorry. My mistake."

"You were, too, Lisa," Nicholas said. "I saw you."

"Nick," Warren said in a mild tone. "Eat your supper."

"But she was!"

"Shut up, Nicholas!" Lisa glared at him.

"Lisa, don't talk like that," Warren said.

"Well, he started!"

"Did not!"

Christ, Alex thought wearily. Where was all this coming from? She yawned. She was still tired most of the day and found herself wanting to go to sleep ridiculously early.

"You're a brat!" Lisa was yelling.

"You're a liar!"

"Lisa!" Warren warned, a referee whose patience was wearing thin. He put down his fork.

"He called me a name, too! Why are you picking on me? Just 'cause I'm older? I'm sick and tired of that!"

"Can we drop this?" Warren said. "Please. Both of you."

All three of you, you mean, Alex thought. He was addressing his children, but she sensed she was being reprimanded, too, being held responsible as the catalyst for the squabble. Warren didn't like scenes, she knew. He wanted a quiet, serene atmosphere at home, he'd explained on one of their first dates; as a divorce attorney, he had enough of screaming, hostile clients and their equally loud opponents.

Lisa took two more bites of her hamburger, then tossed it onto the plate. "May I be excused, please? I have a lot of homework to do."

"You haven't finished your supper," Warren said.

"I'm not hungry, okay?"

Not the right tone to take with Warren, Alex knew.

"No, it's not okay." He fixed stern eyes on his daughter. "We don't waste food in this house. Finish your dinner. Then go."

Alex hesitated, then said, "Warren, I can wrap it up for her and she can have it for lunch tomorrow."

"I don't want a stupid, overcooked hamburger for lunch!"

Silence. Nicholas started to say something, but a look from his father stopped him.

"Lisa, apologize to Alex," Warren said quietly. His lips were set in a grim line.

"It's okay," Alex said quickly. "She didn't mean anything. I know that." Was this the "teenage thing"?

"It's not okay. It was rude. Lisa—"

"Alex isn't eating a hamburger. Why do I have to?"

"Because, young lady, you took one and put it on your

plate. And Alex doesn't have to explain to you what she eats.''

I'm not eating a hamburger because the smell of beef and poultry and numerous other foods makes me queasy as hell. Aloud, Alex said, ''I'm having broiled fish, Lisa. I'm keeping to a light diet because my stomach—''

''Don't lie! I'm not stupid! I know what's going on, even if I'm only fourteen years old! I know you're pregnant!'' Lisa shoved her chair back and ran out of the room.

''What's 'pregnant'?'' Nick asked. His face was almost hidden by the hamburger bun.

''I'll talk to her.'' Warren got up and left the room.

''Just you and me, kid,'' Alex said lightly.

Her face felt hot. She took a sip of water and prepared herself for the next round of questions—with five-year-olds, there were always questions—but Nicholas was chomping methodically on the bun and french fries.

Alex looked toward the doorway. What was Warren saying to Lisa? And how had Lisa known about the baby? Not from Warren, she decided. He'd been shocked by Lisa's outburst. Had she been snooping around Alex's medicine cabinet, too? And then Alex knew: Denise. Aunt and niece were inseparable.

''Finished,'' Nicholas announced after a few minutes. He pushed his chair back and stood up. ''Mommy?''

Here it comes. ''Yes?''

''*I* like your hamburgers.''

''Thanks.'' She watched him leave the room, wondered whether the compliment was sincere or self-serving, or both. She was always amazed at how blatantly children jockeyed for position, taking advantage of another's fall from grace. It happened frequently in the classroom. Alex was an only child, but she had to assume that it happened among most siblings. Among adults, too, but they were more subtle.

She had finished clearing the table and was in the kitchen rinsing the dishes when Warren and Lisa came in. They were holding hands, Alex noticed from the corner of her eye.

Warren said, ''Alex, Lisa has something to say to you.''

''Okay.'' She shut the faucet and turned around, wiping her hands on a towel.

''I'm sorry,'' Lisa said, glancing somewhere over Alex's head. ''I was angry and hurt and . . . well . . . upset, I guess.''

She looks terribly uncomfortable, Alex thought, and felt a rush of pity for the girl. First a stepmother, now a half brother or half sister. Being a teenager was difficult enough without having these complications thrust upon you.

Warren said, "I explained to Lisa why we didn't tell her before. She understands, don't you, honey?" He put his arm around his daughter and pulled her to him. "In a way, this is all for the best. Now we can all plan for the baby together. Lisa's very excited about the baby, Alex." Another hug.

Alex contemplated hugging Lisa, too, but she and Lisa rarely hugged; she decided the gesture would seem forced. She took Lisa's hand. "I'm so glad you're happy about the baby," she said warmly. "And your dad's right. It'll be fun planning things together, buying clothes, furniture." She had seen a yellow spindled crib and a matching French-style dresser in the garage (Nicholas's, no doubt), but she wanted new furniture—all white, all modern—for the spare room next to Lisa's bedroom that they planned to transform into a nursery. "I'll need your advice. And I'm counting on you in a big way to help me with the baby when it arrives." Alex smiled. "Only if you want to, of course."

"Sure. I'd like that." Lisa smiled shyly.

"That's my girl," Warren said. He was beaming at her.

In a voice she hoped was casual, Alex said, "By the way, how did you know I was pregnant?" She knew immediately from Lisa's expression that asking the question had been a mistake, but it was too late to retract it. And she wanted to know.

"I just knew." Lisa withdrew her hand from Alex's and picked up an olive from the wooden salad bowl on the counter. "Things."

"Did someone tell you? I won't be upset with the person, Lisa." Alex's smile felt tight, as if it were cracking a facial mask.

Warren frowned. "Alex, is this necessary?"

"I'm just curious, Warren." She looked again at Lisa.

"I don't remember," the girl mumbled in a sullen monotone.

Drop it, Alex told herself. But a perverse stubbornness made her continue. "Was it Denise?"

"No!" Lisa said hotly. "It wasn't Denise! Look, I said I'm

sorry. I don't want to talk about it anymore, okay?'' She shrugged off her father's arm and left the room.

It *was* Denise. The sudden bright red in Lisa's cheeks had told Alex that. She picked up a towel and reached for one of the dishes draining in the wooden rack.

"Did you have to do that?" Warren's voice was filled with impatience and a hint of anger. "It took me forever to calm her down."

Alex slapped the towel on the counter and turned to face him. "To calm *her* down? She was the one who was rude, remember? You said so yourself."

He sighed and shook his head. "This is difficult for her, Alex. You have to see that."

"You said she's excited about the baby."

"She is, but it'll take her some time to get used to the whole idea." He paused. "It's her age, it's you and me, it's . . . well, it's a lot of things." He shifted his gaze to the counter and ran his finger around the rim of the salad bowl.

"Which is precisely why your former sister-in-law shouldn't have said anything." You're behaving like a child, Alex told herself. Like one of the children in your preschool. You should send yourself to a corner, or to your room.

"Jesus, Alex, give me a break, will you?" He gave the bowl an angry spin, then grabbed it before it knocked over a glass. "I'm doing the best I can, but I don't like being in the middle like this, and you're not helping!"

She took his hand. "I know. I'm sorry." She moved closer to him, put her arms around his neck, and kissed him. "I overreacted. I don't know what got into me."

"Hormones again?" he said quietly after a moment. He was smiling. He stroked her hair.

She was forgiven. "Something like that. I'll talk to Lisa, apologize for being the wicked stepmother."

"Let me talk to her, Alex. I think that's better, okay?"

"Okay," she said, wondering whether it was a good idea to have Warren be the intermediary, again. During the past two years, she'd had the recurring feeling that if she and Lisa could just sit down and talk, really talk, maybe Lisa would open up to her and they could reach an understanding. And possibly be friends.

Alex picked up one of the stoneware plates (Nicholas's—

he'd left all the peas) and scraped the peas into the sink. The olive green reminded her of Sally Lundquist's dress and the slip of paper the woman had dropped.

Alex put down the plate, rinsed and dried her hands, then took out her daily planner from her purse. Under L in the index at the back of the planner, she'd put a yellow 3M Post-It sheet with Sally Lundquist's home number. Alex placed the call. After two rings, an answering machine clicked on. She waited for the beep at the end of the message, then spoke.

"Mrs. Lundquist, this is Alexandra Prescott from the pre-school. When we talked in my office this afternoon, you—"

"This is Donald Lundquist," a voice interrupted. "How can I help you?"

He sounded pleasant, Alex thought, and friendly. Sally Lundquist probably hadn't yet told her husband about her conversation with Alex. "Hello, Mr. Lundquist. I'm Bobby's teacher. Can I speak with your wife, please?"

"Sally's giving Bobby a bath. Can I have her call you?"

"Oh, that's not necessary. She dropped something on the floor of my office, and I didn't want her to worry about it. I'll give it to her tomorrow when she picks up Bobby."

"I'll tell her. Appreciate your calling, Mrs. Prescott. By the way, how's my little guy doing?"

Alex hesitated. "Fine, Mr. Lundquist. Just fine." Now why had she said that? she wondered as she hung up the phone.

Later, when she was reading a bedtime story to Nicholas, she thought again about Bobby Lundquist, who was far from "fine." The boy's grim situation put her own problems with Lisa in perspective, and Alex realized how lucky she was.

She touched the locket Warren had given her. It was a gesture that had become an unconscious habit.

Chapter 6

She lay on her bed in the darkened room, staring at the ceiling. *Don't think about it,* she whispered to herself, but of course she couldn't not think about it. It was like telling herself not to breathe.

Ever since she'd learned that Alex was pregnant, the knowledge had settled like a fiery lump in her chest. It was wrong, all wrong! Alex had probably tricked Warren into having a baby, just as she'd tricked him into marrying her. That was why she'd bought the preschool—not because she loved children, but because she wanted to marry Warren. She'd pretended all along.

She was a great pretender, wasn't she? Smiling at everyone, offering friendship, acting as if she cared—when the truth was that she didn't care about anyone but herself.

And Warren still didn't see through her! He thought she was perfect. "Angel," he called her. "Darling." Sometimes it was infuriating to see him so gullible, but of course, it wasn't his fault. It was Alex's fault.

Until now, she had consoled herself with the knowledge that soon Warren would see Alex for the fake she was. Now it was too late. Even if he did, he would never send her away. Not now. Not as long as she was carrying his child. . . .

Chapter 7

Bobby Lundquist wasn't in school on Wednesday or Thursday. Alex was tempted to call his home, but what would she say? Maybe Sally Lunquist *had* decided to remove Bobby; if so, that was her choice.

On Friday Bobby showed up. There was no improvement in his behavior as far as Alex or Evelyn could see. If anything, he was more belligerent than ever, and Alex spent most of the morning and afternoon separating him from the various children with whom he'd started fights. But then, she hadn't really expected a sudden turnaround; in spite of Sally Lundquist's promise that she would speak to her son, Alex didn't think she had. Or would.

At three o'clock Alex waited in the yard for Sally Lundquist to drive up to the front of the school. A few minutes later Alex saw the Mercedes, but when she escorted Bobby to the car, she saw a man she recognized as Donald Lundquist sitting in the driver's seat. Her memory had been correct; he *was* very good-looking, with piercing blue eyes and a cleft in his chin.

He turned off the ignition and got out of the car. She recognized the light gray suit—an Armani. Warren had bought one just like it a few weeks ago. She wondered what Lundquist did for a living. Whatever it was, he obviously did it well.

"Hi, guy!" Donald Lundquist said to his son. He swung him up high, then returned him to the sidewalk. "Have a good day?"

"Okay." Bobby's tone was desultory. "Where's Mommy?"

"Doing errands. I got home early, so I figured I'd pick you up and we'd stop off at Baskin Robbins for some ice cream on the way home. What do you say? Sound good?"

43

"Okay." The same tone.

Donald Lundquist opened the front passenger door, settled Bobby on the seat, and fastened the seat belt and harness.

Alex hesitated, then said, "He should really have a car seat at this age. He's under forty pounds, I think."

"You're right! I keep telling Sally to get one. I'll do it myself, tomorrow." He shut the door, then turned to Alex. "Poor kid," he said quietly. "I don't think he believed me, do you? About Sally doing errands, I mean."

"Is your wife okay?"

"Is she okay?" he repeated, then shrugged. "Who's to say? One day she is, one day she isn't . . . "

A woman in the car behind the Mercedes honked.

Alex said, "I'm afraid you can't park here. It's very busy at carpool time. If you want to talk—"

"No, that's okay. I don't want to leave Sally alone too long. I'll make this short. She told me you're concerned about Bobby, and I just want to say thank you, and please let me know how he's doing. If you think he needs help—professional help, I mean—well, tell me that, too. Sally . . . Sally isn't coping well right now. A lot of stuff. I can't get into it."

Another honk. The line of cars behind the Mercedes was growing.

"Mr. Lundquist—"

"Sorry. I'm going. The bottom line is, Sally's moods are pretty erratic, and, well, I think they're affecting Bobby. But I'm going to get on top of this situation. That's a promise." He walked around to the driver's side of his car and got in.

After he drove away, Alex remembered the paper she'd planned to return to Sally Lundquist.

On Saturday Alex and Warren were planning to take a two-hour drive with the kids to Sea World in Mission Bay, just outside San Diego. Even though she'd never been to the theme park, Alex would have preferred going to the San Diego Zoo, but Lisa had pronounced zoos in general boring, and Nicholas had been thrilled at the idea of seeing Shamu the killer whale.

Alex put on a pair of loose, elastic-waisted, white twill slacks (the only pair that still fit) and an oversize green cotton sweater that Warren liked. And her Adidas—at least her feet hadn't been affected by her pregnancy. Yet. This week she really had to shop for maternity clothes. She didn't know if there was much of a selection in Venice, but she had an appointment with Dr. Pearson on Thursday, and she'd noticed a maternity shop on Third Street, not far from his office.

The phone rang twice, then stopped. Somebody must have picked up an extension. A few mintues later Warren came into their bedroom, his electric shaver in his hand.

"That was Denise," he said. "She and Ron are thinking of joining us. They'd take their own car, of course, and they might bring Mona and Stuart along. Denise said to check if it's okay with you. I think it'll be fun, don't you?"

Now's your chance, Alex thought. Tell him that it's not okay, not at all okay, that it's important for just the four of us to spend leisure time together, away from the well-meaning people who are constant reminders of a previous wife and a previous life in which I had no part. That we need new, shared experiences to weave the strands that will make us a family.

"Sure," Alex said. "Why not?"

Warren drove Alex's Jeep. He was dressed in a pair of jeans, a white polo shirt, a white windbreaker, and a black Kings cap. Alex thought again how handsome he looked.

It was a pleasant drive, and she relaxed. As they headed south along the San Diego Freeway, Warren pointed out some of the places they passed—Irvine, San Juan Capistrano, Camp Pendleton, La Jolla. Lisa couldn't hear him; her eyes were closed and she was listening to the music coming through the Walkman earphones on her head. Nicholas munched on the snacks that Alex doled out and listened to his father and asked "How much longer?" five or six times, but Alex didn't mind. Every once in a while, she could see flashes of ocean to the right.

She had been vaguely aware that Ron's black Acura was behind them throughout the drive, but she'd forgotten about Ron and Denise and the Hutchinses. When Warren pulled into a spot in the Sea World parking lot and Ron parked right next to him, Alex was annoyed—unreasonably, she told herself. You had your chance to say no, lady.

Denise and Ron got out of the Acura first; then Mona and Stuart, both dressed for a yachting expedition in nautical whites with navy trim and matching captain's hats. Poor Stuart, Alex thought. He was glancing over his shoulder from time to time, clearly embarrassed to be on view, although Alex had to admit that with his tall, trim build, he didn't look half bad. Distinguished, actually. Mona, on the other hand, looked squat and silly, like a giant white mushroom.

Mona stared unabashedly at Alex's abdomen—so Denise had told her, too—but Alex didn't care anymore, didn't really give a damn, wished at that point that she were huge with Warren's child. She met the woman's eyes and smiled. Mona looked away.

Denise came up to Alex. "Thanks for sharing your day with us, Alex. I would've understood if you and Warren had said no."

Alex could detect nothing but affection in Denise's voice and in her warm brown eyes. What the hell, she thought. "I'm glad you could come along."

When they were all inside the theme park, Mona studied a copy of the schedule and map they'd each been given. "If we want to see everything, we'll have to be organized. Stuart, give me a piece of paper and your pen."

"Mom," Denise said, "there's no law that says we have to see everything. The idea is to relax and have a good time."

"A very good time," Ron said, and kissed her.

"Shamu!" Nicholas yelled. "I want to see Shamu!"

They saw the dolphins and a surfing show and a pirate show. And finally, Shamu the killer whale. The stadium was packed. Denise and Ron were off somewhere to the side, snuggling; Mona and Stuart had opted for a shaded spot. Alex sat alone on one of the top tiers in the stadium, well above the Splash Zone. Warren (she could hardly believe this was her husband of the heavily starched shirts and double-breasted suits) was on the ground level with Lisa and Nicholas, getting soaked by the gallons of water that overflowed from the pool with each acrobatic leap and successive landing of Shamu and her companions.

The afternoon sun was hot on Alex's face, and she felt pleasantly drowsy. She was surprised to find herself enjoying the show—the music; the appreciative oohs and ahs of the crowd that applauded the amazing feats the whales performed; the almost human interaction between the trainers and the animals, something that went beyond the reinforcement the trainers supplied by tossing pounds of herring and other small fish into the whales' gaping jaws. The whales themselves, with smooth, glossy black-and-white coats, were beautiful and fascinating—amazingly graceful for their size, almost poetic in their swift, knifelike motion through the light blue water. In one trick, Shamu and her baby swam in tandem. Alex was touched as she watched. Fecundity is everywhere, she thought.

The head trainer announced that he would give one child a special treat, an opportunity of a lifetime—to sit on the giant mammal's back. The trainer swam over to the side, and Alex peered downward to see the lucky child, and it was Nicholas! She jumped up, her heart in her throat, ready to run down the steps. But the audience was clapping, and even from high up she could see that Nicholas was grinning as he sat perched on the whale. And then he was back in Warren's arms.

"Did you see me, Mommy?" Nicholas squealed when Alex joined him on the ground level. "Did you? It was the best! I wasn't scared, not one bit!"

"You're a champ," she said, her heart still thumping. His clothes were wet and he smelled of brine and fish, and she loved him so much it was almost painful.

"Did you bring a change of clothes for him?" Mona asked Alex.

No, she hadn't. Strike one.

"I just hope he doesn't catch cold," Mona said.

"He's okay, Mona," Warren said.

"He's not that wet, Mom," Denise said. "His stuff will dry in no time."

This made up for Denise's telling Lisa about the baby. Alex thanked her silently and remembered why she liked her husband's former sister-in-law so much.

They went to Captain Kid's World next. Warren kept an eye on Nicholas, who was enjoying himself on a multitude of playground adventures. Ron, Denise, and Lisa were inside an arcade, playing games. Denise and Lisa were giggling like sisters. Alex watched them for a while with what she admitted to herself was envy; then she wandered outside to a shooting gallery with pirates for targets. She put in a token, chose a water gun, and aimed.

"Lemme show you how," she heard Ron say. Then he was behind her, his arms around her, guiding her hands. She was uncomfortably aware of how close he was, and of the fact that his arms were pressed against her breasts. She thought of the kiss in the restaurant, and quickly dismissed it, because he was almost engaged to Denise. He was a bit too friendly, that was all.

But she pulled away, forcing herself to laugh, and said, "This just isn't my game. You go ahead."

She found Warren, who was watching Nicholas bobbing and sinking in a sea of multicolored plastic balls in a giant cage. She kissed him. He put his arm around her, and she leaned her head on his shoulder. Bliss.

"Tired?" Warren smoothed her hair.

"A little," she admitted.

"I'll go get Nick. You wait here." He left her and walked around to the opening of the cage.

"Alexandra?"

It was a woman's voice, but Alex didn't recognize it. She's calling someone else, Alex decided.

"Alexandra? Is that you?" The owner of the voice was nearer now.

Alex half turned, curious to see who else bore her name, and the color drained out of her face, leaving splotches of red where the sun had tinted her nose and cheeks. Nancy Beekman and her husband! Alex wished she could turn back, hide somewhere, disappear, but it was too late. Nancy had made eye contact with her.

"It *is* you!" The gray-haired woman turned to the short, rotund man with her. "Victor, I told you I recognized her!"

Victor Beekman didn't seem impressed. He was either scowling or squinting into the sun. "How are you?"

Alex almost laughed. How *was* she? She was nauseated, dizzy with fear. Couldn't they see that? Out of the corner of her eye, she saw Warren lacing Nick's Reeboks.

"We saw your parents in church just last week, dear," the woman continued. "They didn't say you lived here."

"I don't. I'm just vacationing. I'm sorry I can't stay and talk. I'm late meeting a friend." She knew that her words and the lame excuse they formed sounded mechanical, as if she were a robot; she was being rude, but she didn't care. She had to leave, *now*.

She turned. Warren and Nicholas were approaching, hand in hand. Run! Alex told herself. But where? In seconds, Warren and Nicholas would be at her side. She moved a few feet toward them, away from the Beekmans. Not far enough, she knew.

"All set, hon," Warren said. He put his arm around her. "You okay? You look . . . strange, somehow."

Could he feel her trembling? She knew that the Beekmans were staring at her back, wondering about the handsome man and young boy who had joined her. "Too much sun." Her smile was limp.

"Mommy, can I play one game inside? Daddy said I can if you say it's okay. Please?"

"Why don't you take Nick, Warren?" Alex said in an undertone. Please leave, she willed. Please, please, please.

"I didn't know that you'd remarried, Alexandra," Nancy Beekman said. She had come closer. "How very, very nice for you. Is this your little boy? He's darling."

Alex turned to face her. She parted with the answer reluctantly, as if it were a priceless treasure about to be snatched away. "My husband's son."

Warren was looking at Alex with a who-are-these-people? lift to his eyebrows.

She had no choice but to make introductions. "Warren, these are some people from my hometown. The Beekmans." Her tongue felt thick, fuzzy. She wondered if the words coming out of her mouth made sense.

Victor Beekman extended his right hand to Warren. "Victor Beekman. My wife Nancy. Pleased to meet you."

Warren shook Victor Beekman's hand. "It's nice to finally meet people from Alex's past." He smiled widely.

Nicholas said, "Daddy, Mommy said yes, so can you take me?"

"In a minute, champ."

Nancy Beekman said, "When did you get married, dear?"

"Almost two years ago."

"I'm surprised I didn't hear about it. Although under the circumstances, I suppose you had a small wedding." She touched Alex's arm. "We were all so terribly, terribly sorry about what happened."

"Thank you," Alex whispered. "You're very kind." She was shivering and perspiring at the same time. Was that possible?

"Daddy," Nicholas said.

"Are you in touch with Larry's family, dear?"

"Not much." Alex's voice sounded strangled to her ears.

"Well, I can understand that," Nancy Beekman said somberly. "So sad. And I can understand why you left. I know it was a nightmare for you, and I can't tell you how happy we are to see that you've made a new life for yourself." She smiled. "And won't your mother be tickled when I tell her I bumped into you at Sea World, of all places. Do you live nearby?"

Warren said, "We live—"

"Daddy! C'mon!" Nicholas tugged at his father's hand, and Alex almost wept with relief.

Alex said, "Mr. and Mrs. Beekman, I'm afraid we have to go. It was nice seeing you, and I hope you enjoy your vacation."

Alex took Nicholas's hand and started walking quickly toward the arcade. She heard Warren say, "Nice to have met you"; a moment later he was next to her. Inside the arcade, Nicholas saw Lisa and Denise and ran to join them. Alex and Warren followed more slowly.

"Why'd you rush away?" Warren asked. "They looked kind of hurt, Alex. They seem like nice people."

Her ears were assailed by the clanging cacophony of video games. "They *are* nice, but I'm really tired, and I have a horrible headache. Nancy Beekman can go on and on. You know."

"I wouldn't mind hearing what you were like when you were a little girl in pigtails." He grinned and ran his fingers through her hair.

"I never had pigtails. And I don't know the Beekmans all that well."

"They seem to know all about you. And about Larry's death," Warren added in a quiet voice. "Sounds as if everyone was upset by it."

She really *did* have a headache. It was boring its way through her forehead. "People in a small town feel close, Warren. Everybody knows everything about everyone. Look, can we not talk about this? Please?"

He was violating their tacit agreement: She didn't press him about Andrea; he didn't question her about Larry.

"You're upset. I'm sorry," he said gently. "But I don't think it's because of Larry. It's because they mentioned your parents, isn't it? You must think about them, worry about them. It's only natural."

There was nothing natural about her relationship with her parents. "I try not to think about them, Warren." A thought crept through now and then, but she didn't really worry about their welfare. They seemed indomitable, armed with a stubborn righteousness and rightness that she had sometimes thought wryly would cow most illnesses. Even death.

"Alex, I know you don't get along with your folks, and I know how hurt you were when they didn't even come to our wedding. But maybe now, with the baby coming, we should invite them out here. Make a fresh start. Think about it."

"I will," Alex said.

It was a small lie compared with the other, larger ones that, like the dream, were threatening to smother her.

Chapter 8

Alex lay on the padded blue-and-white-striped canvas chaise longue on the stretch of bright green lawn that ended in front of the gates to the pool. Sunday afternoon, and no one was home except for her and Warren. No kids. No company.

A miracle.

Well, no one would be home as soon as Lisa left. She was going roller-skating along the Venice boardwalk with Denise and Ron. Nicholas was at a birthday party. Alex had dropped him off, along with the wrapped Trouble game she'd bought with him for the birthday boy (she'd had to buy another, identical game for Nicholas, who didn't yet understand the fine art of gift-giving and had become sad and pouty in the store).

Warren was in his study, working on briefs (he was always working on briefs, Alex had quickly learned). Earlier, he'd convinced Alex that it was a perfect day to sit out at the pool.

"We don't have to go in the water," he'd told her, "but it's so beautiful outside. And quiet."

"Alone at last." She'd sighed dramatically.

He'd grinned. "Think we need a chaperone?"

"Depends on what you're planning."

He had kissed her then. It had been a long, passionate kiss, and they would have made love if Lisa hadn't been home. Instead, Alex had put on a bikini—her swelling midriff wasn't very attractive, she thought, but no one would see except Warren. Then she'd taken a towel, a paperback, and suntan lotion and gone outside. Warren had promised he'd be right out.

That had been twenty minutes ago. Alex turned onto her stomach (how much longer would she be able to do that? she wondered). Her head was facing the back of the house, and she studied the two-story structure. The stucco walls were pale pink; the doors and window trim were a dark gray. Alex didn't particularly like the combination, but she hadn't picked the exterior or interior colors, or the sofas or tables or beds or accessories or anything in the house. Andrea had done that. Andrea had chosen everything, from the dining room wall-paper with the tiny blue-and-rose flower design to the glass breakfast room table with the white wrought-iron base to the hand-guided, outline-quilted rose-and-blue floral bedspread that had been on the king-size bed she and Warren had shared for thirteen years.

Change anything you want, Warren had said when he and Alex had become engaged, but she hadn't wanted to hurt his feelings, or upset Lisa or disrupt her life any more than it had already been disrupted. A month before the wedding, she'd redecorated only the master bedroom and bath, not just to surround herself with colors and textures she liked, but to strip the room where she and Warren would make love of its layers of memories.

The wallpaper had been replaced with eggshell paint. The blue carpet had hidden a fine hardwood floor. Alex had had the floor bleached and lacquered; a handwoven, creamy white fringed rug protected it from the bed frame. She'd ordered a geometric-patterned bedspread with accents of pale gray and mint green, and simple sheer drapes for the two windows and the French doors that opened onto the balcony. She'd kept the headboard, nightstands, dresser, and armoire. They were beau-tiful, in perfect condition—more contemporary, actually, than most of Andrea's selections; Alex couldn't justify getting rid of the furniture, though she knew Warren wouldn't have ar-gued.

She had bought a new mattress and box spring for the king-size bed. She had also bought perfumed soaps for the dresser drawers that had been Andrea's, but of course, the dead wom-an's scent was long gone when Alex moved into her room.

Alex had changed little in the kitchen or living room or dining room or family room—Lisa's territory. (And Paula's. The woman's proprietary manner was becoming unbearable.) At first it had grated on Alex's nerves, seeing Andrea's touch all over the house, like a ghost gliding silently, hovering. After a while she hadn't minded as much, though most days, when she thought about it, she still felt as though she'd moved into a furnished life.

Today, with the sun warming her back, she didn't want to think about it. She didn't want to think about Sea World and the Beekmans, either, but it wasn't as easy to dismiss them from her mind. She had been almost mute on the drive home to Venice; she'd gone straight to bed, pleading exhaustion and a headache. In the morning she'd been calmer, but even now, lying on the chaise longue a hundred and twenty miles from San Diego, she felt her stomach tighten at the memory of her encounter, at what had been said, at what hadn't.

But that's all it was, she told herself. A chance encounter, one in a million. Yesterday belonged to her past; she couldn't allow it or the specters of all the other yesterdays floating in her mind to shatter her painfully reconstructed life. And she couldn't stay within the cocoonlike protection of her home. That wasn't living.

There had been a moment on the drive back, when she was safe from Nancy Beekman's well-intentioned curiosity and no longer paralyzed by fear, that questions had surfaced, questions Nancy Beekman would have been happy to answer. "How is . . . ?" and "Where are . . . ?" and "What happened to . . . ?" She had pushed the questions from her mind, just as she'd done before when these and other questions had forced their way into her consciousness, stubborn growth poking its way through the cracks in her concrete resolve to turn her back on her past. The first year, when she'd lived alone in an apartment in Los Angeles, had been the hardest; she had kept a constant vigil, yanking by the roots seductive thoughts about her hometown and its streets and the people who had been part of her life for as long as she could remember. Left unchecked, she knew, these tendrils would blossom into a garden of melancholy and regret.

She closed her eyes and willed herself to relax. Her face was only a foot away from the grass, and she inhaled the sweet, spicy fragrance. From a distance she heard a honk. Ron and Denise, she thought. That meant Lisa would be leaving. She hoped Warren would come outside soon, but she felt too languid to stir from the chaise to find him.

A few minutes later she heard the rumble of the sliding-glass door that opened from the family room onto the backyard, then the slap of Warren's sandals on the bricked steps and patio leading to the yard.

"It's about time!" she called softly without opening her eyes. "How about a massage, mister?" She waited for him to reach her, then smiled as she felt his hands kneading her shoulders. "Nice," she said, enjoying the gentle pressure, wanting it to go on forever. "How about putting suntan lotion on me?"

With a teenager and a five-year-old in the house, the opportunities for flirting were rare. Grab the moment, she thought. She reached behind her back and neck, untied the double set of strings to her bikini top, then stretched her arms in front of her. "I wouldn't want a tan line."

"Uh-uh," he whispered.

She knew he was smiling, too. A moment later she felt a cold trickle on her back; she arched instinctively in protest. Warren's hands started smoothing the lotion over the skin on her shoulders and back, around the sides of her waist, the rounded periphery of her full breasts, down the long expanse of her legs, across the soles of her feet, then up again. Now his hand was stroking the inside of her thighs, higher and higher. His fingers teased the elastic of her bikini. Her breathing quickened, and she shivered with pleasure.

"Ron, Aunt Denise says we're leaving."

Lisa's voice, coming from the direction of the family room, was a sonic boom ripping through the still air.

Alex's eyes flew open. There was Lisa, on the top level of the brick steps that led down from the family room. But what was she—Alex turned halfway to Warren, but it wasn't Warren, it was Ron! He was standing at the side of the chaise longue, grinning at Alex and her exposed breasts. She'd forgotten that she'd unlaced the straps of the bikini bra.

Christ! she thought, flushed with anger and humiliation. Had Lisa seen? Alex whirled and clutched her bikini top to her chest. But Lisa was gone.

In a frigid, emotionless voice, she said, "Denise is waiting for you, Ron. I think you'd better go." With shaking hands, she fumbled with the bottom straps of the bikini.

"Lemme help," Ron said. "Two pairs of hands are always better than one."

"No, thank you! I can manage." His hands were on her sides. His touch singed her skin. She twisted away. "Don't!"

He laughed. "Hey! What're you upset about, Alex? As I recall it, *you* invited *me* to give you a . . . massage."

She could hear the grin and the insinuation in his voice. "I thought you were Warren!"

"Did you? Now, how was I supposed to know that? We had a little fun, is all. No harm done. You weren't complaining."

"You *knew* I thought you were Warren! You took advantage of me." I sound like a heroine from a Regency romance, Alex thought. She had finished tying one set of straps and was tying the other. Part of her wanted to prolong the task so that she wouldn't have to turn around and face Ron. The creep.

Warren's friend, the creep—that was the problem. Or part of it. Had she somehow given off the wrong signal, not just today, but another time? Had he mistaken friendliness for flirtation? Was he telling the truth, that he'd thought Alex had known it was Ron, not Warren?

"Well, now, exactly what did I take, huh?" he said. "Your virtue's intact. I've seen breasts before, you know. They're not an endangered species, although yours are pretty impressive."

She turned around. "How could you come on to me, touch me like that? Warren's your friend. You're practically engaged to Denise, for God's sake."

"You're blowing this out of proportion." His eyes had narrowed. He stuffed his hands into the pockets of his shorts.

"At Sea World, you were copping a feel, too. I wasn't sure at the time, but now I am. At the restaurant, you put your tongue in my mouth." She was trembling, but she kept her voice steady.

Ron was shaking his head. "You're really hot for me, aren't you? I've heard that pregnant women get crazy. All those hormones bumping into each other, the whole system out of whack. Aren't you getting enough from Warren, is that it? Some men get turned off by pregnant women. Me, I think they're sexy as hell."

"You're disgusting." She was repulsed by this man standing in front of her. How had she ever considered him attractive, pleasant? Poor Denise, she thought.

Ron sighed. "Shit, Alex, life's too short to get uptight over nothing. Calm down, will you?"

"Ron! Come on!" It was Denise.

Alex said, "Do you think Denise will think this is 'nothing'? Or Warren?"

"Coming, honey!" Ron called to Denise. He waved to her, then turned to Alex. "You planning on saying something to them?"

A breeze ruffled the grass. "Maybe I should. Maybe Denise has a right to know what she's getting into."

Ron stared at Alex for a long time. His eyes were cold, hard; Alex felt a prickle of fear. Then he smiled.

"Go ahead. But don't forget to tell her how much you liked it. Make sure you tell Warren, too. *Ciao.*" He strolled toward the family room.

Bastard, Alex thought. She felt as exposed and humiliated as she had five minutes ago.

Warren was still in the study ten minutes later when Alex went back into the house. He was talking on the phone.

"Any time," he said into the receiver, then hung up. He looked up and noticed Alex standing in the doorway. "That was Patty."

"I forgot to tell you, Warren. She asked me if she could call you about a problem she's having with her landlord. I said you wouldn't mind."

"I *don't* mind." He stood and walked over to her. "You gave up on me, huh?" he said sheepishly. He put his arm around her. "Sorry. I got sidetracked. I promise, Alex, just one minute, and I'll join you outside."

"Actually, I'm a little tired. I think I'll take a nap."

"You're mad, aren't you? I don't blame you." He nuzzled her neck.

"I'm not mad. Just tired." She yawned for effect. "The heat, and everything." Tell him! she commanded herself. "Warren, Ron came outside to the patio, and—"

"Great guy, isn't he? And Denise is so damn happy." Warren sighed. "Ron thinks she's about ready to say yes. He wants me to be best man. I wouldn't be surprised if Denise asks you to be her matron of honor. Terrific, or what?" He grinned.

Alex looked at him for a moment. "Terrific," she said.

Upstairs, she took off her bikini, showered, then put on

shorts and an oversize T-shirt. She undid the bedspread and tried napping, but sleep eluded her. Warren came into the room; she pretended to be asleep. A while later she went downstairs to the study. Warren was writing on a legal pad.

"Caught me," he said. "I was upstairs, but you were sleeping. Want to take a walk along the beach?"

"Maybe later. I'm going to my studio."

"That's a good idea." Warren smiled. "Have fun."

Her "studio" was off the laundry room. It was a midsize rectangle with generous morning and afternoon light. It had been Paula's room, and six months after Alex and Warren married and Paula was no longer living in the house, Alex had used it to store luggage, boxes of books, supplies for the preschool, odds and ends. Empty, the room had been a constant admonishment—a shrine to Paula the Noble, whom Alex the Terrible had banished.

Last Wednesday Alex had asked Warren to move the clutter to the garage. In a local art store she'd browsed through the aisles with quickening excitement as she selected an easel, charcoal sticks, pastels, watercolors, a palette, oils, a large tablet of sketching paper, and several sheets of canvas. She'd also bought a large plastic tarp to protect the carpet. Eventually, she'd have the carpet replaced with linoleum.

On the way home, with the Jeep loaded with all her purchases, she had wondered, suddenly nervous, whether this was a mistake, whether her fingers, still for so long, had forgotten how. Their first strokes had been tentative, as if they were embracing a new lover, but they had quickly found their rhythm. And she had found a measure of peace and contentment that she had thought she'd lost forever.

The next day she'd bought a small easel, sketching paper, and a box of colored pencils for Nicholas, who had been instantly fascinated by the studio, and cautioned him gently that the room and the supplies were off limits.

"Can I draw in here with you?" Nicholas had asked.

"Sometimes. Other times I need to be alone when I draw. Okay, Nick?"

" 'Kay." He nodded solemnly. "Can you draw me now?"

She quickly sketched his face. "This is me!" he exclaimed, grinning, and ran to show Warren. She drew one for Lisa, too. The girl stared at the sketch, then at Alex.

"You're really good," she said quietly.

Was that pride in her eyes? "Thank you," Alex said.

In the studio now, Alex took her sketch pad and sat cross-legged on the small tan corduroy sofa bed. She stared at the blank sheet of pristine white paper, then tore it off and clipped it to her easel over a pastel still life she'd been working on. She picked up a charcoal stick; her hand began moving across the paper in quick, dark, angry strokes. A half hour later she was finished. She stepped back and gazed at the menacing likeness of Ron Gilman with exaggerated muscles and a leer. He looked ridiculous. She felt infinitely better.

She was about to pull the paper off the easel when she sensed that someone was standing behind her in the doorway to the hall. She turned. It was Lisa.

Acutely aware of Ron's leering face and muscular body on the paper, Alex blocked the easel. She smiled. "Have a nice time?"

"Pretty good."

"Hungry? I can fix you a sandwich. Matter of fact, I'll join you. Somehow I skipped lunch, and I'm starving."

"No, thanks." Lisa disappeared from the doorway.

Great, Alex thought, and sighed. Since the "hamburger" confrontation and reconciliation, Lisa had been pleasant if not exuberant, and although Alex still caught the girl staring at her from time to time, she attributed that to normal teenage curiosity. Now Lisa was abrupt, terse.

It was the incident with Ron, Alex decided. She yanked the sketch off the easel, crumpled it up, and tossed it into a trash can. She searched the downstairs rooms. No Lisa. She went upstairs and knocked on the girl's closed door.

"Can I come in, Lisa?"

"Fine."

Alex opened the door and stepped into the room. The pink room, she called it. Almost everything in it was pale pink—the carpet, the tulips on the wallpaper, the ruffled bedspread and canopy, the pleated Roman shades, the lamp on the dresser, the waste basket. The furniture was white with pink handles. Every time Alex stepped into the room, she felt she was being swallowed by a giant cone of cotton candy.

Lisa was at her desk. She didn't turn around when Alex entered. Alex walked over to her.

"Lisa, can we talk a minute?"

"What about?"

"Can you turn around? I'd feel a lot more comfortable talking to your face." She maintained a smile while Lisa swiveled to face her. "Lisa, I sense that something's bothering you."

"Who said?" She picked at the cuticle of her thumb.

"It's just a feeling."

Lisa shrugged.

"You won't even look at me."

"Last time you complained I was staring at you."

Alex clenched her fists and unclenched them. "You're angry with me. Can't you tell me why? Whatever it is, it's better if we talk about it." But was that true? It would be difficult and awkward for Alex to explain to her fourteen-year-old stepdaughter what had happened. And would the girl believe her?

No response from Lisa.

"Lisa, sometimes people are placed in compromising positions. That means that a situation can make it look as if someone is doing something wrong, when really he—or she—is totally innocent. Do you understand what I mean?"

Lisa turned back to her desk. "I have a lot of homework."

It was a curt dismissal, and very effective. Alex felt as if Lisa had slapped her. She left the room and shut the door behind her. She felt anxious because Lisa hadn't let her explain, and curiously relieved for the same reason.

Damn Ron Gilman for being an immature, conceited pig.

And damn the Fates for toying with her. Two days ago, everything had seemed fine. Her life had finally achieved an even keel, and she'd almost convinced herself that she could stop looking over her shoulder at the past. And then the Fates had thrown the Beekmans at her.

Not that she really believed in the Fates. Meeting the Beekmans was a coincidence, that was all. And Ron was just a randy jerk. What was next? she wondered irritably.

Nothing, she told herself quickly, afraid to tempt the non-existent Fates she'd just damned. Nothing is next.

She touched the locket automatically for reassurance.

Nicholas returned from the party exhausted. He'd had a good time, he said, but the whistle in his goody bag didn't work, and could Alex get him another one?

"Absolutely," she told him.

Later she filled the tub in the bathroom off his bedroom. Sometime in the past few months he'd developed a sense of modesty about his body, so she waited in the doorway to the bathroom while he took off his underwear.

"I'm going in!" he called.

"Careful. One foot in, both hands on the tub, then the other foot."

"I know." A moment later: "I'm in!"

She entered the bathroom and knelt on the blue mat at the side of the white tub. She watched as he soaped his arms and chest and sturdy legs with a washcloth. She would have liked to do it for him, but he was proud of his independence.

"Doing my ears," he announced, and she had to smile.

He shampooed his hair but let her rinse out the lather with a spray nozzle attached to the faucet. Then he lay back and submerged his head until only his face was above the water. She knew he was propping himself up on his arms, but it was hard, as always, to keep her hands from reaching out to support his back. His darkened hair floated around his face like a lion's mane.

He sat up, grinning. "All done."

She turned and stood, then picked up a thick blue terry bath sheet lying on the toilet seat.

"Ready." He was standing with his back to her. "Don't look."

"I won't."

With the towel held open in front of her, she leaned toward him. She wrapped him in the towel, picked him up, and carried him in her arms to his bed, savoring the smell of his hair and body, the slick wetness of his skin. He bounced as she dropped him carefully onto the bed, and giggled.

She went downstairs to prepare supper. On the way to the kitchen, she stopped in the studio to put away her supplies. The trash can was filled with several days' worth of aborted efforts. And her sketch of Ron Gilman. She had the urge to see it once more before she consigned it to oblivion, and reached into the trash can for the crumpled ball that had been his face.

It wasn't there.

She rummaged through the papers, uncrumpled two balls,

neither of which was Ron. She went back upstairs to Nicholas's room and knocked on the door.

"Come in!"

She opened the door and walked in. "Nick, when you came back from the party, did you take anything from the trash can in my study?"

" 'Course not. You said not to."

Of course not. "Right. I forgot. Thanks."

Lisa had taken it. Alex had known even before she'd asked Nicholas.

Chapter 9

Driving to Denise's house on Monday morning, Alex wasn't sure she was doing the right thing.

She'd wanted to ask Warren's advice but had decided not to tell him about Ron. Warren liked Ron; she didn't want to be the cause of an end to their friendship. Warren might resent her for it. And he might think that she was overreacting—or worse, that she'd invited Ron's advances. And how could she explain that she hadn't known that another man's hands were touching her?

She would have liked to put the incident behind her, but she was burdened with the knowledge. And Lisa had the sketch of Ron; Alex was sure of that. What if Lisa told Denise about the sketch and what she'd seen—or thought she'd seen? Lisa was close to her aunt—they were like sisters, everyone said.

Of course, Denise might not be home, Alex realized as she turned onto Linnie, the narrow street where Denise lived; she might be with a client. But the BMW (a gift from Denise's parents, Alex knew) was in the driveway. Maybe it was a sign.

Alex parked the Jeep in front of the house and walked up the short flagstone walkway. She'd wondered why Denise hadn't chosen a house near her parents in Pacific Palisades, a wealthy beach community to the south—was it so that she could be closer to Warren and the kids? According to Warren, though, Denise had preferred Venice because there were more singles here. The house, like the car, had been a gift from Denise's parents. A very expensive gift—the small, one-story structure sat on prime property that abutted Linnie Canal. A good investment, Stuart Hutchins had decided.

A year ago, Denise had mentioned that a newly built, two-story house on Sherman Canal had gone into foreclosure.

Were Warren and Alex interested in looking at it? Warren *had* been interested, and Lisa had campaigned madly for the move. But the price had been too steep, and Alex wasn't disappointed. The canals were quaint and charming—strolling along Dell Avenue with Warren and the kids, she had viewed them more than once from the bridges that Dell formed—but she didn't need a canal in her backyard. And she didn't really want to live around the corner from Denise.

Paula answered the door. Alex was flustered—she'd momentarily forgotten that the woman worked for Denise on Mondays. Wednesdays and Thursdays, too.

"Good morning, Alex. How are you?" Paula's large frame filled the doorway, and she made no move to invite Alex in.

She's putting me in my place, Alex realized, letting me know this isn't my turf. "Fine, thanks, Paula. I came to see Denise."

"I'll tell her you're here." Paula left the entry.

Alex stepped inside the house. A moment later Denise appeared. She was wearing a mint-green jogging outfit, and her blond hair was pulled back in a ponytail. She looks Lisa's age, Alex thought.

"Alex! What a surprise!" A frown suddenly crossed Denise's face. "Nothing's wrong with the kids, is there?"

"They're fine. I thought I'd stop by on the way to work. There's something I want to talk to you about."

There was curiosity in Denise's brown eyes. "Sure."

They sat in the living room. Alex had been to Denise's house several times with Warren, but she was struck again by the simple beauty of the room and its furnishings. The walls were light cream. On an Oriental rug with a delicate floral design, pale peach raw-silk love seats faced each other across a square glass table with a clear lucite base. A sleek black baby grand piano sat imperiously in the far corner. Above the emerald-green marble fireplace was a Chagall. Warren had told Alex that, like all the artwork in the senior Hutchinses' home, the lithograph was authentic. Denise's jogging suit matched the green of the flowers in the Oriental rug, Alex noted.

"I'm glad you came by," Denise said. "I was going to call you later this week anyway." She smiled and put her hand on Alex's. "I want to give you a baby shower."

Oh, God! This made it so much harder. "Denise—"

"It's no trouble, believe me. We'll have it outdoors—a luncheon, if that's okay with you. Just give me a list of the people you'd like invited, and I'll take care of the rest. It'll be fun." Another smile.

Alex tried to match it. "That's so thoughtful of you, Denise. Let me think about it, all right?" Five minutes from now, Denise probably wouldn't feel like giving Alex a shower. Or anything.

Denise put her index finger to her lips. "You're not superstitious, are you? About baby showers, I mean."

"No."

"Good. Some people are. They think a shower will bring bad luck. I think that's silly." She smiled again. "But tell me why you're here."

Alex lowered her eyes to the Lalique peacock on the table. "This is awkward, Denise," she began in a low voice. "I'm not even sure whether I should tell you this."

"Tell me what?"

Alex didn't look at her, but she knew that Denise's smile had disappeared. "On Sunday, when you came by to pick up Lisa, Ron . . . Ron flirted with me." Alex told her what had happened. "I thought it was Warren," she added. It sounded lame, even to her own ears. "I didn't want to hurt you, but I thought you had a right to know."

"Of course." Denise's voice was as smooth and impersonal as glass. "Did you tell Warren?"

Alex shook her head. "I don't plan to." She explained her reasons. "I think Lisa saw us, though. I talked to her about it in vague terms, but I don't know . . ."

The silence seemed to pulsate in the air.

"Well," Denise finally said. The word was a sigh. "So much for Ron's undying love for me, huh?"

"Maybe I overreacted," Alex said, seeing the pain on Denise's face. Maybe I shouldn't have come.

"You don't think so, or you wouldn't be here, would you?"

Alex didn't answer.

"I suppose I should thank you," Denise said. "Better to know sooner than later, right?" She paused. "You know what's funny? I feel devastated. Ten minutes ago, I wasn't all that sure I wanted to marry Ron. He's awfully handsome and charming, and he's extremely successful, but he's a little too slick, you know?'' Her lips curved into a half smile. ''I guess you *do* know.''

Alex flushed. ''Denise—''

Denise stood up. ''Thanks for coming by, Alex. I mean that. I'm sure this was difficult for you.''

''Maybe you should talk to Ron. Maybe he doesn't realize—''

''Alex, would you leave, please? Because I really, really, really don't want to talk about this anymore, all right?''

Alex touched Denise's hand. ''I'm sorry, Denise.''

Denise walked out of the beautifully furnished living room and disappeared from view.

Alex let herself out.

''So what do you think?'' Alex asked Evelyn.

They were sitting cross-legged on the classroom floor. It was nap time. The yellow-and-white mini-blinds on all the windows were shut, bathing the room in a soft, tranquil, cozy semidarkness. Most of the preschoolers were asleep, some with thumbs in their mouths. A few stubborn children were lying on their dark blue vinyl mats with their eyes open. Whenever Alex or Evelyn glanced their way, the eyes shut quickly. Patty had arrived early; she was sponging off the tables that were sticky from lunch.

''Evelyn?'' Alex prompted.

''Sorry. I was thinking. I just can't believe what you're telling me. Why would he do it?''

''I can't sleep!'' a little girl cried.

Alex started to get up but saw Patty hurrying to the child's side. ''Who knows? He's got a disease. Or he likes the thrill. Or maybe he doesn't think it's a big deal.'' She shrugged. ''I feel terrible about Denise. You should have seen her. And what about Warren? Do I tell him? Or do I forget it ever happened?'' Not that she could. She would never feel comfortable around Ron again. And how would she hide that from Warren?

''My opinion? Don't say anything to Warren. His ego will probably be hurt. As far as Denise is concerned—''

The side door was flung open and slammed shut. Alex and Evelyn turned. Patty had turned, too.

It was Donald Lundquist. Alex recognized him in the semidarkness. She got to her feet and hurried toward him.

"Mr. Lundquist," she whispered, "all the children—"

"Where's Bobby?" he demanded. His handsome face was furrowed with lines of anxiety.

"He didn't come to school today. I assumed he was sick."

"I went home to check on Sally because she hasn't been feeling well, but she wasn't there. Some of her clothes are missing. Bobby's things are missing, too. I have to find my wife and son!"

Sally Lundquist had run away with Bobby? Why? Alex pictured his dark, curly hair and his beautiful face, so unhappy, so forlorn. From behind her, Alex heard rustling sounds and comforting "Shhhs" from Evelyn and Patty.

"Mr. Lundquist, we're disturbing the children. Let's talk outside, all right?" She opened the door and steered him firmly outside, then pulled the door shut behind her. She squinted at the sudden brightness. Parked in front of the school entrance was a silver Jaguar. Probably Lundquist's, she decided.

"Could your wife have gone to visit relatives?" Alex asked.

"I called her parents in Arizona. They haven't heard from her. Her car's in the driveway, so she must've taken a taxi. I talked to the neighbors. Nobody saw anything."

"What about friends?" Alex suggested.

"They don't know anything." He pressed his hand against his forehead. "What frightens me is that I don't know what Sally will do. I told you before that she's having a hard time coping." He gazed at Alex. "She talked to you last week. Did she mention anything about going away?"

Alex shook her head.

"What did you talk about? Maybe it'll help me figure out what happened."

"We talked about Bobby." She saw the father's face tighten. "Bobby is unhappy, Mr. Lundquist. He fights with the children. He's been having difficulty socializing."

Donald Lundquist nodded, then sighed. "Poor kid. He deserves better than this. What did Sally say?"

"Your wife was distraught, Mr. Lundquist. She was crying. I suggested that she get professional help."

"What else did she tell you?"

"Nothing else."

"She must have said something." His voice rang with desperate urgency. "She must have told you why Bobby's upset."

Alex shook her head. "She said you were both loving, caring parents. That Bobby was a very good boy." She hesitated. "I had the feeling she was trying to tell me something, but couldn't."

Lundquist frowned. "Tell you what?"

"I don't know. I pressed her. That's when she started to cry." Alex saw Sally Lundquist's tear-blotched face, saw her jump up from the chair, heard the clatter of the objects that fell from her purse onto the floor. A lipstick. A compact. Suddenly she remembered the paper Sally had dropped. A paper with a seven-digit number and the letters EMER. *Emergency?* The paper was in Alex's office, in the middle drawer. It was probably nothing. Still . . . She could feel Lundquist staring at her.

"You just remembered something, didn't you?"

"I'm not sure that it's—"

"Tell me!"

Alex flinched at his tone.

"Sorry," he said quickly. He ran his fingers through his dark hair. "I'm just so upset, Mrs. Prescott. I'm desperate for a clue, any clue. I'm sure you can understand."

"Of course." She didn't like Donald Lundquist, she decided. She didn't like him at all.

"So you can also understand why I need your help. What is it that you remembered?" he asked quietly.

"I'm sorry." She shook her head. "I thought I remembered something, but now it's gone." She tried what she hoped was a sympathetic but rueful smile.

"You're lying! You know where she is, don't you? Tell me where they are!"

"Mr. Lundquist—"

He grabbed her arm. "You're helping her, aren't you?"

She felt a flutter of fear. "You're hurting me. Take your hand off me." She tried to move her arm.

He tightened his grip. "What did she tell you, that I hit her? Is that what she said?"

"No. Take your hand off me," she repeated more firmly.

He laughed and released her arm. "Like hell she didn't. I can see it in your face. She went to a goddamn women's shelter, didn't she? She's been threatening to do it, the fat cow."

It was all so clear now—an anxious, almost hysterical mother; a hostile, violent, antisocial child. Mother and son were the victims of the man standing in front of Alex.

"Look," Donald Lundquist said, "tell me where she is, Mrs. Prescott. All I want to do is talk to her. Don't I have the right to talk to my wife? To see my kid?"

His voice was buttery with the false conciliation that Alex knew so well. *C'mon, Alex. Give me another chance.* "I don't know where your wife is," she told Lundquist.

He pointed his finger at her. "You put her up to this, didn't you? Is that the kind of professional help you advised her to get? You and all those other feminist bitches who mess up people's marriages? I want my wife! I want my wife and my son!"

His face was inches from hers now. She fought to keep from cringing. "I want you to leave, Mr. Lundquist. Right now, before I call the police."

"You don't have to call the police, lady, 'cause I'm calling them. They're gonna ask you the same questions I'm asking you, and you'll have to answer them. And if they don't help me find Sally and Bobby, I'll get a private detective to find them. I'll do whatever it takes."

"That's fine." She reached behind her for the doorknob.

"You're enjoying this, aren't you? You gonna report to Sally after I leave?"

Alex sighed. "Mr. Lundquist, for the last time, I don't know where your wife is."

He nodded. "Yes, you do. I know you're lying. I saw it on your face. I'm warning you, Mrs. Precott. Tell me where they are, or I'm going to ruin you and your goddamn school."

Alex turned the knob, pushed the door open, stepped quickly inside, and shut the door. With shaking hands, she locked it.

"You think I'm joking?" he yelled through the door. "I'll shut you down, you meddling bitch! You think I can't do it?"

The door reverberated with his pounding.

Evelyn hurried to Alex's side. "What's going on?" she

whispered. "Patty and I heard all the screaming. The kids did, too. They're scared."

The children, Alex saw, were all sitting up on their mats. Patty was circulating among them. In between the sounds of Lundquist's blows to the door, Alex could hear the sound of crying.

The pounding stopped. The sudden silence was more frightening than the noise.

"Go to the office and make sure the back door is locked," Alex whispered. "I'll explain later."

Evelyn hurried away, then returned a moment later. "Done. Should I call the police?"

"Wait." Alex went over to one of the windows that faced the street and peeked through the closed mini-blinds. There was no sign of Donald Lundquist or the Jaguar she'd seen parked in front of the school minutes ago.

"He's gone," she said. For now, she added to herself.

After helping Evelyn and Patty quiet the children, Alex went to her office. From her desk drawer she took the paper Sally Lundquist had dropped and dialed the numbers written on it.

A woman answered the phone. "Yes?"

"This is Alexandra Prescott. May I please speak to Sally Lundquist?"

"You've dialed the wrong number."

"Is this 555-6803?"

"Yes. But there's no one with that name here. Sorry."

"Are you—"

The woman had hung up. The dial tone blared in Alex's ear. She folded the paper and put it in her purse.

"Press out the bubbles," Alex told Nicholas.

It was after supper, and they were in the kitchen, making an apple pie. Nicholas was standing on a step stool, pushing the rolling pin back and forth over the dough Alex had prepared and placed on the flour-dusted Tupperware plastic sheet.

"Like this?" Nicholas said without looking up.

"Perfect." She leaned down and nuzzled the back of his neck. She loved his little-boy, slightly sour smell.

"Mommy!" He giggled, then frowned. "I'll mess the dough and have to start all over."

"One kiss," she demanded. "A good one."

"Okay." He turned to her, placed his palms on her cheeks, and kissed her.

"Delicious."

The phone rang. Alex wiped her hands on a paper towel and picked up the receiver on the wall phone. "Hello?"

"You bitch!"

The anger in the voice made her wince. How had Lundquist gotten her home number? "Look, if you don't leave me alone—"

"You had to tell her, didn't you?"

It wasn't Lundquist. It was Ron. She glanced at Nicholas. He was busy rolling the dough. "I'm sorry," she said, almost whispering, "but I think Denise had a right to know. I can understand your being angry—"

"Well, isn't that generous of you! I have news for you. I'm not bowing out of the picture so fast, honey. Denise'll take me back. You can bet on it. You stay out of my life. I'll stay out of yours, okay?"

"I hope everything works out for you."

"Sure you do." His laugh was ugly. "You know, I feel damn sorry for Warren. From what I hear, Andrea was one hell of a woman, not some patronizing, moralizing, emotionally screwed-up feminist bitch who meddled in people's lives."

This must be a record, she thought wearily, being called an interfering, feminist bitch by two men in one day. She was aware that Nicholas was looking at her, and she tried to keep her voice pleasant. "Good night," she said.

"Good night my ass. I'm not done. You—"

She felt like slamming the receiver onto the cradle. Instead, she hung up quietly. As she turned toward Nicholas, she saw that Warren had entered the room. He walked over to the counter where Nicholas was working, pinched off dough from the edge, and put it in his mouth.

"Hey! You messed my job!" Nicholas said. "And we can't eat raw dough. Mommy said it can make you sick."

"Oh, no!" Warren clutched his stomach and groaned.

Nicholas laughed. "Daddy, you're silly!"

"Who, me?" Warren's eyebrows formed comic arcs. He turned to Alex. "Who was that on the phone?"

"Evelyn," she said automatically. She felt sick, and not from raw dough. She sensed the color rising up her neck.

"You ought to see your face," Warren said.

Did he know she was lying? "Warren—"

"Flour all over yourself." Grinning, he shook his head, then took a paper towel, moistened it under the tap, and wiped Alex's face. His grin faded. "What's wrong, Alex? Something Evelyn said?"

"I can't stop thinking about Donald Lundquist." This wasn't a lie. She had replayed their confrontation over and over, could still feel his hand gripping her arm, could hear the pounding on the preschool door.

"His wife and son are probably safe, wherever they are. And chances are he won't come back. If he does, or if you're really worried, call the police."

"Is he a bad man?" Nicholas asked. He had stepped off the stool and come closer to Alex and Warren.

"He's an angry man, sweetheart," Alex said. And probably a bad man, although who could define "bad"? Was Ron "bad"?

"Why is he angry at you, Mommy?" Nicholas grasped Alex's hand and turned to Warren. "Daddy, you're not going to let him hurt Mommy, are you?"

" 'Course not, Nick." He put his arm around his son. "No one's going to hurt Mommy. Or any of us."

Chapter 10

*T*he warm water was soothing. She sat in the tub, then slid down until only her head was above the water. She closed her eyes, letting the steam circulate around her head, and felt the tension seep out of her.

Alex would leave. Warren would be upset, of course; Nicholas would be sad, too, but only for a short while. They would both get used to her absence—Warren had gotten over Andrea, hadn't he?—and then everything would be the way it had been, the way it was supposed to be, before Alex came and seduced her way into their lives with her beautiful face and beautiful body and beautiful long, thick black hair. Just like Hester Prynne's. Hester Prynne had been a seductress, too, but at least she'd had to wear a scarlet letter so that everyone would know what she was.

Not Alex. Alex could do anything she wanted and get away with it. And one man wasn't good enough for her! Here she was, pregnant with Warren's child, and she was flirting with another man, practically inviting him to make love to her! It was disgusting, totally disgusting, the way she flaunted her body!

Warren deserved better. Much better.

The trouble was that Warren didn't know the truth about Alex. At first she was going to tell him, she wanted so badly to tell him, he had a right to know! But she realized he wouldn't believe her. Alex would seduce him into believing that she was the perfect wife and lover and mother, "Oh, Warren, I love you so much, I'm so thrilled to be having your baby, how could you even think for one minute . . ." Even though right outside, in his own yard, she was taking off her clothes for another man!

She couldn't tell Warren the truth, but she would find an-

other way. She could send him an anonymous letter. Or she could "accidentally" slip and tell him Alex's version of what happened—"Oh, I'm sorry, I thought you knew," she'd say— and let him wonder. And maybe worry.

And if that didn't work . . .

If that didn't work . . .

She pressed her hands against her temples, as if by doing so she could push the thoughts back into a recess of her mind where she wouldn't hear them.

They were ugly thoughts, evil thoughts. They frightened her and made her wonder if there was something very, very wrong with her. She kept telling herself that she didn't wish Alex harm, that she just wanted her to disappear. Most of the time she believed it, but sometimes she had the feeling that if Alex didn't go away soon, something terrible would happen.

Chapter 11

Alex was half expecting to see the silver Jaguar in front of the school the next morning, but it wasn't there. Relieved, she pulled into the small lot in the back and parked her Jeep.

Carrying two paper bags filled with the beginnings of construction-paper art projects the children would be working on that morning, she made her way to the back door. She almost dropped the bags.

The door and frame were splintered.

Donald Lundquist.

Her heart started thumping. Knowing instinctively that she shouldn't touch the knob, she pushed the center of the door. It opened onto a dark hallway.

She stood rooted to the concrete. She could go in and call the police, but what if he were still there? She hurried to the Jeep, placed the bags in the back of the car, and ran to the nearest neighbor to call the police.

Within minutes, a police siren was piercing the early morning quiet. The sound became louder and shriller—she hated it, really hated it, felt like covering her ears to dull its insistent whine. She waited with clenched fists in front of the neighbor's house for the patrol car.

Two uniformed male officers stepped out of the car. One was young, surfer-blond; the other was older, shorter, darker-complexioned. After speaking briefly with Alex, they drew their weapons and entered the building. Several minutes later—it seemed like an eternity to her—they emerged.

"The place is empty," the older officer told Alex. "Some damage, though."

The blond officer stayed outside. Alex followed the older one into the building and into her office. Papers and manila

75

folders that had been on her desk were strewn all over the linoleum. Her desk drawers were open. So were the drawers of the beige metal filing cabinet in the corner. She walked over to her desk first.

"Anything missing?" the officer asked.

He'd introduced himself and his partner to her outside, but she hadn't concentrated and couldn't remember their names. Now she was too embarrassed to ask.

She examined the contents of the drawers. "I don't think so. I don't keep anything valuable here. Just papers, bills."

"What about here?" He pointed to the open file cabinet.

"I keep a folder on each of our preschoolers." Alex walked over to the file cabinet and scanned the folders. "Lundquist" was there. But then, Donald Lundquist wouldn't have removed it and pointed to himself as the culprit. And the fact that the folder was there didn't mean he hadn't looked through it.

"Everything seems to be here," she told the officer. "What about the main room?" Had Lundquist trashed that, too?

"It's not pretty."

"Not pretty" turned out to be an understatement. Bookcases had been toppled. Posters and children's art projects had been ripped off the walls. Finger paints had been smeared across tables, on the walls and floor, on the mini-blinds. The floor was a sea of books and crayons and toys of all shapes and sizes.

It would take hours, maybe days, to clean the room. The children's art projects were ruined. And how would she explain that to them without frightening them? Alex felt tears welling in her eyes. She was filled with sadness and exhaustion. And rage. Definitely rage.

"Any idea who did this, ma'am?" the officer asked.

She turned to face him. "Donald Lundquist." She explained about Bobby Lundquist and his overweight, tearful mother; about her confrontation with the father yesterday afternoon.

"He thinks I know where his wife and son are. He must've broken in to look for something that would tell him where to find them." The rest was just spite, or, if she wanted to be generous, frustration. But she didn't want to be generous. She wanted to punch Donald Lundquist in the mouth.

"*Do* you know where his wife and son are?"

Alex shook her head.

"Could be Lundquist. On the other hand, could be kids."

"It's Lundquist," Alex insisted. "I'm sure of it."

"We'll pay him a visit, see if we can get his prints. We'll try to raise some prints here. If there's a match, great. If not, well, it'll be tougher to prove. We'll start in the classroom. With the paint and all, we might have some luck. By the way, you'd better call the parents, tell 'em school's closed, at least for today. Try not to touch anything, okay?"

Oh, God! The parents! Alex looked at her watch. It was nine-ten. School opened at nine-thirty. Most of the parents would already be on their way, but maybe she could reach some of them. As she rushed to her office to make the calls, she wondered what she would say. She didn't want to mention the vandalism—that would frighten the parents and make them think her preschool was unsafe. But parents dropping off their children would realize that something serious had happened the minute they saw the black-and-white police vehicle in front of the school. And the news would certainly spread.

She found the parent roster among the papers littering the floor. As she dialed the first number, she rehearsed her speech: the school had been vandalized, maybe by kids. (That wasn't a lie; the officer believed it was a possibility, even if she thought otherwise.) She would say nothing about Lundquist. A random break-in was one thing; in this day and age, it was almost inevitable. A disgruntled, unhinged parent was far more frightening and brought with it images of repeated violence.

Evelyn arrived as Alex completed her eighth call. (Of the eight parents, she had reached only two. "Oh, my God!" both mothers had said. "It's those gangs, isn't it? I heard more of them were coming to Venice!" Alex hadn't corrected the women.)

"What's going on?" Evelyn's dark eyes were wide with fear. "The officer outside said someone broke in and vandalized the school! Why would anyone do that?"

Alex quickly explained what had happened, then handed Evelyn the roster. "Start with the Foleys. Tell whoever you reach that school will be closed today and maybe tomorrow. We'll let them know. Don't say anything about Lundquist, Evelyn."

"Of course not! My God, Alex, he must be crazy to do something like this! What if he comes back?"

"God forbid! You make the calls. I'm going outside. I want to be there when the parents arrive. I don't want them to panic when they see the police car."

It took more than an hour before the last parent had driven away. Alex had had to calm, to explain, to reassure. She walked back inside the building, physically and emotionally drained.

Evelyn was sorting the papers lying on the floor. The police, she told Alex, were still busy in the classroom. Alex went to find them.

"When do you think we can start cleaning up?" Alex asked the officers. Minutes ago, while talking to the parents, she'd exuded confidence and minimized the damage. Seeing the wall-to-wall debris was a fresh shock. Again she felt like crying.

"Couple of hours," the older detective said. "You can go to the station now, if you like."

She frowned. "The station?"

"They'll want you to fill out a report."

"Couldn't you just tell them what I told you?"

He smiled. "Sorry. It's Pacific Division, by the way. 12312 Culver Boulevard. Ask for someone in Burglary. I'll call and tell them you're on your way."

Alex walked back to the office. "I have to go to the police station, Evelyn."

Evelyn looked up at her. "Don't worry. I called Patty. She's coming to help. We'll finish the office. Then, when the police are done in the classroom, we'll start clearing up there." When Alex made no move to leave, Evelyn said, "Go!" and grinned weakly.

In spite of herself, Alex smiled. "Thanks. I don't know what I'd do without you."

It took her twenty minutes to drive to the station. First she had to wait in a small anteroom for almost an hour. Then she had to explain to Detective Dean Brady exactly what had happened, what she'd found, why she suspected Lundquist.

"Could've been kids," Brady said. He twirled the points of his mustache. "We're hearing more and more of that. In which case you should be talking to someone from Juvenile."

"It wasn't kids," Alex insisted, trying to contain her irritation. Why was everyone bent on blaming kids? "It was

Lundquist. He threatened to shut down my school because I wouldn't tell him where his wife and son are.''

Brady nodded. Then he asked more questions. Finally he stood up and handed her a card.

"I'll call you if we find anything, Mrs. Prescott. If you think of anything else, let me know.''

The police car was gone when Alex returned to the preschool. Warren's Lexus was in the back lot. She parked her Jeep next to it, got out, and hurried inside.

"Warren?'' she called from the corridor.

"Alex?'' A moment later he was at her side, his arms around her. "Goddamn son of a bitch! I'm so sorry, Alex.''

She rested her head against his chest. "Who told you?''

"Evelyn called the office, but I was out. I just got back, and when I called Evelyn, she told me you were at the police station. I called there. They said you'd already left, so I came here. How was it?''

"Long.'' She yawned. "I'm so tired.''

"Go home. Rest.'' He massaged her neck.

She wanted to stay in his arms forever. "I want to try to clean everything up today so we can open tomorrow.''

"The others can handle it. Paula's helping them. I called home to see if you were there and told her what happened. She offered to help, so I picked her up on the way here.''

"That's nice of her.'' For once, Alex meant it. Maybe she'd misjudged Paula.

"Denise is here, too.''

"Denise?'' Alex lifted her head.

"She called to talk to you, and Evelyn told her what happened. She came to help. That's just like her, isn't it?''

"Denise is great,'' Alex said, wondering how she could face her after yesterday. "Where is she?''

"In the classroom, with the others. You go ahead. I'll call the office and check in.''

On the way to the main room, Alex passed the open door to the office. It had been returned to normal—there were no papers on the floor, no gaping file cabinet or desk drawers. Paula was standing in front of the desk, holding a sheaf of papers.

"Thanks for coming, Paula,'' Alex said.

Paula looked up quickly. "Oh, Alex! I didn't know you

were back. I'm just sorting these," she said, indicating the papers. She sounded flustered. "I'm almost done," she added.

"I'm sorry I startled you. I really appreciate this." Alex smiled warmly.

"I thought you could use my help here more than at the house. Warren thought it was a good idea."

"It was a *great* idea." Alex felt a rush of gratitude toward the woman she continued down the hall.

The classroom was still in shambles, but the women were making headway. Patty was kneeling on the floor, sorting toy pieces into various boxes. Evelyn was removing torn art projects from the walls. Denise was on a stool, scrubbing finger paint off the mini-blinds with a sponge.

Alex greeted the women, then said, "Sorry I was away so long."

"Trying to get out of the hard work, huh?" Evelyn smiled. "We thought they arrested you."

"You people are great," Alex said, suddenly overcome with emotion. She blinked back tears. "I don't know how to thank you."

Denise stepped off the stool and came over to Alex. "I'm so sorry, Alex." She took her hand. "Whoever did this is unbelievably rotten. Ruining all those kids' things . . . " She shook her head.

"Thanks for coming to help." Alex squeezed Denise's hand.

"I'm glad to do it." In an undertone she said, "I called earlier to tell you I'm glad you stopped by yesterday. It took courage and . . . well . . . thank you." She bit her lip.

"Denise, maybe I'm wrong. Maybe—"

Denise shook her head again and released Alex's hand. "I wasn't sure about Ron, anyway. I think he was more interested in getting my dad to invest with him than he was in me. Please don't worry. I'll be fine. And what I said yesterday still goes. About the shower, I mean."

"Denise, it isn't necessary."

"What isn't necessary?" Warren asked, joining them. He slipped his arm around Alex's waist.

"A baby shower for Alex." Denise smiled up at him. "Didn't Alex tell you? I'm looking forward to planning it."

"Sounds great to me," Warren said. "As long as I don't have to be there." He grinned.

"That's a wonderful idea!" Evelyn said. "I'd like to help." She held rolled-up posters in her hand.

"Oh, that's sweet of you, Evelyn," Denise said, turning to her, "but my mom's already offered, and she tends to take over."

"No problem. I understand."

Evelyn's smile was strained, and Alex could hear the hurt in her voice. She thinks Denise is snubbing her, Alex thought, wondering if Denise was, or whether Evelyn was being over-sensitive. She wondered, too, when Mona had become involved in the shower and wished she could bow out of the whole thing.

Warren left—he couldn't help clean up, dressed in his suit. Alex worked for several hours, then admitted to the others that she was exhausted and was going home.

"Don't come back," Evelyn warned. "We won't let you in."

On the way home Alex picked up Nicholas. In the morning, she'd intended to take him marketing with her after school, but she drove straight home instead. She'd ask Warren to pick up a pizza for supper.

Once inside the house, she went upstairs, unlaced her Adidas, and took off her socks. She walked barefoot down the stairs and into the kitchen, where Nicholas was waiting for his after-school snack. She filled two glasses with milk—low-fat for Nicholas, nonfat for herself—and cut two slices of the apple pie they'd baked together last night.

When Nicholas was finished, Alex rinsed the glasses. She was terribly tired—she could barely keep her eyes open—and would have gone upstairs to nap, but she couldn't leave Nicholas alone. She went with him to the den and lay on the couch, her legs propped up on the arm, while he turned on *Sesame Street*. She closed her eyes.

The phone rang. She groped for the extension that sat on the glass corner table behind her and brought the receiver to her ear. "Hello?" She stifled a yawn.

"Where is she, Mrs. Prescott?"

It was Lundquist. She sat up quickly and swung her legs down. All day she'd thought of a hundred expletives she wanted to scream at him. Now she was too tired to talk.

"I don't know where your wife is, Mr. Lundquist. You ruined my school for nothing."

"I don't know what you're talking about, Mrs. Prescott. I haven't been near your school."

She could hear the contemptuous amusement in his voice. She sensed he was waiting for her to rail at him, to shriek. She wondered if this was what life had been like, every day, for Sally and Bobby Lundquist. She said nothing.

"I'm going to find her, you know. I've hired a detective. And I'm going to find out everything about you, Mrs. Prescott. Where you're from. What your secrets are. Everything. And then I'm going to destroy you."

"Why?" Her question was prompted partly by fear, partly by a strangely disembodied curiosity.

"Because you won't tell me where she is."

"But I don't—" She realized she was talking to a dial tone. What did it matter, anyway? Nothing she said would convince Lundquist that she didn't know where his wife was. He needed to believe that Alex was lying. He needed to harass someone, punish someone. His wife had escaped his reach. Alex made a perfect substitute. Lucky me, she thought.

She hung up the phone and got up off the couch. "Be right back," she said to Nicholas, who nodded as he was listening to Ernie and Bert.

Upstairs, she entered the bedroom, locked the door, and went to her dresser. She opened the drawer and pulled out the gray envelope.

Everything was still there. It had been silly to think otherwise.

Chapter 12

"**W**hat do you think?" Evelyn asked on Wednesday morning.

"Amazing," Alex said, looking around.

The classroom had been restored to its original condition. Almost original—none of the children's artwork had been salvageable, and with the exception of a new Growth Chart and Star Chart that Evelyn had drawn, the walls were bare.

At least the splintered back door was salvageable; the carpenter Alex had called yesterday was repairing it. She had briefly contemplated installing an alarm system, but there was little of material value in the building. And the person who had vandalized her school had been interested in intimidation and punishment, not in theft.

"I can't believe you did all this yesterday, Ev. It seemed so hopeless."

"Everyone pitched in. Lisa was great, by the way. Please thank her again for helping me stencil the charts, okay?"

Last night after supper, when Alex had mentioned she was meeting Evelyn and Patty at the preschool to finish cleaning up, Warren had insisted that she stay home.

"You're exhausted," he'd said. "I'll go." When he'd come downstairs after changing into jeans and a sweatshirt, Lisa had offered to go along.

"That's my girl," Warren said, clearly pleased. Lisa glowed under his approval.

"Can I go, too?" Nicholas asked.

Warren smiled. "You have to stay home and baby-sit Mommy, okay, champ?" He ruffled Nicholas's hair.

" 'Kay."

"That's so thoughtful of you, Lisa," Alex said, thinking, Maybe we're finally over the Ron incident. Lisa said "Sure," but she barely looked at Alex. She's not interested in helping me, Alex realized; she just wants to be with her father. And what's wrong with that?

Five children weren't coming that morning—"something going around," their mothers had told Alex when she'd called last night to tell them school would be open today. Alex wondered if the "something going around" was a latent fear that whoever had vandalized the school would strike again.

She had spoken to Detective Brady earlier in the morning. There were no usable fingerprints, he'd informed her. Sorry. He would call her after he'd spoken to Lundquist. When will that be? she'd asked. Sometime today, Brady had replied, and she'd thought he sounded annoyed. She told him about Lundquist's call to her at home. Did he admit anything? Brady asked, a note of interest in his voice, and she had to say no. Sounds like he's running out of threats, Mrs. Prescott, Brady said. Don't let him rattle you.

That was what Warren had said, too, when Alex told him about Lundquist's call. So let him have a detective check, he'd said, stroking her hair. What will he find out, that you're wanted by the FBI? And of course, she'd had to smile.

Brady and Warren are right, she told herself firmly as she cut construction paper into different geometric shapes. Lundquist is just trying to scare me.

Soon the preschoolers arrived. Usually, parents dropped their children off in front of the entrance (Alex or Evelyn or the aide always waited outside) and sped away. Today, though, most of the parents lingered, asked more questions about what had happened, sought new reassurances. Several mothers parked their cars and escorted their children into the classroom, no doubt to determine for themselves that their children would be playing in a secure facility free of any vestiges of violence. Alex didn't blame them.

The children reacted differently to the bare walls. A few seemed not to notice and, after placing their lunch boxes and sweaters in their cubbies, went directly to the shelves for their favorite toys. Most asked what had happened. Alex explained as simply as she could, and was relieved when they nodded in understanding and acceptance. One three-year-old boy cried inconsolably over the loss of his painting. Alex wished Donald

Lundquist were here to face the little boy, then decided Lundquist wouldn't really care.

Within a half hour the children had slipped into their normal routine. Alex admired their resilience. Several times as she walked around the tables, supervising the different art projects (the walls, she saw, would be covered with new "masterpieces" before the end of the day), she passed by the windows facing the street and looked out, wondering what she would do if she saw the silver Jaguar.

Just before noon, she did see it. Or thought she did. It was inching along the street in front of the school. The driver was a male, but she couldn't see if he was Lundquist. The Jaguar stopped for a moment, then sped away. Maybe it's just a coincidence, she decided.

Five minutes later the car was back, and she knew it was Lundquist. Her first instinct was to call Detective Brady, but then she thought about the police vehicles that were sure to show up, and the sirens. The children would be frightened. The parents would be frightened, too. Alex had reassured them once. The second time would be far more difficult. One parent would remove a child. Then another. And another . . . She knew the pattern all too well.

The Jaguar took off again, a streak of silver against the dark green wall of cypress trees across the street. If he comes back one more time, I'll call, Alex decided. But she didn't see the car again.

During nap time, Alex left Evelyn in charge and went into the office to pay bills. She wrote a check for the monthly mortgage payment, another for the Department of Water and Power. From the bottom left-hand file drawer, she took out a folder labeled "Phone" and opened it. Inside was a stack of phone bills from Pacific Bell and AT&T. She lifted the top one, scanned the total, and frowned.

This was the January bill; she'd paid it already, and February's bill. Where was the March bill? She remembered the papers strewn on the floor. Maybe the phone bills had been among them, and whoever had sorted them hadn't arranged them chronologically.

She thumbed through the stack, checking the dates, but there was no bill for March. Or for February. Suddenly she realized what had happened: Lundquist had taken the bills.

He'd convinced himself that Alex knew where his wife and son were. He probably hoped the location was a toll or long-distance call from the preschool and would be reflected on Alex's phone bills.

He's going to call every number and try to find out who he's talking to. That's what I would do. So what, she told herself, but her hands were shaking as she closed the folder.

She picked up the phone receiver and pressed the long-distance number, but when the receptionist answered, Alex quickly hung up. She was being silly, she told herself. Donald Lundquist wasn't interested in her. And even if he called this number, he wouldn't learn anything.

She reached for another, unlabeled folder at the back of the file drawer (was it her imagination, or was it somewhat askew?), pulled it onto her lap, and opened it. Her fingers were clammy as she counted the receipts for the cashier's checks, but they were all there. The first time she'd counted, she'd thought one was missing, but it had been stuck to another one. She felt tingly—hyperventilation, she guessed—and she breathed slowly, deliberately, telling herself that it was all right, the checks were all there. Not for the first time, she contemplated tearing them up (maybe if she did, she sometimes thought, the nightmares would stop), but she couldn't. They were the only tangible connection she had with the life she'd left behind.

Like the nightmares, and the material in the gray envelope, they were her penance.

They were also her solace.

On Thursday, Detective Brady called Alex.

"I spoke to Lundquist yesterday evening," he told her. "Brought him down to the station. It's no go. He's got an alibi—his secretary vouches for him."

"But I know he did it!" Alex hesitated, then said, "He stole my phone bills. He's trying to track his wife." *And me?* she wondered.

"Listen, Mrs. Prescott, for what it's worth, you're probably right. But we have no prints, nothing. I kept at him for almost two hours, told him if you have any more problems of any kind, at the school or at your home, I'll be on him like a ton of bricks. You want my advice? Forget about Lundquist. Be happy no one was hurt.''

''He drove by the school a few times yesterday morning.''

''I don't have a record of that. Who'd you speak to here about that?''

She heard the rustling of papers. ''I didn't call the police. I didn't want to upset the children.''

''You should have called anyway, Mrs. Prescott.'' Brady sounded annoyed. '''Course, that was in the morning, before I spoke to him. He probably won't bother you again.''

In the early afternoon, as soon as Patty arrived, Alex drove to Los Angeles for an appointment with Dr. Pearson. She'd gained three pounds, the nurse told her, and her blood pressure was normal—which was surprising, Alex thought, considering how agitated she'd been the past few days.

Dr. Pearson seemed pleased when he examined her. ''Baby's got a strong heartbeat. Would you like to hear it?'' He listened through his stethoscope for a few seconds, moved the diaphragm around on her bare skin below her abdomen, then placed the stethoscope plugs in her ears.

She listened intently, straining to distinguish amid what sounded like a sea of rushing waters the sound that was her baby, and then she heard the steady, rapid, incredibly strong *tha-thump, tha-thump, tha-thump*. She grinned at Dr. Pearson.

''Have you felt the baby kick yet?'' he asked.

''No.'' she frowned. ''Should I have?''

''Nothing to worry about. Each pregnancy's different, so I always ask. You could feel something in a week or in five weeks. By the way, I'd like to schedule an amniocentesis when you're seventeen weeks pregnant. That would make it in three weeks.''

She nodded.

''Fine. Anything you want to ask?'' Pearson said, helping Alex to a sitting position. ''Anything bothering you?''

''Everything's great.'' She thought fleetingly about Lundquist and Ron and Denise and Lisa and quickly dismissed the thought. Right now, with the baby's heartbeat still echoing in her ears, nothing was bothering her at all.

After she left Pearson's office, Alex drove to the maternity shop she'd noticed on Third Street near Orlando. She bought jeans, cotton slacks, a bathing suit, shorts, and two dresses.

Everything was ridiculously large. The saleswoman encouraged her to buy an intermediate wardrobe "until you grow into everything, dear," but Alex declined.

She left the shop, a bag in each hand, and headed toward her Jeep. As she was opening the rear door, she saw, reflected in the glass, a man across the street, at the end of the block. He was leaning, arms folded, against a silver Jaguar. He was watching her.

Her heart beat more quickly. She tossed her purchases into the back of the Jeep, slammed the door, and turned to face him. It was Lundquist. He'd followed her! He waved at her, and even from afar, she could see he was grinning. The gall! Angry now more than afraid, she checked for oncoming traffic, crossed the street, and marched toward him.

"Listen!" she yelled as she neared him. "I've had enough of—"

She stopped in mid-stride. It wasn't Lundquist. It was another man with dark, wavy hair. He squinted at her briefly with a who-the-hell-are-you? expression. Then he looked beyond her; Alex turned and saw a blond woman coming up behind her.

"All done?" the man said, walking over to the woman and taking the package from her. He put an arm around her shoulder, leaned close, and whispered in her ear.

Alex didn't wait to see the woman stare at her. Flushed with embarrassment and relief, she hurried back to her Jeep. Get a grip on yourself, she told herself. Not every silver Jaguar belongs to Donald Lundquist.

"Ma'am." The low drawl came from behind her.

What now? Turning, Alex saw the stern face of a motorcycle policeman.

"I watched you jaywalk twice," he told her.

"I'm sorry, Officer." She hesitated. Would it make a difference if she explained? "I thought I saw a man who's been harassing me. I was upset."

"Uh-huh," he replied in a noncommittal voice that said he'd heard them all. He took out a citation booklet. "Do you know that jaywalking is dangerous?"

Alex sighed. "How much is the ticket?"

*   *   *

After Nicholas was asleep, when she was sitting in the den watching TV with Warren, she told him about the ticket.

"Poor baby," he murmured, but there was a twinkle in his eyes.

"You think it's funny!" She punched his arm playfully. Evelyn had thought so, too. Was the cop at least cute? she'd wanted to know.

"Kind of." Warren smiled. "Don't you?"

"I guess." There *was* some humor in it, she supposed. "Every time I think about Lundquist, though, I get so tense."

"Forget Lundquist. He's history. Speaking of tense, something's up with Ron. I called today and mentioned that the four of us should get together this weekend, and he said to talk to Denise. He was barely civil." Warren paused. "I heard he's having money problems. Maybe that's it." He looked at her.

"Maybe." To change the subject, she said, "Want to see how I spent our money today?" She saw his puzzled look. "My maternity wardrobe?"

"Sure." He smiled.

She tried on the shorts first with an oversized T-shirt, then the slacks. "Cute," Warren said to everything. She put on one of the two dresses, a red silk tunic over a short, straight skirt. She pinned up her hair, put on pearl earrings, slipped on a pair of black pumps, and looked in the mirror.

The dress was huge. On an impulse, she took a cushion from the armchair in the bedroom and slipped it under the tunic, behind the elasticized waistband of the skirt. Then she went downstairs and into the den.

"So what do you think, Warren? Is it—oh, hi, Lisa."

Lisa was sitting next to Warren on the couch, staring at Alex's abdomen. So was Warren, Alex noted. No one said anything.

Alex pulled out the pillow; it dangled awkwardly in her hand. "I thought I'd help the dress out a little." She felt suddenly stupid and immature and knew she was blushing. She forced a smile.

"It's very pretty," Warren said. His voice had a strange timbre. "Don't you think so, Lisa?"

Lisa didn't answer. She took the television remote control and raised the volume, then started rapidly switching channels.

"Lisa," Warren prompted quietly.

"I'm going upstairs to change," Alex announced.

Warren took the remote control from his daughter and lowered the volume on the television. "I asked you a question, Lisa."

Leave it alone, Warren, Alex begged silently.

Lisa whirled toward him. "Alex doesn't care what I think about her dress. You don't care, either, so why are you asking me?"

"We *do* care, honey. We care very much what you think. We're all a family, and—"

"It's ugly, okay? It's ugly and I hate it and I think putting in a pillow is dumb!" She jumped up off the couch.

Warren sighed. "That's rude, Lisa. Apologize to Alex."

"She doesn't even need maternity clothes yet. She's just showing off!"

Alex said, "I'd appreciate it if you didn't talk about me as if I weren't here." Her fists were clenched.

Warren said, "Alex, Lisa is just—"

"Everything was fine before! We didn't need another baby. We didn't need her!" Crying, Lisa ran from the room.

"I'll talk to her, Alex." Warren followed his daughter out of the den.

Alex stayed there for a few minutes, then walked slowly upstairs. Lisa's bedroom door was shut. Alex went to her own bedroom, tossed the pillow onto the chair, and changed into a nightgown. She hung up the red dress and put away all her other new maternity clothes. When Warren came into the room, she was reading in bed.

"She's okay now," Warren said. He sat down on the edge of Alex's bed and reached for her hand.

She pulled it away.

"Come on, Alex. Why are you angry with me? I'm the guy in the middle."

"You're coddling her. Every time she's rude and makes a scene, she runs from the room and you follow her. She knows exactly what she's doing."

He shook his head. "You're wrong. She's going through a difficult time. Try to understand."

Alex closed her book. "I *am* trying. We've been married

almost two years, and I still feel like I'm walking on eggshells all the time. She hates me.''

"She doesn't.''

"She hates me. She hates the baby. She as much as said so downstairs.''

"She doesn't mean what she's saying. She's a kid, Alex. She's upset. She's confused.'' He paused, and when he spoke again, he wasn't looking at Alex. "Andrea had a red maternity dress almost like the one you just had on. When you walked into the den, for a minute you looked like her. I have to be honest, Alex. It threw me. I guess it threw Lisa, too. She went through a rough time when Andrea died.''

"I'll give the dress back.'' Did she sound petulant? She didn't want to sound petulant. She wanted so much to belong, to have her own identity in this house, in this family, and it seemed that wherever she went, she bumped into Andrea's ghost.

"That's silly. No one wants you to give it back.'' He sighed. "Try to be patient, please, Alex? I guess Lisa needs more time to get used to the idea of the baby. Maybe we could downplay it for a while. Not talk about it in front of her.''

"The baby's not going to wait to be born until Lisa's ready, Warren,'' Alex said softly. "It's going to grow. I'm going to get bigger. It's not a pillow I can put away.''

"I know that.''

She took his hand and linked her fingers through his. "I'm excited about the baby, Warren. Are you telling me I can't be excited?''

"Shit, Alex. She's fourteen years old. You're a grown woman.'' His voice held weariness and frustration. "I thought you'd be more understanding.''

She removed her hand. "Maybe this was a bad idea, my getting pregnant. Maybe we should have waited.''

"Maybe.'' He sounded lost in thought. He stood up.

It wasn't the answer she'd wanted. She leaned over toward the lamp on her nightstand and shut off the light.

Chapter 13

*S*he ought to thank Donald Lundquist for providing her with such a wonderful opportunity, and for being a perfect decoy. She smiled at the thought. Maybe she would thank him someday. After it was all over.

Breaking the lock on the back door of the preschool had been easy. Much easier, in fact, than she'd expected. She'd been a little nervous, but the door was hidden from the street and the adjacent neighbor by a hedge of cypress trees.

She'd known that Alex would blame Lundquist. She knew how upset Alex was about Donald Lundquist and his wife and little boy. Everybody did. She wished she could have seen Alex's face when she first saw the office and classroom, but seeing her afterward had been almost as satisfying, and having Alex thank her for helping clean up the mess had been a wonderful, secret moment. You think you're so smart, don't you, Alex? *she'd felt like saying.* It wasn't Lundquist. I'm the one who vandalized your school.

Your precious school. If not for the school, she knew, Alex would never have moved to Venice. She would never have taught Nicholas. Never married Warren. Things would have been so different.

She sighed. Maybe it was that thought that had unleashed her anger. She still wasn't certain what had come over her that early morning. Her intention had been to break into the office and search among Alex's files and papers for something revealing, a clue, something that would ultimately help her drive Alex away. Then, to make it look as though Lundquist was responsible—he would be angry, wouldn't he?—she'd swept the folders off Alex's desk (oh, how good that had felt!), emptied drawers, littered the floor with papers.

Then she'd walked into the classroom. Lundquist, she de-

cided, would certainly do some damage here, too—to show his anger, to intimidate. She knocked over several chairs and emptied several boxes of toys and puzzle pieces. She had started tearing one of the children's finger-paint projects thumbtacked to the wall (she would rip just one, she told herself—it wasn't the kids' fault, after all; it was Alex's), but the raspy sound of the paper being ripped struck an elemental chord deep within her, and she found that she couldn't stop. Her hands became messengers of a rage she hadn't known she possessed. They ripped and ripped and ripped, paper after paper. They pushed down bookshelves, sent blocks and trucks skittering across the floor. They opened bottles of finger paint and hurled them across the room, against the wall, on the tables, on the floor, spilling out, in vibrant primary colors, her anguish and fury.

When she was done, she'd looked at her watch and tensed. She'd spent more time than she'd planned. She still had to search through Alex's papers, to find something, anything. But she couldn't do it now. Alex would be arriving soon. She always arrived first, at nine o'clock.

She would have to come back. She would have to find a way.

She needn't have worried. Even with so many people around, it had been easy, while filing papers, to rummage through the folders and find the phone bills. And the cashier's checks—those were interesting, and they were all made out to one place, the same place Alex called once a month.

A mortuary.

She pictured row after row of tombstones. One of them, she knew, was important to Alex. A chill went through her, and she was suddenly and unexpectedly moved by what she recognized as sympathy. For one brief moment she felt as if she had no right to trespass on Alex's grief, but her fledgling sympathy was smothered by her desperate, full-grown resolve.

The signature on the check was "Alexandra Trent." Her first husband's name was Trent. Larry Trent. But why didn't she sign the checks "Alexandra Prescott?" And why did she send a monthly check and make a monthly phone call?

The receptionist at the mortuary had been extremely helpful. "Yes, Mrs. Trent's check arrived just the other day," he said. Was there a problem?

"No, no problem. Mrs. Trent asked me to make sure. It's so important to her, you know."

"Oh, I know," the receptionist said, and sighed. *"Isn't it the saddest thing? We all feel terrible for her, with everything she's been through."*

"Terribly sad. She doesn't like to talk about it, but I know she still grieves."

"Who wouldn't?" he said. *"Such a tragedy. And all the talk. But you know all about that, of course."*

"Of course. Losing her husband like that . . ."

"Well, at least he's found his peace at last. But poor Mrs. Trent, having to leave her childhood home. They say even her parents turned against her, so it's no wonder, is it?"

"Her in-laws must be bitter," she said.

"Oh, yes. A double blow, so to speak. People say . . ."

Chapter 14

"I'm sorry."

Alex pulled on her sweater and turned around. Lisa was standing just outside the bedroom doorway.

"Okay." Alex's voice was noncommittal.

Had Warren put Lisa up to this? she wondered. Usually, Alex and Warren awoke together and enjoyed a few quiet moments before the day began. This morning when she'd awakened after a fitful night's sleep (the aftermath of the quarrel and another nightmare; there was always a nightmare), he'd already showered. They had stood in the bathroom, inches apart, brushing their teeth, and she had welcomed the sound of the water rushing out of the faucets. It had masked the silence. He had dressed quickly, as if eager to escape downstairs. Their conversation had been perfunctory. So had his good-bye kiss.

"Those things I said last night? They were really mean. You must hate me." There was a catch in Lisa's voice.

Alex's anger dissolved. She walked over to her. "I don't hate you, Lisa. I know this is a difficult time for you."

Lisa didn't say anything. Alex couldn't see the girl's eyes; she was fidgeting with the strap of the book bag slung over her right shoulder, and her blond hair had fallen over her face.

"I know you talked to your father last night, Lisa. It's okay to have confused feelings about the baby." Alex hesitated, then put her hand on Lisa's shoulder. "Are you worried your father will love you less when the baby comes?"

Lisa looked up and smoothed her hair behind her ear. "Of course not!"

Had the protest come too quickly? Automatically? "It's normal to have fears like that." Alex saw it all the time in the preschoolers who had new siblings.

The girl shook her head.

"I wish you'd talk about your feelings, Lisa. I'd be happy to listen. Anytime."

Lisa took a step backward. Alex removed her hand.

"I have to get air in my bike tire," Lisa said, "and I'll be late for homeroom if I don't leave right now."

Not a solution, Alex thought as she watched her stepdaughter run down the stairs. But an improvement. If only it would last.

The day was uneventful. All during the morning, Alex glanced nervously out the window facing the street, but there was no sign of the silver Jaguar. By noon she was able to relax. Detective Brady's right, she decided. Lundquist won't bother me, not after Brady's warning. And he's run out of threats. She wondered suddenly how Sally Lundquist and her son were doing.

Paula wasn't in the kitchen or the service porch when Alex and Nicholas came home, but her Ford Escort was parked in front of the house. She's probably upstairs, putting away the laundry, Alex thought. Paula had prepared a plate of Oreos and a glass of milk for Nicholas. Alex left him sitting at the breakfast room table and went to her studio to put away the new art supplies she'd bought on the way home.

Paula was in the room, ironing. She'd pushed Alex's easel against the wall and rearranged several sketch pads and boxes of pastels and charcoals.

"Oh, hello, Alex." Paula smiled. "Did you have a nice day?" With her hand, she smoothed a sleeve belonging to one of Alex's cotton blouses and ran the iron across it.

"Fine, thank you." Alex found it hard to filter the anger from her voice. "Paula, I'd prefer that you iron in the service porch, or, if you like, in the family room. And please don't straighten my art supplies. I'll do that myself."

Paula smoothed the second sleeve. "I noticed this morning that you took all those boxes and suitcases out to the garage. That's a good idea, I think. I always enjoyed ironing in my room. The light is so pleasant, and the room is so cozy."

"This is my studio now, Paula. I don't want you using it."

Paula stared at Alex for a long while. Then she said, "Certainly," in a tone that made Alex feel like a petty, foolish lady of the manor.

The iron had been sitting on the sleeve. Paula moved it now, and there was a tan, iron-shaped design on the white cotton.

"Oh, no! I've ruined your blouse, Alex. I'm sorry," she said, clearly not sorry at all. "I'll pay for it, of course."

"That isn't necessary. It was an accident, Paula." Was it?

Alex left the studio and went to the entry hall. Paula had arranged the mail, as usual. There were several magazines, the usual junk, a large stack of bills. There was a small white envelope addressed to Alex. The flap was tucked inside the envelope, not sealed. She opened it.

Inside the envelope was a folded sheet of white paper. She unfolded it and stared at the words written with a thick black marker in the center of the page:

YOU DON'T DESERVE TO HAVE A BABY!

An icy finger touched her heart. She closed her eyes, then shook her head, as if to dispel the message on the paper in front of her, but when she opened her eyes, it was still there. She looked at the postmark on the envelope. It was dated Thursday. Yesterday.

Lisa had sent the note, Alex decided. But it didn't matter, because she and Lisa had made up that morning and everything would be all right. The girl had really been abject.

Alex decided not to tell Warren about the note. She crumpled it and walked into the kitchen to throw it into the trash bin under the sink, but at the last moment changed her mind. She uncrumpled the paper and smoothed it out on the kitchen counter.

"Alex."

She jumped at the sound of Paula's voice and turned around.

"I'm sorry again about the blouse," Paula said. "I'd really like to pay for it." She was looking past Alex at the paper on the counter.

Was that a smirk in her eyes? "Please forget about it, Paula. It was my fault, really. I distracted you." With a casual movement she folded the paper and took it with her as she went to get her purse from the entry hall, where she'd left it.

She returned to the kitchen and handed Paula two days' pay. "Thank you for everything. See you on Tuesday."

"Tuesday, then. I guess you'll be busy all weekend in your studio, is that right? Enjoy yourself, dear."

The woman was passive-aggressive, Alex decided. There was no doubt about it. She glanced again at the note. "YOU DON'T DESERVE TO HAVE A BABY!"

Maybe Lisa hadn't sent the note. What if Paula had sent it? What if Denise had told her about Alex's incident with Ron? Paula and Denise were close. Paula had been at Denise's house the morning Alex had stopped by to talk to Denise. Paula might even have eavesdropped on their conversation.

And it made sense. Paula resented Alex; naturally, she'd think Alex had invited Ron's attentions. Paula had a fierce, almost unnatural loyalty to Warren, Lisa, and Nicholas. She obviously didn't think Alex was good enough for any of them.

You're being ridiculous, Alex told herself. It was Lisa. And it doesn't mean anything. She tore the note into shreds and threw the scraps into the trash.

Lisa offered to make a salad for supper. Warren came home early (to serve as referee? Alex wondered) and was clearly pleased to find his wife and daughter working amiably together.

After supper, at Lisa's suggestion, Alex, Warren, Lisa, and Nicholas went to an early movie in Santa Monica. After the movie they strolled along the Third Street Promenade. The area, blocked off to automobile traffic, had a carnival atmosphere and was filled on weekends and most weekday evenings with throngs of pedestrians. There were cafés, outdoor Mexican bands, sidewalk artists, mimes, gymnasts who did cartwheels over boxes, a juggler on a ten-foot unicycle. Something for everyone. Warren had an artist sketch the four of them in charcoal. Lisa and Nicholas had ice cream; Warren and Alex, frozen yogurt.

Warren didn't mention Lisa or last night's quarrel. Alex didn't bring it up, either. There was no need. Later, after everyone was asleep, Alex and Warren made love. Lying on her back, his arm on her breast, she knew she'd been right not to mention the note.

It took her a while to fall asleep. Just before she did, she felt it. A tiny flutter, almost imperceptible. She placed her hand below her abdomen and waited several minutes in the comforting silence until she felt it again. She fell asleep smiling, with her hand still in place.

Alex parked the Lexus on a side street and walked two blocks to Rose Avenue and the restaurant that bore the street's name. She'd been to The Rose several times and was always taken by the huge, hot-pink blossom over the entrance. And the food was delicious.

It was twelve-thirty. Denise had said twelve-thirty when she'd called that morning, but Alex hated being late (another quality instilled in her by her parents). She entered the restaurant, unsure whether Denise would want to sit indoors or outdoors.

"Over here, Alex, dear."

Alex turned in the direction of the voice and saw Mona. No Denise. Great, she thought. Denise had mentioned that her mother would be joining them (which made sense, since both mother and daughter were planning the baby shower for Alex), but Alex had assumed they would arrive together. She forced a pleasant expression on her face as she walked over to the table where Mona was sitting.

"Hello, Mona. How are you?"

"Just fine, thank you. But there's no need to ask how you are. You look glowing, dear, positively glowing. One can see that pregnancy suits you." She patted the chair to her right. "Come sit down. Denise will be here any minute."

Alex seated herself, wondering what she would talk about with Mona until Denise arrived. "Mona, it's so thoughtful of you and Denise to give this shower for me. I really appreciate it."

Mona waved her hand dismissively. "I love giving parties. I'm happy to do it. And Denise is fond of you. Very fond." She took a sip of water from the goblet in front of her. Her heavy gold bangle clanked against the table.

"Denise is wonderful."

"To tell you the truth, and I hope you don't take this the wrong way, Alex, I was surprised when Denise told me you were pregnant. Considering everything, I mean." Her dark blue eyes stared at Alex from across the table. They were almost as deep a blue as the large sapphire in the diamond-encrusted ring on the hand holding the goblet.

It's none of your business, Mona, Alex wanted to say. "You mean Lisa. It was an adjustment for her, of course, but she's fine." This morning Lisa had been cheerful, helpful. For the first time in weeks, Alex had felt hopeful about her relationship with her stepdaughter.

"Lisa is a very private person, Alex. She doesn't show her true emotions. She's always been unusually close to Warren, and after Andrea's death. . . . " Mona took another sip of water and put down the goblet. "Well, what's done is done." She sighed. "Can I be honest with you, Alex?"

More honesty? Alex fidgeted in her chair. Where was Denise? "Of course."

"I'm glad Denise isn't here, because there's something I wanted to discuss with you. Stuart and I are heartbroken that Denise has stopped seeing Ron. Now, Denise told me all about what happened that Sunday in your yard—"

"Mona, I don't feel comfortable discussing this."

"The thing is, you see," Mona continued as if Alex hadn't said anything, "I think she's making a terrible mistake. Ron is handsome. He's charming. He's successful. And I think he's perfect for Denise. Stuart thinks so, too."

"Without meaning any disrespect, Mona, I think that's up to Denise to decide."

"Of course. But she has to have the correct information to make the right decision, doesn't she?" Mona smiled and leaned closer. "I've spoken to Ron. He's devastated, poor man. He admits he made a mistake that day, but he says it was all in fun, and I for one believe him."

Alex didn't say anything.

"I've tried to convince Denise of that, but you know, Alex, I think if you talked to her and told her you were mistaken—"

"I wasn't mistaken, Mona. I know what he was doing."

"Of course you do." The smile was almost a leer. "And can you honestly say you weren't partially to blame?"

Alex stared at Mona. Her fingers kneaded the edge of the tablecloth. "What are you talking about?"

"You're a beautiful woman, Alex, and you're not exactly shy. Some men might find you provocative. Ron told me you enjoyed flirting with him."

"That isn't true!" This was ridiculous! Why was she defending herself to this woman?

"I saw the way you were standing together at Sea World, you know. He had his arms around you. I didn't hear you complain. You looked very cozy. Oh, hi, dear," Mona said, and it was clear she wasn't talking to Alex.

Alex turned around. Denise was standing behind her, a curious expression on her face. How much had she heard? And how long had Mona known that her daughter was standing there?

"Hi, Mom, Alex." Denise took the seat across from Mona. "Sorry I'm late."

Was it Alex's imagination, or did Denise sound strained?

"That's all right, dear." Mona reached over and patted her daughter's hand. "Alex and I have been having a lovely conversation, haven't we, Alex? Now that you're here, Denise, we can talk about the shower. I was thinking poached salmon and a trifle for dessert. How does that sound, girls . . . ?"

She had eaten a fresh fruit appetizer and toyed with her salad Niçoise, but when Mona called the waitress over to take their dessert orders, Alex, pleading exhaustion and a headache, announced that she had to leave. (The headache was real enough, a product of Mona's incessant jabbering and the tension Alex had felt from the moment the woman had started talking about Ron and Denise.)

"But you don't want to miss dessert, Alex, dear!" Mona exclaimed. "Dessert is the very best part."

Judging by Mona's figure, Alex could see that the woman practiced what she preached. "Another time, Mona. Thank you so much for lunch. It was delicious."

"Have a little something, Alex. The cheesecake is divine."

"Mom, don't pressure Alex," Denise said. "If she doesn't feel well, she should go home and rest."

Had that been concern, Alex wondered now as she headed for her car, or had Denise been as relieved for Alex to be gone as Alex had been to leave? She was halfway up the block when she became aware of rapidly nearing footsteps. Instinctively, she quickened her pace.

"Hey, Alex! Wait up. This isn't the L.A. marathon, you know."

Alex stopped, not believing her ears, and turned around. "Why are you following me, Ron?" She was annoyed, not nervous, she told herself. There was no reason to be nervous.

"I'm not following you." He smiled. "I want to talk to you. Is that a crime?"

"How did you know I'd be here?" she demanded.

"Mona told me. I figured it was a good opportunity for you and me to clear the air."

"There's nothing for us to clear, Ron. Talk to Denise." Alex turned and started walking.

He caught up with her and grabbed her elbow.

"Don't touch me!" She yanked her arm free and kept walking.

"Sor-ry!" He sprinted ahead of her, then turned and, facing her, began jogging backward. "Hey, c'mon, Alex. Five minutes, okay? What's the harm?"

He would probably follow her all the way home if she refused, Alex thought. She stopped abruptly in mid-stride. He stopped, too.

"What do you want, Ron?" she snapped. "Make it fast."

He nodded. "Okay, here's fast and straight. Number one, I'm sorry for the things I said on the phone the other time. I was mad, but that's no excuse. Forgiven?"

Whatever. "Fine." She just wanted to get home.

"Good. That's out of the way." He smiled. "Two, Mona told me she was going to talk to you about squaring things with Denise. I just want to thank you."

Alex frowned. "Ron, I didn't agree to square anything with Denise."

He raised his hands, palms up. "Look, it's no big deal. I told Denise I was out of line. All she needs to hear from you is that you blew it out of proportion. You knew it was me. It was harmless fun. Then, when Lisa saw us, you got scared and changed the story."

Alex stared at him. "You're crazy, Ron. That's not what happened, and I have no intention of lying to Denise."

"I want her back, Alex." Anger flashed in his eyes.

"Then tell her the truth and beg *her* forgiveness, not mine."

"You don't get it, do you? Sure, Denise is mad at me right now. But you know who she's madder at? You. For telling her and humiliating her. Making her feel like shit."

Alex flinched. "Denise isn't angry at me. She appreciated my honesty."

" 'Appreciate' my ass. She hates you for it, Alex. Any woman would. And she probably doesn't believe your story."

"Is that why she's giving me a baby shower, Ron? Because she hates me so much?"

"That's her pride talking. She *has* to go through with it. C'mon, Alex. Help me out here. I'm begging you. You have no idea how important this is to me. Without Denise—"

"I won't lie to her, Ron. I'm sorry."

He scowled. "What are you, some holier-than-thou prig? You never told a lie in your life, Alexandra the Great? Never did anything you're ashamed of? No secrets in the closet?"

Alex paled. Ron caught the startled expression in her eyes. "There *is* something there. Now what can it be?" He stroked his chin. His forehead was creased in feigned concentration.

"Good-bye, Ron." She started walking up the street.

"Want to tell me about it?" he called. "I'll find out, you know. And then I just might have to tell Warren. Unless, of course, you talk to Denise. What do you say?"

She had an urge to run but refused to give him the satisfaction. She kept walking at a steady pace.

"Warren doesn't know that his wife has a big, bad secret, does he?"

She crossed the street. Only half a block more.

"Hey, Alexandra! You can run, but you can't hide!"

His laughter followed her all the way to her car.

The minute she stepped inside the service porch, she heard Nicholas's whispered "Mommy's back!"

"Come into the studio, Alex," Warren called. "We have something to show you."

She was still reeling from her confrontation with Ron, and it took great effort to erase the agitation from her face. Wearing a fake smile that felt more like a grimace, she walked down the hall to the studio.

A natural-tone oak rocking chair was sitting in the center of the room. Standing behind it were Warren, Lisa, and Nicholas. All beaming. Even Lisa.

Alex felt herself beaming, too, as she joined them. Her family.

"It's for when you have the baby!" Nicholas exclaimed.

"I can't use it till then?" Alex asked Nicholas. She pretended to frown.

The boy turned to Warren. "Can she, Daddy?"

"If she takes good care of it." Warren smiled.

"I promise." She ran her hand across the smooth wood. "So that's why you told me to take the Lexus," she said to Warren. "Sneaky."

"Like it?" His arm went around her.

"I love it." She kissed him.

"It was Lisa's idea. She picked it out, too. I was going to get a white one, but she said you'd like the oak."

"She was right." Alex turned to her stepdaughter and hugged her. "I can't tell you what this means to me, Lisa."

She was filled with a sense of well-being that brought tears to her eyes. Who cared about Mona Hutchins and Ron and their stupid insinuations, anyway?

On Monday a note came to the preschool.

On a bright yellow envelope, tucked in among several catalogs offering preschool educational materials, someone had used multicolored crayons to print Alex's name and the school address in large, uneven, childlike letters. At first Alex had thought that one of her "graduates" had sent it. She often received love letters from the boys and girls who had gone to the preschool. She treasured them. The note was written with the same multicolored crayons on extra-wide-lined gray paper, the kind first graders used to practice their penmanship, and she started to read, smiling in anticipation.

YOU AREN'T FIT TO BE AROUND CHILDREN!

She was still staring at the paper a minute later when Evelyn came into the office.

"Alex, we need—what's wrong? You look like you've seen a ghost."

Alex handed Evelyn the note. Evelyn read it quickly, then tossed it onto the desk.

"What a monster!" Her face was flushed with anger. "I thought he stopped bothering you."

"Who?" Alex's brow was furrowed in puzzlement.

"Lundquist, of course. He's the one who sent this."

Alex shook her head. "I don't think it's Lundquist, Evelyn. I got a note on Friday, at home. How does he know my home address?"

"The phone book?"

"There are several Prescotts in the phone book. How would he know which one to send it to?"

Evelyn thought for a moment, then said, "He could have checked out the addresses. When he spotted your red Jeep, he knew he had the right place. Or he could have sent notes to all the Prescotts." Evelyn hesitated for a moment. "He could have followed you home from school, Alex."

Alex grimaced. "Is that supposed to cheer me?"

"I'm sorry. But maybe you're right. Maybe it isn't him after all. What did the first note say?"

They were just words, but Alex found it difficult to repeat them. " 'You don't deserve to have a baby.' That's another thing, Evelyn. Lundquist doesn't know I'm pregnant, so the note doesn't fit him."

"Maybe he does know. You *are* showing. Maybe his wife mentioned it. Where's the first note? You should show both of them to Brady." Evelyn frowned. "We probably shouldn't have touched the paper. Maybe the police can raise fingerprints."

"I don't have the first note. I threw it out." Alex paused. "I thought it was Lisa."

She explained what had happened when she'd tried on the maternity clothes. "I thought Lisa hated me and the baby, but the next day she apologized, and she went with Warren to buy me a rocking chair for when the baby comes. She's been great."

Too great? she wondered suddenly. Mona had said that Lisa hid her true feelings. What if her stepdaughter was just pretending?

The notes were on Alex's mind during the entire afternoon. She added too much flour to the paste for a papier-mâché project the children were making. She let Patty make the second batch. Then she spilled water paint all over a sheet of poster board. When three o'clock came, she was more than eager to leave.

Usually, Alex was waiting for Nicholas when he came out of the building entrance, but there was heavy traffic, and she was a few minutes late. There were clusters of children on the lawn, waiting for their parents, and as she pulled up in front of the school, she glanced at them but didn't spot Nicholas.

There he was. He was standing sideways, but she recognized his tawny hair and profile. He was talking to a dark-haired male. One of the teachers with yard duty, Alex decided. She honked to get Nicholas's attention, then got out of the Jeep and stood at the curb to wait for him.

Nicholas turned toward her. "Hi, Mommy!" he called, then turned back to the teacher. "That's my mommy," Alex heard him say, and the teacher glanced in her direction and smiled, but it wasn't the teacher. It was Donald Lundquist.

Her heart skipped a beat. She started walking toward them, but Lundquist had taken Nicholas's hand and was heading over to her.

"Great boy you have here, Mrs. Prescott."

"Get in the car, Nicholas." She opened the back door.

Nicholas said, "He's Bobby's father, so he's not a stranger, and it's okay for me to talk to him."

"Nicholas—"

"I remember Bobby from last year, when I was in your school, Mommy. Bobby's father said—"

"Nicholas, I asked you to get into the car. Please do it now." She hated the brusqueness that had crept into her voice and the look of bewilderment and hurt on Nicholas's young face, but the need to get him away from Lundquist was urgent, overwhelming.

"Okay." Without looking at her, he climbed into the back and sat passively while she adjusted the shoulder harness.

She shut the door and turned to face Lundquist. She spoke quietly so that Nicholas wouldn't overhear. "If you ever come near my son again, I'll call the police."

"There's no law against talking to people, is there? Or in checking out elementary schools for your kid. Bobby'll be starting kindergarten in September. As a teacher, don't you think now's a good time for me to see what's available?"

"Stay away from us!"

"I have to tell you, I'm really pissed that you told the police I trashed your school. Sally probably told you to do that, right?" Lundquist moved closer. "I want my wife, Mrs. Prescott. I want my son. I want to be a family again. Don't you understand that? You'd be devastated if you couldn't see your son, if you didn't know where he was. That's how I feel, Mrs. Prescott. Every minute of every day."

She moved away and walked to the driver's side of the Jeep.

"Where is she, Mrs. Prescott?"

She opened the door, got in quickly, and pulled the door shut.

"Where is she?" Lundquist yelled. He was leaning over the hood, his angry face inches from the windshield.

She buckled herself in and turned on the ignition. She saw his hand rising, forming a fist, moving at a downward angle toward the windshield. She flinched. At the last minute his fingers unfurled, and he waved at Nicholas.

"See you soon," he said to the little boy.

Alex released the emergency brake and drove away.

Chapter 15

As soon as they got home, Alex settled Nicholas in the breakfast room with a snack and went into the den. She called Detective Brady and told him what had happened.

"Did he harm the boy?" Brady asked.

"No. There were people around. But he implied that if I don't tell him where his wife and son are, he'll——" She closed her eyes, unable to say the words. "He'll take Nicholas."

There was a pause. Then Brady said, "I doubt it, Mrs. Prescott. He knows if anything happened to your son, especially after today, we'd come straight to him."

"Detective Brady, you're thinking logically. Lundquist isn't logical. Or rational. I want a court order keeping him away from me and my family."

"You'd have to get a lawyer to handle a court order. But it isn't easy. There was no explicit threat, no assault."

"Are you going to wait until he hurts someone or kidnaps Nicholas?" She was practically screaming, she realized. With an effort, she lowered her voice. "I want police protection."

Brady sighed. "Mrs. Prescott, please understand. I sympathize with you a hundred percent. But getting police protection just isn't going to happen. I'll talk to Lundquist again, put the fear of God into him. Now, if you see him, and he says anything explicit. . . ."

Alex thanked Brady (for what? she wondered) and hung up. She called Warren. His secretary told her he was in court and would give him the message. Alex then called Evelyn at the school and told her what had happened.

"I want you to take special precautions when the parents come. Make sure you or Patty escort every child to his car." It had occurred to Alex after she'd talked with Brady that Lundquist might target one of the other children in an attempt

108

to coerce Alex into revealing his family's whereabouts. She wondered suddenly what she would do if she did know where Sally Lundquist was hiding with her son.

She remembered the paper Sally Lundquist had dropped. When she'd called last time, the person who'd answered had said there was no Sally Lundquist there. But maybe that was routine protection for the women and children who stayed at a shelter.

Alex found the paper and punched the numbers. A woman answered the phone after the second ring, and Alex identified herself and asked for Sally Lundquist.

"You've reached the wrong number," the woman said.

"Please tell her this is an emergency. Her husband vandalized my preschool. He's threatening my family."

"I'm really sorry, miss, but—"

"Just tell her, okay? Alexandra Prescott."

The woman hung up. Alex put down the receiver. Probably a dead end, she thought. She turned around and saw Nicholas.

"Finished your cookies?" she asked.

He nodded. He'd been quiet in the car—a rarity for him, but small wonder, considering Alex's unusually harsh tone when she'd told him to get into the Jeep.

"How about a game of Trouble?"

He shook his head and stared at his feet.

She walked over to him and crouched down until they were eye level. "Nicholas, I'm sorry I yelled at you at the school."

"I did a wrong thing, didn't I?" His eyes filled with sudden tears. His lips quivered. "But he's Bobby's daddy, and I saw him last year, so I thought he wasn't a stranger!"

"You didn't do a wrong thing, Nick." She hesitated. "Bobby's daddy is upset with me. That's why I don't want you to talk to him, okay?"

"Is he the angry man you and Daddy were talking about?"

She hesitated. She didn't want to frighten him. "Yes."

"I don't want him to hurt you, Mommy!"

Nicholas threw himself at Alex. Her arms went around him. She felt his trembling. She wondered if he could feel hers.

She stroked his hair. "He won't, Nick. He won't."

At night, long after Warren had fallen asleep, she awoke from her nightmare and lay with forced calm, waiting for the wild pumping of her heart to slow down.

The dreams were worse. Ever since the first note arrived, they had become more frequent, more gripping in their intensity. Especially the sounds. Alex couldn't bear the sounds.

The shrill, staccato ringing of the wall telephone.

The rhythmic clacking of the receiver as it smacks like a metronome against the wall.

The protesting squeak of the uncarpeted stairs that lead from her attic studio. The muffled thump as her bare feet fly down the other, carpeted staircase to the room below.

The oppressive silence that rushes to meet her.

The moaning of the wind in her ears as she runs, her feet skimming the warm, gritty concrete.

The screech of the gate as she pulls it open. The reverberating clang as it slams against the fence.

She is through the gate, but there is another one ahead, and another one, each with its own screech and clang, so many gates, she can never get through them, never! The clanging grows and grows into a frenzy of syncopated noise, a percussion section gone wild, until she thinks her eardrums will burst, and when she is through the last gate, the final sound is the one that has been with her from the first ring of the telephone and emerges now from her throat as a primal scream that wakes her and leaves her shuddering in her bed.

She can never understand how it is possible for Warren not to hear that scream.

On Tuesday morning, after taking Nicholas to his homeroom, Alex spoke to the principal and told her what had happened.

"My husband and I don't want Nicholas waiting outside the building unsupervised, not even for ten seconds," Alex told the woman, and she could see from the expression in her eyes that she was being taken seriously.

Driving to the preschool, she felt somewhat more relaxed. Nicholas knew to avoid Lundquist; he was on guard. So was Lisa. For the time being, she wouldn't bike to school. Warren would drop her off there. Alex would pick her up.

Warren had called Brady from his office, and again that morning. Brady had talked to Lundquist; Lundquist, of course, denied that he was trying to intimidate Alex, but Brady felt he'd made an impression on the man. Warren had also initiated the paperwork for a court order against Lundquist. "Just in case," he had said. "I really don't think we'll need it."

Evelyn's car was in the preschool lot when Alex arrived. Alex had asked her to come in early, in case she was delayed at Nicholas's school. Evelyn was in the office, leaning against Alex's desk, talking on the phone. She waved at Alex with her free hand.

"Hi," Alex mouthed. She put her purse on the desk, then walked to the closet and hung up her denim jacket.

"See you Saturday," Evelyn said into the phone and replaced the receiver. She turned to Alex. "Did you talk to Nicholas's principal?"

Alex nodded. "They're going to be very careful. Who were you talking to?"

"Jerry. He wants me to have dinner with him and his parents on Saturday." She was smiling, her face flushed with pleasure and excitement. "I said yes. Now I'm a little nervous. I hope I'm doing the right thing."

Alex smiled. "Of course you are. You keep telling me how much you like him, how much you have in common. What are you going to wear?"

"I don't know!" Evelyn looked stricken. "I'll have to buy a new dress. Will you come with me, Alex? Unless you're not up to it," she added quickly. "With everything that's going on, I mean."

"I could use the diversion. How about Thursday night? I'll make sure Lisa or Warren will be home to watch Nicholas."

"Thursday night's great. Thanks, Alex." Smiling, Evelyn picked up a stack of stenciled papers from the desk. "I'll set these out before the kids come," she said and left the office.

The phone rang. It was Warren. Had everything gone all right this morning with Nicholas? Alex assured him that everything was fine and that the school had promised to be diligent in supervising him. As soon as she hung up, the phone rang again.

"Is this Mrs. Prescott?" a woman asked.

"Yes. How can I help you?"

"This is Sally Lundquist. I don't know how you got my number or how I can help you, but I feel terrible about what happened. Are you all right?"

"I didn't want to bother you, Mrs. Lundquist, but I don't know where else to turn." Alex repeated the events of the past few days. "I thought you could call your husband and tell him I don't know where you are."

"I see." She was silent for a moment, then said, "But if I call and tell him, he'll know we've talked. How else would I know about all this?"

Alex had given it some thought. "You could say you read about it in the local paper." Alex hadn't seen anything, but Lundquist wouldn't know that.

Another silence. "I want to help you, Mrs. Prescott. I really do. I know what Donald can be like." Sally Lundquist paused. "But I just don't know if I can talk to him."

"I understand." Alex was disappointed, but she *did* understand.

"I ran away before, you know. To my parents. Each time I told myself I'd never go back, but Donald can be so convincing. And Bobby misses him. . . ."

"Mrs. Lundquist, forget that I called. I'll be all right."

"Let me think about it, okay? I'll call you. And please, Mrs. Prescott, tear up the paper with my number. If Donald had any idea that you knew how to reach me. . . ."

The first thing Alex did when she came home with Nicholas was to go through the mail in the entry hall. There were magazines, bills, several envelopes for Lisa. No hate note for Alex.

She sighed with relief and went into the kitchen to check on Nicholas, who was having his daily snack. Then she went upstairs to change.

Paula was in Alex's bedroom, putting Warren's knit shirts into his armoire. She looked up when Alex entered.

"Hello, Alex." She smiled. "Have a nice day?"

"Very nice, Paula. Thanks for asking." She took off her Adidas and placed them neatly at her side of the bed. She put her socks in the bathroom hamper. She liked walking barefoot.

When she came out of the bathroom, Paula had picked up a stack of her underwear and was opening her dresser drawer.

Not for the first time, Alex said, "Paula, you can just leave everything on top of the dresser. I'll put it away."

"I'm used to doing it. I don't mind."

But I do, Alex thought. She didn't like the idea of Paula or anyone looking through her things, touching them. Especially the things in this drawer. It made her feel vulnerable, which

was silly. The gray envelope was well hidden toward the back.
(But it wasn't impossible to find, if someone was looking
for it. She recognized the risk of keeping the envelope in her
bedroom, but she needed to look at its contents daily—it had
become part of the ritual of pain. Sometimes, too, the thought
crossed her mind that she kept it there because subconsciously
she wanted Warren to learn the secret she lacked the courage
to reveal. Once exposed, it would stop haunting her.)

"I saw the rocking chair," Paula said. "It's so lovely."

"Lisa picked it out." Alex wondered why she'd felt it necessary to tell Paula that. To show that they were a "family"?
That Lisa liked her? Probably.

"Lisa's a wonderful girl. And Nicholas." Paula shook her
head. "He's a dear. He reminds me of my nephew. I feel so
close to those children."

"They're very fond of you, Paula. We all are." The dresser
drawer was shut now. Alex started to leave the room.

"Alex?"

She turned around. "Yes?"

"Denise told me about the baby shower she and Mrs. Mona
are giving you. I'm so happy for you and the family about the
baby."

Are you? Alex couldn't tell from the woman's voice or expression. "Thank you, Paula. That's nice of you to tell me."

"It'll be wonderful for Nicholas to have a brother or sister.
Of course, you'll be needing more help around the house and
someone else to watch the baby. Denise said she'll look for someone else to help her so I can be here full-time."

"That's sweet of you to offer, but I'm not sure yet whether
I'll be going back to work." That was a lie, but how could
she tell the woman that most of the time, she didn't want her
around even two days a week, that full-time would be unbearable?

Nicholas had finished his snack and was playing in the family room with his Etch-A-Sketch. Alex admired his creation
and went into the kitchen. She was standing at the counter,
eating leftover salad, when Paula appeared.

"Everything's put away, Alex. There're just two shirts left
to iron, but I'll do those Friday."

"Thank you, Paula. Everything looks wonderful, as always." That was true. Paula was an immaculate housekeeper

and handled everything in the house with care.

"Be good to yourself now, Alex. And that baby." Paula smiled and left.

Alex finished the salad. Whom *would* she hire to watch the baby? she wondered as she rinsed the bowl and fork. She found Paula annoying, but she was the logical choice: she was honest, dependable. The kids loved her. As Paula so often told Alex, she'd practically raised Nicholas after Andrea's death when he was five weeks old. Paula with her irritating habits and proprietary manner might be better than a stranger with yet-to-be-discovered irritating habits. Or worse, someone incompetent. Alex had heard her share of horror nanny stories.

She checked on Nicholas. He was working the Etch-A-Sketch and singing along with Mr. Rogers, who was lacing his tennis shoes and inviting him to be his neighbor.

She walked down the hall to her studio and was instantly on edge. Last night she'd left three sketches on the sofa. Paula had stacked them neatly and clipped them to the easel. She had vacuumed the light tan carpet in parallel rows, and the carpet was perfectly smooth except for the indentations of what Alex knew were the legs of the ironing board.

Paula had also cut the wide yellow ribbon that had festooned the rocking chair. The tightly coiled ribbon and matching bow were lying on the easel ledge. She wondered whether Paula had tested the chair, rocked in it.

Paula wanted me to see the ribbon, Alex realized. Just as she wanted me to see the ironing-board indentations, so I'd know she'd been in this room, doing what she wanted, what I'd asked her not to do. She was asserting her rights, reclaiming what had been her room.

That night, after Warren had helped Lisa with her math homework, Alex told him about Paula. They were in the bedroom, and he'd turned on the television and was lying on his side of the bed, his hands clapsed beneath his head.

"So?" he said when she'd finished. He sounded uninterested.

"So I'm in a constant battle of wills with the woman."

"You're making it into a contest, Alex. So she irons in your studio. Big deal. She's not ruining anything." He turned his attention back to the television.

She felt a flash of irritation. "She ruined my blouse. She rearranges all my things. I've asked her over and over not to. She touches everything. It bothers me, Warren."

He sighed. "Let it go, Alex."

"She sat in the rocking chair, Warren. It was a gift for me, but she cut the ribbon and sat in the chair."

He turned to look at her. "Christ, do you hear yourself? 'She's touching my things. She's sitting in my chair.' You sound like a kid, or one of the three bears."

Tears sprang to Alex's eyes. Maybe she *did* sound childish, but why was his voice so cold, so unfeeling? He'd been strangely quiet all evening. "Maybe I'm not being mature, Warren, but I want her out."

"Who else do you want out?" His eyes were suddenly hard.

She frowned. "What do you mean?"

"How about Lisa? Should I get rid of her, too?"

She stared at him. "How can you say that? You know how hard I've been trying to make things work between us. And it's been much better."

"But it would be a hell of a lot easier if she weren't here, wouldn't it? Just you and me and Nicholas and the baby."

"Why are you being so cruel, Warren? Did Lisa say something to you?" The girl had been subdued during dinner and had gone straight to her room, but Alex had thought it was because she was nervous about a major math test she was taking tomorrow.

"She showed me the application form, the one you had the school send her."

"I don't know what you're talking about."

"The boarding school, Alex. You had the Sheffield School send her an application for next semester. How do you think she felt when she got it?" His anger was like a whip.

"I never contacted a school, Warren. Maybe it's part of a promotion campaign to get students."

Warren got off the bed and walked over to his dresser. When he returned, he held a paper in his hand. " 'Dear Mrs. Prescott: Thank you for your inquiry about Sheffield School,' " he read. He handed her the application.

Alex looked at it, then gave it back to him. She shook her head. "There's some mistake."

"One of the first things that attracted me to you was how

great you were with Nicholas and the other kids in the pre-school. I made it clear from the start that I needed someone who would love *both* my kids.'' There was a steely edge to his voice.

She was suddenly furious. ''Is that the only reason you mar-ried me, Warren? To have a mother for your children, some-one to replace Andrea? Both our names start with A, so you didn't even have to change the monogrammed towels.'' She saw the hurt ripple across his face and told herself she didn't care. He had hurt her, too.

Warren took a deep breath. ''That's cruel, Alex,'' he said softly. ''And it isn't true. You know I love you.''

''This isn't about love. This is about trust. How could you think for one minute that I would send Lisa an application to a boarding school? Do you think I'm that mean, that under-handed?''

''She didn't send it to herself.''

''Didn't she?''

He frowned. ''What's that supposed to mean?'' His tone was ominously quiet.

She hesitated, then said, ''I wasn't going to tell you this, but now I have to. Somebody's been sending me hate notes.'' She told him what they had said and watched his face. ''I think Lisa sent them, Warren. Last week she hated me. Friday she apologized, but obviously she was just pretending. Now she sends herself this application. It's a sure way of getting you to think that I'm the mean stepmother, isn't it?''

''You're wrong, Alex.'' He shook his head impatiently. ''Lisa would never do anything like that. Somebody else sent the notes.''

''Who?'' The same person who had sent the application, Alex decided.

''Where are the notes? Can I see them?''

''I threw them out.'' She saw his skeptical look. ''I couldn't stand having them around. Evelyn saw the second one. Call her if you don't believe me. Why would I make this up?''

''Of course I believe you. I just wanted to see them. Maybe I could have learned something from them.'' He put the ap-plication back on the dresser, then turned quickly around. ''What about Lundquist? He could've sent you the notes. He's out to get you.''

"He wouldn't have sent the application to Lisa. It's too much of a coincidence to think that two people are trying to make trouble for us." Trouble for *me*, she amended silently. Someone's trying to get rid of me. She felt a frisson of fear.

"I know it wasn't Lisa, Alex." His voice was more imploring than insistent. "Who, then?"

Suddenly she thought of Ron.

"It could be Ron," Alex said. Without looking at Warren, she told him about the incident in the yard and her talk with Denise and explained why she hadn't told him before.

"Ron called me last week," she continued, "screaming and ranting. And Saturday he accosted me outside The Rose and begged me to tell Denise I lied. I refused. Maybe this is his way of getting even." She felt immensely relieved. That was one secret off her mind. The others . . .

"I know about Ron and what happened," Warren said.

Alex looked up at him, her eyes wide with surprise. "You know? Did he—"

"Denise told me." Warren's tone was flat. There was an odd expression in his eyes.

Alex felt as if she'd been slapped. She'd told Denise she wasn't going to tell Warren. She'd explained her reasons. Why had Denise told him, if not to cause trouble between Alex and him? And what else had Denise said? Had she insinuated that Alex had invited Ron's advances? Alex wanted to know but was afraid to ask.

"I'm sorry," she said. "Maybe I should have told you. You do understand why I didn't, don't you?"

"I understand, but I wish you'd told me yourself when it first happened. You talked about trust, Alex. It goes two ways, doesn't it?" he said softly.

Warren told Alex he was going to the office to catch up on paperwork.

"Don't wait up for me," he added. "I may be very late."

How late? she wondered. And why couldn't he work in his study? After he left, she decided to get milk and cereal. There was enough for tomorrow, but she felt she had to get out of the house.

Lisa was in her bedroom, sitting cross-legged on her bed, hunched over a text. She was wearing her Walkman earphones. Alex had to call her name twice to get her attention.

"I'm going to the market," Alex told her. "I should be back within the hour."

"Okay." The girl avoided looking at Alex.

Which is just fine with me, Alex thought as she backed out of the driveway. Although she would have liked to see what was in her stepdaughter's eyes. Anger? Hurt? Triumph?

At the market, as she was rolling her half-filled cart along the aisle, looking for the cereals Lisa and Nicholas liked, Alex had the prickly sensation that someone was watching her. Her heart beating faster, she stopped her cart and, pretending to study the stacks of cereal boxes in front of her, glanced sideways.

No one was there.

Calm down, she told herself, but ten minutes later, when she was in the produce section choosing salad greens, she felt it again. She whirled around and caught a flash of startled eyes and a face partially masked by a black cap. The face quickly turned. A second later Alex saw the sleeve of a dark sweatshirt and a jeans pant leg and jogging shoe disappearing around the nearest aisle.

Abandoning her cart, she raced around the island of potatoes and onions, but when she reached the aisle where the person had turned, she saw only a harried-looking young woman with an infant strapped in a baby carrier to her chest. The woman put her arm around her baby and stared at Alex.

"Sorry," Alex said, embarrassment deepening the hue of her face, already flushed with anger and fear. "I thought I saw someone I knew." She backed out of the aisle, quickly checked several other aisles, then, defeated, walked back to her cart.

Maybe I imagined the whole thing, she told herself, but there had been something familiar about the eyes and the face. Outside, she hurriedly rolled her cart along the concrete to her Jeep. When she was buckled in her car, she drove up and down the lanes in the parking lot and scanned the cars.

There was no silver Jaguar. But that didn't mean there hadn't been one.

As she was nearing home, it occurred to her that it might not be Lundquist. It could be Ron. Or someone else. That thought, coupled with the notes, frightened her even more, and she knew she had to tell Warren.

Warren wasn't home when Alex returned. Lisa's bedroom light was on. Alex knocked, opened the door, and poked her head in. Lisa was in the same position on her bed, still wearing the earphones.

"Did your father phone?" Alex asked. "Lisa?" she called sharply.

The girl looked up. "What?" She sounded annoyed.

"I asked if your father phoned."

"Nope. Evelyn called about half an hour ago. She said she called before, too, but I must've been in the bathroom or something." Lisa turned back to her book.

"Or something" could be the earphones, Alex thought irritably as she shut the door and went downstairs. When Lisa had them on, she was in another world. Alex put away the groceries, then called Evelyn.

"No emergency," Evelyn said. "I just wanted to know if everything's okay with Nicholas." She sounded anxious.

"Nick's fine. He was waiting inside the school when I picked him up. I didn't see Lundquist." Alex frowned. "You didn't see any sign of him at the preschool after I left, did you?"

"No. I would've called you if I had. But I have to be honest, Alex. I keep looking over my shoulder to see if he's there. I guess this thing just has me spooked."

"Me, too." Alex debated telling Evelyn about the figure at the supermarket, but what was the point? Telling her would make her more nervous than she already was. And what if Alex had imagined the whole thing?

She intended to wait for Warren to come home, but she fell asleep watching television. By then she'd decided not to tell him. How do you know someone was watching you? he would have asked, and she would have explained that she'd had a strong feeling, that there had been something familiar about the eyes and face. And Warren would have looked skeptical, just as he had hours ago when she'd told him about the two notes, and he would think she was just a little bit crazy.

Maybe she was.

*   *   *

On Wednesday there was another envelope.

She was angry when she saw her name written in capitals in black marker. I won't let this get to me, she told herself as she ripped open the envelope and pulled out the note. Whoever is doing this is playing a childish prank but can't hurt me.

She unfolded the paper.

"MURDERESS!" the blood-red letters screamed at her.

"Oh, God!" she whispered and let go of the paper. It floated silently to the floor.

Chapter 16

Alex had promised herself that if she received another note, she would show it to Brady. But she couldn't show this one to the detective, or to Warren, because they would want to know what the writer meant (MURDERESS!), and even though it wasn't true—no one who knew what had happened could say it was true—how could she explain it without revealing what she'd struggled to keep hidden for three years?

In the kitchen, she stood over the counter and tore the note into tiny fragments until the hateful word was obliterated. Then she swept the fragments into her cupped palm and walked into the bathroom off the service porch. She tossed the bits of paper into the toilet bowl. Those that had been part of the word looked like droplets of blood floating in the water. She flushed and waited until the pale blue water was clear and still.

Nicholas was lying on the den carpet, engrossed with his Hot Wheels cars. Alex passed him on her way upstairs.

"Be right down," she said, amazed at the calmness of her voice.

In her bedroom, she walked over to the dresser (there was no need to run now, was there?) and reached inside the drawer for the gray envelope. It was there, of course, exactly where she'd left it. But what did that prove? Someone looking through her drawers (Lisa? Paula?) would be careful not to disturb their contents, even more careful to return the envelope to its original position.

But it was equally possible that whoever was sending the notes had gleaned information, not from her dresser drawer, but from the missing phone bills. She'd been certain until this minute that Lundquist had taken them in an attempt to trace his wife. What if someone else had taken them? Someone who hated her?

Not Lundquist, Alex decided. The sender of the notes had also sent the boarding-school application. Then who?

It could be Evelyn—she had constant access to Alex's files. Or it could be any one of the people who had come to help straighten up the vandalized preschool. How would Alex face them, not knowing?

At least she wouldn't have to face Lisa tonight. Denise had picked her up from school and was taking her to dinner; Lisa would spend the night with her aunt. A spur-of-the-moment idea, Warren had told Alex in the morning, but Alex knew otherwise. Lisa wanted to avoid her (she'd said good morning when Alex had come downstairs, but nothing else before she left for school). *Because she thinks I sent the application? Or because she sent it to herself and is afraid I'll read the truth in her face?*

"I can't stand this!" Alex said aloud.

Her head was beginning to throb. She pressed her hands against her head and massaged her temples. *You should be angry,* she told herself. *Focus on that, not on fear. Whoever did this violated your privacy, your past.* But her anger wasn't equal to the task, and although the note was gone, the word *MURDERESS!* was still emblazoned on her mind.

Warren called at five and said he'd be home late. An important meeting with an out-of-town client, he told Alex; don't wait supper for me. She broiled two baby lamb chops for Nicholas and a salmon steak for herself. After supper she supervised him while he took his bath. Then she read him Dr. Seuss's *Marvin K. Mooney, Will You Please Go Now!* It was his current favorite, and she read the story with all the humorous inflections and hand gestures he loved. Nicholas didn't have to suffer because her world was falling apart.

After he went to sleep, Alex tried watching a sitcom, but she couldn't concentrate; she found the dialogue tedious and the canned laughter grating. She went upstairs, changed into her nightgown, took off the bedspread, and placed it at the foot of the bed. She was getting into bed when the phone rang. It was Denise.

"I just wanted to know if everything's okay, Alex."

"What shouldn't be okay?" *Receiving a hate note? When*

Evelyn had called earlier and asked much the same thing, Alex had felt the same twinge of suspicion. And hated herself for it.

"I meant Lundquist, that creep. He didn't bother Nicholas again, did he?"

No, Alex told Denise, Donald Lundquist hadn't bothered Nicholas again. "How's Lisa?" she asked dutifully.

"Fine. She'd come to the phone, but she's holed up in the spare bedroom, working on a composition assignment. Is Warren there? He left a message on my machine."

Did he? "No, he's not."

"Is anything wrong, Alex? You sound strange."

"Just tired. I'll tell Warren you called."

"Thanks. And I'll give Lisa your love."

"You do that. Good night, Denise."

Warren came home at ten-forty-five; Alex heard him walking up the stairs and checked the clock on her nightstand. When he entered the room, her eyes were closed, her lamp off.

"Alex?" he whispered. When she didn't answer, he left the room.

She lay as she always did before she went to sleep—deliberately still, her hand below her abdomen, waiting for the fluttery sensations that were her nightly serenade, her lullaby. Tonight they were more important than ever, providing her with an island of serenity.

It'll be all right, she told herself. I'll find out who's behind these notes and put a stop to them. A fetal kick punctuated her thought. She took it as a sign.

She had to.

"You really like the dress?" Evelyn asked Alex on Thursday night as the saleswoman returned her credit card.

"It's perfect. Jerry's parents will be bowled over."

Evelyn laughed. "That's kind of funny, considering that his parents are in a bowling league."

Alex checked her watch again. A little after eight. She'd told Warren she'd be back by nine-thirty.

"I guess it's not that funny," Evelyn said.

Alex looked at her. "What?"

Evelyn repeated what she'd said. "Weren't you listening?"

"Sorry. My mind wandered. That *is* funny," she said and smiled. "Ready?"

"Sure." Evelyn looked as if she were about to say something. Instead, she slipped her charge card into her wallet and folded the plastic-bagged dress over her arm. "All set."

Going down on the escalator, they were silent. From the corner of her eye, Alex could see Evelyn looking at her.

"Are you okay?" Evelyn finally asked. "You haven't seemed yourself all day."

"Just tired." Alex hadn't slept well last night. Thinking. Not knowing who was turning her world upside down. At work, she'd found herself looking at Evelyn from time to time, wondering.

"I shouldn't have dragged you out here tonight. I'm sorry."

"Evelyn, I *wanted* to come. And I had fun. Really." Helping Evelyn choose a dress had taken her mind off her problems, if only for an hour. Now she was eager to get back home.

"You're not upset with me about something, are you?"

"Evelyn—"

"Because if I'm doing something wrong with the kids, or not doing something you want me to do, just tell me. I won't be insulted." Pink stained her face.

Alex put her hand on her friend's arm. "Evelyn, you're a wonderful teacher. The kids are lucky to have you. *I'm* lucky to have you. I just have a lot on my mind."

"The notes?" A frown creased Evelyn's forehead. Her eyes narrowed. "You didn't get another one, did you?" she asked in an undertone.

MURDERESS! Alex shook her head. "I just need a good night's sleep." Suddenly she looked over her shoulder.

"What is it?" Evelyn asked. "What are you looking at?"

Alex hesitated, then said, "I had the feeling someone was watching me. No one's there," she added, but Evelyn, with an abrupt movement of her head, glanced quickly behind her.

"Who would do that?" she asked, turning back to Alex. She was staring, her eyes wide.

"I don't know. I had the same feeling a couple of days ago, at the supermarket. My imagination's overactive, I guess."

They stepped off the escalator and made their way past the shoe and accessories departments. As they meandered around the cosmetics islands, a woman at the Chanel counter offered them a free makeup session.

Evelyn stopped and turned to Alex. "Want to?"

Alex shook her head. "Warren has to go back to the office. I told him I'd be home by nine-thirty to watch Nicholas. Lisa's spending the night with a friend."

"It's only eight-fifteen. Come on, Alex. It'll be fun." Evelyn smiled.

Alex shook her head. "Sorry. Maybe we should've come in separate cars." She had picked up Evelyn from her house in Santa Monica, just north of Venice, then driven to Robinsons.

"No big deal. I'll make a Saturday appointment. Is twelve o'clock open?" Evelyn asked the woman behind the counter. When the woman nodded, Evelyn turned back to Alex. "That's probably better. I'll look glamorous for the big evening." She patted the dress hanging over her arm and smiled.

While Evelyn was giving the woman her name and phone number, Alex examined her face in the large oblong mirror on the counter. She looked pale, and there were faint shadows under her eyes. Hardly the picture of a glowing mother-to-be. I could use a makeover, she thought. I could use a lot of things, like peace of mind.

She was turning away when she saw the face in the mirror. It was about fifty feet away and she thought, but couldn't be sure, that the eyes were riveted on her. Her heart started beating rapidly. She swiveled around and caught a glimpse of a figure wearing a shapeless three-quarter-length tan jacket, jeans, and a black cap with lettering on it. The figure whirled, turned right, and disappeared behind several racks of belts.

Alex started running.

"Where are you going?" she heard Evelyn call, but she had no time to stop and explain, not to Evelyn or to the two women who stepped quickly aside at her approach and stared at her. She had passed the cosmetics department and was turning right, past the belts, when Evelyn caught up with her.

"What's going on?" Evelyn asked, breathless. She grabbed Alex's arm.

"I lost him!" Alex cried.

"Who?"

Alex looked quickly to the right, then to the left. Where had he gone? There were so many people! It was hopeless, she would never—there he was! She saw the backs of the cap and the jacket on the escalator. Going up.

Her heart pounding now, she pulled away from Evelyn and raced across the floor to the escalator. "Alex, wait!" Evelyn cried, but she couldn't wait. The figure was halfway up the escalator when Alex stepped onto it. She climbed the moving steps, apologizing as she wove around the stationary people in her way. An obese man muttered an angry "Hey, lady!" as he flattened himself against the side of the escalator to let her pass, but she didn't care, she was almost at the top.

She half stumbled off the escalator and her heart sank as she looked quickly around. The figure was gone.

She knew it was pointless to search for someone who could have walked into any number of dressing rooms or taken another escalator up, or down, or blended with the people swarming through the myriad departments. Still, with Evelyn beside her, she asked questions of dozens of shoppers, sales clerks, floor managers—"Did you see . . ."—all of whom looked at her strangely, none of whom had seen the figure in the tan jacket and black cap and jeans.

A man or a woman? they'd all asked.

It was a good question. One Alex hadn't known how to answer.

She didn't say anything to Evelyn while they were in the store. Evelyn didn't press her. When they were buckled into the Jeep, Alex said, "Did you see anything?"

Evelyn hesitated, then shook her head. "I'm sorry."

"You do believe me, though, don't you? That someone was watching me?" She studied the expression in Evelyn's brown eyes.

"Of course I do," Evelyn said. But she looked away.

On Friday morning Sally Lundquist called.

"I phoned my husband," she told Alex. "I told him I read in the paper about the vandalism to your school and wondered if he was responsible, and if he was, I wanted him to know that you didn't have any idea where Bobby and I were." She paused.

"And?" Alex said, although she could hear from Sally's low, mournful tone that the news wasn't good.

"He said he wasn't responsible for what happened to your school, and he didn't believe I'd read about it in the paper and connected it with him. So now he's convinced more than ever that you and I are communicating, and that you're keeping my whereabouts from him."

Wonderful. "Thanks for trying, Mrs. Lundquist. I appreciate it."

"I'm sorry I couldn't help." Sally sighed. "I don't want to frighten you, Mrs. Prescott, but I think you should know that Donald is furious at you for telling the police he was to blame. He said you'd be sorry. I feel responsible."

Alex thought about the figure she had seen and felt a spasm of fear. "It's not your fault. I appreciate your calling me."

"He probably won't do anything. It's me he's angry at."

And I'm your proxy, Alex thought as she hung up.

Denise stopped by the preschool in the middle of the morning. Alex was outside with Evelyn, supervising the children as they played. Evelyn was alternating between the slide and the monkey bars, occasionally lifting a child down. Alex was standing by the swings, pushing the children when they needed assistance, making sure no one was swinging too high. She didn't lift them, though. Dr. Pearson had cautioned against that.

"This is a surprise," she said when she saw Denise enter through the chain-link gate that opened onto the street. Denise was wearing her blond hair down, with a red headband. Alex thought she looked like Alice in Wonderland.

Denise walked over to her. "Is it a bad time, Alex? I have to talk to you. It won't take long, I promise."

"Go ahead. We'll have to talk here, though. I can't leave Evelyn alone."

"That's fine." In a quiet voice, Denise said, "Alex, Warren told me about the application thing, and I—"

"Warren told you?" How could you, Alex said silently to her absent husband.

Denise put her hand on Alex's arm. "Don't be upset. He's worried, and he wanted my opinion because I know Lisa so well. Poor kid. She's going through a rough time."

Not as rough a time as I'm going through, Alex thought.

Denise continued. "I know you've been doing all the right

things, but it isn't easy being a stepmother, is it?'' She smiled. "Cinderella's given all of you a bad rep.''

"You could say that.'' Alex paused. "I thought Paula might have sent the application.''

Denise stared at her, then laughed. "You're joking, right?''

"Not really.'' One of the boys was swinging way too high, Alex saw. "Slow down, Brian,'' she called and nodded approvingly when he obeyed. She turned back to Denise. "Paula doesn't like me. She resents my being around. I'm surprised she hasn't talked to you about it. I know you're close.''

A faint blush appeared on Denise's face. "The truth? She thinks you don't like her. She was hurt when she was cut back to twice a week. But you have to understand, Alex. Paula's been with Warren forever. She loved Andy. God, she was devastated when she died! She helped raise Lisa. She *did* raise Nicholas.''

"Until I came along. Maybe she wants to make trouble so that I'll leave.'' So that she can have her room and family back.

Denise shook her head. "Paula wouldn't do that.''

Was that uncertainty in her eyes? "Somebody sent the application, Denise. It wasn't me.''

"Warren told me you think Lisa could have sent it. I've been giving it some thought, and you may be right. Some loyal aunt, huh?'' She smiled again. "With all the fuss about the baby, maybe she did it for attention. Or maybe she needed affirmation that you and Warren would never send her away.''

"Of course we wouldn't!''

"I know that. But Lisa's confused, Alex. She's attached to Warren, as you know. Too attached, I think, but I've read that teenage daughters go through a stage when they're really attracted to their fathers and angry at their mothers.''

"The Electra complex.''

Denise nodded. "Maybe that's part of the problem. And Lisa was always attached to Warren, even before Andy died. Then when Andy died, everybody concentrated on Nick. Now that you're having a baby, maybe Lisa sees the same thing happening again.''

"I see what you mean.'' That could explain sending the school application and the unhappiness that might have prompted it. But it couldn't explain the notes. *MURDERESS!*

"I want to get off," a pigtailed girl called.

Alex walked over to the girl, unlatched the metal-link belt, and helped her slip to the ground. The child scampered toward the slide, her pigtails bouncing up and down. Alex walked back to Denise. "Sorry."

"She's so cute," Denise said, gazing at the little girl. "Do you think you're having a boy or a girl?"

"I don't care. I just want the baby to be healthy."

"You're right. That's what I'd want." Denise sounded wistful. She watched the girl for a while, then turned back to Alex and said, "Last night Lisa told me she wants to live with me for a while."

Alex frowned. "I don't think that's a good idea."

"I don't either. I told Lisa no way. You and Warren are her parents, and she has to work things out with you. I'm not a psychologist, but again, maybe she wants to be told that she's loved, that she's wanted."

Maybe. "So you think she sent the application?"

"It's possible. I'd rather think it's Lundquist."

Alex shook her head. "How would he know I have a step-daughter?"

"You'd be surprised at what people know about you." Denise grinned.

Was that a sly reference to Alex's past? Alex forced herself to smile. "What does that mean?"

"You know how word travels. Most of the parents at your preschool probably know all about you——that you were Nicholas's teacher, that you married his father, that you have a teenage stepdaughter. And I thought of something else. Remember that Christmas play you put on a year and a half ago? The parents were there, of course. Warren and Lisa went to see Nick perform. So did I. Was Lundquist there?"

"Maybe. His son was enrolled then, but I don't remember if the father was there that night." Denise was right. Lundquist was still a possibility, one Alex preferred immeasurably to her stepdaughter or housekeeper or colleague. Or the woman standing in front of her, offering sympathy, support, friendship.

"By the way," Alex said, "I seem to be missing some phone bills from my office files. You didn't by any chance see any lying around when you were helping clear the place up, did you?'' She hoped that her tone was casual and that Denise didn't notice the intensity of her gaze.

"Sorry. I wasn't in the office. I had classroom detail." She smiled. "Why? Is it important?"

"Not really. Thanks anyway."

Denise tapped her finger against her lips. "Now that I think of it, Paula was straightening up the office. I'll ask her for you." She checked her watch. "I'd better be going. I have to choose carpet samples for a client with four children who wants something light but dirt-resistant." Denise grinned and shook her head. In a more serious voice, she said, "I just wanted you to know that I want to help in any way I can, Alex, and that I'm on your side."

Are you? Alex wanted very much to believe her.

Later, when the children were at the tables eating their lunch, Alex told Evelyn about her conversation with Denise. The two women were sitting on barstools near the counter at the left end of the room, filling plastic bowls with buttons, yarn, and circles, semicircles, and triangles of felt—the materials the children would use to glue eyes, eyebrows, lashes, hair, mustaches, lips, noses, and rosy cheeks to the bald, blank-faced cloth puppets Alex and Evelyn had stitched.

Alex cut several strands of dark brown yarn into four-inch lengths and placed them in a bowl. "I hope Denise is sincere," she said.

"Why wouldn't she be?" Evelyn frowned. "You always told me how wonderful she's been to you from the start. And she's making you a baby shower, don't forget." She poured buttons into another bowl.

There was something in Evelyn's tone that Alex couldn't identify at first. Then she remembered: Evelyn was probably still hurt that Denise had rejected her help for the shower.

Alex said, "That could be part of her pretense."

"But why? I can understand Lisa sending the notes and the application. What Denise said, about Lisa's being emotionally needy and all that, makes sense. Why would Denise want to threaten you?"

Alex shrugged. "I ruined her romance. She ruins my life. That's fair, don't you think?" She cut more strands—yellow this time.

"Next you'll decide that she's always had a thing for Warren, that she hates you for coming here and making him fall in love with you right under her nose. Come on, Alex." Evelyn shook her head.

Alex frowned. "I never thought of that."

Evelyn put the bag of buttons on the counter. "God, Alex, I was *joking!* You should see your face."

"Maybe it isn't a joke. You were working for Cybil when Nicholas first started at the preschool. Did you notice anything about Denise and Warren?"

"Come on, Alex, that was over two years ago."

"Think! It's important."

"Okay." Evelyn picked up the bag of buttons and sifted through them. After a moment she said, "Warren dropped Nicholas off every day and Denise picked him up. If he forgot something, like his lunch or a sweater, she'd bring it, or Paula would. If he got sick, we'd call Denise or Paula and one of them would come get him. If we needed extra mothers for an outing, Denise would always volunteer."

"Funny, I remember Denise coming once or twice to pick Nicholas up, but mostly Warren came."

"He wanted to get to know Nicholas's beautiful new teacher." Evelyn smiled. "Anyway, Denise or Paula was always available. Cybil used to say that Nicholas might have lost his mom, but he never lacked for mothering. That's about it. Proves a lot, doesn't it?"

"It proves that Denise was attached to Nicholas." So was Paula. Alex would have to keep the housekeeper in mind, too. "Maybe she wanted to show Warren what a good mom she'd be."

"She was being a good aunt. It's Lundquist," Evelyn said firmly. "He sent two notes and the application, and that's the end of it. You haven't gotten anything else, have you?"

"No." Alex couldn't tell anyone about the last note, not even Evelyn.

"See? It's over," Evelyn said, but the expression in her eyes indicated that she wasn't so sure. "So is lunchtime. Let's go play with some kids."

Lisa came home after supper. Denise dropped her off, but left after saying a quick hello and kissing Nicholas.

"Alex," Lisa began, and there was the by-now-familiar ritual of reconciliation. She was sorry for having been upset; she knew Alex hadn't sent the application.

"I understand how terrible you must have felt," Alex said. "Let's forget it, okay?"

Warren stood by, smiling approvingly. Alex wondered how long this truce would last, whether there was any truth to what she or Lisa was saying.

On Friday, Alex dreaded coming home and dealing with Paula, but the housekeeper was in a cheerful mood and solicitous about her.

"You look so tired, Alex," Paula said as soon as she saw her. "Circles under your eyes, too. I hope you'll try to rest this weekend."

"I plan to." Why the sudden kindness? Alex thought, and felt terribly sad. She was tired of being on guard with everyone, of analyzing every comment, every tone, for hidden meanings or motives.

Nicholas said, "Mommy, you promised we'd go to the beach tomorrow to see the jugglers and go biking."

"We will."

She went to the entry hall and checked the mail chute. There was no note for her today. There hadn't been one yesterday, either. Maybe it *is* over, she thought, then remembered the figure. Or had that been her imagination after all?

After Paula left, Alex went to the studio. There were no ironing-board-leg indentations. Alex wondered whether Warren had talked to Paula.

She slept late on Saturday, something she rarely did, then showered and dressed and ate a leisurely breakfast. Warren left to play a set of tennis. He returned at eleven, and twenty minutes later he drove with Nicholas and Alex to the beach. Lisa had gone roller-skating with friends—someone had picked her up—and would meet her family at the bike-rental shop at one o'clock. From there they would all go for lunch.

Warren parked the Jeep in a lot on Market Street. In Abbot Kinney's day, it had been Aldebaran Canal. Alex tried to visualize what it had looked like then, with gondolas and gondoliers.

"I'll go rent the bikes," Warren told her. "Nick, you want to come with me or stay with Mommy?"

"I'll come."

"Meet you right here in twenty minutes, hon," Warren said.

Alex watched them walk away hand in hand. The day was cool, but the beach was filled with people of all ages in swimsuits. Some were in the ocean, and she wondered why anyone would go swimming in what must be freezing water.

She stopped in front of a corner kiosk that sold T-shirts, visored caps, straw hats, sunglasses, earrings, imitation Gucci and Louis Vuitton purses and totes. She tried on a wide-brimmed straw hat and dark sunglasses and looked in the small, round mirror on the post of the kiosk. She looked so different, unrecognizable, and she had a sudden urge to run away, start over. (Years ago, she'd read, the evangelist Aimee McPherson had disappeared in Venice, maybe right near this spot. Later, she'd shown up in another state.) But of course, Alex couldn't run away. There was Warren, whom she loved. And Nicholas—she couldn't bear the thought of leaving him. And she had run away before, started over before.

She removed the hat and sunglasses and handed them back. Nothing today, thank you, she told the owner.

She turned right onto Ocean Front Walk and strolled about fifty feet until she came to a restaurant; she entered and passed through it into Small World Books. It was a store she frequented for art books and children's books and general fiction. There was a section toward the back called The Mystery Annex; Alex often scanned the shelves for a title or cover that looked particularly intriguing, but not today. *I have enough suspense in my life,* she thought. She found a booklet on names for babies and brought it to the front counter.

"For you?" the pretty, brown-haired owner asked. "I hope you don't mind my asking."

"Yes." Alex smiled. Thinking about the baby always made her smile. It was the one joy that nothing could dim, not even the notes.

She left the store and walked back to the stretch of sand near the parking lot. Thirty feet across from her, a volleyball game was in progress. She liked volleyball; in high school she'd derived satisfaction from playing the game well. (Her parents had dismissed her accomplishment. *Concentrate on your studies, Alexandra.*)

She joined the crowd that had gathered to watch and stayed at the front, turning to her left every now and then in hopes of catching sight of Warren and Nicholas and the bikes. The pace of the volleyball game was accelerating; around her, the crowd was cheering. She stood several feet from the edge of the boardwalk and watched the players and rooted silently for the ball that seemed to stay aloft forever before it came down and was suddenly, miraculously, airborne again.

She wished her life could be like the ball—light, buoyant, full of promise.

The hands that shoved against her back were sudden and strong and swift. Her scream was swallowed in the crowd's roar. She clutched at the air to steady herself, then cradled her lower body with her arms to cushion the baby inside her as she fell and hit the concrete path with a sickening thud.

A cyclist screeched to a halt inches from her, but the momentum propelled rider and bike onto Alex.

By then she didn't feel a thing.

Chapter 17

When Alex awoke, she was lying in a hospital room. Her head was throbbing, and her right cheekbone ached. She lifted her right hand to touch her cheek and yelped at the pain that shot through her arm and shoulder and sides. There was a thick bandage on her cheek.

"You're awake," a woman said. "That's good."

Alex turned her head to the left, in the direction of the voice, and saw a nurse getting up from a chair against the wall. The movement of her head hurt, too, and she wondered if there was anything in her body that didn't hurt. And then she remembered.

"My baby!" She shoved her hands under the blanket, under her hospital gown, and placed them gingerly below her abdomen. Nothing felt different. "Is my baby all right?"

"I'll get the doctor." The nurse headed for the door.

"But is my—"

The nurse opened the door and shut it behind her. Alex closed her eyes and lay still and waited for a communication that would allay her fears. What seemed like an eternity passed; she felt nothing. Her fingers gently prodded. Still nothing. That doesn't mean anything, she told herself. The baby could be sleeping. But her heart was heavy with dread.

The door opened and Warren entered. He looked haggard and tired. He walked to the foot of the bed and put her purse and a paper bag on top of the blanket. She wondered what was in the paper bag, then remembered: the book of baby names. Hot tears smarted behind her eyelids.

"Are you okay?" he asked.

He was avoiding looking at her, but she could see the pain in his eyes, she could hear it in his voice, and she knew the baby was dead. She started to cry.

135

"Hold me," she whispered. "Please hold me."

She pulled herself to a half-sitting position, wincing at the pain, and held out her arms. He walked to the side of the bed and sat down. She put her arms around his neck and leaned her head against his chest and wept.

"Don't cry," he said, but there was no conviction in his voice. He unclasped her hands from around his neck and placed them on her lap. His white knit polo shirt was damp from her tears. "You should rest, Alex. You've had a concussion. You fractured your collarbone and two ribs. You bruised your jaw and cheekbone, too. But the doctor says you'll be fine."

He sounds so odd, Alex thought, like an insurance adjuster citing an inventory of damages, not like a husband. But then, grief took many shapes; she knew that from experience. "I don't care about myself. The baby's dead, Warren, isn't it?" The words quivered on her lips, but she needed to say them aloud.

He looked at her for the first time since he'd entered the room. "No. Pearson said the baby's stable."

"The baby's stable," she repeated, disbelieving. "The baby's stable," she said again and felt a surge of joy. She grabbed Warren's hands. "We're so lucky, aren't we?"

"Pearson said it's amazing you didn't suffer more injuries, especially with the cyclist falling on you with his bike."

She frowned. "What cyclist?"

Warren told Alex what the people in the crowd had reported. "By the time I got to you, somebody had called an ambulance. I told them to take you to St. John's. I asked them to alert Dr. Pearson. They were able to reach him, and he got to the hospital pretty quickly. By then, of course, a resident had checked you and said that the baby seemed all right."

"How long have I been here?"

"Almost four hours. It's three-thirty now."

"Where's Nicholas? He must be so scared."

"In the waiting room with Lisa. I called Mona after I got here and asked her to meet Lisa at the bike shop at one, the way we'd arranged. Mona brought her here to St. John's."

"Why Mona?" Alex knew she was being petty—she should be concentrating on being grateful that she and the baby were all right—but she was annoyed that her husband's former mother-in-law had been involved.

"I called Denise. She wasn't home. I didn't know who else to call." He removed his hands.

"What's wrong?" She frowned. "Where are you going?"

"Nothing's wrong. I'm exhausted, that's all. I figured I'd go have a sandwich and a cup of coffee."

"There's something you're keeping from me. I can tell from your voice. What did Pearson say?" Her own voice had taken on a shrill edge.

"I'm not keeping anything from you, Alex. Calm down. Maybe Pearson should give you a sedative."

"I don't need a sedative, Warren! But if you're lying about the baby because you think I can't handle bad news, please don't. I want to know the truth now." She grasped his hand and held on to it tightly.

"The baby's fine. That *is* the truth. Pearson wants to keep you here for observation for a few days, to see if there's any delayed stress from the trauma of the fall. But he thinks everything's fine."

"So what's bothering you?" Something was wrong. Very wrong.

Warren sighed. "Please, Alex, not now, okay? It's been a long afternoon. We'll talk about this at home." He stood up.

"I want to know now. Tell me!"

"You want to know?" There was undisguised anger in his voice and in the set of his jaw. "I was talking with Pearson after he examined you and said the baby was fine. 'The fetus has a strong heartbeat and it's a good size,' he said, 'although I'd love to have your wife's records here to compare.' "

She felt as if someone had punched her and knocked the wind out of her. "Warren—"

" 'To compare?' I said, not understanding, and Pearson said, 'With her first pregnancy and delivery. We like to compare how things are progressing—her blood pressure, weight gain, the baby's weight gain, blood work, sugar. Your wife said her other obstetrician is out of state and that he lost her records, so that's that.' "

Alex studied the weave in the blanket she was clenching with both hands.

"You want to know what's bothering me, Alex? What's

bothering me is that I can't understand how you could marry me and sleep with me and live with me for two goddamn years and not tell me you had a child.''

"I'm sorry," she whispered.

"You're *sorry?* You *lied* to me, Alex. Why? Why couldn't you tell me you had a baby?" Hurt had replaced the anger in his voice. "When I saw you lying on the concrete, before the ambulance attendants lifted you onto the stretcher, you looked like a broken doll, and I thought I would die. I really did." There was a catch in his throat.

"I can't talk about it, Warren. It's too painful. Please don't do this." She reached for his hand.

He moved it away. "Is it Larry's child?" he asked in a carefully detached tone.

She flushed at the insinuation. "Yes. Of course."

"Boy or girl? Or would that be revealing too much? I'm sorry," he said quickly. "I just feel so angry, so betrayed."

"A boy," she whispered. Her eyes welled with tears.

"Where is he, Alex? Is he—"

She looked up at Warren. "He's dead. He's part of my past, and that's dead, too, and none of it has anything to do with us. I promise."

"Alex—"

"I won't talk about it, Warren! I can't! I've never forced you to talk about Andrea's death because I know how painful that was for you. Why can't you leave this alone?"

The intercom came to life—a female voice asked Dr. Abrams to report to the OR, stat—and then the room was plunged into silence again.

"Maybe you're right," Warren finally said. There wasn't anger in his voice, or hurt, but she knew that something between them had changed. "I guess we're even. One for one. Just tell me this, Alex. Are there any other secrets I should know about?"

She didn't answer. She stared at the framed poster hanging on the wall across from her bed.

"I'll get Nicholas and Lisa," Warren said. "They're anxious to see you." He headed for the door.

"Will you be back?"

He turned to face her. "Of course I will. I love you, Alex. That's why this hurts so much."

It was only after he left that she realized what she'd forgotten to tell him:

Someone had pushed her.

She had plenty of time to consider the possibilities. There was little else to do while she lay confined to her hospital bed.

Until now, Alex had regarded the sender of the notes as someone who, prompted by jealousy or resentment or malice, wanted to intimidate her and drive her away. She had feared exposure—had quaked at the thought—but not physical danger. All that had changed. Someone was trying to hurt her and her unborn child. *To kill us?* The idea seemed impossible, melodramatic, but she had felt the hands against her back. She had felt the hate. She was dealing with someone who was obviously emotionally ill. And dangerous.

In the hospital she felt safe from physical assault (at night she'd entertained and quickly dismissed the idea of propping a chair against the door before she went to sleep), but suspicion creaked each time the door to her room opened. Warren had returned and brought Nicholas and Lisa. Nicholas had run to Alex's side and cried softly as she held him, but he'd been quickly reassured by her smile and her promise that she was all right, and soon he was playing with the controls to her bed and changing the stations on her television. Lisa had approached Alex tentatively and brushed her lips against Alex's unbandaged cheek; then she'd hovered near the doorway, fidgeting with her hands and hair, clearly eager to leave. Was it Alex's imagination, or had Lisa avoided making eye contact with her?

Denise came with Warren on Saturday night. She was warm, solicitous, affectionate. There were tears in her eyes. "We were all so scared!" she'd exclaimed. Alex had tensed under her embrace. On Sunday morning Warren had come again with Nicholas and Lisa. Alex wondered whether it was a coincidence that Warren was never alone with her in the room.

His flowers were there. He'd sent calla lilies, her favorite; the note had read, "Get better soon. Love, Warren." A note you could send to your secretary, she'd thought, but after what he viewed as her breach of trust, could she really expect better? Denise had sent flowers, too; so had Mona—a gargantuan arrangement of exotic blooms that overpowered the room with their size and perfume. Paula had sent her best wishes via Warren. Nicholas had drawn her a card; Lisa had brought a small pink, stuffed kangaroo with a baby in its pouch. I'm so glad you and the baby are okay, she'd told Alex, her voice hushed with emotion. Alex had thanked her, wondering as she kissed Lisa's cheek what that emotion was—genuine sympathy and relief, or disappointment that a plan had failed?

On Sunday afternoon Evelyn came. She hadn't known a thing, she told Alex, until Warren called half an hour ago. She'd been out with Jerry and his parents when Warren called her on Saturday night.

"Thank God you're all right!" she exclaimed softly as she leaned over and gingerly hugged Alex. Her voice shook.

"You should have seen the other guy." Alex had examined herself in the bathroom mirror. Her cheek was still bandaged; her forehead and chin were purple.

"Warren said you fell and a cyclist fell on top of you with his bike. What happened? Did you lose your balance?"

"I was in a crowd, watching a volleyball game. Someone pushed me, Evelyn." The same someone who had been watching her, first in the supermarket, then in the department store?

Evelyn's eyes widened in disbelief. "Maybe it was an accident, Alex. People get jostled in crowds."

Alex shook her head. "I felt the hands. Someone wanted to hurt me. More than that, someone wanted to hurt the baby." That was the most frightening realization.

Evelyn frowned. "What do you mean, 'more than that'?"

"Whoever pushed me probably didn't think I'd die. I had a concussion, and I fractured my collarbone and two ribs. None of that is life-threatening. But I could have miscarried. Dr. Pearson said so." You are a very lucky woman, he'd told her.

"What does Warren think about this?"

"I haven't told him. We haven't been alone to talk. And what will I tell him? That someone hates me and tried to kill our baby?"

Evelyn bit her bottom lip. "It could be Lundquist. You said so before. He's angry at you, Alex. His wife told you he wants to get even. He's been physically abusing her. He wouldn't be above physically hurting another woman."

"Maybe. But I keep thinking about what you said, that before I arrived at the school, Denise was like Nicholas's mom."

"So was Paula, remember? Although—" Evelyn stopped.

"What?"

"You're going to misconstrue this, especially now that you think someone pushed you."

"Tell me."

Evelyn sighed. "You asked me about Denise's relationship with Nicholas? Well, on Saturday I was looking through the scrapbooks I keep of the kids—"

"You keep scrapbooks? That's so sweet." And so like Evelyn, Alex thought.

Evelyn smiled. "Anyway, I came across a snapshot of Nicholas's second-year birthday party, and it triggered a memory. Warren was there, of course, and Denise, and Cybil said something like, 'You're better than most full-time moms,' and Denise said, 'Maybe I *will* be a full-time mom soon.' Cybil told me she thought Denise meant she was going to marry Warren."

"And then I arrived."

"It doesn't prove anything. Cybil could have been wrong. I could be remembering it wrong. Maybe you should call Cybil."

"She's off somewhere in Europe till November, isn't she?"

"Right. I forgot."

Alex sighed. "I don't want to discuss this anymore. It's too depressing. And it's pointless. Tell me about Jerry's parents. How did the evening go?"

"Fine." Evelyn grinned. "I think they really liked me."

"The dress was worth it, huh?" Evelyn had been nervous about the cost; she'd spent more than she usually did.

"Definitely. Jerry kept telling me how great I looked. And I'm glad I had that makeover." She saw Alex's blank expression. "My free Chanel makeup session, remember? At Robinsons? I wouldn't call it free, though, not with all the products I bought." She laughed and shook her head.

"So?" Alex prompted, smiling. She wanted to know about Evelyn's evening; even more, she wanted to prolong this conversation about normal, everyday things and pretend that her life was normal, too. "What happened? With Jerry, I mean. I can tell from your face that something *did* happen."

"Well . . ." Evelyn hesitated, then said, "After dinner Jerry and I dropped his parents off at their place in Van Nuys, and he took me home . . . and . . . well, he gave me this." She extended her right hand toward Alex. On her fourth finger she wore a small, square-cut emerald surrounded with tiny diamonds.

"Oh, Ev, it's beautiful!" Alex exclaimed. "Why didn't you tell me right away?"

"I don't know." Evelyn shrugged and laughed shyly, clearly pleased and embarrassed at the same time. She looked down at the ring and played with it. "Somehow it didn't seem like the right time, with everything you've been through."

"Don't be silly! I could use some good news. You must be so excited, Evelyn. Did you call your mom?"

"God, no!" She laughed. "She'd probably take the next flight out of Baltimore." Her mother had remarried and moved to Baltimore five years ago, after Evelyn's father's death. She had given Evelyn her two-bedroom beach house in Santa Monica. "I *will* tell her, soon. I just don't want to get ahead of myself. This isn't an engagement ring. Jerry hasn't proposed."

"Yet." Alex smiled.

"Yet," Evelyn agreed. She was flushed with happiness.

There was a knock on the door. The nurse entered.

"Mrs. Prescott? One of the other nurses just noticed that this package came for you. Someone left it at the station." She handed Alex an oblong box wrapped in paper with a baby motif.

"Your first baby gift," Evelyn said after the nurse left the room. "Aren't you going to open it?"

Alex tore the wrapping paper and opened the white box. Inside was a twelve-inch doll with long platinum-blond hair that could have been Barbie except for one striking feature: this doll was pregnant. Someone had removed the doll's clothes—a denim jumpsuit and red blouse lay neatly folded at her side—and her swollen midriff was exposed.

"I'm a little old for dolls," Alex said. "I wonder who it's from." She looked in the box. There was no card.

"Maybe it's for Nicholas. Kathy Morton has a doll like that. Remember she brought it to school? Her mother was pregnant.

She told me she thought it would be a good way for Kathy to 'share the experience.' ''

"Who's the doll's father? Does he share the experience?'' Alex smiled.

Evelyn grinned. ''Funny. Actually, I think you can send away for him.'' She took the doll from Alex. ''It's kind of cute. You take off the tummy and the baby's inside. There's a flat tummy insert for after the doll has the baby.'' She removed the egg-shaped, flesh-colored dome.

There was no baby. Instead, there was a narrow ribbon of white paper, the kind found in Chinese fortune cookies.

"You got gypped,'' Evelyn was saying, but Alex was only half listening. With a sense of foreboding, she took the paper and read the typed message to herself:

CONFUCIUS SAY:
SHE WHO TAKES A LIFE
DOES NOT DESERVE TO CREATE A LIFE.

She dropped the paper onto her blanket, grabbed the doll from Evelyn's lap, and hurled it across the room. It bounced against the wall. The head snapped off and landed several feet from the body.

"It's another note, isn't it?'' Evelyn whispered. ''What did it say?'' She reached for it.

Alex picked up the piece of paper and closed her hand around it. ''Just the same stuff.'' *MURDERESS!*

"This has to stop! You have to give Detective Brady the note. Maybe he can trace it.''

Alex shook her head. ''There's nothing he can do.'' She opened her fist, took the strip of paper, and began ripping it.

Evelyn grabbed Alex's hand. ''Don't do that! At least show it to Warren. Let him handle it.''

"I'll tell him about it when he comes later today.''

"Alex,'' she said, and her voice held a mournful chord, ''Alex, I wasn't going to tell you this, but Warren called me. He wanted to know if I'd seen the notes.''

"He didn't believe me!'' The thought knifed through her.

"He's concerned about you. He told me you're under terrible stress. I told him I saw the second note, but you should show him this one so he can see for himself what's going on.''

"You're right. I will.''

Alex put the paper in the top drawer of her bed table, but as soon as Evelyn left, she finished shredding the note and threw the fragments into the paper trash bag taped to the side of the bed table.

It was an effort to get out of bed, but she managed and walked to the nurses' station. None of the nurses, she learned, had seen the person who had left the package for her. She wasn't surprised. When she returned to her room, she almost stepped on the blond-haired, blue-eyed, smiling, disembodied head lying on the floor. She bent down, picked up the head and babyless doll, and dumped both into the waste basket in her bathroom.

When Warren came during evening visiting hours, she wanted to tell him about the doll and the note (not the entire message—she couldn't do that), but the kids were with him. She would tell him tomorrow, when they were back home, alone.

The thought of being alone with Warren filled her with anticipation and anxiety. She wondered how she would begin to repair the damage to their marriage, or whether, like the headless doll, it was fractured beyond repair.

Chapter 18

Warren *would hate her if he found out.*

She knew he would. She would try to explain, if he let her. She would tell him the truth—that she hadn't planned to push Alex, she really hadn't. She'd followed Alex to the kiosk, and to the bookstore—it had been fun to follow her, to stare at her back, to watch her unseen—then she'd stood behind her in the crowd, and her hands had suddenly moved, as if by themselves. She had to admit she'd felt a thrill of pleasure when she heard Alex cry and saw her fall, but she hadn't meant to hurt her or the baby, just to frighten her, to make her go away, so that everything would be right, the way it was before Alex came.

Why couldn't Alex go away?

She'd almost gasped when she'd seen Alex lying on the concrete. She'd wanted to bend down to see if she was all right, but of course, she couldn't. How could she explain what she was doing there?

That didn't mean she was bad. She wasn't bad. No one could say she was bad, because she was happy that the baby was all right, wasn't she? She wouldn't want to harm an innocent baby. She didn't really want to harm Alex, either. She wasn't that kind of person.

Even if something happened to the baby, it wouldn't be her fault. She'd given Alex so many warnings—so many!—and if something happened to the baby, it would be Alex's fault, not hers. Because if Alex really loved her baby, she would leave before it was too late.

Stupid! *she told herself. Alex wasn't going to leave! Not now. Why should she? Everyone was doting on her, sending*

145

*her flowers and cards and telling her how much she was loved.
And Warren felt sorry for her. She could just hear him soothing Alex, calming her. "My poor darling, I'll take care of
you."*

*That wasn't right! That wasn't the way it was supposed to
be! In one instant she had undone everything she'd so carefully planned.*

Stupid! *she screamed at her reflection in the bathroom mirror.* Stupid, stupid, stupid! *Her eyes burned with tears of helpless fury and self-loathing. She picked up a brush and lifted
it, ready to throw it at the mirror and shatter the pitiful image
she saw.* A failure! *Instead, she smacked the brush against her
bare thigh. She winced, but she bit her lips and, watching
herself in the mirror, continued to rhythmically beat her
thighs, first one, then the other, until the skin was raw and
bleeding from the scraping of the steel bristles of the brush
and her pain was strong enough and her whimpers loud
enough to block out the thoughts that were careening wildly
in her head.*

*Later, when she was calmer, she put on a nightshirt and
lay down on her bed. Her thighs ached, but she rolled gingerly
onto her side and curled up in a semifetal position. She shut
her swollen eyes.*

*Everything would be all right, she whispered to the pillow
she was hugging. Warren would never find out that she'd
pushed Alex. And nothing was ruined. Warren felt sorry for
Alex, but that was natural. And it was pity, not love. Pity that
would shrivel the second he found out what kind of person
Alex really was. The terrible thing she'd done. He would hate
her then.*

*She thought again about the call to the mortuary and the
wealth of information she'd uncovered about Alex. It had been
so easy, almost as if she'd been meant to find out, and although she didn't need help from anyone—she was doing fine
handling things by herself—it reinforced the knowledge that
she was doing the right thing.*

It was going to be fine.

*It was just a matter of waiting. Alex wouldn't be in the
hospital forever. Even there she wasn't safe. The doll had
shown Alex that. She smiled at the thought.*

Alex wasn't safe anywhere, not from the truth.
She moved and winced from the pain in her thigh.
The doll had been a very good idea.
She had other good ideas.

Chapter 19

"You and the baby are fine," Dr. Pearson told Alex on Monday morning after he had examined her. "But I want you to take it easy for the next few days. Bed rest, no work. No exercise. Also, I want to postpone the amnio. I don't want any additional trauma to the uterus right now. Come see me Thursday at my office and we'll reschedule."

She nodded.

"Speaking of amnios, Alexandra," Pearson said, "you're not switching health insurance carriers, are you?"

"No. Why do you ask?"

"Didn't think so." He sounded troubled. "A man called Friday, claimed to represent your new carrier, wanted to know all about your pregnancy. How far along you were, did you have an amnio. Stuff like that. Said the company needed the information before they would cover your pregnancy."

Alex frowned. "What did you tell him?"

"Nothing. I wanted to check with you first. I told him I'd phone him back, but he said he'd give me a call next week. I don't think he will."

Alex felt a ripple of fear. Who was trying to find out about her pregnancy? And why? "What did he sound like?"

"Hard to say." Pearson stroked his chin. "Nothing stood out. No accent to speak of. Youngish voice, somewhere between twenty and fifty. Doesn't help much, does it?" He peered at her through his tortoiseshell glasses. "I don't want you to worry about this. Maybe I shouldn't have told you."

"No, I'm glad you did."

"Probably some statistical study for advertising purposes. They do it all the time. Vultures." He patted her hand. "Concentrate on that baby of yours. That's an order."

Pearson left to sign Alex's release papers. Warren arrived

soon after and waited while she changed from her hospital gown into the shirt and slacks he'd brought from home. (No pullovers, she'd told him; it was too difficult and painful to move her arms and shoulders.) He was still avoiding looking at her, and she felt awkward, as if she were getting dressed in front of a stranger.

"Need help with the sleeves?" he asked suddenly.

Was this an overture? "Yes, please."

She handed him the shirt. He stood beside her and eased her arms into the sleeves. It was the first time they'd touched since he'd held her after she'd awakened in the hospital room.

"Thank you." She turned and kissed him lightly on the lips. He didn't pull away, but he didn't respond. "I love you, Warren." I'm sorry, Warren.

"I love you, too."

His words sounded scripted. Her eyes filled with tears, and she turned away. She didn't want his pity.

There was a knock on the door. A blond, Brunhilde-sized nurse entered the room, pushing a wheelchair in front of her. "Ready to go, Mrs. Prescott?"

"I can walk, thank you." Bending carefully, Alex picked up her purse and the book of baby names from the bed table.

"Sorry. Hospital regulations." The nurse waited until Alex was seated on the chair, then asked, "What about all these beautiful flowers? You taking them home?"

"I don't think so." Alex didn't want any reminders of her stay in the hospital, or of the act of hate that had put her there.

The nurse wheeled Alex down the long ramp to the patient pickup area where Warren had parked the Lexus. He opened the front passenger door; the nurse helped Alex onto the front seat.

"Four, five months from now, we'll be wheeling you and your baby out of here," the nurse said. "Now won't that be nice?"

Beyond nice, Alex thought. On the drive home Warren and Alex barely talked, and she wished the nurse had come along to fill the silence. She turned on the radio and selected a station with classical music.

Warren said, "By the way, Paula's at the house."

"Paula? But it's Monday." Alex had looked forward to the

one-day reprieve before she'd have to face the housekeeper.
And wonder . . .

"It was her idea. Denise didn't mind. I told Paula we appreciated her thoughtfulness."

Was that a hint to Alex to be grateful when she spoke to
Paula? "It's very nice of her, Warren," Alex said and lapsed
into silence again. Even if Paula *was* the enemy, she decided,
it was unlikely that she would harm Alex in her own home
and draw suspicion to herself.

When they arrived at the house, Paula opened the front
door. "Welcome home, Alex," she said in the somber tones
of an undertaker. Her eyes were more heavily lined in black
than usual. "I'm so happy you and the baby are all right. I
was praying for you yesterday at church."

Praying for what? "We're fine, Paula. Thank you for your
good wishes. And thank you so much for coming today." Alex
didn't look at Warren, who was standing behind her, but she
knew he was smiling with approval.

Most of her body was still sore and ached in places she
couldn't even identify, especially when she moved; although
Warren was behind her, supporting her back with his hand,
she found climbing the stairs a slow and uncomfortable process. Someone—Paula, no doubt—had removed the bedspread
and folded back her quilt. A cotton nightgown that buttoned
down the front lay on her pillow. It was one of the gowns
she'd bought for later, when she would be nursing the baby.

"I'll be right back," Warren said and left the room.

She undressed and undid all the buttons on the nightgown
so that she could put it on more easily. When Warren returned,
she was lying in bed.

"Paula wants to know if you're hungry," he said from the
doorway.

"Not really. I had breakfast at the hospital."

"I have to get to the office, but I'll call."

She realized with sharp disappointment that she'd expected
him to stay a while. Before his talk with Dr. Pearson, he would
have. Then again, he did have a law practice to run. "Warren,
before you go, there's something I have to tell you."

"I thought you didn't want to discuss your past."

She felt herself flushing, the heat spreading up her neck.

How long would this go on? "It's not that. It's about Saturday. I was pushed, Warren. Deliberately pushed."

He took several tentative steps into the room, as if he were reluctant to be drawn toward her. "Alex, you were in a crowd. People get pushed in crowds."

She shook her head. "I felt someone's hands shoving me."

"I talked to a lot of people who were there, Alex. They all said the same thing—you lost your balance and fell."

He spoke in his "reasonable" voice, the one he used when Nicholas or Lisa—mostly Lisa—was being difficult, childish. It was the same voice her parents had often used on her, long after she was no longer a child.

"Someone has been following me, Warren! Stalking me! First at the supermarket, then on Thursday, when I was at Robinsons with Evelyn. I didn't tell you because I knew you wouldn't believe me."

"Did Evelyn see this person?" The same calm, inflectionless voice.

She was infuriated. "No! But that doesn't mean it didn't happen. Someone pushed me! Someone wanted me to fall. Someone wants to kill our baby! Why won't you believe me?"

Warren sighed. He shut the door, then came over and sat next to her. He took her hand. "Alex," he said, and his tone was tender. "Alex, no one is trying to hurt you. You have to stop thinking that way. You're becoming paranoid, and it scares me."

"I'm not paranoid, Warren. Dr. Pearson told me someone pretending to be an insurance agent called his office asking about my pregnancy."

Warren frowned. "Who?"

"I don't know." Alex repeated what the doctor had told her. "Pearson thinks it's some advertising gimmick."

"It probably *is,* Alex," Warren said gently. "You're probably overreacting."

"But what if it isn't? And what about the notes? I didn't imagine them. I got another one yesterday, at the hospital." She told him about the doll and the note inside it. "There was no baby, Warren. Don't you see? Whoever pushed me sent the doll. The note said I don't deserve to have a baby." *MURDERESS!*

"Can I see it?"

"I tore it up. I threw the doll away." Why hadn't she shown it to him in the hospital? She looked him squarely in the eyes. "Evelyn was there when the doll came. You can check my story, like you did last time."

He had the decency to blush. He dropped her hand. "I called her because I was worried about you, Alex, not because I didn't trust you."

Do you trust me now? she wanted to ask, but was afraid to hear the answer.

"So who do you think pushed you?"

She could tell that he didn't believe her. He was humoring her, being patient. If she mentioned Denise or Paula (not Lisa—she couldn't mention Lisa), Warren would be convinced that she was becoming neurotic. She needed proof before she presented him with a name.

"I don't know. Maybe Lundquist," she said, offering the name like a sacrificial lamb because it would be the most believable and least offensive in Warren's eyes.

"I'll call Detective Brady and tell him."

She almost felt ashamed, but consoled herself with the thought that it *could* be Donald Lundquist.

During the rest of the morning and the afternoon, Alex rested. She napped, watched a little television—some soaps, Oprah, Phil. She read the *Los Angeles Times* and a copy of *Newsweek*.

Paula fixed her a bowl of vegetable soup and a tuna sandwich for lunch. The housekeeper was exceedingly pleasant and doting, and Alex had to admit it was nice being pampered. But she wondered whether Paula was ironing in her studio, rocking in her chair, moving her easel and all her supplies, spraying starch on all her nightgowns. Preparing for when Alex was no longer there.

At twenty to three, Paula came upstairs and told Alex she was leaving to pick Nicholas up from school.

"Denise offered to pick Lisa up," she said.

Alex nodded. "That's nice of her. By the way, Paula, remember when the school was vandalized and there were papers all over my office?"

"Of course. That was terrible, just terrible."

Was it Alex's imagination, or had the woman tensed?

"Well, I seem to be missing some papers, and I'm wondering—"

"I didn't take anything, Alex." The housekeeper stood straighter. "I just sorted what I found."

Almost the exact words she had used that afternoon when Alex had returned from the police station. "Of course not, Paula. I know you wouldn't do that." Alex smiled. "But maybe something got thrown out accidentally. There was such a mess," she added apologetically.

"I didn't throw anything out," Paula said, her voice and face stern with indignation. "Everyone was in the office at one point or another. Evelyn, of course. And your aide—?" She looked at Alex questioningly.

"Patty."

"Yes." She nodded. "Patty. And Denise."

That was interesting, Alex thought. Denise had said she hadn't been in the office. In a casual voice, Alex said, "I thought Denise helped clean the classroom."

"That was later. When I arrived, she was in the office." Paula checked her watch. "I'd better leave now, or Nicholas will be kept waiting. We don't want that, do we?" She turned sharply and left the room.

Well, I've been put in my place, Alex thought.

A half hour later she was still frowning in concentration, thinking about who'd had access to her bills. Then she heard Nicholas charging up the stairs. She smiled even before he entered her bedroom.

"Hi, Mommy!" He ran to her side, leaned over, and kissed her. "Your boo-boo's yuk!" He pointed to her cheek.

A resident had removed the bandage that morning, but the bruise was ugly. "It's much better. How was school, Nick?" She moved over carefully and patted the side of her bed. "Sit."

"School's great." He grinned and sat down.

She smoothed his hair. "Tell me all about it."

"Well, first—"

"Nicholas?" Paula called from downstairs. "Let your mother rest, dear. Come to the kitchen. I have a treat for you."

What about my treat? Alex thought, irritated, but she kissed Nicholas and watched as he bounded out of the room.

Warren arrived home earlier than usual. Alex heard him

talking in the family room. A few minutes later he came up-stairs, and after asking Alex how she was feeling, he told her he had briefs to write before supper. No problem, she said.

"Paula prepared supper," Warren said. "By the way, Denise is eating with us. Lisa invited her to stay."

"That's nice," Alex said. Three suspects in one room.

"Denise wants to say hi. Okay if she comes up?"

"A little later, all right? I'm feeling tired."

She was in no mood to see Denise and accept cheer and comfort that might not be genuine. Then again, it might be, and that bothered her, too. She wondered whether she was so quick to suspect Denise because she was jealous of what her husband shared with his former sister-in-law.

A while later Alex heard bits of conversation floating up the stairs into her room, like the Pied Piper's song, tempting, compelling. She was half out of the bed, ready to join the others, when Paula brought up dinner on a white bed tray. Alex hesitated, then got back into bed and thanked her.

Paula went downstairs. Alex picked at her broiled chicken and baked potato and salad and wondered what they were all talking about. Warren, Lisa, Nicholas, Denise, Paula. The happy family, she thought—exactly as it was before I arrived on the scene. She knew she was feeling sorry for herself, but she couldn't help it.

After supper Warren brought Denise upstairs. How are you, Alex? she asked. She was smiling, but her smile didn't reach her eyes. Fine, thank you, Denise. The conversation lagged; Alex made no move to revive it. After an awkward silence, Denise gave Alex a kiss that barely touched her cheek and went back downstairs. Alex had learned nothing—Denise was suffering under the strain of duplicity or was hurt by Alex's sudden aloofness.

If Warren found her behavior to Denise odd, he didn't say anything. He told her that Paula was spending the night so that she'd be there for her first thing in the morning. Didn't Alex think that was a great idea? Great, she agreed, hating the fact that the woman would be around all night, all day, hating even more the fact that no one had consulted her.

Several minutes later Evelyn came up to visit.

"Look what I brought you, Alex." She deposited an armful

of get-well cards on the bed. "Even Richie finished one, and you know he takes forever choosing which crayon to use." She smiled.

"These are wonderful." Alex had tears in her eyes as she read the loving messages from each child.

The phone rang. A moment later Lisa yelled, "It's for you, Alex. Line one. A guy. He didn't give his name."

Alex pressed the button marked "Line 1" and put the phone to her ear. In the background she heard Warren calling to Nicholas, and the laugh track from the television.

"Just a minute, please," Alex said into the phone. "I'll be right with you." She pressed the Hold button. "You can hang up, Lisa," she called downstairs. She pressed Line 1 again. The sounds from the television were still there. She wished Lisa would remember to hang up the receiver. Or use the Hold button.

"I'm sorry I kept you waiting," Alex said. "My daughter—"

"I saw who pushed you."

Alex's heart beat faster. "Who is this?"

"Don't play games, Mrs. Prescott. I saw who pushed you. You know where my wife is. We can make an even exchange of information. What do you say?"

Her hands were suddenly clammy. "Mr. Lundquist, for the thousandth time—"

"You don't know where she is. I know." He snickered. "But you *do* talk to her. She as much as admitted that the other day."

Evelyn whispered, "What does he want?"

Alex put her finger to her lips. "Mr. Lundquist, you said you saw who pushed me. How do I know you're telling the truth?"

Lundquist laughed. "How would I know someone pushed you if I didn't see it happen? Or did the local paper report it, like they reported your school being vandalized?"

"Maybe you know because you pushed me."

"It wasn't me! Why the hell would I do that?" he demanded angrily. In a calmer voice he said, "Look, we meet, you agree to give my wife a message, then I'll tell you."

"I don't know where to reach her." That was a lie. Alex hadn't destroyed the slip of paper with the number for the shelter. Now she regretted not having done so, because she would be tempted to call the woman.

"Yes, you do. Anyway, she'll call you. I know she will. When she does, I want you ready to tell her what I want."

"What if she doesn't call?"

"That's my gamble. All I'm asking is that you meet me, talk to me. I'm not a bad guy, Mrs. Prescott. I admit I've made some big mistakes. But I want to tell you my side, and okay, I'll be honest. I'd like your help in getting Sally to come back to me. I have to talk to her."

"When do you want to meet?"

"Tomorrow night, nine o'clock, at my house." He gave her the address. "Is it a deal?"

"I'd prefer to meet in a restaurant."

"Well, *I'd* prefer my house. I'm having some business problems right now and I want to keep a low profile. Tomorrow at nine, at my house, or forget the whole thing. But then you'll never know who pushed you, will you?"

And wrote the notes. And is trying to kill my baby. "Okay. Tomorrow at nine."

She held the receiver for a moment after Lundquist cut the connection, wondering if she'd lost her mind by agreeing to meet with him, then hung up. The red light for Line 1 was still on, which meant the downstairs extension was off the hook. Someone would notice eventually. Until then, anyone who called would get a busy signal, but Alex didn't really care.

She turned to Evelyn. "Lundquist knows who pushed me, Evelyn. He's going to tell me."

"I heard. You're not going to meet with him, are you?" She stared at Alex.

"I have to find out who's behind all these notes."

"What if *he* is?" Evelyn grabbed Alex's hand. "Don't go, Alex. It's crazy."

"He said he's not, and I believe him. He's convinced I'm a conduit to his wife."

"Are you going to tell Warren?"

"No. And I don't want you to say a word to him."

Evelyn frowned and released Alex's hand. "Alex, I—"

"Promise!" Her eyes bored into Evelyn's.

Evelyn was silent. "I won't let you go alone!" she finally

said. Her voice quavered. "If you won't tell Warren, let me come with you."

Alex shook her head. "He won't talk in front of you. You know that."

"I'll wait in the car. He won't know I'm there."

Alex considered for a moment, then nodded. "Okay."

Later, when Warren came upstairs, he asked her who had called.

She thought about the downstairs receiver that had been off the hook. Was this a test? "Donald Lundquist. He wants me to try to get his wife to come back to him." That much was true.

"Jesus, when will that son of a bitch stop hounding you?"

Warren undressed quickly, shut the light, and got into bed. Alex reached over to take his hand, but he rolled away from her onto his side.

"Good night, Alex. Sleep well."

"Good night."

She shut her eyes, not knowing whether she should welcome sleep or fight it. Sleep would allow her to forget about her problems with Warren. It would also open the door to her dream.

She opened her eyes and glanced at Warren. He had rolled onto his back and was staring at her. When he saw her looking at him, he shut his eyes.

At eight-thirty the next evening, Alex heard a honk. She looked out the living room window and saw Evelyn's blue Toyota Corolla in the driveway. She went into Warren's study.

"Evelyn's here," she said.

He looked up from his papers. "I still think you should be resting."

"We're just going for coffee. I'm feeling better today, almost like new, and to tell you the truth, I'm stir-crazy." That wasn't a lie. She'd been edgy all day, watching the minutes crawl by, waiting for the moment when she would finally learn the truth.

Then she would go to Warren, and together, they would put an end to this. *Unless it's Lisa*, a voice whispered. *If it's Lisa, there is no end to this.* But she refused to think about that now.

Lundquist lived in Marina del Rey, an affluent area south of Washington Boulevard. Evelyn found the street easily, but passed the address and had to double back. It was eight-forty-five when she parked in front of Lundquist's wide ranch-style house. They sat in silence, too tense to talk. Alex checked her watch every few minutes. At nine, she opened the car door.

"Are you sure you want to go through with this?" In the meager light of the street lamp, Evelyn's eyes were dark pools.

"I'm scared," Alex admitted. "But this is the only way I can find out."

"I just wish you were meeting him somewhere public."

"I called him an hour ago like you suggested and asked him to meet me in a restaurant. But he refused." *Don't you trust me?* he'd asked. "I told you that."

"I know you told me. But I still don't like it." She touched Alex's arm. "Why don't we leave? Let the police handle it."

"I can't."

"Then let me come with you." Her voice was hushed with urgency. "Why should he care if I'm there?"

Alex shook her head. "Wish me luck," she whispered.

Getting into the car had been relatively painless. Getting out required careful maneuvering. She moved her legs to the right and, holding on to the door handle, pulled herself off the seat to a standing position. She grimaced and bit her lip at the spasms of pain that shot through her, then shut the door.

All the lights were on in the house. She walked up the flagstone path to the white double doors and rang the bell. No one answered, but she knew Lundquist was home. She rang the bell again, then noticed that taped to the doors was a white piece of paper, folded in half. She pulled it off and opened it.

Mrs. Prescott—The bell is broken. The door is open. The house is yours. I'm in the Jacuzzi. Yell when you arrive, and I'll be right there—or you can join me. Just joking! Fix yourself a drink.   *D.L.*

She was annoyed and a little nervous—was this a trick?—and felt tempted to turn around, get in the car, and tell Evelyn to take her home. She twisted the knob, pushed the doors open, and stepped into a large entry hall with a white marble tile floor.

There were closed doors to her right and left. Directly ahead of her was an enormous sunken living room with three un-curtained French doors that offered a view of the backyard. There was no furniture except for two gray silk sofas and a glass coffee table with a black granite base. The floor was the same white marble. The walls were painted pale gray. Alex wondered where Bobby Lundquist played—certainly not in this austere, icy room. Probably in one of the rooms hidden behind the doors.

She walked down the marbled steps and crossed the room to one of the French doors. It was ajar. She pushed it open and called out, feeling silly addressing someone she couldn't see.

"Mr. Lundquist? This is Alexandra Prescott. I'm here."

She turned around. On a black granite bar to her right, Lundquist had set up decanters with amber liquids, crystal tumblers, Perrier, various sodas. Lundquist was a good host, if not a good husband, Alex thought. She filled a tumbler with Perrier and sat on one of the gray silk sofas.

Five minutes passed, then six. She put the tumbler on the glass coffee table in front of her and stood up. She would announce herself again; maybe he hadn't heard her. Then she would wait a few more minutes and leave.

She walked back to the French door, called out to him once more. She pressed her face against the glass, but the Jacuzzi and pool were hidden from view by a circlet of trees.

She stepped outside onto the flagstone patio. She heard music. Maybe Lundquist hadn't heard her call after all. She followed a path that turned left. There was the pool, and several steps up, the Jacuzzi. And there was Lundquist, sitting on the Jacuzzi steps. His back was toward her.

"Mr. Lundquist!"

She walked around the edge of the pool until she was in front of the Jacuzzi. Lundquist's head was bent toward his chest. His elbows were propped on the tile ledge. She reached out with one hand and touched him lightly on the shoulder. One elbow slipped on the tile, and then the other, and before her horrified eyes, Donald Lundquist slid into the swirling water and sank to the bottom.

Chapter 20

Alex screamed.

Even in the darkness, she could see from the moonlight that Donald Lundquist was dead. His face was drained of color. There were dark, jagged gashes in his neck and chest, and his blood was tinting the bubbling water in the Jacuzzi a pale pink.

She gagged and staggered backward, then turned and vomited on the concrete. When her heaving had subsided, she held her bruised, aching sides and ran as quickly as she could toward the house and through the French door, across the living room, past the entry hall. Finally, she was outside.

Pain tore through her tortured rib cage, but she couldn't stop. She hurried to Evelyn's car, yanked open the passenger door, got in, and pulled the door shut.

"Drive!" she croaked. Her throat was raw from vomiting.

Evelyn stared at her. "Alex—"

"Now!"

Evelyn started the engine and drove several blocks, then pulled over to the curb. She put her hand on Alex's shoulder.

"I shouldn't have let you go in by yourself! What did he do? Did he attack you?"

"He didn't attack me." Alex paused. There was no way to soften this. "Lundquist is dead, Evelyn. Someone killed him."

Evelyn jerked back her hand. "He can't be!" Her eyes were wide with fright. She was shaking. "What happened? Did you—"

"He was dead when I got there. In the Jacuzzi. It was awful, Evelyn. I touched him, and he slid into the water. Someone stabbed him in his neck and chest. The blood . . ." Alex gagged again at the image that flashed through her mind; she covered her mouth but had nothing left to vomit.

"Oh, God!" Evelyn moaned. She closed her eyes briefly.

Beads of sweat had formed above her lip. "I know he was beating his wife, and he was a horrible person, but to kill him . . ." She sounded as if she were about to cry.

"I know. I have to call the police."

"You can't! They'll want to know why you didn't call from his house. Don't get involved, Alex!"

"I can't leave him like that, Evelyn! Let's find a pay phone. I won't give them my name. *Please*," Alex urged when Evelyn didn't move.

They drove without talking, and after what seemed like endless minutes to Alex, they found a mini-mall with a 7-Eleven and a phone booth. There were several people inside the 7-Eleven and two unkempt, scruffy-looking men in torn clothing sitting on the strip of pavement in front of the store, their backs against the stucco wall of the building.

"Let's find another place," Evelyn whispered.

Alex wanted to go home, crawl into her bed, pull the covers over her head, and forget. As if she could. "I want to get this over with."

She got out of the car and avoided looking at the two men, but was conscious of their gaze and strode as purposefully as she could to the phone booth.

"You got fifty cents?" one of them asked. He had a raspy, slurred voice.

She'd left her purse in the car. "Sorry," she said, not stopping, and heard him call, "Bitch," in an uninterested tone.

She stepped inside the booth and shut the bifold door. From the moment she'd run out of Lundquist's house, she'd been overwhelmed with the need to pass on the knowledge of his death to someone in authority, to rid herself of the responsibility, but as she reached for the receiver, her hand shook. She took a deep breath and pressed the buttons for 911.

"Police Department, emergency line," a male operator said.

"There's been a—"

There was a sudden pounding on the phone booth door.

Alex whirled and gripped the receiver in her raised hand, prepared to use it to defend herself against the man who'd called her a bitch. Instead, she saw a white-faced Evelyn.

Evelyn opened the door an inch. "Hang up!"

Alex looked at her, uncertain.

"You haven't thought this through!" Evelyn hissed.

"You're going to need a lawyer." She reached into the booth and put her hand over the phone. "You found a murder victim!" Her panic-filled eyes locked onto Alex's dazed stare.

Alex heard squawking from the receiver. The two men, she saw, were looking at her and Evelyn with interest. She replaced the receiver on the hook, then left the phone booth and headed back to the car with Evelyn, her eyes fixed resolutely ahead.

"Fifty cents?" the man asked in the same uninterested voice, and burped loudly.

They got into the car. Evelyn drove out of the mini-mall lot and parked around the corner but left the engine on.

"How much did you tell the police, Alex?"

"Nothing. I didn't have a chance. Do you really think I need a lawyer?" she whispered. "Warren will be so upset," she added in a small voice.

Evelyn nodded vehemently. "A lawyer and an alibi. First we'll go for coffee, like we said we would. After that, you can call."

Alex stared at her. "Are you crazy? I can't go for coffee now! Lundquist is lying in his Jacuzzi *dead*."

Evelyn grabbed Alex's hand. "You have to! You need the alibi."

"But I *have* an alibi! I was with Warren, and now I'm with you."

"Alex, wake up!" Evelyn's voice was shrill with urgency and a hint of impatience. "Lundquist must've been killed right before you got there." She paused. "That's why we're going for coffee," she said firmly, as if she were talking to one of the preschoolers. "You told Warren you were going for coffee. That's what he'll tell the police if they ask. You can call in anonymously and no one will ever know you were at the house."

"The police?" Alex paled. "Why would they talk to Warren?" She felt her chest tighten.

"Alex, you accused Lundquist of vandalizing your school. You filed a complaint against him for harassing you, for talking to Nicholas. Of course they'll want to talk to you!"

Alex covered her mouth with her hand. "Oh, God!" she whispered. She was trembling. "Oh, God!" She slumped against the seat.

"You talked to him at eight o'clock," Evelyn said in a calmer voice. "So he was alive then. You said you touched him. Was he . . . was he cold?"

"No," Alex said, remembering. "He felt normal."

"That's good." Evelyn nodded. "So he wasn't dead for long. We'll go for coffee, like you told Warren. The waitress won't remember exactly what time we came or left. You'll have a confirmable alibi." She frowned. "Did you touch anything at the house?"

In her mind, Alex replayed her movements from the time she'd arrived at Lundquist's. "I opened the front door. I touched the French door that leads to the backyard." Her forehead was creased in concentration. "I had some Perrier." She looked at Evelyn. "My fingerprints are all over the goddamn house!" Her voice was almost inaudible. "What am I going to do?"

"Okay." Evelyn stared into the windshield. Her knuckles were white from gripping the steering wheel. "Okay," she said again, as if she were trying to convince herself. "You'll tell the police that you were there earlier in the day to talk to Lundquist, that he was fine when you left him."

"What if they find out I was there later, after he was killed? What if someone saw me?" An approaching car caught her in its high beams. She cringed and ducked her head.

"You'll tell them the truth—you ran from Lundquist's house because you were terrified they'd suspect you."

"I don't know, Ev. I think I should just call the police and tell them everything."

"But—" Evelyn took a deep breath and looked away. When she looked back, she said, "Maybe you're right. It's all so complicated. I wish you hadn't touched anything." She sounded listless, tired. "I'll drive you home. Warren's a lawyer. He'll know what to do."

The idea of facing Warren, of admitting she'd lied to him tonight, was suddenly more than Alex could bear. "I can't think straight. Do what you think is right."

"But I don't *know* what's right!" Evelyn's voice trembled.

For a moment, the only sound was the rumbling of the engine. "Let's go to the coffee shop," Alex said.

They found a coffee shop they'd never frequented and parked in the almost empty lot. Evelyn shut off the engine, but neither woman made a move to leave the car.

"Okay," Alex finally said. "Let's go." She opened the door.

"Wait!" Evelyn said. "Fix your hair. Put on some lipstick and blush. You look so pale."

Evelyn didn't look much better, Alex thought as she brushed her hair. Her hand shook as she applied lipstick. Evelyn's hand, she noticed, was shaking, too, as she did the same. It dawned on Alex that Evelyn was putting herself in jeopardy.

"Nervous?" she asked.

Evelyn nodded rapidly.

"You don't have to do this. We can go home."

"No. I'll be okay." She took Alex's hand and squeezed it. "Friends, right?"

"Thelma and Louise," Alex said, smiling grimly, and immediately wished she hadn't made a reference to the two celluloid women who had eluded the police and ended up driving their car into the Grand Canyon.

Walking to the coffee shop, Alex felt wobbly, as if her legs were made of rubber, but Evelyn's arm supported her. As they entered, Evelyn began to laugh. Startled, Alex turned her head sideways to look at her friend—was Evelyn hysterical?—but she realized Evelyn was acting, trying to set a carefree mood.

"That's so funny!" Evelyn exclaimed. "I'll have to remember that."

She linked her arm through Alex's (Alex could feel her trembling) and steered her toward a booth. When the waitress appeared, Evelyn ordered two coffees and a slice of cheesecake.

"Just one slice?" The waitress glanced at Alex's rounded middle. "Thought you'd be eating for two," she said to her.

Evelyn said, "She's eating for two. I'm trying to diet for one." She smiled.

"Uh-huh," the waitress said and left.

"Talk," Evelyn whispered to Alex. "Say anything. Tell me something about the kids at school."

"I can't."

But when the waitress returned with their orders, Alex found that she could. She drank the coffee—it felt wonderful going down her throat—but the sight of the cheesecake with a cherry glaze dripping down the sides nauseated her; it made her think of Lundquist's pasty-white face and his neck and chest, covered with blood.

Fifteen minutes later they paid and left. They drove to a movie theater complex and found a phone booth. (There was a phone booth inside the coffee shop, but Alex had worried that the 911 operator could trace her call to the shop.) Alex made an anonymous call, reporting the body and giving Lundquist's address. She hung up before the operator could ask any questions.

Alex and Evelyn were silent again on the drive to Alex's house. When they arrived, Alex half expected to see black-and-white police cars waiting for her, their red lights flashing.

"Thanks," she said to Evelyn when they pulled into the driveway. "I'll call you tomorrow at school."

"Do you want me to come in with you?"

Alex shook her head. "I'll have to face Warren alone sooner or later."

"What are you going to tell him?"

"I don't know."

The house was quiet when Alex entered. The light in the kitchen was on. So was the one in Warren's office, but he wasn't there. Alex went upstairs to see if he was in their bedroom watching television, but the room was empty. She checked on Nicholas. He was sound asleep, tented by his Ninja Turtle comforter. She stroked his cheek and bent down to kiss him. Then she walked down the hall to Lisa's room and knocked. No response. She opened the door and stepped inside.

The room was dark and filled with faint music from Lisa's CD player. Lisa was on her stomach, her head facing the wall. "Lisa?" Alex called softly. The girl was sleeping, or pretending to. After a moment, Alex left the room.

She went to her bedroom. On her dresser, she found a note: "I'll be out late. Don't wait up. Warren." She called his office. No one answered. She ran a bath, undressed, and stepped into the tub. The water was too hot at first, but she lowered herself gradually until she was reclining with her head against the tile-covered backboard.

The water felt wonderful, soothing her muscles and sore ribs. She lay in the tub for half an hour, crying quietly, wondering how her life had suddenly gone so wrong.

After her bath, Alex put on a nightgown and got into bed. She turned on the television—she was determined to wait up for Warren and tell him about Lundquist. She watched the eleven o'clock news, then *Nightline*. Then the second half of Letterman. Sometime during the show she fell asleep.

When she awoke it was morning. She remembered immediately what had happened and turned toward Warren, but he wasn't in bed. She looked at her clock. Nine-forty. There was a note on her nightstand:

Sorry I was so late last night. You were tossing and turning in your sleep, so I didn't want to wake you this morning. Call when you're up.   *Warren*

P.S. Denise will bring Nicholas and Lisa home unless you tell her otherwise.

No "love." No explanation for why he'd been so late. If she asked him, he'd probably tell her "briefs." She wondered if they would be communicating with notes from now on.

She got out of bed and washed up in the bathroom. Then she called Warren's office. His secretary told her he'd been called to an emergency deposition and would be gone all morning and most of the afternoon.

"Please have him call, Gwen," Alex said. "It's important."

She took her time in the shower, letting the warm water relax her muscles. Then she dressed and went downstairs. The *Los Angeles Times* was on the kitchen counter. Her hands shaking, she checked the Metro section. There was no mention of Lundquist.

She wasn't hungry, but she knew she should eat something, for the baby. She'd barely touched her dinner last night; she'd been too nervous. She sliced a bagel and placed the halves in the toaster. The phone rang. She wasn't sure whether she wanted the caller to be Warren. It was Evelyn.

"Are you all right, Alex?" Her voice was funereal.

"Yes." The bagels popped up. She put them on a paper plate. "There's nothing in the *Times*. And the police haven't called." Even if they found her fingerprints, she'd decided, they wouldn't know the prints were hers; they had no basis for comparison. Without arresting her, they couldn't force her to have her prints taken, could they? And could they arrest her without having good reason to suspect her? Those were some of the questions she wanted to ask Warren.

"I know," Evelyn said. "I didn't hear anything on the radio, either. What did Warren say?"

"I didn't tell him. He came home late last night, after I fell asleep. He left early this morning, and now he's away from the office. How's everything at school?" She longed to be back at the preschool, with her children. Tomorrow, when she saw Pearson, she would press him for permission to return to work.

"Fine. I'll call you later. Alex, if you need anything . . ."

She needed a miracle, she thought as she spread cream cheese on the bagel, something neither Evelyn nor anyone else could provide. Last night she'd been too stunned by finding Lundquist dead to think clearly. In the shower, she'd started considering the possibilities but had pushed them to a corner of her mind. Now she had to confront them.

It was possible that Lundquist's murder was an isolated event, not connected with her. She knew next to nothing about the man—nothing about his occupation, his friends, his enemies. She knew that his wife feared him, but from what she had seen, Sally Lundquist was a timid, cowed woman. A victim. Alex couldn't see her viciously stabbing her husband.

Still waters run deep, Alex's mother had always told her, but although fear sometimes transformed victim into aggressor, as far as Alex knew, Sally Lundquist hadn't seen her husband since she'd run away to live in a shelter for abused women.

The fact that Lundquist was going to reveal who had pushed Alex could be a coincidence. But it wasn't likely. Which meant that Lundquist had been killed by someone who wanted to prevent him from talking to Alex. Someone who had learned that Alex would be meeting him. Someone desperate to silence him.

Alex shook her head. She had accepted the fact that someone close to her was harassing her with notes, had pushed her and tried to harm her baby. *But kill Lundquist?* The idea was ridiculous, grotesque, impossible to believe—especially about Lisa. She was fourteen years old!

But it was impossible to dismiss.

Lisa had answered Lundquist's phone call. And she'd left the extension off the hook, Alex remembered.

Of course, if Alex wanted to be objective, she had to include Warren and Evelyn on her list. Anyone could have picked up the receiver and listened, and Evelyn had been in the room with Alex when Lundquist called. But Warren had no motive to silence Lundquist. If anything, he would have welcomed finding out who had written the notes to Alex and pushed her. (With Lundquist dead, Alex suddenly realized, she still had no way to prove to Warren that someone *had* pushed her.)

Evelyn had no motive, either. She'd been visibly horrified when Alex told her Lundquist had been killed. *Not proof,* Alex could hear Warren saying; *you're excusing her because she's your friend.* But Evelyn couldn't have killed him—there had been no time. Lundquist had been alive a little after eight; that was when Alex, at Evelyn's urging, had called to ask him to reconsider and meet her in a public place. He'd refused. Alex had called Evelyn back and told her; then Evelyn had left her house in Santa Monica and picked Alex up at eight-thirty, less than twenty minutes later.

Alex had no idea where Denise and Paula had been last night between eight and nine. Lisa had spent the evening studying for a history exam at her friend Valerie Haines's home—or so she'd said. Lisa had biked there after school with Valerie; Valerie's father was supposed to drive her home.

Alex could call Valerie's mother on some pretext and find out if that was true, but she didn't know Valerie's phone number. Yesterday, Lisa had scribbled it on a slip of paper that she'd left on the refrigerator door, attached to a magnet, but the paper was no longer there. Lisa's friends' names, addresses, and phone numbers were written in her pink vinyl daily planner, but she always kept the planner with her. Warren might know the number, but Alex couldn't very well ask him, even if she could reach him. Valerie lived on Millwood Avenue, Alex knew. She checked the phone directory. There was a long column of Haineses, many without addresses. Maybe there was another address book in Lisa's room.

Alex went upstairs and, feeling like a traitor, entered Lisa's bedroom. On the floor near the canopied bed was a giant pink ladybug with plastic green eyes. They seemed to glare at Alex and question her presence in the room.

The room was immaculate, as always. Somebody—Andrea or Paula—had trained Lisa well. Or maybe it was just her nature. Alex checked Lisa's desk. There were neatly stacked magazines, a paperback romance. A Scotch tape dispenser and a stapler. A pencil holder in the shape of a ladybug. No address book.

Alex opened the desk drawers. She told herself she was looking for an address book, but she knew she was searching for damning proof, praying she wouldn't find it. God, she didn't want it to be Lisa! The slim center drawer was locked. Alex wondered what it contained.

She searched among the books on the hutch above the desk, through the dresser drawers, under the bed. She didn't find the address book, but on the top shelf of the walk-in closet she found Warren's black Kings cap.

What was it doing here? she wondered, and her mind flashed to the figure in the three-quarter-length jacket who had been watching her. He—or she—had been wearing a black cap with an insignia. Alex had seen the cap from a distance, and only for an instant. She couldn't be certain that it had been a Kings cap.

She couldn't be certain that it wasn't.

Warren had a three-quarter-length tan jacket.

You're jumping to conclusions, she told herself. Thousands of people have Kings caps. She stared at the cap for a moment before she closed the closet door.

She looked around the room one more time, making sure that she had left no evidence of her search, then pulled the door shut behind her. She wondered whether Denise knew Valerie's number—aunt and niece were so close. Alex went downstairs and called Denise.

Paula answered the phone. "Denise isn't home," she told Alex. "How are you feeling?"

"Much better, thank you. Please tell Denise I'll pick up Lisa and Nicholas from school. Speaking of Lisa, I think she left something at Valerie's and I wanted to check with her mother, but I don't know the phone number offhand. Do you think Denise might have it? It's Valerie Haines," she added.

"I'll check Denise's Rolodex." A moment later, Paula was back on the phone. "Sorry. I don't see anything."

"Thanks anyway." It had been a long shot. But maybe the

call wouldn't be wasted. "By the way, I really appreciated your coming Monday."

"You're very welcome, Alex. It's nice of you to say."

"As a matter of fact, I called last night to thank you, but you weren't in. It was sometime after eight, I think."

"Last night? Oh, yes, I remember. I went marketing."

"Well, thanks again," Alex said lamely. "See you Friday." She had learned nothing and proved nothing.

She took the phone directory and started calling, skipping the listings with addresses other than Millwood. Each time she introduced herself as Alex Prescott and asked for Sandra Haines, Valerie's mother. "You have the wrong number," some people told her. Three calls were answered by housekeepers with Latino accents who said, "Missus no home"; Alex had no way of knowing whether she'd reached the right number. Two calls were answered by machines. Several parties she called weren't home.

She called Warren's office again. The secretary told her she hadn't heard from Warren. Alex returned to the phone directory. On the eighteenth call she reached Sandra Haines. Alex was so flustered by success that for a moment she didn't know what to say, but she quickly regained her composure.

"Mrs. Haines, I wanted to thank you again for having Lisa over for supper."

"Anytime, Mrs. Prescott. We all like Lisa."

"Did the girls get much studying done? I was out when Lisa came home, and she was asleep when *I* came home. And this morning I overslept." You're explaining too much, Alex told herself.

"They were in Val's room until just before eight—that's when Lisa left—but I don't know how much studying got done. You know how teenage girls are." Sandra Haines laughed. "I know Lisa was concerned about her history, though. That's why she went home early, because she'd forgotten some of her notes at home."

"It was nice of your husband to bring her home. I hope he didn't have any trouble with the bike."

"Actually, George didn't take Lisa home." Sandra Haines sounded uncomfortable. "She wanted to bike home. I hope that's okay. It was still light outside, and she said you wouldn't mind, or we would have insisted."

"No problem." Alex thanked her again and hung up, feeling dizzy with tension. Where had Lisa gone from Valerie's? Not home—it was a ten-minute ride and Alex hadn't left the house until eight-thirty. Lundquist's house was several miles from the Haineses'. Lisa could have biked there and. . . .

And nothing, Alex told herself. Lisa probably stopped off at a drugstore or a market. Alex went to her studio. She clipped a fresh sheet of paper to the easel and picked up a pastel stick. She wanted to draw something light, airy, but all she could see was Donald Lundquist's bloodied neck and chest.

Fifteen minutes later the paper was still virgin white. Alex sighed, put down the pastel, and left the studio. There would be no release for her today.

When she was in the kitchen eating the hardened bagel, she heard the mail being dropped into the chute. She walked into the living room and reached inside the chute. She scanned the envelopes. Bills, mostly. There was an envelope for her without a return address. She braced herself (please, God, not another hate note!) and tore open the letter.

It was a get-well card from Ron. "Heard you fell, Alex," he'd written. "Glad you and the baby are okay. I said some nasty things the last time I saw you. I hope you can forget and forgive. As far as Denise and I are concerned, maybe you did both of us a favor."

That was a surprise. Alex still remembered the ugliness of their last meeting. The threats. She wondered how Ron had heard about her fall and what had prompted his change of heart. If, in fact, he'd had one. And what did he mean by "maybe you did both of us a favor"?

She put the mail on the entry hall table (Warren liked to see it there when he came home from work) and noticed the book of baby names. She hadn't seen it since she'd come home from the hospital, and she'd forgotten all about it. She took the book upstairs and sat cross-legged on her bed, flipping through the pages. One of the pages was dog-eared. She frowned and turned to it. A moan escaped her lips.

Someone had taken a black marker and crossed out the name she whispered to herself sometimes at night, the name she shrieked in her dreams.

She dropped the book onto the bed and fell back against

the headboard. It was daylight, but the sounds pierced her ears. First the shrill ringing of the phone, then the intermittent sounds—the clacking of the receiver, the squeaking of the stairs, the thumping, the moaning of the wind, the screeching of the gates; finally the clangingclangingclangingclanging-clanging, a giant alarum bell that swung madly in her head.

She pressed her hands against her ears. "Stop it!" she screamed. "Stop it! Stop it! Stop it!"

Chapter 21

She wondered what the police were doing. Maybe they were knocking on Alex's door right now—"Sorry, Mrs. Prescott, but there are a few questions we have to ask you."

She would love to be in the room with Alex when Warren found out, to watch her face turn pale with terror and shame, to witness the disgust and horror in Warren's eyes. She had waited so long for him to see Alex for what she was: a murderer!

God punished murderers.

She wasn't sorry Donald Lundquist was dead.

It wasn't her fault. He'd brought it on himself, calling Alex and promising to tell her who'd pushed her. She'd felt angry and helpless—and frightened. Anybody in her situation would have been frightened. Because if Alex knew, she'd tell Warren.

And then she'd never see Warren again, never be part of the family. You're crazy! he would tell her, and she wouldn't have a chance to explain, not with Alex there, telling him lie after lie.

Still, she hadn't meant for Lundquist to die. She'd hated him. She'd wanted to make him stop. But she'd never said aloud that she wanted him dead, never even thought it. Killing was wrong. She knew it was.

God punished murderers.

Her head was starting to throb again. She pressed her palms against her temples. She had to stop thinking about Lundquist's death, blaming herself for it. If she didn't, she'd go crazy. She really would. And she couldn't let that happen, not now, not when everything was starting to go right.

She had to be strong. To stay in control.

She wondered fleetingly whether she'd made a mistake—

maybe she should never have made the first phone call to the mortuary, never have started sending the notes. It was like opening a Pandora's box. Now things were escalating, like a top spinning out of her reach, out of her control. She couldn't stop the top from spinning, and it was too late to put the lid back on the box.

But it wasn't a mistake! Of course it wasn't. She'd learned so many things about Alex. So many interesting things. And soon everyone would know about Alex, too.

Warren would know. That was the most important thing. Warren would never forgive Alex. And even if there was the remote possibility that he would, he could never trust her again. Certainly not with Nicholas. And not with the baby.

God punished murderers, but she wasn't a murderer.

Alex was.

She deserved to be in jail.

She pictured Alex being led off in handcuffs. No pretty maternity outfits now, Alex. She smiled at the thought.

Maybe Alex would give birth in jail. Hester Prynne had done that, and the judges had let her keep her baby. But, of course, the judges wouldn't let Alex keep the baby. She wasn't fit to be a mother.

That was the truth, and she had proof.

Alex had thought she was so smart, getting pregnant to trap Warren. But she wasn't so smart after all. She was going to lose everything—Warren, Nicholas, and the baby.

It was sad, in a way, to think of a baby without a mother. But it wasn't a problem. She would help Warren take care of the baby. She had helped him with Nicholas, and she would help him now.

She touched the heart-shaped locket and nodded.

She wasn't sorry about Lundquist. He had deserved to die.

She wasn't sorry about Alex, either. Alex had brought this on herself.

She wasn't sorry about anything.

Chapter 22

"**M**ommy? Are you sleeping?" Nicholas whispered.

Alex opened her eyes. Nicholas was standing by her bed. Smiling, she pulled herself up carefully to give him a hug (no sudden movements, Pearson had warned). Then she frowned. "Nick, what are you doing home? How did you get here?"

"Aunt Denise picked me and Lisa up from school."

Alex looked at the clock on her nightstand. Three-forty. Oh, God! She'd told Paula she would pick the kids up today.

Denise entered the room. "There you are, Nick." She smiled. "Sorry, Alex. I told him not to wake you."

"Denise," Alex began.

"Paula said you told her you'd pick up the kids, but when you didn't show, both schools called me, because Warren had told them I'd pick the kids up. Did Paula get the message wrong?"

Alex felt hot with embarrassment. "No. I overslept." She'd been drained from crying, and had apparently fallen asleep. Some mother, she thought. "I'm sorry. I should have been there."

"No problem. I'm glad I was available. Hey, kiddo," she said to Nicholas, "I peeled and sliced an apple just the way you like it. Finish that, and you get a cookie."

" 'Kay." He kissed Alex and headed for the door.

"He's terrific, isn't he?" Denise said, watching him as he skipped out of the room. "I've been thinking, Alex. The kids can stay with me until you're better."

"Thanks, but it's not necessary."

"I know it's not, but you could rest more, and you wouldn't have to worry about cooking or car pools or—"

"I'm capable of taking care of the kids, Denise. I won't

oversleep again. And I don't need that much rest.'' As if to prove her point, she swung her legs off the bed and stood up.

"I didn't mean to suggest you weren't capable, Alex,'' Denise said quietly. "And I didn't mean to upset you. I'd like to make things easier for you. You're a wonderful mother, Alex. Everyone thinks so.''

"Who is 'everyone'? Do you and Warren and Paula and your mother get together and rate my performance? What about Lisa? Does she get a vote, too?'' Alex walked to her dresser and brushed her hair. Looking in the mirror, she could see Denise staring at her.

"Of course not! I don't know what's wrong with you, Alex. You've been acting strange since your accident. In the hospital, and here the other night, you barely talked to me.''

Alex put down the brush and turned to Denise. "Not everyone thinks I'm a wonderful mother, Denise. I've been getting hate mail that says I don't deserve to have a baby.''

"Oh, Alex! How awful! No wonder you're upset.'' She reached out to touch Alex's arm.

"Why do you sound surprised? Didn't Warren tell you about the notes?''

Denise's flushed face answered for her. She dropped her hand to her side.

"He *did*, didn't he? I don't know why *I'm* surprised. The two of you tell each other everything, don't you?''

"Alex—''

"Why did you tell him about the incident with Ron?'' Alex demanded angrily. "I told you specifically I wasn't going to tell him.''

Denise's color deepened. "I'm sorry, Alex. It just slipped out. Ron told Warren that I'd broken things off, and Warren asked me what happened, and, well . . . I'm really sorry if I caused trouble. It certainly wasn't intentional.''

Wasn't it? And exactly what had Denise told Warren? "Did Warren also tell you that my fall wasn't an accident, that someone pushed me?''

Denise glanced quickly toward the open doorway. She walked to the door, shut it, and returned to the foot of the bed. "Warren's concerned about you, Alex. He thinks you're under terrible stress, and he wants to help you but doesn't know how.''

"He doesn't believe me."

"He doesn't know what to believe." Denise hesitated. "He's also worried about how your . . . emotional state is affecting Nicholas and Lisa."

"Nicholas is fine," Alex said defiantly.

"Lisa isn't. In the car just now she was like a zombie. Something's wrong, Alex. Maybe it's the boarding-school thing—"

"I didn't send the application! You said yourself she might have sent it to herself."

"Even if she did, doesn't that tell you something?" Denise ran a hand through her hair. "When Lisa suggested moving in with me, I didn't think it was a good idea. Well, now I think maybe she should, just for a while, until things settle down."

"Is that the plan? First Lisa comes to live with you. Then Nicholas. Who's next? Warren?" The words, so long on her mind, had tumbled out, and there was no retracting them. In a way, Alex wasn't sorry.

"Is that what you think? That I'm trying to take your place?" Denise's dark brown eyes widened. "You think I wrote the notes? That I *pushed* you?"

Alex wished she could define the emotion that played across Denise's face and resonated in her quavering voice—anger? fear? hurt? She fixed her eyes on the door to the balcony.

Denise said, "I'm trying to remind myself that you've just suffered a concussion and that pregnant women are moody, but—"

Alex whirled to face her. "Don't patronize me, Denise! Someone wrote those notes. Someone pushed me, damn it!"

"Well, it wasn't me!" In a quieter voice, Denise said, "From the day I met you, I tried to make you feel welcome. I'm not going to pretend I thought we'd be best friends. And it was a little awkward at first, seeing someone take my sister's place. But I liked you. You seemed nice, you were good with the kids, Warren was in love with you, and I thought, why not make things easier for everyone? God knows the kids needed a mother. And Warren needed a wife."

"Why not you, Denise?"

"I thought about it. Is that what you wanted to hear?" Her face had reddened. "I had an adolescent crush on Warren from the time he started dating Andrea. God, I was jealous!'' She smiled faintly. ''I loved the kids. And the guys I was dating were such immature jerks compared to him, you know? I think Lisa wanted me to marry Warren. So did my parents, and Paula. That made it even more appealing.''

''Why didn't you?'' It was strange listening to Denise tell her story, as if it were a fictional narrative that didn't concern Alex.

Denise shrugged. ''It was over before it even started. I think a part of me realized even then that everyone—my parents, Lisa, Paula—wanted me to marry Warren so they could pretend that nothing had really changed, that Andy didn't die.''

''No regrets?'' Alex asked softly.

''None.'' Denise looked at her squarely. ''Do you believe me?''

''Someone is sending me hate mail. Someone pushed me and tried to harm my baby. Do you believe *me?*''

Denise paused for a moment. ''I believe you're convinced someone pushed you. You could be wrong. Isn't that possible?''

Donald Lundquist saw someone push me, Alex wanted to say. But of course she couldn't. Not anymore. ''And the notes?''

Denise sighed. ''I believe someone sent you the notes and the doll. Donald Lundquist—''

''It's not Lundquist. He's—'' Alex broke off. ''I just don't think it's him. The anger in the notes is more personal. And I realized something this morning—the notes started after everyone knew I was pregnant. It's as if my becoming pregnant is a threat to someone.''

Denise considered this, then said, ''You think it's Lisa, don't you? Or Paula.'' She sounded terribly sad.

''What do you think?''

She met Alex's eyes. ''I don't know.''

Alex was silent for a moment. Then she said, ''By the way, Denise, remember the papers I'm missing, the ones from my school office?''

Denise put her hand to her mouth. ''I said I'd ask Paula, didn't I? I forgot. I'm sorry.''

''I asked her myself. She said she didn't throw anything out.'' Alex paused. ''I'm a little confused, though. She said when she arrived you were helping clear the office." She watched Denise's face.

Denise frowned. "I don't know why she'd say that, Alex. I wasn't in the office at all." She hesitated, then said, "Maybe Paula was afraid you'd blame her because she's a housekeeper."

"Maybe." Alex had to admit that was a plausible explanation.

"Did she mention that anyone else was in the office?"

"Evelyn and Patty."

"But they work for you. Paula and I are the only outsiders." Denise nodded. "I'm sure that's why she said that. Poor Paula." She sighed. A few moments later she left.

Alex sat on the bed, staring at the open doorway, thinking about what Denise had said, wanting to believe her, wondering whether she could. Suddenly she frowned.

How had Denise known about the doll? Alex hadn't mentioned it. She was positive of that. She hurried downstairs to ask Denise, but Nicholas told her that his aunt had already left.

Warren probably told her, Alex decided. She would ask him about it later, just to make sure.

Warren called a while later. Gwen had given him Alex's messages, but he hadn't been able to call till now. Was anything wrong? By now the urgency to talk to him had passed. He would be home soon enough. She would tell him about Lundquist then. And ask him whether he'd told Denise about the doll.

She prepared supper—meatballs and spaghetti, Nicholas's favorite—and noticed that she'd spotted her blouse with sauce. She went upstairs, changed her blouse, and took the stained one into the laundry room. She squirted Spray 'n Wash onto the orange spots and lifted the washing machine lid to toss her blouse in. There were several towels in the machine, towels Paula had just washed and folded yesterday. Peeking out from underneath one of the towels was a white fabric. Alex pulled at it and found she was holding Lisa's school blouse, a white Oxford. There were rust-colored stains on the front and sleeves.

Alex's heart sank. Her mouth was dry. She hadn't seen her

stepdaughter all afternoon, but according to Nicholas, Lisa was in her bedroom. Taking the blouse with her, Alex went upstairs and knocked on Lisa's door. When Lisa didn't answer, Alex opened the door and walked in.

Lisa was lying on her bed, her arms locked behind her head. She was staring at the underside of her canopy.

"I'm sorry to bother you, Lisa, but I noticed your blouse in the washing machine. Where did you get those stains?" Alex asked as casually as she could.

Without looking at her, Lisa said, "I had a nosebleed when I came home from Valerie's. I washed the blouse last night. I thought I got everything out, but I guess not."

"That must have been some nosebleed."

Lisa turned to look at her. "Is it ruined? Is that why you're upset?"

"It's probably not ruined. I'm not upset, Lisa. I just wanted to know how to treat the stains. By the way, since when do you get nosebleeds?"

"I don't know. I don't keep a record. Why?"

"Just curious. I don't remember your having nosebleeds."

"Well, you don't know everything about me. Why are you always giving me the third degree, Alex?" She was facing the canopy again. "Can I be alone in my own room, please?"

"Of course. Supper will be ready in about thirty minutes."

"I'm not hungry."

Alex nodded and left the room. Downstairs, in the laundry room, she took a cotton swab, dipped it in bleach, and watched the stains pale, then disappear. She rinsed the blouse with cold water and tossed it into the machine.

Warren came home early. He kissed Alex and Nicholas, then went to his office to put away his briefcase. After a few minutes, she went to find him. He was sitting behind his desk, studying a manila folder.

"Supper's ready, Warren."

He looked up. "Okay." He put down the folder and followed her to the breakfast room.

Nicholas was sitting at the table, a white paper-napkin bib tucked into his collar.

"Where's Lisa?" Warren asked.

"Upstairs. She doesn't want to eat supper."

"I'll go talk to her."

He left the room. Alex went to the kitchen to prepare the platter with the meatballs and spaghetti. Several minutes later Warren returned, alone.

"She said she might eat later. She won't tell me what's bothering her." He paused. "Did you and she quarrel?"

"No! Why do you always assume I'm the cause of Lisa's bad moods?"

Warren sighed. "I'm sorry. That's not what I meant."

"I'm hungry," Nicholas called from the breakfast room. "Can we eat yet, Mommy?"

Warren, Alex could see, was as relieved as she was to end this conversation. He carried the platter to the table. During supper Alex was grateful for Nicholas's constant chatter. Afterward, Warren and Nicholas cleared the table. Then Nicholas went to the family room to play. Warren went to his office.

Alex was rinsing the dishes and putting them into the dishwasher when she heard the front doorbell.

"I'll get it!" Warren called. A moment later he appeared in the kitchen.

"Alex, there are two detectives here who want to talk to you. They won't say what it's about. Did you call the police and tell them that Lundquist pushed you? I didn't have a chance."

She looked at her husband and felt a rush of love and despair. She put down the plate she was holding.

"Warren." She cleared her throat. "Warren, Donald Lundquist is dead. I found him in his Jacuzzi. I went there last night—" A sob escaped, and she had to wait until she was in control before she could continue. "He called Monday and told me he saw the person who pushed me at the beach. He said he'd tell me if I was willing to give his wife a message."

"Go on," Warren said when Alex stopped. His face was a mask of steel. His voice was ice.

"He was dead when I got there." She described what she'd seen. "Evelyn said the police would talk to you and me because of the complaints I made against Lundquist. So we went to a coffee shop, because that's where I told you we were going. Then I called the police and told them Lundquist was dead. That's it. Except that my fingerprints are on the doors and on a glass tumbler. I was going to tell you last night—I swear I was—but you weren't home. I tried to wait up for you but fell asleep. I tried reaching you all day. I'm so scared, Warren," she whispered. "I didn't kill him, but it looks so bad, doesn't it?"

In a gentle voice that told her nothing, Warren said, "Alex, you have to talk to them. I'll be right there with you."

"But what should I tell them? Evelyn said I should say I was at Lundquist's earlier in the day. The waitress will remember us, I think, and it's about the same time the police probably found the body."

"Alex." Warren's voice was colder now. "Alex, that is stupid advice. Either say nothing or tell the truth."

"Which one?"

"Right now, say nothing. Let me hear what they ask you."

"What if they ask you questions?"

"Let me worry about that. Okay, let's go. They'll wonder what's taking you so long."

She dried her hands on a towel, then turned quickly. "What about Nicholas? I don't want him to see the police, Warren. He'll be frightened."

Warren's look told Alex what he didn't say—that her concern had come too late. "I'll have him play in his room until the detectives are gone. Wait here."

He left the kitchen. When he returned, he took her hand and walked with her to the living room.

The two detectives—one male, one female—were sitting on the blue damask L-shaped sofa. They stood when Alex and Warren entered. The man was tall, with black, curly hair and a mustache. The woman was almost as tall and had short blond hair.

"How can I help you?" Alex said.

"I'm Detective Rowan," the man said. "This is my partner, Detective Medina. Could we all sit, please? My feet get tired at the end of the day." He smiled at Alex.

"Of course." She sat on the section of the sofa opposite the detectives. Warren sat next to her.

Rowan said, "We understand you know a Donald Lundquist."

His nasal voice grated on Alex's ears. She nodded. "His son has been attending my preschool."

"But not anymore, is that right? Detective Brady from our

division told us Lundquist's wife took the boy with her to a women's shelter.''

"Yes.'' If they knew that, they knew everything about her relationship with Lundquist.

"Do you know where that shelter is?''

Alex shook her head.

"Have you been in contact with the wife?''

"She called me twice.''

"Why was that?'' Detective Medina asked.

There was no reason not to reveal what Brady had already told them. "Her husband was upset with me because I wouldn't tell him where his wife and son were. I told him I didn't know, but he wouldn't believe me. He . . . he threatened to cause me trouble.''

Rowan said, "You told Detective Brady that Lundquist was responsible for vandalizing your preschool.''

"I'm not positive about that anymore. Detective Brady thought kids did it. So did the patrolmen who responded to my call. And Detective Brady told me Lundquist had an alibi.''

"But according to Detective Brady, you insisted Lundquist was responsible. You also told him Lundquist threatened to harm your son if you didn't help him get his wife and son back.''

She felt Warren's hand on hers. "I interpreted it as a threat. Lundquist was upset. Maybe I overreacted.'' She paused. "That's when I called the shelter.'' She explained about the slip of paper Sally Lundquist had dropped in her office. "Mrs. Lundquist called me back. I asked her to call her husband and tell him I didn't know where she and her son were. She did that, and called to tell me so.''

"That's the last you heard from her?'' Rowan asked.

Alex nodded.

"When was that?''

"About a week ago. I don't remember exactly.''

Medina said, "Do you have that slip of paper?''

Warren said, "May I ask what this is all about?''

Rowan's gray eyes were somber now. There was no smile. "Donald Lundquist was murdered yesterday. We're trying to locate his wife. If we have the phone number of the shelter, the phone company can give us an address. If you could get us the paper, Mrs. Prescott?''

''Certainly.'' Alex left the room and found the slip of paper in her purse. When she returned, she handed it to the detective. ''Is that it?''

The smile was back. ''A few more questions, Mrs. Prescott.''

Alex sat down again next to Warren.

Rowan said, ''This is a routine question, and we're going to be asking it of anyone who knew Mr. Lundquist. Can you tell us where you were last night?''

''Just a minute,'' Warren said.

''It's okay, Warren.'' Alex turned to Rowan. ''I fixed supper for my family. Then a friend and I went for coffee.''

''What time was that?''

''I don't know exactly. We got to the coffee shop around nine-thirty.''

''Which coffee shop is that?'' Rowan had his notebook out.

''I don't remember the address or the name, but I can tell you where it is.'' Alex described the location near the theaters.

''Your friend's name?''

''Evelyn Goodwin.'' Alex gave him Evelyn's phone number.

Medina said, ''Mrs. Prescott, did you go to see Donald Lundquist yesterday?''

''Detective, I don't understand the purpose of these questions.'' Warren's tone was sharp. ''Is my wife a suspect?''

''I didn't say that. But if your wife saw Mr. Lundquist, she might be a material witness. He might have told her something that would help us find out what happened.'' She opened her purse and took out a white piece of paper. ''Mrs. Prescott, we found this note addressed to you. It was on the bar in Mr. Lundquist's living room. Did you leave it there?''

Warren's hand pressed against Alex's arm. She said nothing.

Medina read the note aloud, then looked at Alex. ''Mrs. Prescott, it's obvious Mr. Lundquist was expecting you. If you have nothing to hide, I don't understand why you can't answer our questions. And you could help us.''

Alex stared at the fireplace.

Warren put his arm around her shoulder. ''I'm going to

advise my wife not to say anything until she speaks with an attorney.''

Rowan smiled. ''*You're* an attorney, I understand.'' He exchanged looks with his partner, then turned to Alex. ''One more thing. When we checked through Mr. Lundquist's house, we came across some papers that concern you, Mrs. Prescott.''

''What kind of papers?'' Warren asked.

Rowan picked up a dark manila envelope from the sofa. Alex hadn't noticed it before. He opened the envelope and pulled out a sheaf of papers. ''Newspaper clippings, mostly. They're from three years ago, when you were living in the Midwest.''

Tight bands formed around her chest. There was a humming in her ears that made it difficult for her to hear the detective.

'' . . . didn't know it was you in the photos . . . Brady recognized you . . . wondered why Mr. Lundquist would have these clippings . . . do with them?''

The humming was louder. Rowan's lips were mouthing words she couldn't hear. The room was beginning to spin.

Now the detective was extending the papers to her, but she made no move to take them. He dropped them onto the dark cherry coffee table. A copy of an already grainy reproduction of her face stared up at her. Above it in black letters a caption screamed, ''MY WIFE KILLED OUR SON!'' ANGUISHED FATHER INSISTS.

They were waiting for her to say something, but her tongue was a block of wood. She looked to her right. Warren was a statue. His face was expressionless.

'' . . . trying to blackmail you?'' Rowan asked Alex.

Warren said, ''I've already told you that my wife is not going to answer any more questions. I'll have to ask you to leave now, please.''

Rowan stood. So did Medina. ''We'll see ourselves out,'' he said. ''Thanks for your time.'' They walked toward the living room arch that led to the entry.

Warren said, ''You forgot your papers.''

Rowan turned. ''Oh, you can have those copies, Mr. Prescott. We have the originals.'' He and his partner left the room.

A moment later Alex heard the front door open and close. ''Warren, I . . . ''

Without a backward glance, he walked out of the room.

Chapter 23

Except for the light that entered from the hallway, the studio was dark.

Alex had no idea what time it was or how long she'd been sitting in her chair, rocking back and forth; she sensed that several hours had passed since Warren had left her in the living room. She had sat on the sofa, frozen by fear and indecision. After a while she'd gotten up and walked, almost trancelike, to the studio. She didn't know why. Certainly not to paint.

She supposed that eventually she'd have to go upstairs, but right now she wanted to stay in this room, in this chair, forever. The movement of the chair was comforting in its monotonous regularity and, muffled by the carpet, almost noiseless except for the gentle whoosh as the rocker rails pushed the air away and a tiny squeak on every third forward roll. Alex had counted over a thousand squeaks.

The light from the hallway was suddenly obstructed, and she knew without turning that Warren was standing in the doorway.

"It's after twelve, Alex. Are you coming upstairs?"

The absence of emotion in his voice pained but didn't surprise her. She rocked for a moment and counted two more squeaks. She saw from the movement of his shadow that he was turning to leave.

"His name was Kevin," she said. It was strange, after three years of whispering his name to herself, to say it aloud. "He was four years old when it happened. He was a beautiful child, so bright and full of joy. I used to tell him he was a butterfly that floated into our life. He loved hearing that." Unconsciously, her fingers stroked the arm of the chair.

"It was a Sunday in June, a very warm day, and Kevin

wanted to go swimming in our pool. I wanted to finish a painting I was working on. At that time my painting was very important to me. Larry always complained that I was obsessive about it, and maybe I was. It was a haven from all my troubles. Larry's accounting practice was failing because he was preoccupied with money problems. He'd lost most of our savings in the stock market, and we were basically living on what I earned from my preschool. Larry hated that.'' She could still see his face, hear his voice, angry with bitter self-pity that ultimately turned into recrimination. *If you were a better wife . . .*

"Our marriage was burdened with difficulties almost from the start. For years the only thing we'd agreed on was our love for Kevin, but that was no longer enough for me, and I'd told Larry I wanted a divorce. The painting was an escape. Larry understood that. I think that's why he resented it so much, because it gave me a measure of peace he couldn't find. That Sunday when I said I wanted to paint, I was sure he'd make some snide comment, but he didn't. He said he'd go swimming with Kevin so I could be in my studio.'' At the time, and so many times later, she'd wondered whether Larry had been pleasing himself or making a gesture of reconciliation— *See how nice I can be, Alex?* Not that it mattered.

"Kevin changed into his yellow swim trunks. I put sunscreen on him, and I remember he giggled because he said the lotion was tickling him. Really, it was me.'' Her eyes filled with tears. "I gave him a towel and his white terry swim robe, and he went downstairs with Larry and out through the family room to the pool. I made lemonade and took out a pitcherful and a plate of oatmeal cookies with chocolate-chip eyes and smiles. They were Kevin's favorite.'' Her voice was quavering; she fought for control. *Tell the story. It's just a story.*

"My studio was a small room in the attic, on the side of the house away from the pool. It wasn't air-conditioned like the rest of the house, but I was wearing shorts and a tank top, and I opened a small dormer window. With the ceiling fan on, the room was sultry but bearable—perfect, I told myself, for the palm tree I was painting.

"I don't wear a watch when I paint, so I don't know how long I'd been working on the tree when Larry beeped me on the phone intercom from the family room. An hour maybe.

He said it was ten minutes after twelve and that he and Kevin were taking a break. He was going to the store for milk and soda and a pack of cigarettes. Then he'd take Kevin for another swim. I asked him if he could wait five minutes so I could finish something. He said five minutes was fine because Kevin was in the bathroom anyway. I asked if he'd closed the sliding-glass door in the family room. I was nervous because the latch to the gate to the pool was broken. 'I'm doing it right now,' he said, and I heard the rumble of the door in the track. Then I heard him call good-bye to Kevin. 'Mom'll be right down, Kev,' he said. 'Buzz her when you come out of the bathroom. 'Bye, Alex,' Larry said. He turned off the intercom, but a moment later I pressed it and the family-room code number so that I'd hear Kevin when he came into the room. I called his name a few times—at least twice, I'm sure of that— but he was still in the bathroom. I wasn't anxious. He was such a good boy. He always listened, and I'd told him over and over not to go out of the house by himself.''

Alex rocked for a while in silence. She couldn't hear Warren breathing, but she knew he was there; the shadow hadn't moved. ''I was working in oils, and I'd just gotten the shade of greenish black for the shadow of a frond that was giving me trouble. I thought I'd finish the one frond. I didn't think it would take long. It was very quiet in the studio—just the whirring of the ceiling fan—and when the phone rang I was startled. I picked up the wall-extension receiver. It was Larry. He was at the store. He'd promised to get Kevin ice cream and he'd forgotten which flavor. Chocolate or strawberry. 'I'll go downstairs and ask him right now,' I said.

'' 'What the hell do you mean, you'll go downstairs?' Larry said. 'I left the house over twenty minutes ago. Are you telling me you're still in your damn studio? That you left Kevin alone all this time?' I could hear the edge of panic underneath the anger in Larry's voice. I remember that my heart was pounding and that I was instantly drenched with sweat. 'It can't be twenty minutes,' I said, knowing that it could, that I'd lost track of the time once or twice before when I was painting, that hours had felt like minutes. 'It's twelve-thirty-five,' Larry yelled. 'Is your goddamn painting more important than your son?' '' She was rocking faster now, her hands clutching the arms of the chair.

"I dropped the receiver and ran out of the studio and down the narrow flight of stairs to the second floor. I checked Kevin's room—he liked to play in his room. He wasn't there. I ran down the main staircase, then along the hall to the family room. I called his name over and over, but he didn't answer. I knew he wouldn't be in the bathroom, but I checked anyway.

"I thought I would die when I entered the family room. The sliding-glass door was open. Kevin's red step stool was in front of the opening. He'd taken it from the bathroom to reach the door latch and the top bolt. I ran outside. The gate was closed. I pulled it open and raced to the pool. I didn't see him at first. Then I looked down. He was . . . he was . . . " Her voice broke. She started crying.

"Alex, you don't have to tell me this," Warren said.

"Yes, I do," she whispered. She wiped her eyes; after a moment she continued. *Tell the story.* "He was at the bottom of the pool. I took a deep breath and dove into the water. I swam to him and grabbed him by his yellow swim trunks and lifted him. Then I put my arms around him and pushed my way to the surface. I didn't look at his face. He was heavier now. I swam to the shallow end of the pool, then lifted him in my arms and ran to the grass. I laid him on the grass and started CPR. His face was gray. His lips were blue and cold. His eyes were glassy, like marbles. I couldn't find a pulse, but I pumped on his chest. Water came gushing out of his mouth and nose. I breathed into his mouth, and pumped, and breathed, and pumped. I knew he was dead. I couldn't stop."

"Alex."

The word was a sigh, hushed with pain and pity. Still, he made no move to enter the room, and she was relieved; if he came nearer, if he touched her, she knew she couldn't finish.

"There was a cordless phone on the patio table. I called 911. Then I went back to Kevin and continued doing CPR. Larry and the ambulance arrived together. I heard the siren, then Larry's scream when he saw Kevin. He shoved me aside and knelt at Kevin's side. He cradled Kevin and started crying. It was more like a roar, really, the kind a wounded animal makes. Larry loved Kevin more than anything in the world.

"The paramedics took over, but of course there was nothing they could do. 'I'm sorry,' they said, 'he's gone,' and Larry pointed at me and said, 'She killed him.' They looked at me.

I turned away and went to sit on the patio steps. There were more sirens. Two uniformed police officers arrived. One of the paramedics walked over to talk to them. They all glanced in my direction. One of the policemen talked to Larry. Then he came over to me and asked me what had happened. I told him.

"They said I'd have to come to the police station. They let me change my clothes first. They put me in the police car. My neighbors were all watching. At the station, I had to repeat my story over and over to the detectives. They finally took me home. Larry's car was gone. I found out later that he'd left to stay with his parents. I called my parents, but they'd already heard from Larry. He told them I killed Kevin.

"I told them what had happened, that it was an accident, a horrible, tragic accident, that I loved Kevin with my whole heart and being and would have given my life for him. I was sobbing. I could barely speak. My father said"—her voice broke again—"my father said that leaving a four-year-old alone with access to a pool was negligence, not an accident, that he and my mother had warned me that my painting was a frivolous hobby and that my time would have been better spent trying to be a supportive wife. He said that tears would not atone for my guilt, that he and my mother could not forgive me, but that I should pray to God for forgiveness and they would do the same.

"The next morning I was arrested and charged with criminal child endangerment. I called a lawyer. The judge set bail at five thousand dollars. I paid a bail bondsman with a check from the account I had for the preschool I owned. There was next to nothing in our personal accounts. I was released later that day. Someone must have told the media—maybe Larry. I don't know. There were newspaper reporters and photographers and a reporter from the local TV station." She'd been assaulted by a cacophony of merciless questions amplified by microphones. Her eyes had been blinded by endless flashes from the cameras.

"The phone didn't stop ringing from the minute I got home. It's amazing how quickly news travels, especially in a small town. People I hadn't talked to in years called. They said they wanted to offer condolences. Really, they wanted details. Some skipped the charade of caring. Several close friends offered to come over to stay with me, but I refused. I didn't want to be with anyone.

"The funeral was scheduled for Wednesday. My parents came over Tuesday night and told me Larry didn't want me there, and didn't I think I would cause a spectacle by showing up? I told them nothing would keep me from my son's funeral. They said I was being selfish and spiteful. I asked them to leave my house.

"There were reporters and photographers at the chapel. I should have expected them—I was providing the town with news and notoriety. I pushed my way past them and walked to the front of the chapel. I felt hundreds of eyes staring at me, but I was determined not to show that I cared. Larry and his parents were sitting in the front row, to the right of the aisle. My parents were next to them. I sat on the left side. I don't remember much about the funeral service or the burial, but I will never forget the sight of the small coffin being lowered into the ground." She saw it again now and bowed her head. She closed her eyes. The image was still there.

She shifted in the chair. "I thought the best thing would be to throw myself into my work. I went to the preschool on Monday and learned that over half the parents had pulled their children out. My assistant hadn't wanted to tell me. By the end of the week only three children were left. I made phone calls and was given evasions that didn't fool me or the people who made them. They didn't want to leave their children with me.

"I closed my school and took a job as a secretary. The charges against me were dropped—no concrete evidence, my lawyer told me—but Larry was pestering the police to reopen the case. And the whispering never stopped, or the stares. Then, when I sensed that even my loyal friends were wary about trusting their children with me, I sold the house. I left the town where I was born and married and gave birth to my only son and moved to Los Angeles. I never told anyone where I moved to, not even my friends, especially not my parents. I never thought I'd find happiness again, but then I met you and Nicholas. And then I became pregnant, and I thought it was God's way of telling me He'd forgiven me, because by giving me another child, He was giving me another chance."

That was when she'd resumed her painting. After Kevin's death, she'd avoided the studio and everything in it. There was no peace for her in that attic room, only evidence of her pre-occupation and guilt. She had never finished the tree.

She was barely rocking now. "I've wanted to tell you the truth every day of our marriage. I was afraid that you wouldn't love me if you knew, that even if you would, you wouldn't want me as the mother of your two-year-old son. Was I wrong?" She wanted to turn to see his face but didn't have the courage.

Warren didn't answer. He was silent for several moments. "When did Larry die?" he finally asked.

Alex hesitated, then said, "Larry didn't die. We were divorced right after Kevin's death. Three months later—this was before I sold the house—I came home from work one day and found him in what had been our bathtub. He'd slashed his wrists." There had been blood everywhere. She shuddered, remembering. "He was unconscious but alive. I called the paramedics. Now he's in an institution for the mentally ill. His business was a failure. So was his marriage. With Kevin gone, he had nothing to live for." She sighed. "The media raked everything up again, of course." More microphones, more camera flashes.

"Have you told me the truth about anything, Alex?"

There was anger in his voice, and a wistfulness that made her want to cry. "Yes. I love you, and Nicholas, and Lisa, even though she and I haven't been getting along lately."

"Did you kill Donald Lundquist, Alex?"

She could hardly blame him for asking. "No. I told you the truth. He was going to tell me who pushed me, who wrote the notes. One of them said I was a murderess. Someone found out about my past, Warren." She told him about the missing phone bills, about the cashier's checks. "I have them put fresh flowers on Kevin's grave every few days."

"Lundquist had the papers. He could have written the notes. He could have pushed you."

"Then who killed him?"

Warren didn't answer. Alex waited. She plucked at the sleeve of her blouse.

"Alex," he said, and she could tell that he wasn't going to discuss Donald Lundquist. "There's a part of me that wants to take you in my arms and comfort you and tell you everything's going to be all right. But I can't. I don't know you, Alex. I've kissed you and touched you and made love to you, but I don't know you."

What had she expected? "I understand."

"I need time." He moved out of the doorway. "Come upstairs. It's very late."

Their conversation had come full circle. "Soon."

After he left, she sat for a while rocking gently. Then she lay down on the sofa bed in the room and fell asleep. Sometime during the night she dreamed that Warren whispered her name and caressed her cheek.

When she awoke, she found herself covered with a blanket.

Chapter 24

Alex pulled the blanket closer around her, taking comfort from its soft warmth and from the fact that Warren had cared enough to cover her with it. She pictured him upstairs in their bed. She wondered whether he was awake, whether he was thinking about her and about her previous life as Alexandra Trent.

With a jolt, she remembered the newspaper clippings. She'd left them on the coffee table where the detective had dropped them. She got off the sofa bed and hurried to the living room.

The clippings were gone. Alex panicked at first—what if Lisa had taken them? Or Nicholas?—but she reminded herself that it was six-thirty in the morning, and Lisa and Nicholas were still asleep. Warren must have taken them. She wondered whether he'd read them before or after he'd listened to her as she sat in the rocking chair. Maybe he'd done both. She had a copy of the clippings and a photo of Kevin upstairs in the gray envelope in her drawer. She looked at them every night.

Alex washed up in the small bathroom off the studio and returned to the sofa bed. She didn't plan to sleep, but she dozed off for a while. Sometime later when she awoke, she contemplated going upstairs, but she wasn't ready to face Warren. She laced her hands beneath her head and stared up at the ceiling, thinking about Donald Lundquist and Warren and the police, and the person who was tormenting her.

"How come you're sleeping here, Mommy?"

Alex turned. Nicholas was standing in the doorway. "Hi, Nick." She propped herself on her elbow. "Everything okay?"

"I looked for you upstairs, but Daddy said you were here. He said not to wake you, but your eyes were open. How come you're here?" he repeated.

"I was working on something and I guess I fell asleep."

Nicholas looked at the blank paper on the easel. "There's nothing there."

"I was working it out in my head."

"Oh." He shuffled his right foot back and forth along the carpet. "Lisa said you were sick." His eyes looked troubled.

She smiled. "I'm fine." She heard Warren's voice calling Nicholas. A moment later Warren was beside him in the doorway.

"Ready to go, Nick?" Warren asked. "Teeth brushed?"

"Not yet." He ran to the bed, bent down, and kissed Alex soundly on her cheek. "'Bye, Mommy." He skipped out of the room.

"Thank you for the blanket, Warren."

"I didn't want you to be cold." His tone was matter-of-fact. He adjusted the knot in his tie. "I'll call you from the office, Alex. If you need anything, call me. About the police—"

"Warren, I want to tell them the truth." She was tired of living with lies and evasions. The penalty was too stiff. "The police have that note Lundquist left for me. I touched it, and other things in the house. They'll find my prints and identify them. They can get a copy from my arrest record, can't they?"

"Yes." Warren frowned. "I have two morning appointments I can't cancel. After that, I'll come home and take you to the station. I'll have Gwen reschedule everything else."

She couldn't tell if he was annoyed at having to interrupt his day. Probably. She could hardly blame him. "Thank you."

"You don't have to thank me, Alex. I'm your husband." He took a step into the room, then stopped. "See you soon."

After Warren left, Alex lay on the bed for a few minutes, then went into the kitchen and poured herself a glass of orange juice. She hesitated, then picked up the wall-phone receiver and punched the number for Pacific Division. She knew it by heart. When the operator answered, she asked to be connected with Detective Rowan.

"Detective Rowan is away from his desk. Do you want to leave a message, or is there someone else who can help you?"

Alex had forgotten the partner's name. "This is Alexandra Prescott. I'd like to come down to the station to talk to him later this morning, and I want to be sure he'll be there."

"He should be back momentarily. I'll have him call you."

Alex gave the operator her phone number and hung up. Then she called Evelyn. "It's Alex," she announced when Evelyn answered the phone. "The police were here last night."

"Oh, my God!" Evelyn exclaimed. "What happened?"

Alex told her about the detectives' visit, about the note she'd left behind. "I had to give them your name and phone number, Evelyn. I told them we went to a coffee shop around nine-thirty. I didn't tell them about going to Lundquist's, but I don't want you to lie for me."

"Alex—"

"Tell them the truth about everything. I'm going to. I can't stand this anymore."

"I guess you're right." Evelyn sounded dubious. "Anyway, even if you tell them you were there, you don't have a motive for killing Lundquist."

"I hope the police agree." The police might see a motive in the newspaper clippings they'd found in Lundquist's home. What had the detective asked?—*Was Lundquist blackmailing you?*

"Alex? Is there something you're not telling me?"

"Sorry. I'm just tired." Maybe someday she would tell Evelyn about her past, but not now.

Alex called Dr. Pearson's office and left a message with the answering service that she was canceling her appointment and would call to reschedule. Then she went upstairs to shower and wash her hair. She took her time in the shower, relaxing under the gentle pressure of the water. She was toweling herself when she heard the front doorbell. She grabbed her terry robe from the bathroom door and put it on, then hurried downstairs to the entry hall. The bell rang again.

"Coming!"

At the front door she looked through the peephole and grimaced when she saw the two detectives who had been there last night. She opened the door and stepped aside to let them enter.

"I was in the shower," she said, feeling the need to explain her robe and wet hair.

Rowan said, "I got your message, Mrs. Prescott. I'm glad you've decided to help us out. You could be a material witness."

"I told the operator I'd come down to the station. I know where it is," she added with a touch of petulance.

Rowan smiled. "I was in the neighborhood."

"Can you come back a little later? Better yet, I'll come to the station as soon as I'm ready." A moment ago she'd been willing, if not eager, to tell her story to the police. Now she was filled with reservations and wanted more than anything for Warren to be by her side.

"We can wait while you get dressed, Mrs. Prescott," Detective Medina said. "We can talk here or at the station."

"My husband was planning to come with me. His office is in Century City."

Rowan said, "The station's better, then. Why don't you call him and have him meet you there? We'll give you a ride."

Feeling manipulated, Alex went upstairs. From the bedroom phone she called Warren and told him what had happened.

"You shouldn't have called them." Warren sounded annoyed. "All right. Don't say a word until I get there. I'm leaving right now. I'll be at the station in twenty minutes."

She dressed quickly in a pair of maternity slacks and an oversize sweater, then blow-dried her hair. A woman has to look good when she's being interrogated, she told her reflection in the mirror, but she wasn't smiling, and her hand shook as she applied lipstick and blush.

Walking downstairs, she was struck by the unsettling thought that three years ago two other police officers had waited for her to dress so that they could take her in for questioning. She tried to brush the thought away—this was different, after all. She wasn't a suspect. She was a material witness, Rowan had said. She hadn't done anything wrong.

But although today there had been no police sirens, and the car parked in front of her house wasn't the police vehicle with the flashing red-and-yellow lights of three years ago, two neighbors across the street were staring at her as the detectives escorted her from her house to the backseat of the gray Chevy, and she had the prickly sensation that other neighbors were watching her, too, from their windows.

Everything was different. Everything was the same.

Warren was in the waiting room at the station when Alex arrived with the detectives. He was sitting next to a woman who looked vaguely familiar to Alex. When he saw Alex, he stood up and walked over to her.

"Can I have a word in private with my wife?" he said to Rowan and Medina.

"Sure." Rowan stepped to the side. So did his partner.

"I brought Margot Leibman, Alex," Warren said in an undertone. "You met her at a party. She's a criminal attorney, and I've retained her for you. She'll handle everything."

"But I want you to be with me," Alex whispered.

"Margot's the best. And it's not a good idea for me to represent you." He squeezed her hand lightly, then released it. "It'll be all right." He turned to Margot and beckoned to her.

Margot Leibman was slim and tall, Alex saw as the woman stood and walked toward them with a graceful, purposeful stride. She was wearing a well-cut gray career suit and low-heeled gray pumps. She was pretty, with wonderful, large brown eyes that contrasted dramatically with her highlighted, short blond hair. Alex guessed that she was in her early forties.

Warren made the introductions, and the women shook hands. Margot's handshake was firm. Alex's own hand was clammy.

"I'm a little nervous," Alex told the attorney.

Margot smiled. "Understandable. But you'll be fine. Warren explained what happened and what you told the detectives last night. I'd like you to tell it to me again."

Rowan approached. "Ready?"

Margot introduced herself, then said, "I'd like to confer with my client in private first."

"Your client?" Rowan looked at Warren. "I thought you were an attorney." There was a hint of a smirk on his face.

Warren didn't answer him. Something twitched in his cheek.

"Is there a room we can use?" Margot asked.

Rowan escorted Margot and Alex to a small cubicle crowded with a table and four chairs, two on either side of the table. The metal walls were painted a dreary pale yellow and filled with graffiti. The air reeked of cigarette smoke.

"Enjoy," Rowan said and left them.

"Okay," Margot said when they were both seated. "Tell me exactly what happened."

Alex spoke for over ten minutes. She told Margot about everything—the vandalizing of the school; the notes; the feeling that she was being stalked; her being pushed at the beach; the doll. Lundquist's offer to tell her who pushed her. Finding Lundquist dead in the Jacuzzi. She told Margot about the detectives' visit last night, about the papers they'd found in Lundquist's house. Finally, she told her about her past. She studied the attorney's face for some sign of disapproval but found nothing but intense interest.

Margot tapped her fountain pen against a pad of yellow, legal-size paper. "It's probable that they found or will find and identify your fingerprints. That places you at the scene of the crime, but it doesn't tell them when you were there. You wouldn't talk last night, so they're suspicious. They think you know something they want to know, or they think you might have killed Lundquist."

"But I didn't!"

Margot covered Alex's hand with hers. "I believe you. But this is how they may be thinking." She removed her hand. "You were angry at Lundquist. You were afraid of him. You believe he vandalized your school. He made oblique threats about kidnapping your stepson. That might not add up to a motive for murder, but then we have the newspaper clippings. The police will say that Lundquist was threatening to expose your past, that you were desperate to stop him and killed him. You feared the ruin of your good name, of your preschool." Margot paused. "Warren says he didn't know about the death of your son, but the police don't know that, and a husband can't be made to testify against his wife."

Reassuring news, Alex thought, but she was hot with embarrassment, wondering what the attorney was thinking about a woman who had lied to her husband from the beginning of their relationship. Would Margot Leibman think Alex was lying now, too?

"But if I killed him because I didn't want him to expose my past, why didn't I take the papers?"

"You searched for them but couldn't find them. Was Lundquist's place ransacked?"

"Not from what I saw, but I was only in the entry hall and living room."

Margot stood up. "Okay. We're done. I'm going to tell them what you told me."

"I thought I was going to make a statement."

Margot shook her head. "Bad idea. You might say something incriminating."

"But I didn't do anything wrong!" Alex paused. "I'd really like to clear this up myself, Margot."

The attorney frowned. "All right. But follow my lead, and don't jump to answer questions. If I touch your arm, don't talk. My job is to be your advocate and your witness, to make sure they don't abuse your rights or try to trap you into making incriminating statements."

Margot left the cubicle. A moment later she returned with Rowan and Medina. Margot took the seat next to Alex. Rowan and Medina sat across from them. Rowan had brought a tape recorder with him. He placed it on the table, turned it on, identified himself, stated the date, time, and place, and that he was speaking to Alexandra Prescott.

"Mrs. Prescott, you called the station this morning to talk to me. I assume it's about the death of Donald Lundquist."

"Yes. I want to make a statement."

"We're eager to hear what you have to say. Before you begin, I'm going to advise you of your rights."

"Just a minute." Margot's tone was sharp. "Mrs. Prescott has come here to volunteer information about the death of Mr. Lundquist. Are you saying she's a suspect in his death?"

"We're pursuing that and other possibilities. I want to make sure everything's kosher."

Margot leaned closer to Alex. "Alex, this changes everything. No statement."

Alex shook her head. "I want to get this over with. I have nothing to hide." She turned to Rowan. "I'm aware of my rights," she told him, but he was already reciting the Miranda litany.

"... anything you say can and will be used against you. Do you understand everything I've just told you, Mrs. Prescott?"

"Yes." She understood it all too well. She'd heard it all before.

"Okay. Tell me about Donald Lundquist."

She cleared her throat. "On Monday evening Donald Lundquist called me. . . . '' She spoke slowly and so quietly that once or twice Rowan had to ask her to speak up. When she finished, he studied her for a moment. She met his gaze.

"We've verified that the note you found on Mr. Lundquist's front door is in his handwriting,'' the detective said. "The note told you he'd be in the Jacuzzi. That corroborates the medical evidence, which says he was killed near the Jacuzzi, then propped up on the Jacuzzi steps.'' He paused.

Why was he telling her this? Alex wondered. She waited.

"Not easy to do—drag a dead body,'' Rowan continued. "But not impossible, even for a woman.'' He leaned back in his chair. "You didn't see any blood around the Jacuzzi area?''

Alex shook her head. "It was dark.''

"Quite a bit of blood,'' the detective commented. "Whoever killed Lundquist didn't take any chances. Slashed him in the neck, in the chest. Severed the jugular. Punctured the aorta.''

She winced at the image but said nothing.

"We still haven't found the murder weapon. Probably a kitchen knife, according to the medical examiner. Not too hard to come by.''

Margot said, "Detective, thank you for sharing all this information with us. Do you have questions for my client? If not . . . ''

Rowan smiled at the attorney. "I have *several* questions for Mrs. Prescott.'' He turned to Alex. "Mrs. Prescott, why didn't you tell me all this last night?''

She was prepared for this question. "I was scared. I didn't want to be implicated in Lundquist's death.''

"Because he was blackmailing you?''

Margot touched Alex lightly on the arm. "Detective, you're putting words in my client's mouth. She never said or intimated that Mr. Lundquist was blackmailing her. In fact, she made it clear that Lundquist had offered to give her vital information about the person who has been harassing her and her family.''

"Thanks for that clarification.'' Rowan smiled. "Mrs. Prescott, what time did you get to Lundquist's house?''

"A quarter to nine. I talked to him a few minutes after eight o'clock, by the way, so I know he was alive then.''

"That's helpful information. Thank you." He nodded. "How long were you at the house?"

Alex concentrated. "I waited in the living room about six or seven minutes. Then I went out to the pool area. At the most, I'd say ten minutes."

Medina asked, "Why'd you go to the coffee shop? Why didn't you call the police and wait for them to arrive?"

"Again, I was scared. I didn't want to get involved. Lundquist was dead. There was nothing I could do to help him. I'd told my husband I was going out for coffee with my friend. I thought that's what I should do. I know it was stupid, and wrong. I'm sorry."

Rowan said, "It didn't bother you that Mr. Lundquist was lying at the bottom of his Jacuzzi with his chest and throat slashed?"

Rowan's voice was soft. Alex had heard voices like that, and the softness had been deceptive. "It bothered me a great deal," she said. "That's why I called the police."

"*After* you had coffee, Mrs. Prescott. *After*." He glanced at his notebook. "And a slice of cheesecake. We spoke with the waitress last night." He looked up at her. "You have a pretty good appetite, I guess. I don't know too many people who could eat cake after finding a dead body."

"I didn't eat the cake," Alex said, knowing it sounded lame. Her hands were gripping her knees.

"Can we please move on?" Margot's tone was polite but firm.

"Did you look around the house, Mrs. Prescott?"

"No. I went from the entry to the living room, then out the French doors to the backyard."

"You weren't in the office or bedroom?" Medina asked.

Margot said, "Mrs. Prescott has already answered that question."

"You're right. Sorry." The detective smiled at Margot.

Rowan said, "Somebody ransacked the place looking for something. Maybe it was the clippings. What do you think?"

Alex said, "I wouldn't know."

"They were in an envelope taped underneath his desk, by the way." Rowan leaned back in his chair. "So how do you think Lundquist got these newspaper clippings?"

Margot said, "You're asking my client to speculate."

"We're not in a court of law here, Ms. Leibman."

"Detective Rowan, we don't even know that Mr. Lundquist, in fact, acquired the clippings. Someone could have planted them in his house to implicate my client in Mr. Lundquist's death."

"The bedroom and office were trashed."

"If I were planting something, I'd do the same to make it look as though my client had searched for the clippings."

"And how would this someone have gotten the clippings?"

Alex looked at Margot. Margot nodded.

"After my preschool was vandalized, I found two phone bills missing. I told Detective Brady that. I think that whoever took the phone bills traced the number of the cemetery where . . . where my son is buried, and talked to the people there, and learned about what happened. Then he probably contacted the local paper and asked them to send him copies of the newspaper clippings."

Medina said, "*He?*"

"Or *she*. I was using the generic term."

Rowan said, "According to Detective Brady, you were convinced that Mr. Lundquist was the one who vandalized your school. Which means that he stole the phone bills and traced you to your hometown and got the clippings. Did he show you the clippings when you got there?"

Margot said, "My client told you that Mr. Lundquist was dead when she got there. Come on, Detective."

"What do you think he was planning on doing with these clippings, Mrs. Prescott?"

"I don't know that he had them. I told you last night—I'm not sure anymore that Donald Lundquist vandalized my school."

"So you said. I mentioned that to Detective Brady, and he found it confusing. He said you insisted again and again that Lundquist vandalized your school. What changed your mind?"

The boarding-school application. The notes. The doll. It all seemed out of character for Lundquist. But if she explained that, she'd be pointing the finger at someone close to her. She wasn't prepared to do that.

"It's hard to say," Alex said.

"I see." Rowan exchanged looks with Medina, then

frowned at Alex. "I read the clippings, Mrs. Prescott, and I want to tell you I feel terrible about what you went through."

Do you? "Thank you."

"It's a terrible thing to lose a child, especially like that." Rowan shook his head. "Unfortunately, people can be awfully cruel. I wonder how the parents in your preschool would react if they knew about this. Did that worry you?"

Alex shifted in her seat. "No. I didn't know that anyone had the newspaper clippings."

"But someone was sending you notes that alluded to your past. You said so. That person could have been Donald Lundquist."

"I suppose. But it could have been someone else."

"But if it *was* Lundquist, it would make sense that he was the one who pushed you, wouldn't it? So he invites you over on the pretext of telling you who pushed you, then tells you that *he* pushed you and—"

"Detective Rowan," Margot warned.

"Did he tell you that unless you told him where his wife was, he was going to expose your tragic past to everyone— the community, the parents in your school? By the way, did your husband know you'd been arrested for the death of your son?"

Alex felt Margot's hand on her arm. She stared at the yellow wall above Medina's head.

Margot said, "You're badgering my client. I'm cautioning you to stop, or she won't answer any more questions."

"Lundquist was convinced you knew where his wife was. And you wouldn't tell him. Maybe he wanted information, Mrs. Prescott, or maybe he wanted to punish you."

"Who do you think killed him?" Medina asked.

Alex was startled by the change in tactics. Was this the good cop-bad cop routine? She looked at Detective Medina. "I don't know."

"You must have given it some thought. Who's this 'someone' who planted the clippings to frame you?"

"I don't know," Alex repeated. She saw the skepticism in the detectives' eyes. Had they noticed her hesitation? "Maybe a business associate," she offered. "He mentioned something the night he called about wanting to keep a low profile. That's why he wanted me to come to his house."

Rowan said, "We've been checking into Mr. Lundquist's business life, and we'll continue checking. He was in the import-export business, and it seems he was in debt. Did you know that his wife was the one with the money?"

Alex shook her head.

"Maybe that's why he wanted her back so badly, huh? Do you think she could have killed her husband?"

Am I no longer a suspect? Alex was confused and somewhat disoriented from having to move her head back and forth to answer questions first from Rowan, then from Medina, then from Rowan again. "She was at the shelter."

"No, she wasn't. Not that night, anyway. Mrs. Lundquist left the shelter that Tuesday and hasn't returned. Interesting, isn't it?" Rowan smiled. "I think that's all for now, Mrs. Prescott. Thank you for cooperating with us." He stood up.

His dismissal was so sudden that Alex felt like a marionette whose strings had been snipped. Margot stood. Alex did the same and followed the attorney out of the cubicle and back to the waiting room.

Warren got up from his seat and hurried to join them. "How was it?" he asked. His face was tight with anxiety.

Margot smiled and put her hand on Alex's shoulder. "She did great. They Mirandized her, but I think they're just fishing. They're checking Lundquist's business past, and it seems his wife has flown." She glanced at her wristwatch. "I've got to get back to my office. Call if anything comes up. And Alex, if the police call you, refer them to me."

"Thanks, Margot," Warren said.

"No problem." She smiled again and walked away.

"What did they ask you, Alex?" Warren said.

"I'll tell you in the car." She was suddenly drained. "Can you take me home, Warren? Right now, please."

He steered her by the elbow out of the waiting room. At the entrance he held the door while she stepped outside.

"Mrs. Prescott!" she heard someone call.

She turned in the direction of the voice and was startled by the flash of a camera. She bent her head and raised her hand to block her face.

"Shit!" Warren muttered.

"Mrs. Prescott! Can you tell us . . ."

Warren put his arm around Alex. "Let's go." He hurried her to the sidewalk.

"Mrs. Prescott!"

"Alexandra Trent!"

Everything was different. Everything was the same.

Chapter 25

"**I**'ve asked Paula to move in," Warren told Alex when they were in the breakfast room after supper. "It's just temporary, until things settle down."

She wondered what he meant by "things"—the police investigation into her involvement with Lundquist and his murder? The media attention (a persistent reporter from the local Venice newspaper had called repeatedly all afternoon)? The precarious state of their marriage?

"Fine." She took a sip of her herbal tea.

"With all this stress on top of the pregnancy and your fall, you could use help. Pearson told me you should be taking it easy, not lifting anything, especially with your injuries. Paula can do the marketing. She can pick up the kids from school if you're not available."

"Like if I'm in jail for Lundquist's murder, you mean."

Warren put down his cup and stared at her. "If that's a joke, it's not funny. Why don't you want Paula to come?"

"Why do you *want* her to come?"

"I told you. She'll be a big help, Alex. She'll—"

Alex sighed. "Do what you want, Warren." It's your house, your children. "Where is she going to sleep?"

"I can get a bed and put it in the nursery. Or she can stay downstairs."

"In my studio, you mean." Alex hated relinquishing the studio to Paula. She could just see the housekeeper's triumphant smile. On the other hand, the nursery was next door to Alex and Warren's bedroom, and the idea of having Paula in such intimate proximity didn't thrill her.

"We don't have extra rooms, Alex." His tone and the expression in his eyes added, "Why are you being so difficult?"

"I know." She took another sip of tea. "Downstairs, I

guess. We'll move my easel and supplies to the nursery.'' The light was passable; she would make do. Right now she didn't feel like painting anyway.

"I'll do it tonight. This is only temporary, Alex."

"So you said." Alex put down her cup and began stacking the dinner plates.

"I'll do that." He took the plates from her. "Alex, one more thing. I think we should tell Lisa about Lundquist and . . . well . . . everything before she reads about it in the paper or hears about it at school."

"We don't know that the paper will run a story on me."

"A photographer snapped your picture. A reporter called all day. Think how hurt and shocked Lisa will be if she hears it from someone else."

"I guess you're right." She cringed at the thought of having her stepdaughter know about her past—then remembered that maybe Lisa already knew. That she'd known for a long time. "You tell her."

"All right." He nodded. "We won't tell Nicholas, of course."

"Or Denise, or anyone else." Even when she'd called Evelyn in the afternoon, Alex had told her only parts of the police interrogation. She hadn't mentioned anything about her past; she wasn't ready to. "Did you tell Paula?"

Warren frowned. "Of course not. Why would I do that?"

He cleared the table and loaded the dishes into the dishwasher, then left the kitchen. Alex wiped the counters and put the leftovers away. She was still achy and limited in her movements and had to admit that having help made sense—if only it weren't Paula.

Alex went into the family room. "Bedtime," she announced to Nicholas.

He was lying on the carpet on his stomach, working on a jigsaw puzzle. "'Kay." He sat up, scooped the puzzle pieces with his hands, and dumped them into the cardboard box.

"Don't you want to leave it for tomorrow?" she asked.

He shook his head.

"Okay. Meet you in your room."

She went upstairs. Lisa's door was closed. Warren was probably in the room with her. Alex changed into a nightshirt and a pair of loose shorts. She turned down the bedspread.

She brushed her hair. She wondered what words Warren was choosing to explain to his daughter that his wife was a suspect in a murder investigation, that she had let her only child drown. She felt a twinge of sympathy for Warren and Lisa, but realized that most of all, she was feeling damned sorry for herself.

On the way to Nicholas, she passed Lisa's room. The door was still closed. She walked down the hall and knocked on Nicholas's door. "Ready?"

"Yes."

She opened the door. Only the lamp on his nightstand was on. Nicholas was in bed, his hands on top of his comforter. Alex walked over to him and sat on the edge of the bed.

"Which story tonight?"

"I don't care."

Nicholas *always* cared. He had his favorites, and enjoyed hearing them over and over. She studied his face. He looked more serious than usual, or maybe it was her imagination.

"Is something bothering you, Nick?" Alex asked softly.

He shook his head.

"Something *is* bothering you. Can't you tell me what it is?" She stroked his hair. "Maybe I can help."

"It's a bad thought, Mommy. Lisa said you're not supposed to say bad thoughts or they'll come true."

"Lisa's wrong, Nicholas." She took his hand. "It's good to tell people what's bothering you."

He curled his fingers around hers and squeezed her hand. "Are you going to die, Mommy?"

Her heart lurched. "Everyone dies sometime, Nicholas. People get old. But I'm not going to die for a long time. Why are you worrying about that?"

"My first mother died, and she was young, just like you. Lisa said so."

"Oh, Nicholas," Alex whispered.

"She died right after she had a baby, and you're going to have a baby, and you fell, and you were in the hospital, and that man is angry at you, and Lisa said you were sick this morning, and you said you weren't, but I'm scared, Mommy!" His eyes had filled with tears. They were coursing down his cheeks. "I don't want you to die."

She leaned over and put her cheek next to his. His arms

went around her. His small body was shaking. She held him tight against her chest and smoothed his back with her hand in slow, slow circles.

"I'm not sick, Nicholas. And women don't die from having babies. Your mother did, but that hardly ever, ever happens."

"Promise?"

"Promise."

She held him for a while. Then she said, "Would you like a story now?"

He shook his head. "Can you stay till I fall asleep?"

"Sure." She shut the lamp on the nightstand, then lay down next to him. "Would you like to feel the baby kick?"

"Could I?"

"It's not a strong kick yet, more like this." She flicked her finger lightly against his palm. Then she took his hand and placed it below her abdomen. She left her hand on his.

"I don't feel anything," he whispered.

"Wait."

They waited together in the silence and darkness.

"I felt it!" Nicholas said. "Can he do it again, Mommy? Can he?"

Alex smiled. "Maybe. Let's see."

Minutes later Nicholas was asleep, his hand still on her abdomen. Alex moved his hand and got off the bed. When she stood, she saw Warren standing outside the doorway.

She left the room and pulled the door shut. "He had a hard time falling asleep." She told Warren about Nicholas's fears. "I think I've reassured him."

"You're a good mother, Alex." His tone was almost solemn. "Nicholas is lucky to have you."

What about you? she wanted to ask. Are you lucky to have me? "Did you tell Lisa?"

"Yes. She was wonderful, Alex, very supportive. She feels terrible about what you've been through."

That was what Rowan had said in the interrogation room. Alex wondered if her stepdaughter was more sincere than the detective had been. "I guess you were right to tell her."

"She won't bring it up—she doesn't want to embarrass you—but I think she wouldn't mind talking to you about it. When you're ready," he added, seeing Alex's expression. "Right now I'm going to take your stuff to the nursery."

Warren found a box in the garage. While Alex filled it with her supplies, he took up her easel and the rocking chair. The box was last. The room wasn't a nursery yet—it was a spare bedroom with nothing but white mini-blinds and blue carpeting.

"I'll get a cabinet for your supplies," he said.

"It's fine." It wasn't fine, but what could she say?

"Don't wait up, okay? I have a lot of paperwork to do."

Warren went downstairs. Alex tried reading in bed but couldn't concentrate. She turned on the television and became engrossed in a movie. Two hours later, when she was watching the news, Warren came into the bedroom.

"I thought you'd be sleeping by now," he said.

"Sorry to disappoint you."

He flushed. "That's not what I meant. I just meant—shit, Alex." He unbuttoned his shirt.

"I really *am* sorry. I know I'm making this difficult. If you want, I can sleep downstairs tonight." Tomorrow night Paula would be here.

"No, that's not what I want!" In a calmer, more controlled voice, he said, "I don't think it's a good idea, not for us and not for the kids." He undressed and got into bed. "Good night, Alex."

"Good night." They were in the same bed, but she felt as if there were an imaginary wall between them. *I need time,* Warren had said last night. She didn't blame him, but she wondered how much time. She shut off her lamp and closed her eyes, willing sleep to come.

"Alex?"

She turned toward him. Even in the dark, she could see that he was staring at her.

"I know today was terribly upsetting for you, and I'm sorry I haven't been more . . . emotionally supportive."

"You came to the police station with me. You brought a lawyer to help me."

"I would do that for a client, Alex. You're my wife." He paused. "I'm trying to understand why you lied to me. I tell myself that after everyone turned against you—even your parents and friends—you felt you couldn't trust anyone. But I can't get beyond the hurt, Alex, the fact that you couldn't trust *me.*"

"But they were right, Warren—Larry, my in-laws, my parents. It was my fault that Kevin died."

"It was a tragic accident, Alex," he said gently.

"It was negligence. I left him alone for twenty minutes so I could paint. Are you saying you wouldn't have blamed me? That you don't blame me now?"

"I can understand how it happened. You read all the time about children drowning. You have to let go of the guilt."

"I can't," she whispered. "I relive Kevin's death in my dreams every night." Last night she'd been emotionally spent yet somewhat relieved, the burden of secrecy having been lifted from her shoulders, and she'd thought that the dream might be behind her. But it had invaded her sleep and held her captive, image by image, sound by sound.

"For years I kept waiting for God to punish me," she said. "When I met you, I was afraid to get involved. I thought I didn't deserve happiness. There's a part of me that still feels that way." Sometimes she wondered whether the notes were her punishment. And the sender?

"Last night you said you loved me," Warren said. "I believe that, but I have to know. . . . "

She tensed. "What?"

"Did you marry me because you loved me, or because you loved Nicholas and wanted someone to replace Kevin?"

Her eyes welled with tears. It was a cruel question, she thought, but a fair one. "I asked myself that when we were dating," she said softly. "I never consciously tried to replace Kevin. I could never do that. I wouldn't want to. I fell in love with Nicholas when I was his teacher because it was impossible not to love him. And I fell in love with you because it was impossible not to."

"I've hurt you. I'm sorry." He reached out and wiped the tears from her cheek.

She longed to put her hand on his. "Do you believe me?"

"Yes. Good night, Alex. Sleep well."

Had there been a beat of hesitation before he'd answered?

"Good night," she said.

Chapter 26

"**W**here shall I put these?" Paula asked Alex, pointing to the two suitcases she'd deposited in the service porch.

As if you didn't know, Alex thought, but she kept her voice light and pleasant when she replied, "In my studio."

"What about your things, Alex? I hate to put you out."

"It's no problem. Warren moved my materials to the nursery. It's thoughtful of you to help out," she added, wondering why she and Paula were dancing this stilted minuet of congeniality.

"There's nothing I wouldn't do for this family, Alex. It'll be like old times, won't it? Me in my own room, and a baby on the way." Paula smiled at her. "Oh, I almost forgot." She handed Alex a newspaper. "This was on the lawn." She picked up her suitcases and walked toward the studio.

It was the local paper. With anxious fingers, Alex unrolled it. There was nothing on the front page, she saw. She expelled her breath but drew it in sharply seconds later. There were two photos of her on page 3, one taken yesterday by the photographer as she was leaving the police station. Next to it was the photo of Alexandra Trent. The caption ran above both photos: VENICE PRESCHOOL OWNER QUESTIONED BY POLICE IN LOCAL BUSINESSMAN'S MURDER IS HAUNTED BY TRAGIC PAST.

If it's so tragic, why can't you leave it in the past? Her fingers were tingling; so was her face, and she was having difficulty breathing. She was starting to hyperventilate, she knew. She forced herself to take deep, even breaths and tried not to think about the people who were staring at her photos this very moment and reading of her shame. Denise, Mona, Evelyn, Patty. The parents of her preschoolers. There were thousands more, strangers to her, but she would no longer be a stranger to them. They would see her at the supermarket, in a restaurant, in the park. *Oh, look! There's that woman who let her son drown. . . .*

In the kitchen she found a paper bag and breathed into it until the tingling stopped. As she folded the newspaper and rolled it up tightly, she wondered whether Paula had read it. There was usually a rubber band around the paper. Today there hadn't been one. Of course, that didn't mean anything.

The phone rang. She reached her hand toward the receiver, then pulled it back. It could be a reporter, or any one of a number of people she didn't want to talk to.

Another ring. "Paula! Can you get that, please?"

There was a third ring, then silence. A moment later Paula came into the kitchen.

"It's Warren," she told Alex. "By the way, can I look at that paper I gave you? They usually have coupons. . . . "

"I'll be done with it soon." Alex realized she was clutching the paper to her chest and dropped her hand. "Thanks, Paula." She waited until the housekeeper was leaving the kitchen, then picked up the receiver. "Hello?"

"How's everything working out?" Warren asked.

"Horrible. My picture's in the local paper."

He sighed. "I wanted Paula to keep the paper from you. Everyone's been calling me about it."

"I'm not surprised. It's a great story, isn't it? They probably want to know all the details."

"They're concerned, Alex. They're upset for you. Denise. Evelyn. Patty. Mona. Brenda Judd. Mort Green. There were tons of messages when I got to the office. They wanted to alert me. They don't know if you want to talk to them."

"I don't!"

"You don't have to. Have Paula answer the calls. It'll be terrible for a day or so, and then someone else will make the headlines." He paused. "Alex, if you want me to come home—"

"That's silly. I'll be all right."

After she hung up, she walked to her studio—Paula's room, she corrected herself, but she was too tired to care. Paula's suitcases were lying open on the sofa bed. She was hanging dresses in the closet when Alex entered the room. Alex noticed that her framed photos—the one of Paula with her late husband, and the one of her nephew—were already on the dresser.

"Paula?" Alex waited until the woman was facing her. "I know why you wanted the paper. Thank you for trying to help my husband protect me."

"I'm sorry," Paula said quietly.

"Here." Alex extended the newspaper to the housekeeper. "This doesn't concern me."

"I want you to read it. You're probably wondering what they wrote, and that makes it worse for me." Unless you already know, Alex thought. "I didn't kill Donald Lundquist, but everything about my past is true."

Paula blushed and averted her eyes. "I'm sorry for your pain." She made no move to take the newspaper.

Alex dropped it on the sofa bed. "Would you please answer the phone if it rings? Except for my husband, I can't think of anyone I want to talk to, but I'd appreciate your taking messages." She turned and left the room.

From her bedroom, Alex called Dr. Pearson's office and had the nurse schedule her for an amniocentesis the following Thursday. Alex also spoke to Pearson. He agreed that she could go back to work on Monday.

"Don't overdo," he warned. "And avoid stress."

Alex almost laughed. "I will," she promised. "By the way, Dr. Pearson, did that man call again? The one who said he was from the insurance company, I mean."

"No. I told you it was nothing, Alexandra. Don't give it another thought."

Maybe it *was* nothing, Alex thought as she hung up. Or maybe the caller had been Lundquist. And dead men don't make phone calls.

As if to echo her thought, the phone rang. She was startled by the sound but made no move to pick up the receiver. Paula answered the call after two rings.

A few minutes later the phone rang again. Alex turned off the sound on her extension, switched on the radio on her nightstand, and, lying on the floor, did some prenatal stretches recommended in her Lamaze book. They helped her body relax, if not her mind. Afterward, with the radio still on, she sat cross-legged on her bed and jotted notes on a pad for new arts and crafts projects for the children. If they're still in school when I get back, she said to herself, and quickly banished the thought.

She realized midway through the morning that she hadn't eaten breakfast. She was hungry. More importantly, the baby needed nutrition. She went downstairs to the kitchen. Paula was there, washing the refrigerator shelves. There was an awkward moment when the two women saw each other.

"You had several calls, Alex. Here's the list." Paula handed it to her.

"Thanks." She tucked it into the pocket of her blouse. Then she filled a bowl with cereal and sliced in a banana.

"Can I say something, Alex?"

She turned toward Paula.

"It's very cruel what they did, printing that. I lost a husband many years ago, when I was very young. Cancer. It was terrible, but I can't imagine the pain of losing a child, of knowing—" She put her hand over her mouth. "I'm sorry. That's not what I meant to say."

Didn't you? "It's all right."

"You have much to be grateful for. A husband who loves you. Two children. A baby coming. Make that your strength."

"I'll try."

Alex poured milk into the bowl and took it into the breakfast room. From her pocket she removed the slip of paper and scanned the phone messages as she ate the cereal. Jim Battaglia, the reporter who'd called yesterday, had phoned twice. He'd left a number where he could be reached. Several friends had called, including Evelyn and Patty ("Give Alex my love") and Denise. Denise had offered to pick up the kids from school. Alex was tempted to accept—she dreaded meeting the stares of the other parents at the car pool—but she'd have to meet the stares eventually. Ron had called, too—to gloat? Then she remembered the get-well note he'd sent after she had fallen, and the apology. Maybe they had been sincere.

She called Denise. When the answering machine clicked on, she thanked God silently that Denise wasn't home and left a message that she would pick up the kids herself. Then she called Ron at his office. His secretary answered. Alex introduced herself, and a moment later Ron came on the line.

"Alex!" he exclaimed. "I'm glad you called."

"Thanks for the note. It was sweet of you."

"It's the least I could do after the shitty way I've been behaving. Look, I'm not one for being subtle, so here goes. Number one, no one who knows you is going to believe for one minute that you killed someone. Number two, I think it's a goddamn shame they dragged out this stuff from your past, and I want you to know I think you're one hell of a woman. End of speech." He laughed.

"Pretty good speech," she said softly. "Thanks, Ron."

"Your friends will stick by you, Alex. Wait and see. And those who don't, well, they're not friends." He paused. "Speaking of which, I know I behaved like a total jackass last time, outside The Rose. Not to mention when I came on to you in your backyard. But I'd like to think that you and I can still be friends, Alex. So . . . uh . . . do you think you can forgive me for what happened?"

It seemed like ages ago, and so unimportant now. "Maybe I overreacted."

"No, you didn't. Don't let me off easy, Alex. I don't deserve it. I did a dumb thing. It was immature and sleazy, and when you called me on it, I got pissed. The only defense I have is that I was jealous."

Alex frowned. "Jealous? Of whom?"

"Of Warren, of course. In my eyes, he's got everything. A beautiful wife. A great family. A terrific career. And then Denise—" Ron stopped.

"What about Denise?"

"Forget it. It's nothing."

"Come on, Ron. What about Denise?"

"I thought she had a thing for Warren. It didn't do much for my ego, let me tell you. That's why I acted so stupid. Denise was gaga over him. I figured I'd even the score."

"What makes you think Denise was interested in Warren?" She tried to sound casual. "It's natural that they're close. Denise was his sister-in-law."

Ron sighed. "Alex, this is awkward, okay? Just take my word for it."

"You're making it up, aren't you?"

"No way!" He paused. Finally he said, "Sometimes when we were making love, she'd call out Warren's name."

"Oh."

The line was silent for a moment.

"Yeah," Ron said quietly. "I told you it was awkward. Look, you're not going to say anything to her or to Warren, are you? I'd hate for Denise to be embarrassed. Or him. It's not his fault. I only told you so you'd understand where I was coming from."

"I appreciate it."

"So, friends?"

"Friends," she said, wondering if she could believe him, wondering whether she wanted to.

Warren kissed her when he came home from the office. Alex was surprised, and gladdened, then wondered if it was for show, to demonstrate to Paula and Lisa and Nicholas that they were a happy couple, a happy family. But she welcomed his touch. His mouth seemed to linger on hers, and later, while they ate the rolled roast and scalloped potatoes Paula had prepared ("Just like I used to make!" she'd exclaimed, beaming), Alex found Warren looking at her from time to time.

After supper she played with Nicholas. He was giggly and mischievous and seemed to have forgotten his fears of the night before. She read him a story and tucked him into bed. Then she went downstairs. The kitchen was spotless. Alex thanked Paula, grateful for the help, but wondered how she was going to survive days and weeks and possibly months of Paula's rearranging Alex's linens, alphabetizing her spices, putting her own stamp on every room in the house.

That night was no different from any other night. It amazed Alex how she and Warren and Lisa and Paula were conducting their lives under the guise of normalcy. Warren was working in his study. Lisa was doing homework in her room. Paula was in her reclaimed room, watching TV. (Warren had brought back the twelve-inch color set that had been there before Alex converted the bedroom into her studio.) Maybe I should buy some yarn to knit a blanket for the baby, Alex thought.

Upstairs, she sat on her bed and turned on the television with the remote control. Too restless to watch, she jumped from channel to channel. Finally she clicked off the television, lay back against the headboard, and thought about Lundquist's murder.

It was strange and illogical, she knew, but from the time the two detectives had confronted her with the newspaper clippings, her main concern had been not Lundquist's death, but Warren's reaction to the revelations of her past.

Of course, she'd been frightened by the detectives' questions, and yesterday, in the cramped, smoke-filled cubicle, even more by their insinuations that she'd killed Lundquist. But her fear had been visceral, and she'd been fortified all along—and still was—by the knowledge that she was innocent and by the belief (maybe this was naive, she realized) that in time the police would know it, too.

In the meantime, there was nothing she could do about their suspicions. And now that the paper had dredged up her past, there was nothing she could do about that, either, but wait and hope that Warren was right, that she would quickly become yesterday's news. In a sense, the worst was behind her—her tormentor no longer had any ammunition to use against her.

Still, she wondered who had sent the notes, who had pushed her, wondered if that same person had killed Lundquist. It had seemed so clear to her two days ago—the connection was impossible to overlook—but the police had mentioned that Lundquist was in serious debt with his business partner and that Sally Lundquist had left the shelter on the day of her husband's murder. Two more suspects, not connected with Alex; she'd embraced the possibilities. (She'd felt sad about Sally Lundquist, but the woman wasn't her friend or family.)

But if Lundquist's business partner or wife had killed him, why had he—or she—positioned him on the Jacuzzi steps for Alex to find? And who had placed the newspaper clippings in his house? Who would want to implicate Alex in his murder? That made no sense—unless Warren was right, and it was Lundquist who had sent the notes and pushed her, Lundquist who had uncovered her past and the newspaper clippings and was planning to blackmail her with them.

As for placing Lundquist at the ledge of the Jacuzzi, the killer had obviously taken advantage of Lundquist's note to Alex and tried to set her up as a suspect. Or tried to make it look as if Lundquist were still alive at nine o'clock so that the killer could establish an alibi for himself. Or maybe the killer just had a bizarre sense of humor.

Today, Alex had almost convinced herself that Lundquist's murderer and her own tormentor were separate individuals, drawn together by a grim coincidence. Then Ron had phoned.

His call had upset and confused her and awakened her suspicions.

Alex went downstairs, resolved to ask Warren about Denise, but when she stepped into his office, she realized that this wasn't the place. Here, sitting against a background of bookcases filled with heavy tomes, he was a lawyer, not a husband or a friend.

"Are you coming to bed, Warren?"

"Soon." He looked up at her briefly, then returned to his papers. "Don't wait up for me."

Don't call us. We'll call you. His earlier embrace *had* been for show, Alex realized.

She waited anyway. When he came upstairs, she was pretending to read, but she was busy rehearsing how to begin. Nothing seemed right. She put her book on the nightstand. Simpler is better, she decided.

"Ron called today," she said. "He was very supportive. He apologized for his behavior and explained it."

Warren emptied his pockets and put his wallet and coins on the dresser. "I'm sure he was inventive. Ron's very smooth."

"Until a few weeks ago, he was your best friend."

"Best friends don't paw each other's wives." He took off his slacks, held them upside down, aligned the creases, and hung the slacks on his valet hanger. "So what did he say?"

"That he was upset because Denise had a thing for you."

Warren turned toward Alex. "That's ridiculous! Denise and I are close friends, nothing more. Ron's trying to make trouble."

"Maybe." The thought had occurred to her. "Did you ever go out with Denise?"

"Alex." His voice was tight with impatience. And warning.

She didn't care. "Denise told me that after Andrea died, people thought the two of you would get together."

"Where is this leading? Are you trying to prove that Denise sent you the notes and pushed you? Christ, I thought you agreed Lundquist did that. It's the only thing that makes sense."

"Did you tell Denise about the doll?"

"What doll? Oh, the doll." He frowned. "No. Why?"

"She knew about it. She mentioned it to me the other day, but I never told her about it."

Warren was silent. He started unbuttoning his shirt.

"Whoever wrote the notes found out about my past by using my phone bills, Warren. Denise was at the preschool, helping clean up after the place was vandalized. It was the perfect opportunity for her to have access to my files, unnoticed."

"A lot of people had opportunity. Evelyn, Patty, Paula."

And Lisa, Alex added to herself. Had Warren forgotten that Lisa had gone with him at night to help clean up the preschool, or was he deliberately not mentioning her name and hoping that Alex had forgotten?

"Evelyn and Patty didn't need to wait for an opportunity," Alex continued. "They have access all the time." She paused. "Denise claims she wasn't in the office. Paula insists she saw Denise there when she first arrived. You brought Paula, Warren. Did you see Denise in the office?"

"I'm not sure. There were so many people around."

"Why are you trying to protect her, Warren?"

"I'm not trying to protect her, damn it!" He yanked at one of the buttonholes on his shirt. The button snapped off and dropped soundlessly to the floor. He made no move to look for it. "I said I'm not sure because it's the truth, all right?"

"All right."

He undid the rest of the buttons, rolled the shirt into a ball, and tossed it into the corner.

"Did you go out with her?" Alex asked again.

He hesitated, then said, "I wouldn't call it *dating,* Alex. We saw each other once in a while. Mostly, we talked about Andrea, how we missed her."

"Did you sleep with her, Warren?" She knew the answer from the expression on his face.

"Once." His clipped, terse tone told her he was angry at the question.

"I'm sorry. I guess *your* past is none of my business."

"I suppose I deserved that." He paused. "We both knew right away it was a mistake. We did it out of loneliness, I guess. Or maybe subconsciously we thought that if we got together, everything would be almost the same as before Andy died. I don't know." He sat on the edge of the bed and faced Alex.

"It was just the one time," he repeated. "I didn't tell you because I thought it would make things awkward between you and Denise, and I really wanted the two of you to get along.''

"I understand."

"Don't let on that I told you. She'd be terribly embarrassed.''

"I won't." Alex picked up her book.

"Denise didn't send the notes or the doll. She's not like
that."

"Somebody sent them. If it wasn't Lundquist—"

"Of *course* it was Lundquist! My God, do you realize what
you're saying? If it wasn't Lundquist, then someone planted
those newspaper clippings in his house, and that person killed
him. Do you really believe that Denise is a murderer?''

Denise. Or Paula. Or Lisa, whose bloodstained blouse had
been hidden under a pile of towels.

"I guess not," Alex said, opening her book.

Chapter 27

What was taking so long?

By now the police should have arrested Alex for Lundquist's murder and put her in jail. Alex didn't kill Lundquist, but she killed her own child, so that was exactly where she belonged—in jail.

She knew the police suspected Alex—they had to! They'd found the packet of photos and the newspaper clippings. That had been a wonderful idea, putting the clippings in Lundquist's house. And Alex hadn't reported finding Lundquist's body. That was very damning. And stupid.

She'd been upset when Warren had hired a lawyer for Alex—why would he do that! After everything Alex had done! But of course Warren had to do it, so people wouldn't talk. She was his wife, after all. The mother of his new baby.

But it didn't mean he loved Alex. And it didn't mean he'd forgive her. How could he forgive her for killing her own child, and for lying to him all this time?

Warren had talked to her about Alex—"This is very hard for Alex," he'd told her. "She needs our help and understanding." At first she'd been shocked—how could he want to help her?—but then she'd realized he was just going through the motions, saying the things he thought he should be saying. He didn't believe them.

She had gone through the motions, too—"I feel terrible for Alex. Tell me how I can help, what I can do." But of course, he hadn't known she was pretending, and he'd been touched by her concern and understanding.

Still, she didn't know what was taking so long! She wanted it to be over. She wanted Alex out of her life so that things could be the way they were before she arrived and ruined *everything. But what if the lawyer found a way to get Alex off? That could happen, and she would hate it!*

But it won't be a disaster, she told herself. She was sitting on her bed, hugging herself and rocking steadily back and forth. Alex would still have to go away. Her picture had been in the paper—both pictures—and even if the police couldn't prove Alex had killed Donald Lundquist, everyone would think so. Alex would feel everyone staring at her wherever she went, wondering if she'd killed Lundquist, knowing she'd killed her son. Her husband, Larry, had said so, so it was true.

Soon Alex would see that she couldn't stay here, that she was ruining Warren's life, and Nicholas's, too, that she had to leave and start over somewhere else. At least she'd have the baby.

She nodded. Everything was going to turn out all right. All she had to do was be patient.

And careful. She frowned. She had to be very careful. Lately, Alex was asking a lot of questions. The other day she'd had the feeling that Alex was seeing right through her, that Alex knew what she'd done!

That was silly. Alex couldn't know.

It was taking too long!

She was rocking faster. What if Alex convinced Warren that she hadn't done anything wrong? She could try to seduce him with her body. He was only human. What if she tricked him into making love to her again? What if she made him believe her? That could happen. She knew it could. Alex had done it before. She'd gotten him to marry her. She'd tricked him into making her pregnant.

If that happened, she decided, if she had the slightest sus-picion that Warren was weakening, she would have to prove to him that Alex couldn't be trusted. But how could she do that? How . . . ?

She stopped rocking. Nicholas, she whispered.

If she had to, if things started going wrong, she would get Warren to believe that Alex was negligent around Nicholas. Warren would never forgive her then. Never.

Of course, she wouldn't let anything bad happen to Nich-olas. She loved Nicholas. Nobody could say she didn't. She would do her very best to make sure he was all right. And if something did happen to him—some little thing—everybody would know that it was Alex's fault.

She would do it only if she had to.

Chapter 28

Everyone was watching her—Warren, Paula, Lisa. Alex was aware of their furtive looks, the awkward smiles that didn't cover their embarrassment. Only Nicholas was carefree, oblivious. Being around him was a balm to her jangled nerves.

There was nothing in the *Los Angeles Times* on Saturday morning. Alex had checked. There were several phone calls about the story and the pictures in the newspaper. Warren handled them all. They were mostly from friends, he reported, one from the persistent reporter who wanted Alex to tell her side of the story.

Denise called in midmorning. Alex was in the family room with Warren when he answered the call, and she knew immediately that it was Denise from the awkward, guarded note that crept into his voice and from the fact that he wasn't looking at her. "Everything's fine," he said into the receiver. "Alex appreciates your call, and she'll get back to you."

Toward noon, Paula left to go shopping. Warren was taking Lisa and Nicholas to a movie. Did Alex want to come along? No, thanks, she told him. She was in no mood to see a movie, and the truth was that she relished being in the house by herself, not having to watch people watching her.

A short while after they left, the phone rang. Alex hesitated. What if it was the reporter again? Or Denise? After three rings she picked up the receiver. If it was someone she didn't want to talk to, she would just hang up.

"Yes?"

"Alex?"

It was Evelyn. Alex would have to talk to her sooner or later. And explain. "I know you called yesterday, Evelyn. I wasn't up to talking. I hope you understand."

"Of course I understand. I just wanted to make sure you're all right."

"Evelyn—"

"God, that's dumb! Of course you're not all right! You must be going through hell. I'm so sorry, Alex."

This was the hard part. "Evelyn, you're probably wondering why I never told you about my son. It's just—"

"Alex, that's none of my business. Don't apologize."

"It isn't that I didn't trust you, Evelyn. You know how much I value our friendship. I couldn't talk about it to anyone, not even Warren."

"Is he angry?" she asked quietly.

"More hurt than angry. I can't blame him."

"He'll come around, Alex. He loves you."

"I guess. In the meantime, it's awful around here. Evelyn, did the police contact you?"

"Thursday afternoon. They asked me what time I picked you up, how long you were in Lundquist's house. I said less than ten minutes. Is that all right?"

"It's fine, Evelyn. That's what I told them, too."

"I told them it was my idea to go to the coffee shop. I don't know if they believed me."

"It's okay. I'm not the only suspect, thank God." Alex repeated what Detective Rowan had said about Lundquist's wife and his business associates. "I hope it's not Sally Lundquist."

"She's not your problem. The main thing is that this whole ordeal will be over soon, and your life will be back to normal."

Alex had forgotten what "normal" was. "I hope so. In any case, I have to get on with my life. I'm coming to work Monday."

"Are you sure that's a good idea?"

"Pearson said it's okay. I'm still sore, but I'm managing."

"I didn't mean physically. I meant—"

"I have to face the world, Ev. I can't hide forever."

Although that's exactly what I'm doing today, she thought as she hung up. Hiding at home, putting my life on hold until the police exonerate me and Warren forgives me. That could take weeks, months. She wondered whether she would still be living under a cloud of suspicion and guilt when the baby arrived, less than four months from now. She hated the thought.

She was filled with a sudden need to be busy, to do something positive. She would start remodeling the nursery. The room needed wallpaper, and linoleum instead of the worn carpeting. Or maybe she'd have the floor refinished. She found Warren's tape measure in the tool chest in the service porch and was measuring the walls when she heard the doorbell.

She felt a pang of anxiety—she didn't want to see anyone— but reminded herself that she wasn't hiding anymore. She left the tape measure in the room and went downstairs.

It was Mona and Stuart, she saw through the peephole. Alex hesitated, then opened the door.

"Hello, dear," Mona said when she was in the entry hall. "How are you?" She was scrutinizing Alex's face.

"Fine, thank you." Alex forced herself to smile. "Warren and the kids went to a movie."

"Oh? Well, we'll wait."

"I don't know when they'll be back. They might go somewhere else after the movie."

Stuart said, "We can come later, Mona." He sounded uncomfortable.

He probably doesn't know what to say to me, Alex thought. "I'll tell Warren and the kids that you were here."

Mona touched Alex's arm. "Alex, dear, Stuart and I know this is a difficult time for you, and we want to help. I've discussed this with Stuart, and he agrees. We'd be happy to take the children for a while, for as long as you need, until you get your life back together."

"That's not necessary, Mona. Although I appreciate the offer. I'll be fine."

"And what about the children? Will they be fine?"

"I don't know what you mean." Her hands were fists. Her nails dug into her palms.

"Alex, dear. Your photo has been in the paper. They'll probably run more articles about you. We don't blame you, of course, but do you really want to subject Nicholas and Lisa to that kind of notoriety?"

Stuart said, "Mona, let's discuss this another time."

Mona turned to him. "You said it was a good idea."

"Alex obviously doesn't think so. Let's not force the issue, all right?"

"I'm only saying what other people are thinking, Stuart." Mona turned back to Alex. "You should go away for a while, dear. Maybe you could stay with your parents, or with friends. You must have some friends back home."

"Mona!" Stuart's tone was a whip. His face was red.

"Would you excuse me, please?" Alex said quietly. "I'm in the middle of fixing up the nursery for our baby."

"I apologize for my wife, Alex. Let's go." He opened the door, took Mona's arm, and steered her outside.

"I'm only thinking about the children," Mona said. "You don't want them traumatized by this, do you, Alex? They've been through enough, especially Lisa, poor thing. First her mother's death, now this. They need stability. They need—"

Alex shut the door and leaned against it. Then she went upstairs, picked up the tape measure, and started writing figures on a pad of paper.

"I'm sorry." Warren's lips were set in a grim line. "Mona had no right talking to you like that."

They were in their bedroom. With Nicholas and Lisa in the family room and Paula a ubiquitous presence wandering around the house, this was the only refuge for private conversation.

"She claims she's saying what everyone else is thinking," Alex said. "She's probably right."

"She's *not* right. She's a meddling fool. I'll talk to her."

My hero, Alex thought, pleasantly surprised. She'd never heard him upset with Mona before. In fact, she'd debated telling him what Mona had said; she had dreaded his reaction— a stoic what-now? sigh, and a defense of his former mother-in-law.

"Don't," Alex said. "You'll just make it worse."

There was a knock on the door.

"Come in," Warren called.

The door opened; Nicholas entered the room. "I'm ready for my bath, Mommy. Can I have bubbles?"

"Absolutely." She smiled at him—he always made her smile, she realized—and waited until he left the room. "Let it go, Warren. Really. I'm not upset anymore. I just had to vent.''

He squeezed her hand. "I'm glad you told me."

In Nicholas's bathroom, Alex turned on the tub faucets, adjusting the water so that it wasn't too hot. She poured in bubble lotion, waited until the tub was filled, then shut off the faucets. She went into Nicholas's bedroom. He was sitting at his desk, coloring.

"The water's set, Nick. Lots of bubbles."

" 'Kay." He put down his crayon and got off his chair.

"Call me when you're ready."

She waited in the hall outside his partially closed door while he undressed. A minute passed. "Nicholas?" she called.

"Not yet!"

She saw Warren walking up the stairs and smiled at him.

"Bath done?" he asked.

"Not even started."

"I'm in, Mommy!" Nicholas called. "I surprised you!"

"Be right there!" Alex said.

"You let him get into the tub by himself?" Warren was frowning.

Alex felt her face getting hot. "He's five years old, Warren. He's shy about getting undressed in front of me."

"He could hurt himself."

"I've taught him how to do it safely. Usually I wait right outside his bathroom door."

"I still don't think it's a good idea. It's dangerous."

"You never worried about my giving Nicholas a bath before. What's wrong, Warren? Are you afraid I'll let him drown? Are you going to have me supervised from now on?"

He reached for her arm. "Alex—"

She jerked her arm out of his reach, pushed the door open, and slammed it behind her.

"Mommy?"

"Coming, sweetie." Biting her lip to keep from crying, she entered the bathroom. "Okay, mister. Let's see who can make bigger bubble balls."

Ten minutes later, when they were done, she barely remembered sitting at the side of the tub, watching him bathe himself. Because of her ribs and collarbone, she couldn't lift him after he stepped out of the tub into the towel she wrapped around him, but she followed him to his room and completed the ritual by tickling him as he lay on his bed.

When he was in his pajamas, she came back into his room and sang him a lullaby. Then she kissed him good night.

Her purse was in her room. She took it downstairs with her. Warren appeared at the foot of the staircase.

"Alex, can we talk?" he said quietly.

"Not now." She walked by him and headed for the side door.

He followed her. "Where are you going?"

She didn't answer. She opened the door and walked out. She would have liked to slam the door, but she didn't want to give Paula the satisfaction of knowing that everything was rotten in the house of Prescott.

She wasn't sure where she wanted to go, but she had to go somewhere, anywhere away from the house. She decided to go to Evelyn's. It was a fifteen-minute drive, not a terrible waste of time in case she wasn't home. Alex didn't want to be alone with her thoughts, so she turned on the radio. Billy Ray Cyrus was singing "Achy Breaky Heart." She turned off the radio and drove the rest of the way in silence.

The lights were on in the front rooms of Evelyn's house. There was another car in the driveway, behind Evelyn's Corolla—Jerry's car. Alex remembered that Evelyn had told her she and Jerry would be spending the evening together at her house. Alex turned the Jeep around and headed north.

By now her anger had seeped out of her, like pus from a wound, but she still didn't feel like going home. She drove around for a while, all the way north of Malibu, then east along Sunset, following the serpentine boulevard past the darkened, secluded gated community of Bel Air, past the flats of Beverly Hills, to the garish, neon-lit Strip. On La Brea she turned left to Hollywood Boulevard, then right.

She decided to see a movie. She parked in the theater lot, walked from the lot around the corner to Hollywood Boulevard, and asked for a ticket.

"The movie started twenty minutes ago," the cashier said.

"That's okay."

She paid for the ticket and went inside. The theater was crowded, but she found an aisle seat toward the front. She had to tilt her head back to see the figures on the screen, but she didn't care. From the audience's laughter, she figured the movie was a comedy.

"Want some popcorn?" the man next to her asked.

"No, thanks."

"You sure?"

"I'm not hungry."

"I am, sweet mama."

She turned her head. He was grinning and ogling her breasts. She stood up, left the theater, and drove home.

Warren was in their bedroom when she came home. He clicked off the television when he saw her and stood up.

"I'm glad you're back, Alex," he said quietly. "I was worried."

"I'm perfectly capable of taking care of myself." She put her purse on the floor near her side of the bed. She didn't want to stay in the room with him. She didn't want to leave.

"I know you're hurt, Alex." He walked around the bed until he was standing in front of her.

"You're a lawyer, Warren. You're paid to be observant."

He sighed and ran his hands through his hair. "Look, I know how it must have seemed. I want to explain—"

"There's not a goddamn thing to explain, all right?" She was yelling, and she didn't care if Lisa or Paula or the world heard her. "You don't trust me as a mother, Warren. Mona doesn't, either, but at least she's honest enough to say so."

"Mona's wrong, Alex. I told you that."

"You've been watching me. Don't you think I've seen you? You asked Paula to come back so she could watch me, too."

He shook his head. "That's ridiculous."

"Is it? Can you honestly tell me there isn't a tiny part of you that's worried about leaving Nicholas in my care? Can you?"

"I trust you with him implicitly, Alex." He rested his hand on her shoulder. "I swear it."

"I would never leave him alone in the tub, never! I'm always right there."

"I know," he said softly. He drew her toward him. She didn't resist. "I overreacted. I wasn't thinking."

"I'm always careful around water, don't you know that?" she said in a mournful voice. Her face was against his chest. "In Sea World I thought I would die when Nicholas was on the whale's back. I almost didn't marry you because of the swimming pool. I *hate* the pool!''

"We'll sell the house if you want, Alex. I mean that.'' He stroked her hair.

"I don't want to sell the house. I want you to trust me.'' She was crying.

"I trust you, Alex. I love you. And I am so goddamn sorry. Please forgive me.''

He lifted her face and wiped her tears. He kissed her. His lips were gentle at first, almost tentative, then more insistent.

"Alex.'' His whisper was almost a groan.

They undressed quickly, and then he was touching her, kissing her mouth, her neck, her breasts. She clasped her arms around him, pressing herself tight against him, loving the feel of his bare skin against hers. There was something different in their lovemaking, something tender and at the same time bittersweet, more urgent and intense than usual. She wanted it to go on forever.

Later, as she was falling asleep, she wondered if the "something different'' was shared guilt.

Chapter 29

On Monday morning only eleven of the twenty-four preschoolers showed up.

"Maybe they're late," Evelyn said, but her voice lacked conviction. "Or maybe they have chicken pox. Jason had chicken pox last week and—"

"It isn't chicken pox," Alex said. "And they're not late. They're not coming back." Just like three years ago. *You can't run away from your guilt, Alexandra,* her parents had said. Obviously, they were right.

Ever since her picture had appeared in the Venice paper, Alex had worried about the reaction of her students' parents, but she hadn't been prepared for this wholesale defection. In a sense, the weekend had calmed her fears. The police hadn't bothered her. Friends had called again to offer their love and support. Most importantly, Warren had forgiven her—Sunday night they had made love again. Now she was angry with herself for deluding herself, for not fortifying herself against what was inevitable. She couldn't blame the parents, not really. Who would entrust a child to the care of a woman who was a suspect in a murder investigation? A woman whose only child had died because of her own neglect?

The morning passed quickly enough. At noon, the parents for the part-time preschoolers came to pick up their children. Alex could have sent the children outside with Evelyn, but she forced herself to lead them to the curb and smile as their parents drove up. Did they know? she wondered. Some seemed to stare at her; others seemed to be avoiding looking at her directly. Maybe not. Maybe it was all in her imagination.

During nap time, Alex went into her office, pulled out the school roster, and made the first call.

"Mrs. Alters?" Alex said when the woman answered.

"This is Alexandra Prescott, from the preschool. I wondered if Jennifer was all right."

"Oh, Mrs. Prescott. Jennifer has a cold."

"Will she be coming tomorrow?"

"Tomorrow?" A short pause. "I don't think so. Actually, I'm not sure when she'll be back. Her resistance is low, and I don't want her picking anything up. You understand."

"Of course. Please tell Jennifer we miss her and hope to see her soon."

Alex hung up and called the next name on her list.

" . . . always felt Jeremy was a little young for preschool, so we're letting him take a few weeks off. You understand."

" . . . and Shawn's been unhappy with some of the children in the school, you see, so we're trying a different school. I should have called earlier. . . . "

Only one mother was honest. "I'm sorry, Mrs. Prescott. You seem like a very nice person, but my husband and I don't feel comfortable leaving Peggy there, under the circumstances. First the vandalism, and now . . . Maybe it isn't fair to you, but we have to do what we think is right for Peggy. If things change . . . "

Alex had been pained by the conversation but had found it refreshing after all the blatantly false excuses she'd heard.

After she made the last call, she walked into the classroom and looked at the sleeping children. There were only four left. *Ten little Indians . . .*

She wondered how many there would be tomorrow.

"Bastards!" Warren exclaimed in an undertone. His eyes and the tight line of his mouth showed his anger. "Why didn't you tell me right away?"

"I wanted to enjoy our night out."

Warren had called after she'd come home from work and suggested that they go out to dinner. "Just the two of us," he'd said. "You pick the place."

She'd hesitated—what if she encountered people she knew? Worse yet, what if strangers who recognized her from her photo in the paper accosted her or stared at her? *That's Alexandra Trent!* But she'd said yes. It was important for her and Warren to reestablish the rhythms of their marriage out of the bedroom, and she craved an evening away from Paula, who made her feel like an interloper, and from Lisa. Alex was filled with awkwardness around her stepdaughter, alternately reading pity and guilt into everything the girl did or said. As far as facing other people, Alex would have to do it sooner or later. Sooner was better; hiding would only be interpreted as a sign of guilt.

So she'd made reservations at the beachfront restaurant where they'd had their first date, and they had both been careful to keep the conversation light and unencumbered. Then Warren had asked how her first day back at work had gone.

Now he reached across the table and took her hand. "You don't need the school, Alex. In a few months you'll be busy with the baby, and you won't miss it."

"That's not the point. I love running a preschool. I love the kids. I don't want to give it up."

"Do you want me to call the parents?"

Alex shook her head. Evelyn had offered the same thing. "It won't help. Right now they don't have confidence in me, Warren. I don't really blame them. I don't know that I'd want my child in a preschool owned by a murder suspect."

"That's going to be cleared up, Alex."

"When? A week from now? A month? By then all the parents will have pulled out their kids."

"You said yourself that the police are checking into Lundquist's wife and business associates." Warren squeezed her hand. "You'll see. They'll find out who killed him, Alex, and all this will be behind us."

And what if it's not Lundquist's wife or a business associate? she wondered. Will it still be behind us?

Eight children showed up at the preschool on Tuesday. Alex called Patty and explained the situation.

"So there's no point in your coming in today," Alex said. "Of course, I'll pay you for today. About tomorrow—"

"I'm sure this is just a fluke, Alex."

"I hope you're right. I'll have to let you know."

Alex felt a rush of gratitude toward Patty. From Evelyn, Alex knew that the aide had read of Alex's plight, but there had been no clandestine stares yesterday, no awkward silence, just cheerful support.

To Alex, the classroom seemed to echo failure. The children

were busily working on collages, but four of the six activity tables were pointedly empty. Later, during story time, the eight children formed a pathetically sparse circle. Alex went through the motions—playing, showing, coloring, reading.

At one o'clock, Paula called. "I just brought Nicholas home," she told Alex. "The principal phoned and suggested that I get him."

Alex paled. "What's wrong? Is he sick?"

"Not exactly." She paused. "He's upset. One of the older boys taunted him about . . . well . . . what appeared in the newspapers. He told Nicholas you were going to jail."

"Oh, God!" Alex cried.

"Apparently Nicholas called the boy a liar and hit him. The boy hit him back, and Nicholas has a cut lip. The school nurse put ice on it, but it was still quite swollen when I got there. I'll put ice packs on it for a while."

"Thank you, Paula. I'll be right home." Three of the children had gone home at noon, leaving only five. Evelyn could easily handle them by herself.

"You don't have to rush. I have everything under control."

In spite of the housekeeper's reassurance, Alex went home early. She entered through the side door, as she usually did, and found Paula in the kitchen peeling potatoes.

"Where's Nicholas?" she asked.

"In his room, playing with Lego."

"How's his lip?"

"Better. The swelling's almost gone. I told you that you needn't have come home early, Alex."

"I want to talk to Nicholas."

Paula frowned and put the peeler on the counter. "Do you think that's a good idea? It'll only upset him all over again. It took me forever to calm him down, poor boy."

The implication was clear—all this was Alex's fault. "Thanks for your advice, Paula."

Nicholas was sitting on the carpeted floor surrounded by tiny red, yellow, blue, and white Lego pieces. He was building a tower. Alex walked over to him and sat cross-legged beside him.

"Rough day?" she said quietly.

He nodded.

"Want to talk about it?"

He glanced at her quickly and shook his head. She was pained by the split in his lip and by the bewilderment and awkwardness in his eyes.

"How's your lip?" she asked.

"Okay."

"Paula said you punched someone. He must have made you angry, huh?"

Without looking at Alex, Nicholas said, "Christopher Rakin said you might go to jail for killing someone. Then he said . . . he said you let your own son die, so I hit him. He hit me back." He looked up at Alex. His lips were trembling.

Alex took his hand. "Nick, I'm so sorry you had to go through this. You're a smart boy, and I hope you'll understand what I'm going to tell you. Remember that man who was talking to you at school? The one who was bothering us?"

Nicholas nodded. "Bobby's father."

"Right. His name was Donald Lundquist. Someone killed him, and the police asked me questions about him because I knew him and Bobby was in my school."

"Were you scared?"

"Yes. But the police will find out who killed him." God, she hoped that was true! "About letting my son die—"

"I told Christopher he was a stupid liar! I told him you don't even have a son, right, Mommy?" His eyes were riveted on her face.

"I *did* have a son, Nicholas," Alex said gently. "He drowned in our swimming pool. And it *was* my fault, because I left him alone and he went outside."

"But that's not on purpose." His eyes were somber. "Is that why you always tell me not to go near the pool by myself?"

"Yes."

"What was his name?"

She cleared her throat. "Kevin. He was four years old."

"Do you miss him?"

"Very much," Alex whispered. She stroked Nicholas's hair.

"I don't miss my mother. I was a little baby when she died, so I don't remember her. I asked Lisa and Daddy, but they don't like to talk about her." He paused. "Paula tells me about her, and sometimes she shows me pictures, like today. Paula says my mother's in Heaven and she's watching over me.''

"I'm sure she is, Nick. I'm sure she loves you very much.''

Nicholas picked up a blue tile and snapped it into place. Alex handed him another tile, and another, and wondered what he was thinking.

Nicholas suddenly looked up at Alex. "Maybe she's taking care of your little boy. My mother, I mean. 'Cause you're taking care of me.''

"Maybe.'' Her eyes glistened with tears.

Nicholas nodded and continued erecting his tower. A moment later he said, "I'm not sorry I punched Christopher.''

"Punching is never the answer, Nick. Talk to me if you're upset about something. Or talk to Daddy.''

"Okay.'' He moved closer to Alex. "But you're not going to jail, right?''

"Right.''

Lisa and Nicholas ate supper at six o'clock. Alex had told Paula that she would eat with Warren, who had called to say he'd be late. "I'll wait, too,'' Paula had said, and Alex didn't know how to tell the woman politely that she preferred eating supper alone with her husband. Had Paula always eaten with Andrea and Warren?

At dinner, Paula did most of the talking. "How are the minute steaks?'' she asked Warren.

"Delicious. Aren't they, Alex?''

"Delicious.''

"I prepared them just the way you always liked them, Warren. Nicholas loved them, too. He seems much better now. I hope nothing happens tomorrow to upset him again.''

Alex tensed.

"What do you mean?'' Warren looked puzzled. "What happened?''

"I'm sorry, Alex.'' Paula smiled self-consciously. "I assumed you'd told Warren about Nicholas's fight and his lip.''

Warren glanced at Alex. She felt herself blushing.

"I'll get dessert.'' Paula stood and left the room.

Was that a smirk on the housekeeper's face? "Nicholas got into a fight with Christoper Rakin,'' Alex began. She told Warren what had happened. "I talked with Nicholas. He understands.''

"Why didn't you tell me?"

"I was going to tell you, after supper. I didn't want to bother you with it when you were at the office."

"Okay," Warren said. His eyes said otherwise.

"She did this on purpose, you know. She's trying to make trouble between us."

Warren sighed. "Alex, we've been all through this. Paula is a good woman and she's dedicated to the family."

"She talks to Nicholas about Andrea. She shows him pictures of her."

"Alex." He sighed again. "I can understand how that might make you feel awkward, but is there anything wrong with it?"

Was there? "I guess not," Alex admitted.

On Wednesday there were nine children—the same eight who had come yesterday and one more: Bobby Lundquist. Alex stared as he walked into the classroom with his mother, then quickly regained her composure.

"Hi, Bobby. It's nice to have you back." He looked pale, Alex thought, and there were dark circles under his eyes.

"Hi." He marched to his cubby and put his lunch box inside.

Sally Lundquist said, "Can I talk to you privately, Mrs. Prescott?"

Alex led her into her office. "I'm glad to see that you and Bobby are all right."

"I don't know about 'all right.' We're managing. I had to tell him Donald was dead. It was awful."

How had she known her husband was dead? Where had she been? "The police questioned me about the murder," Alex said. The statement came out more accusatory than she had intended. She blushed.

"I know. I've been in contact with someone at the shelter, and she told me there'd been an article in the local paper." Sally sighed. "I feel responsible about what happened to you."

"You're not. It was just a coincidental chain of events."

"Maybe. I know the police tried to reach me. I left the shelter the same day Donald was killed. I was afraid the police would think I killed him." She paused. "I went to the house that night. I didn't know you'd be there. I'd called him again that afternoon. Bobby wanted to talk to him, and I didn't think it was right not to let him. After Bobby talked to his father, Donald asked to talk to me. I should have said no, but I couldn't. I could never say no to Donald.

"Anyway, he was real sweet on the phone. He promised he'd be different. He swore he'd get help. I wanted to believe him, I guess. I was tired of living at the shelter, and Bobby was so miserable. So I decided I'd talk to him alone. I didn't tell Donald I was coming. I just went to the house. And I found him dead, sitting in the Jacuzzi. At first I thought he was alive, but then I saw his neck and his chest." She shuddered. "Whoever propped him up like that is really sick."

If Sally Lundquist found her husband *sitting* in the Jacuzzi, she could prove he was dead before Alex arrived! "What time was this?"

"Around eight-thirty. I went back to the shelter, packed, took Bobby, and got on a flight to Phoenix. That's where my parents live."

"Why did you come back?"

"I heard from someone at the shelter that the police suspected you. It isn't right. I'm going to the police right now and tell them Donald was dead before you got there."

Alex felt like hugging her. "Thank you." She hesitated, then said, "They might think you killed him."

"I know. But I couldn't live with myself if I didn't tell the truth. I didn't kill him, you know," she added.

After Sally Lundquist left, Alex called Warren and told him what had happened.

"I'll tell Margot right away," he said, "and have her call Detective Rowan in an hour or so."

An hour? "Why not now? I want this nightmare to be over!"

"So do I, Alex, but we have to give Mrs. Lundquist time to talk to the police. Try to be patient."

It was almost two hours before Warren called back.

"Rowan spoke with Mrs. Lundquist, Alex, but he said that since they don't have a time of death, the fact that she saw him at eight-thirty doesn't prove much."

"But I spoke to him at eight!"

"They have only your word for that, Alex. You can't prove that, can you?"

"No." She thought for a moment, then said, "What about the phone company? Don't they keep a computer log of calls made?"

"I thought of that. And yes, they do, even for local calls. I mentioned that to Rowan. He said he'll subpoena the records."

"So I'll be cleared!"

"Not really," Warren said quietly. "According to Rowan, even if the records show that a call was made from our number to Lundquist's, that doesn't prove that Lundquist was alive when you called."

"But I talked to him, Warren! He answered the phone! Won't the records show that the call was answered?"

"The records will show that the call was answered," Warren said patiently, "but Lundquist had an answering machine. Rowan suggested that the answering machine picked up your call."

"That doesn't make sense. If that happened, the tape would still have my message."

"Not if you erased it when you went back at nine. That's what Rowan suggested, Alex." Warren added quickly, "I know that's not what happened. He's implying that you killed Lundquist earlier, called him at eight to establish that he was alive and give yourself an alibi, then erased the tape later."

"But I *couldn't* have killed Lundquist earlier, Warren. I was home all day. Paula can vouch for that." She could sense Warren's hesitation in the silence that followed. "What's wrong?" she asked.

"The police already talked to her, Alex. She left the house twice that Tuesday—to go marketing, and to pick up Nicholas and Lisa from school between three and four in the afternoon."

"This is ridiculous," Alex protested, but of course it wasn't, not to the police. They were just doing their job.

She managed to push thoughts of Donald Lundquist and the police out of her mind by keeping busy with the children. Later, on the way to pick up Nicholas, she was glum again, but her mood lightened when she saw his smile. Everything had gone well today, he told her. Christopher Rakin hadn't bothered him.

Paula was rearranging the linen closets when Alex and Nicholas came home. She was refolding all the towels and sheets the way she liked them, and Alex was instantly annoyed. She'd shown her a hundred times . . .

Alex went into the kitchen and opened the refrigerator to take out the package of ground beef she'd removed from the freezer to defrost. There was no ground beef. She walked back upstairs to Paula.

"Paula, did you see the ground beef in the fridge?"

"I put it back in the freezer."

Alex counted to five. "Paula, I told you this morning that I was planning to use the beef for tonight's supper."

"We had steak yesterday. I don't think it's a good idea to have meat so often. I prepared breaded chicken. It's Lisa's favorite, you know."

"I planned to make meatballs and spaghetti. That's Nicholas's favorite, and Lisa loves it, too." This is totally idiotic, Alex told herself, and it's not about chicken or meat. In a calm voice, she began, "Paula—"

"I'll defrost the ground beef in the morning. We can have it tomorrow night." She took a sheet, folded it in half, held it against herself, and smoothed it.

"Paula, I appreciate everything you've done to help since I had my fall. I don't know how we would have managed without you. The fact is, though, that everything has settled down, and my bruises are basically healed." She was still achy and had to be careful about lifting objects, but she would manage. "So you see, we don't need a live-in housekeeper anymore."

Paula looked at Alex. "Warren asked me to move in. I didn't force myself on anyone." Her angular chin had a defiant thrust. She continued smoothing the sheet.

"Of course not." Alex forced patience into her voice.

"You'll need me when the baby comes. I'm very good with babies. I practically raised Lisa. I did everything for Nicholas after Andrea died."

"I know," Alex said gently. "I'm not sure yet what my plans are for after the baby comes."

"I don't believe you." She folded the sheet in half, then in thirds. "Why don't you admit it, Alex? You don't like me. That's why you're trying to get rid of me."

Maybe the woman was right; maybe this was the time for honesty, not diplomacy. "Paula, you have your ideas about running a household, and I have mine, and—''

''If you want, I'll defrost the ground beef.''

''It isn't just the ground beef. It's your attitude, Paula. You do the laundry the way you like to do it. You starch my nightgowns after I've repeatedly asked you not to. You rearrange the pantry and my closets and my drawers even though I've asked you not to. You often do the opposite of what I ask you.'' The grievances sounded petty even as she recited them, but Alex couldn't voice what she felt: *you're trying to be the mistress of this house.*

''It's hard to change. I'm used to the way I did things for Andrea.''

''I know. It must be difficult for you, seeing me in Andrea's place. I know you loved her very much.''

''She was the most wonderful woman I ever met.'' Paula's voice broke. Her lips quivered. ''And Nicholas, poor boy, doesn't even know her. No one even *talks* about her!'' She hugged the folded sheet to her body. ''That's why you don't like me, isn't it? Because I remind Warren and Lisa about Andrea. Well, they *should* be thinking about her. Denise remembers. We talk about her all the time, about the way things used to be.'' Her eyes filled with tears. She made no move to wipe them.

''Paula, I'm sorry for your pain. Really, I am.'' Alex paused, then said, ''I think you'd be happier working somewhere else.''

Paula stared at her, then blinked rapidly. ''What are you saying? That you're firing me?''

''I really think you'd be happier elsewhere,'' Alex repeated. ''Of course, I'll write you a recommendation. You have wonderful qualities. Or maybe Denise knows someone who needs help. And you can visit the kids. I know they'll want that.''

Paula shook her head. ''You can't fire me. Warren hired me. He *wants* me here. I'm part of the family.''

''Paula—''

''I can learn to do things your way. I didn't realize you were unhappy, but now that I know . . . ''

Even though Alex knew Paula was lying—every action had been calculated to make her feel unwanted—she was moved by the woman's near desperation, and for a second she was tempted to give in. Then she thought about the notes, and the doll, and she wondered why Paula was so anxious to stay.

"I'm sorry, Paula. I think we both need a change."

"I'm not going until Warren tells me to." Paula put the sheet in the linen closet. Then she bent down, picked up another sheet from the laundry basket, folded it in half lengthwise, and snapped it taut.

Alex turned and walked down the stairs.

Chapter 30

Alex had been keeping a vigil near the living room window from the time Warren had called to say he was on his way home. When she saw the Lexus turn into the driveway toward the two-car garage, she walked out the front door.

She didn't know where Paula was. The housekeeper had eaten supper with Lisa and Nicholas, then reset the table for Alex and Warren and disappeared into her room. Hurrying to meet Warren, Alex felt foolish, like a squabbling preschooler racing to tell teacher her side of the quarrel first. When she reached him, he'd pulled into the garage and was getting out of the car.

He looked at her, surprised. Then he frowned. "What's wrong? Is it Nicholas? Did that boy bother him again?"

The anger in his voice was tinged with weariness. She felt suddenly sorry for him, and wondered when she would stop being a source of concern, a burden. "Nicholas is fine. It's Paula. Can we talk in the backyard?"

Impatience flickered in his eyes. "Sure. Let me put my briefcase in my office."

Alex went outside to wait for him. It was still light out, and on an impulse, she walked to the redwood gym set she and Warren had picked out for Nicholas almost two years ago, and sat on one of the swings.

She heard the rumble of the sliding-glass door in its track. A moment later Warren was standing in front of her. His jaw was set, his eyes impassive.

Alex said, "Basically, I fired Paula, but she said you hired her, and she won't leave unless you tell her."

"What happened?"

Was that a sigh, she wondered, or the sea breeze ruffling the leaves on the nearby trees? "It isn't just today."

She told him about the ground beef, about the linens, about her starched nightgowns, about her feelings of being constantly undermined. "You probably think I'm being petty." She watched his face for signs of disgust but found only sadness.

"She told you she'd try to do things your way?"

Alex shook her head. "It won't work. I don't want her here, Warren. Not to live in, not twice a week, not even for an hour." She paused. "Paula's too attached to you and the kids. She's a part of your past with Andrea, and I can't live with it anymore. I *won't* live with it. You have to tell her."

"She's a good woman, Alex. She's trustworthy. The kids love her. You need more help in the house, and when the baby comes—"

"When the baby comes, I'll get a bonded sitter or a daytime nanny. But it won't be Paula. For now, I'll hire someone to help with the housework." She was silent for a moment. "You asked Paula to move in after you found out about Kevin. You wanted someone to watch over Nicholas when you weren't there to do it. I can't live like that."

"That's not true!"

"Isn't it? Be honest with yourself, Warren. Didn't the thought cross your mind, even for an instant?"

When he spoke, his voice was subdued. "I don't know. Maybe that was part of it. When I saw those papers, I felt as if my whole world had been turned upside down. You'd lied to me, Alex. You'd lied about everything. How could I trust you?"

"Thank you for being honest. I mean that."

"But that's all in the past. This has nothing to do with trust. I *do* trust you. It's just damn hard to tell a woman who's been with the family for over fourteen years that you don't want her around anymore."

Alex didn't answer. She pushed her foot against the grass and set the swing in motion.

"I'll tell Paula," he finally said.

She wondered whether part of his reluctance to fire Paula was that she was a reminder of his life with Andrea. He still couldn't discuss Andrea, not even after Alex had revealed her past. She'd broached the subject several times in the past few days; each time Warren had rebuffed her quietly but firmly.

She watched him as he walked back to the house and disappeared into the family room; then she turned her head toward the pool. She hated the pool, but she forced herself to stare at it, as if by doing so she could rob it of its power to torment her with images of her four-year-old son's cold, lifeless body.

She flashed to Lundquist's lifeless body sinking to the bottom of his Jacuzzi. *Bad things come in threes, Alexandra,* she heard her mother whisper in her ear. *Be careful.* That's ridiculous, Alex told herself. It's a stupid, superstitious old wives' tale. She reached underneath her sweater, grasped her heart-shaped locket, and waited for Warren to return.

"She's leaving tonight," Warren reported ten minutes later. His voice was devoid of emotion.

"What did she say?" Alex was still sitting on the swing.

"Not much. I asked her if she wanted to finish the week, but she said no, she wouldn't stay where she wasn't wanted. She was struggling to keep from crying. I felt like shit."

And I'm the villain, Alex thought, suddenly plagued by doubts. "I really tried to get along with her, Warren."

He shrugged. She slipped off the swing, and they walked back into the house together, though not arm in arm.

"What about supper?" she asked when they were in the hall off the family room. The table was set. The breaded chicken was on a platter on the counter, ready to be warmed.

"I'm not hungry. Maybe later."

Warren went to his office. Lisa and Nicholas were nowhere in sight; they were probably in their rooms. Reluctant to stay downstairs alone and confront Paula, Alex decided to go to her bedroom. Along the way to the staircase, she had to pass Paula's room and was relieved that the door was closed.

In her bedroom, as she lay on the floor and did leg stretches, she wondered how many children would show up in the morning. Today there had been nine, one more than yesterday, but that was because Bobby Lundquist had returned. She couldn't maintain the school with nine children. At some point she'd have to let Patty go, then Evelyn. At some point she'd have to close the school.

When Warren came in, Alex was studying the wallpaper samples she'd picked up for the nursery.

"Paula's packed," he said. "I'm going to put her luggage in her car. She's saying good-bye to the kids, and I thought you might want to say good-bye, too."

"Of course." She didn't want to, but she had to.

She followed Warren to the front hall. Paula was there, with Nicholas and Lisa at her side. All three wore funereal expressions.

Alex said, "Paula, I want to thank you again for everything you've done for us."

"You're quite welcome, Alex. I wish you all the best with the baby." She avoided looking at Alex. She turned to the children. "One more hug before I go."

Lisa and Nicholas hugged Paula simultaneously. Warren opened the door and picked up Paula's suitcases. Paula followed him outside and pulled the door shut behind her.

Nicholas said, "Lisa said you had a fight with Paula and you made Paula cry and that's why she's not going to be here anymore. How come, Mommy?"

Alex felt her face becoming flushed. "It's complicated, Nick." She didn't look directly at Lisa, but she could see from the corner of her eye that the girl was blushing, too.

"You have a big, fat mouth, Nicholas Prescott! I told you not to say anything." Lisa was glaring at her brother.

"But how come?" he repeated.

Alex said, "Paula's a wonderful woman, but she and I just didn't agree about some things. She's sad about leaving, of course, and I know you and Lisa will miss her."

"Paula said she'd visit. Do you think she will, Mommy?"

"Maybe." I hope not, she thought.

Nicholas nodded, then skipped off in the direction of the family room. Alex started to leave the entry hall.

"Alex," Lisa said.

Alex stopped and turned to face her stepdaughter.

"I'm sorry." Lisa was studying her hands. "Paula told me you had a fight. She was crying. And then Nicholas saw her packing and asked me why she was leaving. But I shouldn't have said anything to him." She looked up at Alex and pushed the curtain of blond hair behind her ear. "I'm sorry," she said again.

She sounded sincere, almost forlorn. Alex put her hand on

Lisa's arm. "I know the two of you are very close. I wouldn't blame you for being upset with me."

"I'm not upset with you. I can see why you'd want to get someone else. To tell you the truth, sometimes it's spooky, the way she keeps talking about my mom."

This was the first time Lisa had mentioned her mother to Alex. Was it an overture? If so, why now? "I didn't know you felt like that, Lisa."

The girl shrugged.

Alex hesitated. "Do you think—"

The door opened and Warren entered. "You women look serious." He put his arm around Lisa, then turned to Alex. "Everything okay?"

Alex wondered if by ridding the house of Paula she was not only helping banish Andrea's ghost but getting rid of the enemy. Unless, of course, the enemy was still within. She thought about the stained shirt and glanced at Lisa. The girl was leaning against her father, her arms around his waist.

"Everything's fine," Alex said.

On Thursday morning Bobby Lundquist didn't show.

"You can't count Bobby, Alex," Evelyn said after she and Alex had settled the preschoolers into their morning routine. "We still have eight. We're holding steady. That's a good sign."

"Eight kids do not a school make, Ev. I'm going to call Patty and tell her to look for another job. It's only fair. I think you should do the same."

Evelyn shook her head. "No way. I think you're right about Patty, though. You and I can manage until things are back to normal. And they *will* get back to normal. You'll see. Then, if Patty's already found another job, we can get someone else."

"You're an optimist." Alex smiled. "And a good friend."

Midmorning, Bobby Lundquist arrived. He looked paler, if possible, the circles around his eyes darker.

"I'm sorry he's late," Sally Lundquist said. She was speaking to Alex, but her eyes followed her son as he made his way to his cubby. "He was up most of the night, and when he finally fell asleep, I didn't want to wake him. We're staying at a hotel for now. I can't decide if I want to move back into the house, especially with the way Bobby feels.''

"Has he said anything about your husband's death?"

The woman closed her eyes briefly. When she opened them, they were moist with tears. "He blames himself. He says that once or twice when he saw Donald hitting me, he prayed Donald would die, and now he's dead. That's why Bobby can't sleep."

"Poor thing," Alex murmured.

"I'm going to take him to a child psychologist. The people at the shelter gave me a few names. I feel so bad for him." She sighed and wiped her eyes. "By the way, I *did* speak to the police. I told a detective that Donald was dead when I got to the house, which was before you arrived, so that should be the end of it for you. Did they call and tell you?"

"They don't know when your husband was killed. They think it could have been much earlier. I spoke to him at around eight o'clock in the evening, but I can't prove it."

"I'm sorry."

"It's not your fault. I really appreciate your trying. What about you? Are you . . . "

"A suspect?" A half smile pulled at Sally's lips. "Probably. The police weren't mean or anything. They just kept asking me the same questions over and over. To tell you the truth, I'm too worried about Bobby to be scared about myself."

"Who do you think killed him?"

"My lawyer thinks it was one of Donald's business connections. It seems Donald owed a lot of people a lot of money." Sally Lundquist looked at her watch. "Speaking of lawyers, I have to meet mine. I'll be back in time to pick up Bobby. By the way, I couldn't help noticing how few children there are. Yesterday I thought it was because I'd come early. Is there a virus I should know about?"

A virus of fear, Alex thought. Quietly, she told the woman her suspicions. "I can't prove it, of course. Only one of the parents I called was honest with me."

"This is terrible! And it's my fault, isn't it? If I hadn't talked to you about Bobby, and if Donald hadn't found out . . . "

"It isn't anyone's fault, except for the press's. And I really can't blame them for reporting news. Please don't worry about me, Mrs. Lundquist. You have enough on your mind."

"But your school—"

"I'd be lying if I said I wasn't worried or that I didn't care. I care very much. But worrying isn't going to help. I'm going to do what my husband advised, and take one day at a time."

It was sound advice, mature advice, and Alex tried to follow it. On Friday morning, as on every morning since the day Lundquist had been killed, she checked the local paper for regurgitated news about herself and was relieved to find nothing. (She would have loved to see herself exonerated in the press, but that belonged to the realm of fantasy.) She dropped Nicholas off at his school. She went to work—there were still nine children.

During recess, she called Warren. Had he heard anything from Margot Leibman? Nothing yet, he told her; he'd call as soon as he heard anything. Warren was probably becoming impatient with all her calls, she realized, but she knew that wouldn't stop her from calling him during lunch, and later, when she was home.

After work she picked up Nicholas, and, once home, she checked the mail chute. No hate note. There had been none since the one that had been tucked into the cavity in the doll. Alex wondered today, as she did every afternoon, whether the note-writer had stopped writing, permanently or temporarily, or whether the note-writer was Donald Lundquist, who lay in the morgue awaiting an autopsy. Warren believed it was Lundquist.

Alex wanted terribly to believe it, too. Until Lundquist's murder was solved, her life was in limbo.

Denise called the house late Sunday evening. Alex answered the phone.

"How are you, Alex?"

"I'm fine, thanks." Alex could hear the awkwardness in Denise's voice. "Did you want to talk to Warren? Or Lisa?"

"Actually, I called to talk to you about the baby shower."

Was the woman crazy? "Denise, you know my situation. A baby shower is the last thing on my mind right now."

"I think it would be the best thing for you, as a matter of fact. You need to have positive thoughts, and I can't think of anything more positive than the arrival of your baby, can you?''

"Denise—"

"Think about it, okay? Look, this is a tough time for you. I just want you to know that I'm behind you one hundred percent. So are all your friends, Alex. Remember that.''

"Thank you.''

"By the way, Paula told me you fired her.''

Alex was instantly on guard. "It wasn't working out.''

"Actually, I think it's for the best, for all of you. I've been thinking about what you said a while back. Maybe Paula *is* too attached to Warren and the kids.'' She paused. "I don't know if I should be telling you this, but I think Paula's problem might have to do with the fact that she had to give up her own child for adoption when he was three years old.''

Alex was stunned. "Paula has a child? I never knew that! I know she has a nephew. She kept his picture on her dresser.''

"There is no nephew.''

"But Warren—"

"Warren doesn't know the truth. I do. Paula confided in me long ago. She was young, and her husband had stomach cancer. They had no money, no support. She had no choice. She had to put her little boy in a foster home. She thought it would be for a short while, until she could get back on her feet. But her husband's illness dragged on, and, well, a wealthy family wanted to adopt her son. She thought it was the best thing for him.''

"My God!'' Alex whispered. "That's so sad. I feel terrible for her.''

"I do, too. But I'm wondering if her grief and bitterness over losing her child, plus the fact that you married Warren and more or less made her feel unnecessary—'' Denise stopped, then said, "Maybe she got carried away.''

"What are you saying? That Paula sent the notes?''

"I don't know. I don't think so, but I just don't know.''

Driving to school on Monday morning, Alex decided that if one more child dropped out, that would be a sign to shut down the preschool. At nine-thirty she stared at the boys and girls who filed into the classroom. When they were seated at the tables, she counted them twice, and then a third time. There were seventeen preschoolers.

Evelyn was staring, too. Then she broke into a wide smile. "It's a miracle. What did you do, call every parent over the weekend and promise them all free tuition?"

Alex shook her head. "I didn't call anyone."

The mystery was solved in the afternoon, when Maeve O'Connor arrived to pick up her daughter, Peggy. Maeve was the woman who had been honest with Alex when she'd called the Monday before.

Alex approached her car and helped Peggy into the backseat. Then she walked around to the driver's window.

"It's nice to have Peggy back, Mrs. O'Connor," Alex said. "Can I ask you something? What changed your mind?"

The woman looked at Alex directly. She spoke in a low voice. "Sally Lundquist phoned. She said she was calling all the parents. She explained that she found her husband dead before you arrived."

Bless Sally Lundquist! "I have to be honest, Mrs. O'Connor. The police don't know the time of death. They may question me again, and my picture may be in the paper again. And the article about my son's drowning is true. So if you have doubts—"

"You've always impressed me as a caring, dedicated, responsible teacher. I should have trusted my judgment. I'm sorry."

"Please don't apologize. You were doing what you thought was best for Peggy. But I can't tell you what this means to me, that you're placing your trust in me."

When Sally Lundquist came into the classroom to get Bobby, Alex went over to her.

"There were seventeen children here today, Mrs. Lundquist. You're a miracle worker. I don't know how to thank you."

Sally blushed. "It was the least I could do. I'm glad I was able to help. How was Bobby today?"

"The same. Quiet, reserved."

His mother nodded. "He's starting therapy this afternoon."

"I'm sure that will make a difference. Thanks again, for everything."

"You're welcome. You deserve it, Mrs. Prescott."

*   *   *

Warren was delighted with Alex's news and insisted that they all go out to dinner to celebrate. Lisa seemed genuinely happy, too. She even hugged Alex.

On Tuesday there were twenty children. And in the middle of the morning, the phone rang. Evelyn went to answer it, then returned to the classroom. It was Warren, she told Alex.

Alex hurried to the office and picked up the receiver. "Warren?"

"Margot Leibman just called me. She—"

"They have the autopsy results, don't they? What time was Lundquist killed?" Alex held her breath.

"Based on the autopsy, anywhere from two that afternoon to ten that evening. But—"

"I don't understand. Can't they be more specific?"

"In the movies, they can establish exact times of death. In real life, that's almost impossible to do. Too many variables. Forget the autopsy, Alex. Margot said—"

Her face sagged. "Then why are you calling?"

"Just listen." Warren was clearly excited. "Margot said that the detective we hired—"

"You hired a detective?"

"Of course! I wasn't about to sit around waiting for the police to clear you, Alex. Anyway, Margot gave him a copy of Lundquist's phone bills—she badgered Detective Rowan into accessing them from the phone company. Lundquist made several long-distance and toll calls that Tuesday. The detective called the numbers and verified that Lundquist himself had made the calls. One was at seven-thirty that evening, and that, Alex, lets you off the hook, because I was home with you then, up until you left with Evelyn at eight-thirty!"

"Oh, God!" Alex started crying.

"Margot said Rowan told her they're focusing on Lundquist's business associates. There could be drug trafficking involved. Who knows? Who cares, as long as you're out of it."

They talked for another minute. Then Alex hung up the phone, wiped her eyes, and walked back into the classroom.

Evelyn hurried over to her. "What did Warren want?" She studied Alex's face. "You were crying. Why? What's wrong?"

"Nothing's wrong." Alex repeated what Warren had learned.

"You're kidding!" There were tears in her eyes, too. She hugged Alex. "Thank God! It's finally over."

Was it over? Really over? Alex was no longer under suspicion, but the police didn't know who had killed Lundquist. Business associates, Warren had said. Drugs might be involved.

She checked the mail that afternoon, but there was no note. There were no notes on Wednesday or Thursday or Friday or Saturday. By Sunday she allowed herself to believe what Warren had insisted on from the start:

Donald Lundquist had written the notes and sent the application to harass her. Now he was dead, and Alex and Warren and Lisa and Nicholas could finally get on with their lives.

Chapter 31

*I*t was over.

The taste of defeat was so bitter and galling.

All her carefully thought out plans—all her hopes!—had turned to ashes, and she was left with a moldering despair over her failure, and with the guilt that was gnawing at her over Donald Lundquist's death, guilt that really wasn't hers. She had done nothing wrong. He'd brought it on himself, hadn't he? She wasn't responsible for the actions of others.

Donald Lundquist had died for nothing. The vandalizing, the phone calls to the mortuary, the notes, the boarding-school application—all had been for nothing. Alex was in her glory, euphoric, and why not? Her past, once exposed, was no longer a weapon to be used against her, to drive her away. Her precious preschool had been saved. She was no longer a suspect in Lundquist's murder. And Warren had forgiven her—for lying to him about her past, for letting her son, her only child, drown!

It pained and infuriated her that Warren could be so blind, so stupidly magnanimous, but, of course, he had no choice. It wasn't because he loved Alex, she knew. It was because of the baby. If not for the baby, Warren would have divorced Alex when he found out about her past. But he couldn't divorce her, not if she was pregnant with his child.

If it weren't for the baby, everything would be all right. She walked over to her bed, picked up a round pillow, lifted her shirt, and tucked the pillow inside the elastic of her sweatpants. She dropped her shirt so that it covered the pillow and looked in the mirror at her rounded abdomen. She ran her hands across her abdomen and wondered what it felt like to have life moving around inside her.

Alex knew. Alex was getting bigger, flaunting her pregnancy in everyone's face. Every day the baby was growing. Soon it would be born, and then it would be too late. Forever too late.

Go away, Alex! she whispered. *Go away! Her body shook with waves of rage and frustration. She yanked the pillow out and grabbed a letter opener from her dresser and stabbed at the pillow, again and again, making gash after gash in the pale pink chintz until the pillow was shredded and the room was filled with clumps of cotton batting.*

She would find another way.

She tapped the letter opener against her hand.

She knew what she had to do.

She had no choice.

Chapter 32

"You're sure you don't mind my going?" Warren asked Alex as he hooked his garment bag over the door.

"It's just for overnight. And you should be with your mom. I think it's wonderful that she's being honored."

It was Sunday morning. Warren was flying to Chicago to surprise his mother when she received an award for her work in helping combat illiteracy. The award dinner was at night in a downtown hotel. Warren was returning early Monday.

A half hour later Warren and Alex went downstairs to the garage. He was driving the Lexus to the airport and would leave it in the parking lot overnight.

"I'll call you as soon as I get there." Warren held Alex tight and kissed her. "I'll miss you."

"You do that." She smiled.

He kissed her again, then pulled away reluctantly and got into the car. She waited until he had backed out of the garage, then walked into the house.

Three weeks had passed, and she had finally relaxed into happiness. Her relationship with Warren was healed—better, in fact, than it had been before, now that she was no longer living with the strain of keeping her past a secret.

She had made inroads in her relationship with Lisa, too. They had gone together to a furniture store and picked out a crib, a changing table, and a dresser for the baby. Alex had also consulted with her about wallpaper and linoleum for the nursery.

Last Thursday Alex had had the amniocentesis. The results would be available in two weeks, but she wasn't worried. For the first time in years, she felt that God was smiling on her, and she felt confident that everything, including the baby, would be all right.

The dreams were still there, of course; they would probably be there forever. They still tormented her, though not with the same intensity as in the weeks leading up to Lundquist's death, but she had come to accept them as part of her life. She was contemplating going to a therapist to deal with her guilt about Kevin. Maybe that would help diminish the frequency of the dreams.

Lisa left soon after Warren; she'd made arrangements to spend the day with Valerie and stay overnight. Alex took Nicholas shopping in Santa Monica for new tennis shoes, pants, and short-sleeved tops. Afterward, they went to a pizza shop for lunch, then to a new, full-length Disney animated film he'd been wanting to see.

They got home at five-thirty. The phone was ringing. It was Warren, calling from the hotel. Alex spoke to him, then to Bea and Phil.

"Congratulations, Mom," Alex said. "I wish I could be there with you tonight. So do Nicholas and Lisa."

"I wish you could be here, too, Alex. But we'll see you when the baby's born."

Alex put Nicholas on the phone. The boy talked to his grandparents, then to his father. Alex wondered what her own parents would think of her stepson, and of the baby when it was born. They had loved Kevin, and had lavished him with the affection and approval they had doled out so sparingly to Alex ever since she could remember. Warren wanted her to contact them, but she wasn't ready to do that. She wasn't sure she ever would be.

She made Nicholas a hamburger and broiled a trout for herself. After they ate, she filled his tub, then supervised him as he bathed. When he was done and dressed in his pajamas, he sat on the floor of his room and played with his Lego tiles.

Alex went to her bedroom and put her wristwatch on her dresser. She took off her Adidas and socks and walked downstairs to her studio. Two weeks ago, she'd had the carpet replaced with white linoleum. Warren had brought down her easel and art supplies. The rocking chair had stayed upstairs, in the nursery.

She was working on a portrait of the family—Warren, Lisa,

Nicholas, and herself. She was going to surprise Warren with it on his birthday, two months away. She'd made preliminary sketches from one of the Polaroid photos Lisa had taken months ago at her birthday party.

Alex removed the sheet of canvas from the closet (she kept it hidden there when Warren was around) and clipped it to the easel. She would start with Lisa's eyes. She assembled the small tubes of oil pigments she wanted, took her palette, and mixed some pigments until she had the shade of brown she wanted.

When she was ready to start, she went upstairs. Nicholas was building a helicopter, following the directions that had come with the Lego kit.

"Everything okay?" she asked.

He looked up at her and smiled. "Sure. Will I see Daddy tomorrow morning before I go to school?"

"I don't think so. I'll be in my studio now if you need me." Back downstairs, she left the door to her studio open so that she could hear Nicholas if he called her.

Alex picked up her brush and started painting. After a while she noticed that the natural light was quickly fading. She turned on the overhead lighting and went back to the canvas. Lisa's eyes were exceptional, a dark, velvety brown with hints of amber around the pupil. Alex wanted to get the shading right.

She'd been working for some time when the phone rang. She was startled and her hand jerked, extending a jagged line of brown outside the oval of the eye.

"Damn!" She put down the brush and reached for the receiver on top of the cabinet behind her. Maybe it was Warren, calling again from the hotel. "Hello?"

"Look in the pool, Alex," a voice whispered.

Her heart stopped for a moment, then jumped in her chest. "Who is this?" she demanded, but all she heard was a dial tone.

She dropped the receiver into the cradle and ran to the family room. The sliding door was open.

"Nicholas!" she cried.

She clamped her hand over her mouth to stifle her scream. She raced outside and down the three brick steps, across the lawn to the gate that separated the pool from the yard.

It was unlocked. There was a mild screech as she pulled it open. She flung it wide and ran. She heard it clang shut behind her.

She was past the gate now, her eyes straining to pierce the graying light. She didn't see anything, and she thought, Please, God, let it be a cruel hoax. But then she saw the small, clothed body lying facedown in the dark aqua waters at the bottom of the far end of the pool.

"Nicholas!" she shrieked.

She ran along the concrete. Her heart was pounding against her chest wall and her ribs were on fire. Her legs felt like lead. She knew she was moving too slowly, she would never get there in time, her legs were heavy, so heavy! she could barely lift them, and it seemed forever until she reached him.

She jumped in.

The water was freezing. She swam toward him, shivering, ignoring the pain that ripped through her body as she made her way through the endless gallons of water.

He was only a few feet away. She took a deep breath, dove down into the water, and when his head was within arm's reach, she grabbed it to lift it out of the water.

His hair came off.

She screamed, then realized she was holding a wig. She looked at what she had thought was Nicholas's body. It was an inflatable doll—only partially inflated. That was why it hadn't floated. It was dressed in pants and a knit shirt that she recognized as Nicholas's.

She swam to the edge of the pool and dragged herself out. The air was frigid. She was shivering with cold and dread. Her teeth were chattering. She reversed her steps, running back to the house, up the brick steps, into the family room. She pulled the sliding door closed and bolted it, wondering as she did so whether the person who had placed the doll in the pool was outside or in the house, with her and Nicholas.

Nicholas!

Her heart pounding, she bolted up the stairs to his room and exhaled the breath she hadn't realized she'd been holding. He was in his room. He'd turned on the light. He looked up as she entered and smiled.

"You're all wet, Mommy!" He laughed, pointing at her dripping hair and clothes. "What happened?"

"I fell in the pool." She didn't want to frighten him, but she had to ask. "Nicholas, did you open the sliding door in the family room?"

" 'Course not, Mommy." There was a hint of reproach in his voice. "You told me not to. And anyway, I can't even reach the lock on top. Is something wrong, Mommy?"

"Nothing to worry about, Nick." She closed the door to his room and walked from one bedroom to the other, trembling with fear as she opened each door and switched on the light. The closets were the hardest. She had visions of someone jumping out at her from the black recesses, but no one did.

She stood in the hall, mentally retracing the day's events, trying to remember when she'd last been in the family room. Not since they'd returned from their shopping and movie expeditions, she realized. In the morning, after Lisa had left, Nicholas had been in the family room watching TV. Alex would have noticed an open door when she shut off the TV. She was sure of it.

Someone had opened the door while she and Nicholas were away from the house, she decided. She'd been working in the studio, but with the door to that room open, she would have heard the rumble of the sliding door being opened.

Except for when she was upstairs, giving Nicholas his bath. That had taken at least half an hour, time enough for someone to enter the house, walk into the family room, open the door, and leave.

She hurried down the stairs and checked the side door. It was locked and bolted. So was the front door. The one that led to the garage was locked but not bolted. She slid the bolt. She checked the downstairs rooms, turning on lights everywhere, telling herself that no one was in the house, that the caller had left a while ago.

Look in the pool, Alex. The voice had been muffled, but it had sounded like a woman's voice.

Who was she?

For the past three weeks, Alex had convinced herself that her troubles were behind her. Now all her tortured suspicions sprang to life, full-grown. It was someone who had access to the house, someone who had known that Warren wouldn't be home. Lisa knew, of course. Had the girl told Denise? Had Denise casually mentioned it to Paula? Denise had a key to the house. Paula had had one, too. She'd returned it when she was no longer a full-time, live-in housekeeper. But what if she'd had a copy made?

Of course, it was possible that someone had taken the spare key Alex and Warren kept hidden in a fake rock among other decorative rocks that formed the border of the landscaping in front of the house.

Ron! she thought suddenly. Had his apologetic phone call to her been a sham, a ruse to throw her off guard? Was he playing one last trick now that her troubles were behind her?

Alex unlocked and opened the front door, walked outside, looked around to make sure no one was watching, then knelt and picked up the rock, the third from the right edge. The key was there. But that didn't mean that someone hadn't used it and returned it.

She went back inside the house, locked the door, and bolted it. She wanted to phone Warren, but he was in Chicago at a banquet in a hotel whose name she didn't remember. In the kitchen, she picked up the phone receiver and punched the number Lisa had left on a piece of paper on the refrigerator. "I just want to make sure she's all right," Alex said aloud. "I'm not checking up on her."

Valerie Haines answered. "Oh, hi, Mrs. Prescott. How are you?"

"Fine. May I speak to Lisa, please?"

"She can't come to the phone right now."

"Tell her I have to talk to her now. It's important."

"It might be a while, Mrs. Prescott."

Valerie was stalling; Alex was sure of it. "Where is she, Valerie?" Her palms were sweaty. "I want the truth."

A pause. "She went to meet some boy for pizza. She said she wouldn't be back late and asked me to cover for her if you called. I *told* her I didn't want to get involved."

"What boy?"

"I don't know. She wouldn't say."

There was no boy. Alex went back upstairs, entered Lisa's room, and walked directly to her stepdaughter's desk. The center drawer was locked. There was a pink enamel jewelry box on the dresser. As a young girl, Alex had kept the keys to her diary and her desk drawer in her jewelry box. Maybe Lisa did the same.

Alex opened the box. Inside was mostly inexpensive fashion jewelry—earrings and watches and bracelets. There was a key chain in the shape of a hand with manicured nails. Alex searched for a key that might fit the drawer. She didn't find one, but as she was rummaging through the box, her hand came across a heart-shaped, hammered gold locket.

For a moment she thought it was hers, but of course it couldn't be; she was wearing hers. She reached beneath her sweater, just to make sure, and touched the metal warmed by her body. She picked up the other locket and opened it. Warren's image smiled at her from one half. Lisa's face was more serious; her eyes, dark brown pools, seemed to stare at Alex.

Alex snapped the locket shut and put it back in the jewelry box. So what if Lisa had a locket almost identical to the one her father had bought Alex? A locket didn't prove anything. But she could feel the rapid beating of her heart, and her hand was shaking as she took the letter opener on Lisa's desk and, after a moment's hesitation, inserted it into the keyhole of the locked drawer.

A minute later the drawer was open.

Like everything else in the room, the drawer was neat. On top of the other contents was a slim white envelope, addressed to Alex. With shaking hands, she opened it and pulled out a slip of unlined paper hand-printed with large, red, capital letters.

NOW YOU MUST BOTH DIE.

"My God!" Alex whispered. She felt suddenly nauseated and light-headed. She gripped the edge of the desk to steady herself and breathed deeply.

The envelope had been lying on top of a pink diary. Alex picked up the diary, snapped off the lock, and thumbed backward until she found the page printed with today's date. It was blank. So were the pages for the preceding three weeks. Finally, she found two pages, dated several days earlier, filled with Lisa's small, cramped handwriting. Alex started to read:

... and soon Alex will die. She might even die before the baby is born. Maybe that's better for the baby. It's

*so sad to be born without a mother. Daddy will be sad,
and so will Nicholas. I could feel sad if I let myself, but
I won't let myself. I can't. It won't change what's going
to happen.*

*But I'll be here to help Daddy and Nicholas, and we'll
be a family. We'll be all right, just like we were before
Alex came. And if the baby does live, I'll take care of it,
too, just like I took care of Nicholas. Sometimes I feel so
bad . . .*

Alex shut the diary. She couldn't read any more—there was
no need. She took the diary and note and locket to her bedroom, then hid them at the back of her closet. She would need
them as proof, when she told Warren.

She paled at the thought. How could she tell her husband,
who was this minute sitting in an audience with all the friends
and colleagues who had gathered to honor his mother, that his
beloved fourteen-year-old daughter was mentally unbalanced?
That her attachment to her father had mushroomed into an
obsession, that the obsession had propelled her to harass Alex
and contemplate killing her and her unborn baby?

That, maybe, she had already killed someone.

Soon, very soon, Alex would have to tell Warren, but right
now she was glad she couldn't reach him.

She couldn't stay here alone with Nicholas. The inflated doll
had been a crude joke; the handwritten message had been
clear. Where was Lisa? What was her stepdaughter planning
next?

Alex called Evelyn. The phone rang and rang and rang;
finally, just when she was about to hang up, Evelyn answered.

"Thank God you're home!" Alex exclaimed. "I don't
know if I should come to you or if you should come here.
I'm—"

"What's wrong?"

Nicholas's room was down the hall, several rooms away,
but Alex whispered anyway. "It's Lisa. I'm convinced
she—"

The line went dead.

Stunned, Alex listened to the silence, then pressed the button for the other line. There was no dial tone. Nothing.

A second later the lights went out.

"Mommy?" Nicholas's voice held more uncertainty than fear.

"I'm right here, Nicholas! Stay right there. I'm coming to you. There's nothing to worry about."

The circuit breakers were in a box in the garage. That meant that Lisa was in the garage, too. She had a key to the door that led from the garage, but Alex—thank God!—had bolted the door from inside the house. But what if she broke down the door? There were countless tools in the garage—shovels, a saw, hoes.

There was still enough natural light so that Alex could see. She hurried to Warren's nightstand, opened the double doors, and reached toward the back for the 9 mm. gun he kept there. The clip was on the top shelf of his closet, buried among a box of papers.

The gun wasn't there.

Lisa had it.

They had to leave.

Now.

"Mommy, it's dark!"

"I'm coming in a sec, Nicholas!"

She slipped on her Adidas; her fingers fumbled as she tied the laces. She was almost out of the room when she remembered the locket and diary and note. She couldn't risk leaving them in the house. Lisa would find them and destroy them. Then there would be no proof, and Warren would never, believe Alex.

She grabbed the items, stuffed them quickly into a shoe bag, and took the bag with her as she ran down the hall.

"Mommy's here," she said as she entered Nicholas's room. "Get your slippers, sweetie. We're going for a ride."

"But I'm in my pajamas."

"That's okay, Nick. Just do what Mommy says."

"Are the lights coming back on?"

"I don't know, Nick." She struggled to filter panic from her voice. "Come on. Please hurry." She walked to the doorway and stood there, listening for sounds, any sounds, from downstairs.

It seemed like an eternity until Nicholas put on his Big Bird slippers. Finally he was ready. She drew him close and whispered in his ear.

"Nick, I want you to be very, very quiet when we go downstairs, okay?"

"Why, Mommy?"

"Just do what I ask and I'll explain later, okay?"

" 'Kay."

"Not a sound, right?"

He nodded.

She stepped into the hall first. The silence enveloped her. She grasped Nicholas's small hand, and they walked down the stairs together. At the foot of the stairs, she looked at Nicholas and put a finger to her lips. She stood for a moment, listening. Then she touched his elbow, and they made their way to the kitchen, where she took her car keys from the hook, then went to the side door.

Alex opened the bolt, wondering if Lisa was standing on the other side of the door, waiting to push her way into the house, the gun in her hand.

She turned the knob and jerked the door open. No one was there. She pulled Nicholas out and shut the door behind them. Then she hurried with him to her Jeep. The garage doors, she saw, were open.

She checked the Jeep's doors. They were locked. She peered inside. There was no one there. She unlocked the Jeep, buckled Nicholas into the backseat, then got into the driver's seat and buckled herself in. Her hands were shaking so badly that she could barely insert the key into the ignition.

"You okay?" she asked Nicholas. He hadn't said a word since she'd cautioned him in his bedroom.

"Yes." His voice was tiny, filled with fear.

She thought about driving to Denise—her house was much closer than Evelyn's—but what if Lisa came there? What if she was already there? Alex drove several blocks, then pulled over to the curb and called Evelyn on her cellular phone.

"What happened to your phone?" Evelyn asked when she answered. "I called you back but couldn't get a connection. Then I called the operator. She said the line was out of order."

Alex held the receiver close to her mouth. "I'm calling you from my Jeep," she whispered. "Lisa cut the house phone line. She has Warren's gun. She's trying to kill me, Ev, and the baby. Maybe Nicholas, too. I don't know."

Evelyn didn't answer.

"Did you hear me, Evelyn? I can't talk louder. I don't want Nicholas to hear. We're in my car."

"I heard you." Evelyn was whispering, too. "I just can't believe it. How can you be sure?"

"I have proof, Ev."

"Mommy? I want to go home."

Alex turned her head to face Nicholas. "Just a minute, sweetie. Mommy will be off the phone soon." She turned back and brought the receiver close to her mouth again. "Ev?"

"Where are you now?"

"A few blocks from the house."

"Did you call the police?"

"Not yet."

"Alex, you have to call them! You can't handle this on your own."

"No!" Warren would never forgive her. "Lisa needs a doctor, Ev. She needs help. I don't know what to do. I can't stay in the house. I can't go to Denise. Can we come to your house?"

"Sure," Evelyn said quickly. "Of course."

"It would just be for the night, till Warren comes home."

"You can stay as long as you like."

"Ev, I have to warn you. Lisa knows you and I are close. What if she figures out I'm with you? She knows where you live. She has a gun. What if—"

"We'll deal with it, Alex. If we have to, we'll get help."

Alex hung up and turned toward Nicholas again. "We're going to Evelyn's house, okay, champ?"

"To sleep?"

"Yes."

"Daddy won't know where we are. Can we go home? Please?"

"We can't go home, Nick. The lights don't work, or the phones. It's just for tonight, sweetie. Till Daddy comes home. We'll call Daddy from Evelyn's house."

"What about Lisa? Lisa won't know where we are, either, Mommy. She'll be scared. Can we call her, too?"

"We'll call her, too, Nick," Alex lied.

Nicholas was silent. It was dark now, and the street lamps were blinking at her. Alex drove slowly, forcing herself to concentrate on the streets as she thought about Lisa's cleverness, the flawless accuracy of her cruelty.

Like on that Sunday afternoon three years ago, Alex had been in her studio. It was a different studio in a different house in a different city, and Lisa had obviously read the newspaper account of Kevin's death and tried to re-create it. But the sequence of events had been eerily parallel. It was her nightmare, come to life again.

The ringing of the phone—

I'm at the 7-Eleven, Alex.

Look in the pool, Alex.

The family room door is open.

She runs, barefoot, down the steps.

Even the sounds were the same. The moaning of the wind in her ears as she runs. The screech of the gate as she pulls it open; the reverberating clang as it slams against the fence. Her scream of terror when she finds the body in the pool.

This time, though, it is a plastic, inflated doll, not a real body. This time, there are more sounds. The pounding of her feet on the concrete as she races back to the house. The rumble of the sliding-glass door as it slides along the track. The click as she slips the latch up. The thunk as she drives the top bolt home.

The rumble . . .

Alex's hands clenched the wheel.

The click . . .

She strained to hear the sounds . . .

The thunk . . .

. . . sounds not of today, but of three years ago.

With a sudden motion, she checked her rearview and side mirrors, then pulled quickly over to the curb.

"Mommy? Are we there?"

"Nicholas, please, be quiet for a minute, okay?"

She had to hear the sounds. She knew they were there, but she couldn't hear them. Why couldn't she hear them? Night after night in her dreams she heard all the other sounds, so why not these three?

She hadn't heard those sounds today, but that was because Lisa had opened the family room door either when Alex and Nicholas hadn't been home, or when they'd been upstairs, filling Nicholas's tub. But three years ago, Alex should have heard the rumble of the sliding door when Kevin opened it. The intercom was on; she'd turned it on herself after Larry shut it off. It picked up and amplified every sound.

Why hadn't she heard the sound?

"Mommy?" Nicholas whimpered. "I'm tired."

"One minute, angel."

She listened again. Still she couldn't hear the rumble of the sliding door when Kevin opened it. She had heard it earlier, of course, when Larry had closed the door before he left. She nodded. There was the rumble; she could hear it.

She frowned. Where was the click of the latch? And the thunk of the bolt being closed? She and Larry always closed the latch and the bolt. Always.

Maybe Larry had forgotten that day. Maybe that was why he'd been so hysterical, because he couldn't admit he was partially to blame for Kevin's death. If only Larry had closed the latch and the bolt—

But Kevin's red step stool had been in front of the door. That meant he'd used it to open the bolt. So where was the rumble as he opened the door?

She sat in her Jeep, parked at the curb. She listened again. And again. She listened, but she couldn't hear the sounds, because they weren't there.

Liar! she whispered. Liar! Liar! Liar! You never shut the door at all. You opened it. It was you, not Kevin! And you put the red stool there.

But why?

I left the house over twenty minutes ago, Alex. Are you telling me you're still in your damn studio? That you left Kevin alone all this time?

It can't be twenty minutes, Larry.

Is your goddamn painting more important than your son?

She shook her head. Why would he leave the door open, knowing that Kevin could walk outside to the pool and drown?

Did you close the sliding door, Larry?

I'm doing it right now, Alex.

Unless . . .

I left the house over twenty minutes ago, Alex. . . .

It can't be twenty minutes.

Unless . . .

She never wore a watch when she painted. Larry knew that.
Unless, oh God, oh my poor, sweet baby, unless he knew Kevin was already dead, and he wanted me to think it was my fault.

Chapter 33

"**A**re you okay, Alex?" Evelyn looked paler than usual. Her eyes telegraphed her anxiety. "It took you so long, I didn't know what to think."

"I had some thinking to do, so I pulled over to the curb for a while. I'm sorry." She touched Evelyn's arm. "I didn't mean to alarm you."

"As long as you're all right." Evelyn turned to Nicholas and bent down so that she was eye level with him. "Quite an adventure, huh? Going out in your pj's and Big Bird slippers."

"Our lights don't work and my daddy's in Chicago and the phone is broken, too." He was clutching Alex's hand.

"I know. But you're here now, and everything's going to be okay." Evelyn patted his head, then stood up. "Alex, I prepared the back bedroom. I have some toys . . ."

"He's exhausted, Ev. I think he'll go right to sleep." She turned to him. "Okay, Nick?"

He squeezed her hand. "Are you going to call Daddy and Lisa? You said."

The two women exchanged looks.

"I'll call Daddy right now, Nick." There was a phone on the lamp table next to the brown-and-black-plaid sofa. Alex picked up the receiver and phoned her in-laws. After fifteen rings, she hung up.

"Daddy and Grandma and Grandpa are still at the party, Nick. I'll call again in a while."

"And Lisa? What if she goes to the house and gets scared 'cause it's dark?" There was a tremor in his voice.

"I'll call her soon. First let's get you settled."

They followed Evelyn out of the living room and down a narrow hall to a small bedroom with two beds and a short

273

wooden dresser. A French door opened onto a small patio that faced the beach.

"I'll leave you two alone," Evelyn said and closed the door behind her.

Alex folded down the top sheet and blanket on one of the beds. Nicholas climbed onto the bed and lay down. He was rigid, his arms straight sticks on top of the blanket.

"Will you be sleeping in the same room with me, Mommy?"

"Absolutely, kiddo." She forced herself to smile.

"Can you stay with me now till I fall asleep?"

"I have to talk to Evelyn. But I'll come back in a while to check on you. Okay?" She smoothed his hair.

"Okay." He nodded quickly. "I love you, Mommy."

"I love *you*, Nicholas." She leaned over and kissed him. His arms went around her and pulled her close. She could feel his heart beating rapidly. After a long moment, she gently removed his hands and adjusted his blanket. She kissed him again, then returned to the living room.

Evelyn was sitting on the sofa. "Come sit down." She patted the cushion next to her. "You must be drained."

"I hope he'll fall asleep. He's so tense." Alex looked behind her toward the room where Nicholas was. "Maybe I should stay with him," she said, turning back to Evelyn.

"He'll be fine, Alex." Evelyn's voice, like her words, were softly reassuring. "Kids are resilient. You know that." She pointed to a tray on the cherry wood coffee table. "Have a brandy."

Alex shook her head. "I'm edgy as hell, but alcohol isn't good for the baby."

"One drink won't hurt you. God knows after what you've been through, you need it. I know I do. I still can't believe it's Lisa." Evelyn picked up one of the tumblers and handed it to Alex. She picked up her own and took a sip.

"I guess you're right." Alex sat next to Evelyn and took a sip of the brandy. It felt warm sliding down her throat. She shivered. "I'm so cold."

"No wonder! Your clothes are drenched!" Evelyn touched Alex's hair. "So's your hair. Do you want to change into something of mine? I should have offered right away."

"In a minute. I just want to sit a while." Where was Lisa

now? she wondered. Could she bike all the way here?

"I'll get you a blanket." Evelyn left the room. When she reappeared, she handed Alex a flannel blanket and sat down again. "Now tell me what happened. Oh, before I forget. Patty called. She tried reaching you first, but your line was out of order. She won't be able to come in tomorrow. I told her she could reach you here later."

Patty was the least of her problems. Alex removed her Adidas, tucked her feet under her, and wrapped the blanket around herself. "I was in the studio . . ." she began. She told Evelyn about the phone call and the half-inflated doll in the pool. About the phone call to Valerie.

"All of a sudden, I knew it was Lisa." From the shoe bag, Alex took out the heart-shaped locket and the note and the diary and put them on the couch. "I found these in her room."

Evelyn looked puzzled. "That looks just like the locket Warren gave you."

"I know. Open it."

Evelyn picked up the locket and looked at the two photos. "My God!" she exclaimed softly.

"Read the note."

Evelyn removed the note from the envelope. " 'Now you must both die,' " she read aloud. She shuddered and looked up at Alex. "She's crazy, isn't she?"

"She needs help," Alex said quietly. "Sitting here, I can talk about it calmly. When Nicholas and I were in the house alone, and I thought Lisa was out there, waiting to break in . . ." Alex pulled the blanket more tightly around her. "I don't know how I'm going to tell Warren. This will destroy him." She picked up the brandy glass and took another sip.

"Alex—"

The phone rang. Alex started at the sound. Her hand jerked, sloshing the brandy.

Evelyn reached over and picked up the receiver. "Hello?" she said. She turned quickly toward Alex and pointed sharply to the receiver. Her face looked tight with tension. "Oh, hi, Lisa. What can I do for you?"

Alex froze. Her mouth was suddenly dry. She raised the tumbler to her lips with shaking hands but couldn't drink.

"No," Evelyn said, "Alex isn't here. What makes you

think she would be?'' She placed the receiver close to Alex's ear.

'' . . . tried calling the house, but the line is out of order,'' Alex heard Lisa saying. ''I biked home, and the house is all dark, Evelyn. I'm really worried.''

She *did* sound worried, Alex thought. What a great little actress. She shivered again.

''Where are you now, Lisa?'' Evelyn asked.

''At my friend Valerie's. Are you sure you don't know where Alex and Nicholas are?''

''I'm sorry, Lisa. I don't. Maybe your aunt knows.''

''I called her. She doesn't. If you hear from Alex, would you please have her call me here?'' Lisa dictated the phone number.

Evelyn put the receiver to her ear. ''Of course I will, Lisa. What? No, I haven't talked to Alex since this morning. Yes, I promise.'' She hung up, then turned back to Alex. She placed her hand on her chest. ''God, my heart is beating fast! I'm surprised she didn't hear it over the phone.''

Alex raked her fingers through her hair. ''You think she knows we're here?'' She closed her eyes briefly.

''I don't know. I *think* she believed me.'' Evelyn frowned. ''But you have to call the police.''

''I can't! They'd take her into custody. Warren would hate me.''

''Alex, you don't have a choice! You said she has Warren's gun. What if she comes here?''

Alex shook her head. ''Evelyn—''

''What about Nicholas? The note threatened both of you.'' Evelyn picked up the phone and put it on the sofa next to Alex. ''Call the police.'' She lifted the receiver and handed it to her.

Alex took the receiver, pressed the buttons for 911, then quickly hung up. ''I have to talk to Warren first.''

''It's too dangerous! You can't wait for Warren.''

''I *have* to!''

''Okay. I hope you know what you're doing.'' Evelyn bit her bottom lip. ''I don't want to upset you, Alex, but even if you don't call the police, this will affect your marriage. You must have thought about that.''

''Up until three weeks ago, when I thought it might be Lisa,

I thought about that all the time. Imagine having to choose between your wife and your daughter.''

Evelyn shook her head. "It doesn't seem fair, does it? Warren finally forgives you for keeping your past a secret, for not telling him you were responsible for your son drowning—"

"But I *wasn't* responsible for Kevin's death!" Alex exclaimed. "I just figured that out on the way here!"

"Of course not," Evelyn said gently. "It was a terrible accident. I didn't mean to imply that it was your fault."

Alex shook her head impatiently. The strands of wet hair slapped her cheeks. "You don't understand. It wasn't my fault at all. It was *Larry's* fault!"

Evelyn looked distraught. "Alex, you're upset," she said gently. "You're probably in shock. Let's talk about this in the morning, all right?"

"No. I have to tell you!" She explained about the sounds she'd heard, the sounds she hadn't heard. "Larry knew Kevin was dead, Ev, don't you see? All these years I've been consumed with guilt, and it was Larry all the time."

"You think Larry killed him?" Evelyn's eyes were wide.

"No. Larry *loved* Kevin. The drowning must have been an accident. But Larry couldn't bear to take the blame, because it would be another failure, you see, on top of all his other failures. His business. Our marriage. So he made me and everyone else believe that I was absorbed with my painting while Kevin went outside and drowned. Maybe he convinced himself, too. I don't know. But it wasn't my fault! You can't imagine how I feel, after all these years. The guilt . . . ''

"That's wonderful, Alex." Evelyn hesitated, then said, "Still, it doesn't solve your problem with Warren and Lisa."

"I know." Alex sighed. "But we'll work it out." Would they? She took another sip of brandy.

"All along I've been encouraging you to hang in there, but now . . . '' Evelyn shook her head again. "Warren's so attached to Lisa. I don't see how it's going to work. Not this time."

Alex felt a ripple of annoyance. This wasn't what she needed to hear. "You're wrong."

"I'm sorry, Alex. I've always been honest with you. I won't lie now." She touched Alex's arm. "I think you should move away, before it's too late."

"I love Warren and Nicholas," Alex said firmly. "And I'm not going to run away from my problems. I did that before, and it was a serious mistake. I won't do it again, Evelyn."

"What if Warren blames you for what happened to Lisa? That could happen, you know." She leaned closer to Alex. "Look, you just realized you weren't to blame for your son's death. You can go back home now and tell everyone, pick up the pieces of your life. Who knows? Maybe you could get back with Larry."

Alex put the tumbler on the tray. She was beginning to regret that she'd come. "Evelyn, is this supposed to be some sick joke? Larry's in a mental institution, where he belongs. I don't want to talk about this anymore."

"Well, I do. I think it's important. But I guess you don't care what I want, do you, Alex?"

Alex felt a chill that had nothing to do with her wet clothing or hair. "What are you talking about?" Evelyn was talking strangely. Maybe it was the brandy. Her face was unusually flushed.

"You always get everything you want, don't you? You waltzed into the preschool and bought it right out from under my feet."

Alex stared at her friend. "I never knew you were interested in buying the school. Cybil never said anything."

"I never had the chance! You took over the school, and the children, and then you wormed your way into Warren's life. Through Nicholas. I was Nicholas's teacher first! I met Warren before you did!"

Finders, keepers. It was a phrase Alex often overheard among the children. "I thought you were my friend, Evelyn." Something was wrong, Alex thought. Terribly wrong. She felt a tightening in her groin.

"I thought you and I were friends, too, but you knew I liked Warren. You knew, but you didn't care. If you hadn't come, Warren would have been interested in me. I know it."

"I didn't know, Evelyn." Alex edged away from her. "I never knew you felt like this. What about Jerry? I thought—"

Evelyn laughed. It was an ugly, shrill sound. "I'm not dating Jerry! He asked me out that one time only because he wanted me to talk you into buying his stupid computer system.

I pretended we were dating because I didn't want your pity."
She caught Alex's glance at the ring on her finger. "My
mom's. Pretty, isn't it?" She smiled. "I really had you fooled.
You're not so smart after all, are you, Alex?" Her smile deepened into a grin.

She's ill, Alex realized with a flash of fear. Evelyn is mentally unbalanced. Be careful! she told herself. "I'm sorry if I
caused you pain, Evelyn. I really am."

"It doesn't matter anymore. It's over now. You see that,
don't you?" Her voice was gentle again. "Go away, Alex. Go
back where you came from, before it's too late. Warren
doesn't need you. He needs someone who can take care of
him and love him selflessly, someone who won't bring him
problem after problem, someone who won't lie."

"You wrote the notes, didn't you, Evelyn?" Alex whispered, wondering if it was dangerous to ask, needing to know.
"You wrote the notes, and sent the boarding-school application and the doll in the hospital. You put the inflated doll in
the pool today." Her hands were clammy. "How could you
be so cruel, Evelyn? Why do you hate me so much?"

"I don't hate you, Alex. I love Warren, and I know you
aren't right for him. But I don't hate you, and I don't want to
hurt you or the baby."

"What about the note? 'Now you must both die.'"

"It's just a warning, don't you see? Just like the school. *I*
vandalized it, not Donald Lundquist." Her sudden smile had
a grotesque, impish quality. "I wanted to find out all about
you, Alex. What your secrets were. But I had to make it look
like someone broke in. If I didn't, you would've known right
away that I was behind everything. And it worked, didn't it?
You thought it was Lundquist. You never knew, did you?"

"I never knew," Alex repeated. My God! she thought. No
one knows I'm here. Not Warren, not Lisa, not Denise. No
one.

"But if you go back home, everything will be okay." Evelyn's tone was urgent. "You'll still have your baby, and I'll
marry Warren and take care of Nicholas, and everything will
be the way it's supposed to be. No one will be hurt, not you
or the baby."

"You pushed me, Evelyn. You tried to hurt my baby."

"I didn't mean to push you! It's just that . . . it just happened. But I never wanted to hurt you, *or* the baby. I never wanted to hurt anybody! Not even Donald Lundquist. He saw me! He was going to ruin everything! But I said I didn't want anything to happen to him, so it isn't my fault that he's dead. No one can blame me."

There were things here that didn't make sense, but Alex couldn't sort them out now. "How did you get the note into Lisa's desk drawer? It was locked."

Evelyn smiled. "I slipped it in. It was easy. I used the key you keep in the rock to get into the house. I put the locket in her jewelry box. I took out my photo first and put in one of Lisa. I took a set of Nicholas's clothes. And I took the gun to frighten you." She paused. "So will you listen to me, Alex? Will you go away? It's for the best, don't you think?"

Alex stood and dropped the blanket onto the couch. She had to get Nicholas and leave, right now. She fought to keep her voice calm. "You've given me a lot to think about, Evelyn. Right now, though, I think I should get Nicholas and take him home."

"You said you'd stay here. You *have* to stay here!"

"Evelyn, I'll see you in the morning, and we'll discuss everything then, all right?"

Evelyn stood up. In her right hand were Alex's car keys. She extended them to Alex, then quickly drew back her hand.

"First you have to promise you're going to leave Warren. I won't let you leave otherwise. I mean it! But it'll all work out. You'll see. I'll marry Warren, and you—" She broke off. "I have a surprise for you. I'll be right back. Don't go away." She giggled like a schoolgirl and hurried off toward the kitchen.

As soon as Evelyn was out of sight, Alex raced toward the back bedroom and opened the door. "Nicholas," she whispered, "we're going home."

Nicholas wasn't in the room.

Her heart thumping, Alex ran back down the narrow hall to the kitchen. Evelyn wasn't there. The side door was open. A blast of cool, salty air was coming through it.

"Evelyn!" Alex screamed. She ran out the door. "Evelyn!" she yelled again. Except for the light of the almost full moon, it was dark outside. Alex looked toward the street, then toward the beach. Which way should she go?

"Evelyn!" she called. "Where's Nicholas? Please, Evelyn, I just want to know that he's all right."

No answer.

"God damn you, Evelyn!"

Suddenly, from the direction of the beach, she heard a shriek. Then she heard Evelyn—she knew it was Evelyn—scream, "Bring him back!"

Alex ran toward Evelyn's voice. The sand was cold but smooth under her feet. In the distance she could see the moon's twin, floating on the ocean. As she neared the water, she saw two figures standing on the beach. One looked like Evelyn. The other was a man.

But where was Nicholas? her mind screamed.

She scanned the horizon. There was no sign of her stepson.

"No!" Evelyn's desperate yell pierced the air.

Alex turned quickly in the direction of the sound. Her eyes had adjusted to the darkness, and she could see Evelyn grabbing at the man's arm. The man flung her loose and started walking away. Evelyn hurled herself at him. He pushed her down. She stood up. Then Alex watched in horror as the man raised what appeared to be a large piece of driftwood and brought it crashing down on Evelyn's head.

"No!" Alex screamed.

She rushed toward Evelyn. The man hit Evelyn again. She fell. The man looked at Alex. He turned, ran into the water, and swam toward the left and around a cluster of large rocks that jutted into the ocean.

Evelyn had fallen on her side. She was motionless when Alex reached her. Blood was seeping from a huge gash on her forehead. Her eyes looked glazed. Alex lifted her wrist. There was a faint, erratic pulse.

"Evelyn?"

Her eyes flickered open. "He took Nicholas. Wants to hurt him."

She was barely audible. Alex leaned closer.

"I tried to stop him," Evelyn whispered. A whistling sound came from her throat. "For Warren. Couldn't."

"Who hurt you? Who is he?"

"He killed Lundquist. Not my fault. His."

"Evelyn—"

"Tell Warren I tried." Her eyes closed.

The pulse was still there. Alex could run back to the house to call for an ambulance, but she had to find Nicholas. Who had taken him? Where—

"Alex!"

She dropped Evelyn's wrist and whirled toward the water. Then she gasped. The blood came pounding into her head.

Standing in the water twenty feet from the shore, holding Nicholas, his hand clamped over the boy's mouth, was an apparition. It couldn't be real.

But it was.

Chapter 34

For a second Alex remained frozen with disbelief and fear. This was the "surprise" Evelyn had mentioned! Then she ran toward the water.

Larry wasn't standing any longer. He was swimming on his side toward the cluster of rocks, dragging Nicholas with him. Nicholas was kicking and his mouth was free now, and Alex thought she would die as each pitiful cry—"Mommy! Mommy!"—reached her.

At last she was at the ocean's edge. She plunged in. The water was freezing, and she gasped as she started swimming after them.

"Come get me, Alex! Come on! You can do it," Larry called, sounding like a high school coach.

She couldn't see his face, but she could imagine the way her ex-husband's lips were curving into a taunting smile.

"Mommy!"

She swam faster, pushing away the inky water with her arms and legs, her bruised ribs remembering their pain. She looked up between strokes and saw that she had narrowed the distance between them. She was close enough now to see Nicholas's face, bleached of everything but fright.

"I'm coming!" she yelled. "Mommy's coming!"

She was gaining with every stroke. She wondered why Larry had slowed down—had Evelyn injured him?—and now Larry wasn't swimming at all. He was standing in the crevice of one of the rocks, holding Nicholas to the side, his arm anchored around the boy's waist.

"Mommy!" Nicholas cried. "Mommymommymommy!"

Larry laughed. Alex realized he was playing with her, allowing her to come closer, to reach him. When she was five

283

feet from his side, he grinned at her. Nicholas was whimpering.

"Hello, Alexandra," Larry murmured. "Is this your new son? He's such a *beautiful* boy."

Alex held on to the craggy surface of a rock. She ached to reach out and grab Nicholas, but she was afraid of what Larry would do. "Don't hurt him," she said quietly.

"Why would I want to do that? Just because you took my son away from me? Is that a good reason?"

"Larry—"

"Your friend Evelyn called me and told me you had a whole new family. And that you were *pregnant!*" He spit the word. "Do you know the pain I felt when she told me? *Do you?*" he roared.

Alex flinched.

"Do you know how to swim, Nicholas?" Larry asked in a taunting voice. "Did Mommy Alex teach you how to swim? She taught Kevin."

"Make him let me go, Mommy!" Nicholas cried.

"Please, Larry," Alex said, forcing calm into her voice. "You're angry at me, not him. Let me take him back to shore. Then we can talk. I promise." She propelled herself closer.

"That's what Evelyn kept saying. 'Don't hurt Nicholas.' She's afraid Warren won't love her if something happens to his son. She's pathetic. She wouldn't even—"

In one swift motion, Alex lifted her free hand out of the water, raised it high, and slammed the rock she'd picked up from the shore onto the side of Larry's head.

Larry grunted and drew back. He tightened his grip around Nicholas and started swimming away on his back. Alex caught up with him and hit him again, in the center of his forehead.

Still he held on to Nicholas. He kicked at Alex.

She smashed the rock onto his nose. She heard the sound of bone splintering, Larry's scream.

She dropped the rock. It fell soundlessly into the water. She pulled a dazed Nicholas out of Larry's unresisting arm, anchored the boy to her side, and started swimming to shore. She didn't know how badly she'd injured Larry—there had been a great deal of blood. She looked back. He was bobbing in the water, his head barely visible. When she looked back again, he was gone.

After they reached the shore, she lay panting on the wet sand for a minute, trying to catch her breath. Then she drew herself to her feet.

"Let's go," she said to Nicholas. Her throat was raw.

She took his hand and they started walking across the sand. A hand grabbed her ankle.

She felt herself falling; instinctively, she cushioned her abdomen with her arms. Her chin hit the sand. The impact jarred her jaw. Now a hand was on her other ankle, and she felt herself being pulled toward the water.

"Run, Nicholas!" Her mouth was full of sand. "Run!"

Nicholas stood frozen.

"Run! Go to Evelyn's house! Call the police!"

The boy started running, looking backward at Alex as he did, and was quickly swallowed by the darkness.

Alex tried kicking as Larry dragged her farther across the sand, but the grip on her ankles was too tight. Now her face was submerged in the shallow water. She wondered how long she could hold her breath before she would die.

Suddenly he released her ankles. She pushed herself up with her arms and lifted her head, gasping for breath. Anchoring her fingers in the wet sand, she pulled herself out of the water. Then she felt herself being turned over, like a flounder beached on the shore.

She blinked the water from her eyes. He was bleeding, she saw, from the wounds she'd inflicted on his forehead and temple and nose. Why wasn't he dead? She wanted him dead.

He straddled her. His legs pinned her arms to her sides. One large, muscular hand clamped itself around her throat. The other went under her sweater, stroking her rounded abdomen. She wanted to scream, but when she opened her mouth, no sound came out.

He lifted her sweater and pushed down the elastic waistband of her pants until her entire abdomen was exposed. "You're big," Larry said softly. "Much bigger than I realized."

He traced a circle around her navel. "I think it's going to be a boy. You had an amnio, Evelyn told me, so you'll know soon. I called your doctor. I told him I was an insurance rep and needed information about your pregnancy for your policy, but he wouldn't tell me anything about the baby. Evelyn told me. Evelyn told me everything. I'm so glad your good friend found me and told me where you were." He smiled.

Poor Evelyn. She was probably dead by now, Alex thought. She tried moving. The pressure on her throat increased. She decided to lie still.

"It was fun following you at the supermarket and at the store." He saw the startled expression in her eyes. "Yeah, that was me!" He laughed. "I had you spooked, didn't I? I told Evelyn you wouldn't recognize me, not the way I was dressed. And I was the last person you would've expected to see."

He was stroking her abdomen again. "Evelyn didn't think it was a good idea. She begged me to stop. And she was so scared when Lundquist said he was going to tell you who pushed you. 'What am I going to do?' she kept whining, 'what am I going to do?' So I took care of Mr. Lundquist."

He killed Lundquist. Not my fault, Evelyn had said.

"He made it so easy, leaving the door open for you. He didn't hear me until I was about ten feet away from the pool. When he saw me, he got out of the Jacuzzi and tried to run. He didn't get very far." Larry paused. "I had to do it, Alex. I couldn't let you know about Evelyn. It would have ruined my plans. You can see that, can't you?" His eyes demanded an answer. His hand tightened again around her throat.

She felt the blood rushing to her head. She nodded.

"Evelyn had everything planned, you know." He smiled. "She and Warren would get married. You and I would get back together and raise this baby." He leaned closer until he was breathing on her. "Do you want to get back together, Alex?" He relaxed the grip on her throat. "Do you?"

Her words came out as croaks. She cleared her throat and tried again. "If that's what you want, Larry." She would say anything to stay alive. To keep herself and the baby alive.

"What about Warren, Alex? And your beautiful stepson? Won't you miss them?"

What was the right answer? "I want to make you happy, Larry."

"Do you think we could be happy together? Evelyn thought so."

"Yes."

"And we could raise the baby, your new baby, in Kevin's place? And be a family again?"

"If you want to."

He leaned even closer and she thought he was going to kiss her. The thought repulsed her, but she would bear it.

When his mouth was just above hers, he said, "No one could take Kevin's place, Alex." His voice was cold, dead.

"Of course not," she said quickly. "I didn't mean—"

"No one!" he hissed. "Do you think for one minute that I would want to live with you? You killed Kevin, and you think I would want to be in the same *room* with you?"

Her heart thudded. "Larry—"

"I'm going to kill you, Alex," he whispered, "you and your precious baby. It's only fair. You killed my child, so I have to kill yours." Both hands were around her throat now.

"I didn't kill him! It was an accident!"

"You were painting while he was drowning. *Painting!*"

"No! He was dead already!" She had nothing to lose now. "It was your fault, Larry. *You* let Kevin drown, not me. You didn't close the door. You opened it."

"Liar!" His face was mottled with anger. "Lying bitch!"

She saw from his expression that he had lived with the lie too long to give it up. He started squeezing her throat, then loosened his hands. In an instant he was standing.

"Not like this. In the water, like Kevin. I want you to feel his pain."

He yanked her to her feet, put his arm around her middle, and dragged her, fighting, kicking, into the water until it reached his shoulders. His hands were around her throat again. He was staring at her with crazed, hate-filled eyes, pressing downward on her neck. She knew he was going to push her head under the water and that she would die.

She jabbed her fingernails into his eyes. He screamed. His hands flew from her throat to his face. She jerked her knee swiftly upward and kicked him in the groin. He roared and doubled over, clutching himself.

Gasping for breath, Alex swam away. She knew that soon he would be behind her, coming closer and closer, but she couldn't look back. She couldn't waste the time or risk being paralyzed with fear by seeing him.

She reached the shore, stood up, stumbled, and pulled herself up again. She started running. A moment later she could hear his ragged breathing and his feet slapping the sand.

She ran over to where Evelyn was lying and picked up the

bloodied piece of driftwood Larry had thrown down. She turned to face him.

He was five feet away.

She raised the driftwood above her head. He staggered toward her, then fell to the ground.

Chapter 35

"I spoke to the police," Warren said to Alex. "Larry told them Evelyn found out about his attempted suicide from the mortuary where Kevin is buried. Then she called the institution. Larry had been released into his parents' custody— according to the chief of staff, he'd improved considerably. Evelyn traced him to his parents. I guess when she told him you were married, and pregnant, it drove him over the edge again."

They were in their yard. Alex was lying on the padded blue-and-white-striped canvas chaise longue. Warren was sitting sideways on a matching chair next to her. It was Tuesday afternoon. Alex had just come home from St. John's. The baby, miraculously, hadn't been harmed.

"But then, babies are tough," Pearson had told her, smiling. "And so are you, my dear. I admire your pluck."

Sunday night she hadn't felt tough or plucky. She'd felt terrified and vulnerable and desperate.

After Larry had fallen to the ground, she'd collapsed to her knees at Evelyn's side and cried. She was tired, so tired that she couldn't imagine getting up, but the thought of Nicholas alone in a strange house, not knowing whether she was alive or dead, helped her pull herself to her feet.

As she hurried toward Evelyn's house, she heard the sirens. For the first time since Kevin died, she welcomed the shrill sound. She walked to the front of the house and met the two patrol officers who were coming up the winding, narrow walkway.

"Are you the one who called?" one of the officers asked.

"My son," she told them. She was shivering.

"What happened?" the officer asked.

"I have to see my son first." She rang Evelyn's front doorbell. When she heard footsteps approaching on the other side of the door, she said, "It's me, Nicholas. Mommy."

A moment later they were in each other's arms, crying.

While one of the officers stayed inside with Nicholas, Alex explained what had happened as she led the other officer around the side of the house to Evelyn and Larry.

Evelyn was dead.

Larry was alive but unconscious. He'd lost a lot of blood, the officer said. An ambulance took him away. The siren's blare thinned into a faint whine and disappeared.

Using Evelyn's phone, Alex called Warren at his parents'— they had just returned from the banquet—and Denise. She was too tired to explain, so each time she said the same thing: Evelyn was dead. Her ex-husband, Larry, was here, at Evelyn's, and had tried to kill her, but she and Nicholas were all right. She asked Denise to call Lisa at Valerie Haines's.

She called Dr. Pearson; he urged her to go to the hospital. She waited until Denise arrived with Lisa. There were more hugs, more tears. There were unasked questions that Alex couldn't deal with, not tonight. Then, after Nicholas went with his sister to his aunt's home, Alex allowed herself to be taken to St. John's.

Warren took the earliest flight home from Chicago and arrived at the hospital in midmorning. Alex was sleeping when he entered the room, and when she opened her eyes, he was standing at the side of her bed. She started crying. Warren cried, too. "I could have lost you," he said, his lips trembling. He didn't mention Nicholas, not then. He didn't ask questions.

He stayed until she told him to leave, and to see Lisa and Nicholas. They need you, too, she said. In the afternoon, he came back with the children. And today he'd brought her home. She had walked through the rooms as if seeing them for the first time. And in a way, she was. Sunday night, when she had felt the life being squeezed out of her throat, she'd thought she would never see this house or Nicholas or Lisa or Warren again.

The house was back to normal. Yesterday Warren had arranged for the telephone company to repair the wires Larry had severed just before he'd switched off the circuit breakers in the garage. She assumed that Warren had removed the inflated plastic doll from the pool. It wasn't there anymore.

"Larry got into the garage through the house, using our spare key," Warren explained now. "After he cut the phone lines and flipped the breakers, he opened the garage doors from inside. He had to leave them open. He didn't have the remote control to shut them."

"I know that Larry's in custody in a psychiatric ward, and Nicholas and I are okay, but when I think he was here in the house while I was upstairs giving Nicholas a bath . . . " She shuddered.

Warren took her hand. He held it tightly. "Don't think about it, Alex."

She turned onto her side to face him. "He wanted me to drown, like Kevin. He said so. He could've done it when I was in the pool. But I guess he'd planned it differently, with Evelyn. They were in this together."

Warren frowned. "Then why did he kill her? I asked the police, but Larry hasn't said anything about it."

"Evelyn was struggling with him because he took Nicholas out through the French door of the back bedroom." *Bring him back!* Alex had heard her scream. "I think she was terrified that if Larry hurt Nicholas, you'd hold her responsible. And then you wouldn't love her, or marry her." Alex wondered why she felt so sorry for the woman who had been her enemy.

"And maybe he wanted to silence her," Alex continued. "Because she knew he killed Lundquist. That explains why she was so shaken when I came back to the car and told her Lundquist was dead." She paused. "Warren, did Larry tell the police anything about Lundquist?"

"No. He claims he came here to reconcile with you."

"He tried to kill me—and the baby!" She shivered again, remembering. "That was *his* plan, not Evelyn's. Evelyn wanted me to leave. The notes were meant to scare me away. Larry wanted to punish me for letting Kevin drown."

"But now you know Kevin's death wasn't your fault," Warren said softly. He tightened his grip on her hand. "It's ironic, isn't it, that something good came out of your seeing the doll in the pool? It made you remember correctly."

"It could just as easily have been my fault. Every year hundreds of children drown, children with loving, caring parents. Children like Kevin. People don't realize how quickly a child can drown. I never knew until I read up on it after Kevin died. It can take less than a minute. You can turn your back for twenty seconds, and it's too late.'' What had happened that day? Had Larry made a call? Read the paper? She would never know.

"Alex, are you going to call your parents and tell them?"

She had thought about that earlier. "They betrayed me, Warren." She slipped her hand out of his and lay back against the padded canvas. "I can't forgive them for that. Not yet, anyway. They were very cruel."

"*Evelyn* was cruel. She seemed so straightforward, so sweet, so kind." Warren shook his head. "She told me you wrote the notes to yourself. She said she found evidence in your office and was afraid you were becoming paranoid."

Alex nodded. It made sense.

"I believed her." He was looking out toward the pool as he spoke. He turned back to Alex. "I'm sorry," he said quietly.

"Don't blame yourself. I believed everything she told me, too. She was a terrific liar." Alex smiled weakly. "Did you ever go out with her?"

"No. She was always friendly. I picked up signals that she was interested in me, but she wasn't my type." He shrugged.

"You never told me." Her voice was filled with gentle reproach.

"It was awkward." He paused. "You and Evelyn were so close."

Alex hesitated, then said, "I thought it was Lisa." Her face was flushed, but she looked directly at him. "I broke into her desk drawer, Warren. I'll have to tell her. I'll have to apologize for that, and for thinking that she . . . '' Alex couldn't finish the sentence.

Warren nodded. He linked his fingers through hers.

Lisa, it turned out, had told Valerie the truth: she'd been with Ricky Parks, a boy two years her senior. They'd gone for pizza and a walk. She hadn't told Warren or Alex about Ricky because she thought they'd disapprove. Denise had known, Warren told Alex. It was strange, but Alex no longer felt jealous of her stepdaughter's closeness with her aunt, or threatened by it.

Alex told Warren about the locket and the note, about the diary entry. "Evelyn said she put the note in the drawer, and the locket in Lisa's jewelry box. But I don't understand about the diary. Slipping the note inside the locked drawer was easy. Anyone could do that. But how could Evelyn have gotten the diary and written in it? Lisa always kept it and the drawer locked.''

Warren removed his hand. ''Alex, there's something I should tell you, something I should have told you a long time ago. It has to do with Andrea's death.'' He sat hunched over, his elbows on his knees, his forehead resting against his clasped hands. ''Andrea wasn't herself after Nicholas was born. She was moody and jittery. She cried all the time. Severe postpartum depression, her doctor told me.''

Alex waited.

His knuckles were white. ''I let you think Andrea died of birth complications. The fact is . . . the fact is, she killed herself by taking an overdose of tranquilizers.''

Alex was silent for a moment. Then she said, ''Why couldn't you tell me?''

He lowered his hands and turned to face her. ''I tried—you have no idea how many times I tried! It was too painful.'' He studied the ground. ''There were all the memories. There was the stigma, too, I guess. I realize it was a mistake to keep it from you.'' He looked at her.

''But what does that have to do with Lisa's diary?''

''Lisa was traumatized by Andrea's death. I think she connected pregnancy with dying. So when she found out you were pregnant. . . .''

''She thought I was going to die,'' Alex finished. *Oh, Lisa.*

Warren nodded. ''We had a long talk last night. She told me she received a note months ago, telling her you were pregnant.''

Evelyn again? Alex wondered. ''So it wasn't Denise who told her.'' Or Paula. Alex had so many silent apologies to make. And some not so silent. Although as far as Paula was concerned, Alex still felt she'd made the right decision in letting her go.

''Lisa was hurt when you badgered her about it,'' Warren continued. ''And worried by your behavior. She saw you that afternoon with Ron and didn't know what to think. She said you came to her room later and talked about compromising positions, but she'd seen a sketch you'd drawn of him, and she was worried Nicholas might find it and show it to me, and then I'd be angry at you. So she took it and threw it in the trash outside.''

Lisa a protector? The thought was ironic and touching. Alex voiced her feelings aloud to Warren.

''She thought it was because of the pregnancy,'' he said. ''And to her mind, things became worse. Her moodiness? Her snippy behavior toward you? I think she was trying to distance herself from you, to keep from becoming attached to you, from loving you. And when you became nervous and suspicious, I think it convinced her more than ever that you'd be depressed, like Andrea.''

What had Lisa written in her diary? The words had etched themselves on Alex's memory.

. . . and soon Alex will die. . . . I could feel sad if I let myself, but I won't let myself. . . . It won't change what's going to happen. . . .

''Lisa shouldn't have to deal with this alone, Warren. She should get help.''

''She was in therapy for the first year after Andrea died. She didn't want to continue. She said she was fine. When she started acting up, after you got pregnant, I told myself that all she needed was time. But we talked about it last night, and she's agreed to start seeing someone again.''

The silence was heavier this time.

''I know what you must be thinking, Alex. I talked about trust. I was hurt and angry because you'd kept your past from me. And I did the very same thing.''

He looked miserable, and her inclination was to excuse him, but that was not the road to honesty. ''You're right,'' she said quietly. ''You shouldn't have kept that a secret.''

There were too many secrets, she thought. Her secrets. Warren's secrets. Lisa's. Denise's. Secrets, Alex realized, were fertile ground for breeding suspicion and nurturing it. All of them—especially Alex herself, Warren, and Lisa—had been Evelyn and Larry's victims, but their inability to communicate honestly with one another had made them easy prey.

She took Warren's hand. ''No more secrets.''

''No more secrets,'' he echoed.

''Are we married, Warren?'' she asked suddenly. ''Legally,